For Your glory, Lord

1

Usually Wyatt, goalie for the Minnesota Blue Ox NHL team, could shrug off his mistakes. Ignore the horn blaring behind his ears, block out the cheering—and occasionally the gloating of the opposing players.

Not today.

Wyatt Marshall hadn't come all the way to Russia only to fail.

He glanced at the clock overhead, ignoring the sweat coating his body despite the cool breath of the arena, the slap of the puck at the other end of the rink.

Because if he failed, his entire life could be over in twelve minutes and thirty-two seconds.

He might be a little melodramatic, but it felt that way.

Lives were at stake.

No. *One* life.

The life of the woman he couldn't get out of his head.

Especially since he'd made promises. To himself. And had, in fact, blurted out to his entire family that he would rescue Coco Stanley. *I promise.*

He wasn't going home without her.

As long as he kept the Polish team from scoring, he bought himself more time in the Far Eastern town of Khabarovsk, where this international tournament was being held, to track down Coco and rescue her from a country trying to kill her.

Maybe that was overstated. Not all of Russia was trying to

kill Coco. And in fact, it might be only one very determined assassin by the name of Damien Gustov.

Even *that* Wyatt wasn't sure of.

Just that the woman he loved had been shot.

Left in Siberia.

Hadn't been heard from since.

She'd even been absent from their messaging forum, the Paulies, an online club just for fans of the Minnesota Blue Ox. He knew that *Kittycat1* was Coco, even if she never responded to his private messages. But she occasionally said something about his life before he joined the Blue Ox—something only Coco Stanley from Montana would know. At least she hadn't complete deleted him from her life after the fiasco in Moscow two years ago. The one he'd like to rewrite. No, erase completely and start over.

But first he had to get Coco out of the former Communist—now mafia-ridden—country. Which was why he'd finagled a way to get his team into Russia for this international tournament. Every game they won gave him one more day to search for her.

He was close. *Very* close.

Now, going into the third period, one score up, he had exactly twelve minutes and—oops, fourteen seconds—before he won this game and headed back to his hotel to meet a man named York.

An American. A spy, according to his CIA-analyst sister.

More importantly, York knew how to find Coco.

Wyatt banged the pipes of the goal with his stick and settled down as the puck dropped at center ice.

Now. *Stay in the now.*

He settled himself in the center of the crease, eyes on the movement of the first line. He knew these guys so well, he could have almost predicted that after the drop, right wing Deke Stoner would get out of traffic and their center, Crawford, would shoot the puck out to him in the slot, where Deke would take it down for a quick shot on goal.

The Polish goalie—Warkowski—had kicked it out, and

one of their defensemen shot it down the ice.

A wing on the Polish team—Lutz—wrangled it over the blue line, and now Wyatt stared him down, eyes on the puck.

The key was to center himself on the puck, to stay loose and let his reflexes kick in. He'd practically lived in the crease since he was thirteen. It was his own private island, his eight-by-six-foot cage.

It could choke him with the expectations.

Turn him into a man he either loved or hated.

The shot came hard, through traffic, and he dropped quick, his legs in a butterfly position, his pads flat against the ice, his arms in close.

The puck bounced off his leg pads, and he slapped the rebound away with his stick.

His defenseman, a rookie named Brummer, took it behind the net, and Wyatt caught his breath, his heart a hammer in his chest.

Breathe. Stay cool.

Except his hips were practically on fire, and shoot, but he should have iced down better after yesterday's game.

If he didn't stay loose, Kalen would take over, and Wyatt would get bumped to the second line. Wyatt could nearly hear Jace Jacobsen, one of their coaches, in his ear. *If you're not 100 percent in, you can't be at your best.*

Oh, he was all in.

His body just didn't want to agree.

His head might not be in the game either, because even as the play went deep, back over the center line, into the Polish end of the ice, Wyatt's brain went to Coco.

To the words of his sister, Ruby Jane, six weeks ago when Wyatt had met her, of all places, on a billionaire's yacht in the middle of the Caspian Sea. He'd never felt more in over his head than when he'd jumped on a plane with his former-Ranger brother, Tate, and flew over the Atlantic to the country of Azerbaijan to rescue their sister and a woman whose last spoken words to him were, *We have to talk, Wyatt.*

It was a conversation they'd never had, even online.

He'd gone cold when they tracked down Ruby Jane, nearly human trafficking prey on a Russian freighter and rescued her, only to hear her grim sit-rep. *Coco's been shot.*

Of course there was more—so much more. Namely the fact that RJ had barely escaped Russia with her life after being framed in an assassination attempt of a Russian general. Along the way, she'd met up with Coco, had dragged her into the chaos, and then left her in some remote hospital in Siberia, the KGB on her tail.

No. *FSB.* It was hard to keep up.

As Wyatt was trying to get his head around that, and more—namely that RJ was some sort of Jack Ryan CIA analyst—he also had to assimilate the fact that Coco was the daughter of said Russian general.

A fact that she'd left out the entire time she was living in Montana. With his family. Probably for KGB-slash-FSB security reasons, but yeah, that was a Big Omission that now had her hiding.

Somewhere in Russia.

Because, you know, bad people wanted to kill the general. And Coco could too easily be a pawn in the Russian game of cat and mouse.

He'd tried to contact her through their forum and gotten a shutout.

And in the back of his head, as his defensemen chased the Poles down the ice, as Wyatt dropped to one knee and deflected a shot, kicking it away, he knew he was probably in over his head. Again.

Another shot, and he caught it in his glove. Dropped it behind the net. Brummer brought it down the ice, passed off to Deke. Shouts from the audience—mostly Russian in this newly built sports complex—thundered through him as the clock ticked down. Eight minutes, twenty-four seconds.

Wyatt heard Ford's voice in his head. *You don't have a visa, you don't speak Russian. You're a hockey player, for cryin' out loud.*

Ouch.

Especially when superhero Ford the SEAL added, *I nearly*

got RJ and Red killed, and I actually know what I'm doing.

So Wyatt wasn't a superhero. He wasn't Tate or Ford or big brother Reuben, who jumped from airplanes to fight fires, or even Knox, who stared down bucking bulls.

Wyatt merely stopped pucks flying 110 mph straight at his head.

The Poles had the black and were slapping it down the ice, passing, playing with it. Another shot on goal, and Wyatt hit his knees, slamming them together. He felt the puck hit his chest, bounce down, and he clamped a glove over it.

Around him, ice chipped into his face. The sounds of sticks on ice always reminded Wyatt of gunshots across the fields—a crazy comparison because he'd barely spent time hunting with his father. That was something Tate and Ford and probably Knox and Reuben had done.

Wyatt had always been at practice. Or a game. Or on a trip for a tournament.

But still, shots, sharp and bold, and the crowd was on their feet as he kicked out the puck to the refs for a new drop.

The puck came out, and Brummer shot it down the ice to Deke, and Wyatt was back at the hotel last night, reading the email from his sister.

York will meet you after the game in the lobby of the Intourist Hotel. He will connect you with Coco.

Wyatt felt a little like he might be in a Jack Higgins novel, but he was game—

The puck flew down the ice, along the boards, and he moved out of the crease into the corner to field it, slap it back to Brummer.

The hit came hard and fast. One of the Poles, a wing maybe, checked him into the boards.

Pain exploded through Wyatt's body as his feet went out from him and he landed on his hip.

And sure, he was wearing pads, but sometimes he hit just right—he bit back a word, and realized the wing had fallen with him.

Maybe it was the frustration of the game, maybe the fact

that his entire body turned to flame, but Wyatt rolled over and slammed his fist into the Pole's helmet as he got up.

He didn't want a fight. Just a reminder.

You didn't check the goalie.

Except it seemed that the Poles didn't like his gentle reminder, and suddenly the benches erupted in a brawl. Brummer plowed into a nearby Polish player, and then Deke was there, and the entire second line poured off the bench, and Wyatt went down again.

He lay like a freakin' turtle, pushing off attackers, throwing his own punches, and for a second, he was thirteen again.

Marshall—what are you doing?

He started it!

Whistles and shouts and the refs were pulling players away, but helmets spun on the ice, and guys were pulling off their jerseys, and the Russian roar of the crowd seemed to fan the flames.

Wyatt rolled to his feet, only to have someone jump on him. His helmet and face mask went flying.

And yeah, he'd had it, so he boxed the guy with his elbow, rolled, and added another punch. This one mattered because the guy's helmet had also been kicked off, and then there was blood.

Some of it his.

His nose was bleeding, and his eye burned, getting fat, and shoot, they might not have anyone left to play after the penalties were assessed.

The refs finally broke it up and hauled Brummer and Deke to the box, along with the Pole who'd boxed Wyatt.

Which left the Blue Ox two men down and the Poles on a power play.

Wyatt shoved cotton up his nose and took the net. He fielded twenty shots before one ricocheted in off his glove.

Tie game with two minutes left, and Wyatt just tried to breathe.

Goaltending is mental. You have to be able to handle your emotions. This from his juniors' coach. Or maybe his uncle John.

He couldn't remember. But he hunkered down and tried to pry Coco from his brain as the last two minutes ticked down.

He couldn't help her if he was shipped out of the country.

C'mon, Deke. Deke came over the wall, and dove in, swiping the puck and slapping a quick shot on goal. Warkowski stopped it, but Deke followed with another.

Another save.

It was times like this that Wyatt missed Max Sharpe. He'd played forward for Wyatt's first two years, a champion sidelined by injury— and a cruel disease—just this past year.

Max had a toughness about him that had rallied the entire team. Wyatt could nearly hear him off the bench. *Thin the herd!*

A defender stole the puck and shot it to Lutz. He was still bleeding from the mouth a little, and Wyatt recognized him now.

C'mon, sweetheart, try me.

He stared down the guy, watching him handle the puck—nice moves—bringing it down the ice. Traffic tried to catch up to him, but no, it was just one-on-one, and Wyatt had his number.

Lutz pulled back and bulleted a shot, mid-chest, stick-side.

Wyatt shot out his glove across his body and nabbed it. Felt the puck hit his glove with a hot thud.

Yeah. That's right.

He held up his glove, shooting a look at the clock. Five seconds—

Behind him, the siren sounded.

What—?

He looked down, behind him.

Went cold.

The puck had fallen from his glove and bounced back into the goal.

He stared at it as the crowd erupted, his heart hammering into his ribs.

No.

Brummer skated up and Wyatt looked at him.

"Sorry, Guns." Brummer clapped him hard on the

shoulder pads.

Skated away.

On the other end of the ice, the Polish team was falling apart, sticks littering the ice, the celebrating practically un-clothing them.

His Blue Ox skated around, some of them heading back to the bench, a little bewildered, the others watching the Poles celebrate.

Wyatt dropped his stick, his gloves, and took off his hel-met. Then he pressed his hands to his face, bending over.

Breathe.

Tonight. He had to find Coco tonight.

Because tomorrow, he was getting kicked out of Russia.

Coco knew it would be dangerous to see Wyatt in the flesh.

Her brain always went a little haywire when she watched Wyatt play hockey. She only had to get near his vortex for it to peel her heart away from her body and then she'd be running in a full-out sprint for the man she couldn't forget.

The man who'd forgotten her.

Coco folded her arms against her parka, aware that she was probably overclothed, even if she was in an ice arena. The air held a tautness to it, the blades on the ice slicing the air, the shouts of the players echoing against the metal girders overhead. Flags of all the participating countries hung on the far end, and in the middle a scoreboard and screen displayed the dismal final score.

On the ice, Wyatt was quietly losing it.

She knew because, well, she *knew* him.

She knew how hard he worked at not falling apart. At pretending he had everything together. At playing the role of an elite NHL goalie.

What was he doing in Russia?

She closed her hand around the USB drive in her pocket

and tried not to imagine herself strangling York.

When York said that his contact, Wyatt Marshall would be in Khabarovsk, that she should meet him at the Intourist Hotel to drop off the evidence that would clear RJ's name, he should have clued her in on the fact that...

Well, that...

So maybe York *didn't* know all the painful details of her colorful and heartbreaking past with Wyatt. But he did know she knew him.

Or maybe York hadn't been paying attention to that part, what with the bullets flying and escaping the FSB and fighting the mafia and...

In truth, the man might have his brain focused on tracking down the assassin who killed his girlfriend.

And who'd tried to kill General Boris Stanislov.

Aka, Coco's father, but no one really knew that.

Except now for York and RJ.

So much for lying low with her secrets in Russia.

But Coco couldn't leave, ever, which meant she had to get the information that could exonerate her foster sister, RJ, to York's contact.

Wyatt.

Really, it made sense.

Wyatt was a Marshall. And Marshalls had a tendency to jump on their proverbial white horse and save the day.

At least for members of the family.

So, yeah, it completely made sense that he could be her contact.

Especially since he was oh-so-conveniently here in Khabarovsk, in Far East Russia, playing a Polish team in an international tournament.

Coco's heart had practically turned to hot wax when she saw his picture on one of the flyers for the event posted in the hotel. And at a nearby restaurant. And in a grocery store. And outside the Platinum Arena on a larger-than-life banner.

The man still looked good, too, if this was a recent shot. Probably because he looked older. Tougher than his twenty-six years. Square jawline, whiskey-brown eyes that looked straight into the camera with a sort of dare, and a slightly crooked, flattened nose, evidence of one too many ice brawls.

She had loved to trace her finger down it.

The broken nose made him larger than life, added a toughness to his charming smile, even with the cute dimple on the right cheek, and suggested he was the kind of man who wouldn't be afraid to dive into a fight. He was a big man—nearly six-three, with wide shoulders and a body honed by hours upon hours on the ice and in the gym. The man was practically religious about his health and body—he called it the triad of success—health, body, mind.

She called it pure heartbreak because Wyatt Marshall couldn't walk into a room without stealing her heart.

And inevitably, destroying it.

As she watched him press his hands to his face—probably for privacy as he put himself back together—she lost her heart all over again.

Oh, Wyatt. Breathe. It's just a game.

Clearly, it had been a terrible idea to come to the game. Roman would kill her when he found out. A month of keeping her safe as she healed from her gunshot wound, and she could be blowing it all by sneaking out into this crowd.

Except, it was a crowd. No one was going to find her. First, she'd dyed her hair black. Pitch raven black instead of her natural red. Okay, not completely natural, but she liked to experiment. And she wore a jacket, the hood up.

She might have blown it when she'd shouted the Blue Ox cheer—*Thin the herd!* That emerged in English, pretty loudly, during a lull in the game, right after the fight, but that Polish player, Number 32, had taken a cheap shot at Wyatt.

Her goalie had come up bleeding, wearing a lethal expression. But after the scuffle, he'd tucked it back inside and fielded what seemed like a thousand shots on goal.

Including that last one. Coco still couldn't believe it had dropped out of his glove.

He'd deserved the save.

The stands were thinning as she watched Wyatt pick up his stick, his face mask, his glove and head toward the bench in long, slow, dejected strides.

Her chest ached.

She'd just follow him back to the hotel, make sure he wasn't being tailed. Then…

Then what?

Just knock on his hotel door? Um, she'd tried that once and didn't want to think about the rest.

She loved him more than her very breath.

He most likely thought of her as a one, no-, two-time fling.

And really, she couldn't blame him.

Wyatt Marshall was a big deal. The Hottie of Hockey, according to the Twittersphere. Was dating Miss Minnesota, by the looks of it.

He'd long ago moved on from the angry young man who needed comfort.

She'd fallen not for the strong, steely-eyed athlete who stood alone between the posts, not the cover-model hockey player, the one who made a few pin-up and most-eligible lists on social media, but the rare, quiet man inside who tried to sing country music, donned a cowboy hat, and took her riding. The man who listened when she was hurting and asked for nothing.

But gave her everything when she asked.

Wyatt left the bench, walking back down the tunnel to the locker rooms, and she moved out with the crowd. It was better not to be jostled, anyway. She still held her arm close to her body over the wound in her abdomen.

She'd lost part of her small intestine, but after two weeks in the hospital, York guarding the door, she'd discharged herself and headed east.

To Siberia.

Outside, the evening bore the early scents of autumn, the oak and linden trees along the boulevard that led away from the arena already turning. The sun had splashed down beyond the Amur River, leaving a deep, simmering hint of red along the horizon. The red-bricked Russian Baptist church cast a shadow over the square, on a hill overlooking the arena parking lot. Flags fluttered overhead.

She slipped around the side of the building, past the three stories of steps, and toward the back entrance, hiding herself in a shadow.

Prevyet, Wyatt.

No. English might be better.

Hey, Wy…I heard you were looking for me.

She shoved her hands into her pockets. Maybe she'd simply get on the elevator with him, see if he recognized her—

What if he *didn't* recognize her?

She hadn't considered that, but hello, that was the point of her disguise, right? And what if he hadn't been looking for her, but…

Except she'd read his postings on the board. *ISO Kittycat1. Pls contact me. Scooby87.*

She couldn't exactly reply. She had no doubt that Damien had access to her computer, knew her alias, had probably even drained her bank account.

Of course, she had her own security backups, but if she wanted to make sure that proof of RJ's innocence got into safe hands, she needed to do this the old-fashioned way.

The players began to exit the building. She knew most of the Blue Ox by their pictures on their website—followed their games. Knew Deke Stoner, a forward, and his rookie brother Brendon, who played defenseman. Knew Kalen Boomer, who looked in decent health after his hip replacement two years ago. It was his injury that opened up the door for Wyatt's promotion to the pros.

The guys came out with their duffel bags over their shoulders, a couple equipment handlers pushing out the gear into a big bus.

She waited, the entire team climbing aboard, about to give up when she saw him.

Wyatt had showered, his brown hair wet and shorter,

clearly cut after the Stanley Cup loss. He hadn't shaved, a thin layer of dark whiskers along his strong jaw. He dressed like an elite warrior in a pair of suit pants, an oxford shirt, a tie. A suit jacket that made his shoulders look about a mile wide.

Oh, the press conference. He'd probably stopped in for a five-minute interview after the game.

She'd bet that was fun—reliving the moment when his mistake turned them from leaders to losers.

No wonder his mouth was pinched tight, his hand gripping his bag in a whitened clench.

He got on the bus.

She headed to the parking lot.

Roman had loaned her his Lada, a cute hatchback called a Kalina, and she slid into the front seat and took off her parka, leaving on her hoodie. The sounds of the past stirred inside her as she backed out of the lot.

You need to learn how to drive, Coco. All Americans know how to drive.

She'd been fourteen. Trying to embrace her American heritage. The year her mother got so sick.

Two months before she died.

Wyatt sat at the wheel of the pickup, two years older than her. He wore a black T-shirt, a pair of faded jeans, and a cowboy hat, just home from hockey camp.

"C'mere. It's easy."

It was the first time she noticed how big he really was, even at sixteen. He'd slid the seat of the pickup back and she'd crawled between his legs, sitting in front of him. He put his arms down, on his strong thighs. "You steer, I'll work the gas. Just get a feel for it."

They were in a field off the long road that led to the Marshalls' massive log house, and he gunned it, probably knowing perfectly well that she couldn't run into anything except a few cow pies.

And, of course, the Marshall family's Cessna, parked on the runway. She'd gotten too close and he'd grabbed the wheel. "Whoops! Let's not total my dad's favorite toy."

She'd laughed, happily cocooned in his arms as they veered down the runway.

"When do you leave for Helena?" she asked as he put her hands on the wheel again. She'd hated it when she'd heard the news—that he'd be spending the school year in Helena, playing on a traveling team. If he hadn't switched positions, turned into a hotshot goaltender...

Well, she couldn't expect that he might feel the same way about her.

But she'd given her heart away to Wyatt Marshall the day when she walked into his barn, shortly after moving in with their family and he'd said, "Shoot at me."

He'd pointed to a basket of tennis balls. And by the end of the afternoon, had her laughing with his antics to save the goal. He'd ended up dirty, scraped, bruised, and grinning.

He'd made her laugh.

For the first time, she didn't feel like the girl in the shadows, the Russki, the foreigner.

With Wyatt, she felt like she could belong.

Even when she nearly drove them into a ditch. He'd slammed on the brakes, shaken his head, and told her that by the end of the week, when he left for Helena, she'd be driving like Danica Patrick.

Whoever that was.

But now, as Coco pulled into the Intourist Hotel, not far behind the bus, the memory slid a warmth through her that she had nearly forgotten.

Wyatt would remember her.

Because the last time she'd knocked on his door, he'd chased her down the hallway, shooed everyone in his private party out of his room—men *and* women, so apparently she'd let her worst fears dream up trouble—and invited her inside.

She couldn't let herself think about the rest if she hoped to hand over the USB drive and walk away.

And walk away she would. Because Wyatt had to stay alive. If not for her, then for Mikka.

Because someday, her son had to meet his superstar father.

18

2

S o, that was fun. Any more sunshine from you and we might need shades."

Wyatt looked over at Coach Jace as he caught up to him in the lobby.

Jace "J-Hammer" Jacobsen had been their leading enforcer before he'd taken one too many hits to the head. A big guy, dark hair, a few scars on his square chin, Jace was a straight shooter, with a pretty wife and a family. He became a coach right about the time Wyatt was moved up to the show.

Wyatt's hair was still wet, dripping into the collar of his shirt, and frankly, he just wanted to get upstairs, stow his duffle bag and get back down to the bar where he was supposed to meet York.

But he had a job to keep and a coach to respect so, "Sorry, Coach. I just didn't have much to say."

No, correct that. He hadn't had *anything* to say—his focus on getting on the bus and back to the hotel.

His focus on finding Coco. Tonight. *Please.*

"We're always representing," Jace said. "And, if I remember, you pushed us to get into this tournament. I expected a little more than a few mumbles about playing better in the zone and congratulating the Polish team. We count on you to woo the press. You're not just our starting goalie but a team leader."

Jace sort of reminded Wyatt of his father. Serious.

Hard-hitting. The kind of guy who didn't rattle easily. But he knew how to mix it up on the ice—rumor was he'd ended someone's career in his early days with his fists. At least Wyatt's mistakes only cost games.

It must have changed him because Jace occasionally spouted Bible verses and quotes by C.S. Lewis.

Very much like Orrin Marshall.

Maybe that's why Wyatt tried to steer clear of him.

Wyatt's mouth tightened around the edges. "I wasn't in the mood for an interview." He didn't slow at the desk but headed right for the elevator bank.

"Wyatt, I need to talk to you," Jace said, following him to the elevators.

It was his tone that stopped Wyatt. Sent a cold fist around his chest.

Jace lowered his voice. "How are your hips?"

The question was like a shot on goal Wyatt hadn't seen coming. He could nearly hear the sirens blaring in the back of his head. "Fine."

"You're moving pretty slowly—"

"I'm in top shape, Coach. I promise."

Jace gave him a thin-lipped shake of his head.

"What?"

"You know Kalen is ready to come back. And your contract is up next year, and…well, after the Stanley Cup—"

"It was a *shootout*. Three overtimes—"

"You're slipping, Wyatt. And I'm not just talking about today. Yes, the Stanley Cup overtime loss was hard. But before that—and again during this tournament—your game is off."

"I'm focused."

"Yeah? We need you all in, Guns. On the ice and off. You were always the guy who wooed the press. You're a personality. A star. The face of the Blue Ox. So what's with today's surly press conference?"

"Sorry." Wyatt glanced at Jace, taking his gaze off where he was scoping out the lobby for anyone who looked like York, or at least his sister's description of him. Dark hair, lean, capable.

"Wyatt, I'm not sure what's going on with you, but you've always played with a crazy amount of passion. You're driven like no one I've ever seen before. Up early for extra practice. Staying late. And I know you aren't a partier. But I can't get past the idea that all this isn't enough for you. As if you're still looking for something, moving around the crease, trying to grab something that just keeps flying by you."

He had Wyatt's attention now. "It's enough, Coach. I love playing for the Blue Ox." A fist began to squeeze his chest. "Hockey is all I have. It's my whole world."

Jace was staring him down with those blue-as-ice enforcer eyes. "Maybe that's the problem, huh?" He clamped Wyatt on the shoulder. "What if it crumbled? What would you have left?"

Wyatt stood there, a little stricken.

"Take a breath, Wyatt. I'm not saying I'm starting Kalen anytime soon. I'm just wondering…well, do you even *like* the sport?"

"I've been breathing hockey since I was seven years old. It's who I am."

The elevator arrived and dinged.

"That's not an answer." Jace got into the elevator with him. "You're pretty hard on yourself, Guns. But the more you focus on your failures, the more cluttered your brain will be. Give yourself a little grace. And stop trying so hard. You're your own worst enemy, sometimes."

Wyatt looked at him, not even sure where to start. Except, "Coach, I'm good, really. I'm just…tired."

"Mmmhmm," Jace said. His tone changed. "Listen, there are some media folks joining us for dinner. Show up and show off that Wyatt Marshall charm."

"I'll try and stop by," he said, not wanting to make promises. Who knew what might happen after he met York. In fact, he was dearly hoping he'd be in a cab on his way to meet Coco.

The very idea had his throat thickening, his heart racing.

The thought of meeting her was worse than pregame warm-up. But then again, Coco had always made him feel alive, his real self. Or at least the man he wanted to be.

He'd lost that guy along the way, somehow.

"Okay. Hope to see you. But if not, get some rest. We need to be on the train to Vladivostok tomorrow morning, early."

Jace got off the lift and Wyatt followed him down the hall. He let himself into the adjoining room, dropped his duffel bag on the bed, draped his suit jacket on a chair, and pulled off his tie.

The room had former Soviet Union written all over it, spare and cold. It even came with an old-fashioned room key that he had to use to lock and unlock his door. He'd slept on softer bleacher seats than the double bed, and the blond furniture was either retro or hadn't been replaced since the early seventies.

Still, it was clean, and the balcony overlooked the Amur River. The final hues of red turned the river to fire, the sky above a steel gray.

Wyatt checked his watch. Five minutes to the meet. He changed into a pair of jeans, tennis shoes, grabbed his wallet, passport, and key, and headed back out to the elevator.

Waited.

It seemed to be stuck on an upper floor so he took the stairs down and emerged into a hallway off the bar.

He was still entrenched in the seventies. Gold chandeliers, red leather high top chairs, gold carpet, and even a disco light over a small, empty stage at the back. A karaoke machine was shoved into the corner. So that accounted for the screeching last night. Now, the overhead speakers pumped out a Russian pop song.

He recognized a few Blue Ox players sitting at some of the round tables. They sat with players from other teams, a few making friends with fans.

No one resembled York's description.

Wyatt stood at the edge of the bar, scanning the room

again.

"Why do they call you Guns?" The question came from a woman with long sable-brown hair. She wore a sleeveless velvet top and a pair of black jeans. And around her neck, a laminated sports pass card. He glanced at it, back to her.

"You probably know the answer."

"Because you've got great guns?" she said, winking. She pressed her hand to his arm, squeezed.

He pried her hand off him. "No. Because my last name is Marshall. Sheriff. Gun. Get it?" He tried to move past her, but she stepped in front of him.

"Who are you looking for?"

He looked down at her. Maybe five-seven, lean, deep blue eyes. Pretty, late thirties. She raised an eyebrow, and for a second, he paused.

York? Yes, he was supposed to be male, but he'd seen enough *Mission: Impossible* movies to know that sometimes things go south so, "I'm looking for a friend." He lowered his voice. "His name is York."

He waited.

"Sorry. I don't know anyone named York." She glanced around the room and lowered her voice also. "But I'm pretty good at finding people."

And now he just felt silly.

She smiled, and it felt genuine. But, no. He wasn't interested in help or anything else she might offer.

Maybe she figured it out because she added, "My name is Nat. Why don't you let me buy you a drink while you wait for your friend?" She winked and pressed her hand to his chest. "You can tell your secret at how you stop pucks."

"I don't stop pucks, if you happened to catch the game." He touched her hand, intending on moving it.

"You caught it. You just dropped it."

He looked at her. "Even worse. Sorry, I really don't want to talk about it. Besides, I need to find my friend."

York, show up.

He'd heard about the man from RJ—in fact, she couldn't

stop talking about the American agent who had saved her life.

And apparently, Coco's life.

No, Wyatt wasn't jealous, but…fine, maybe a little. Because *he* wanted to be the one to save her life. Be a hero in her eyes, back before he'd screwed it all up.

He pushed past Nat and scanned the room again. The bar was filling up with players from other teams—Czech, Polish, Lithuanian, Russian. The press had found them—he noticed more than a few women with press passes. Waiters carried drinks to tables.

Jace stood in the corner of the room, his back to the lobby, talking with Deke.

Movement behind him caught Wyatt's attention.

A woman. Petite. A little curvy, but mostly just small, athletic. Wearing a hoodie.

She turned and met his eyes.

Coco.

Seeing her hit him like a punch, right to his sternum, knocking the wind from him.

Time stopped as her luminous gray-green eyes stared him down.

Then the past grabbed his heart, and he was standing on the other side of his hotel room door, staring down at her, laughter spilling out behind them. *Coco. What are you doing here?*

Coco whirled and took off across the parquet floor of the lobby.

Not *again.*

He launched after her, pushing through the room, past Jace, and straight out into the lobby. Her name stung his lips, nearly pouring out, but she wasn't just fleeing him, but a known assassin, probably, so he clamped down on his shout and lengthened his strides as he followed her path.

He hit the far hallway.

Gone.

Yeah, well, he had longer legs. He sprinted, rounded the corner, and caught sight of her quick-walking down the hall.

"Coco!"

He couldn't help the shout and his voice practically boomed down the hallway and lit a fire under her.

For the love of— "*Stop running!*"

She pushed through the back doors out into a courtyard.

He caught the doors before they closed. She'd opened up now, moving fast as she wound her way around flower beds and planted trees in the landscaped garden.

He didn't bother dodging them and ran right through the gardens, a straight line toward her.

She was cutting through a gazebo that overlooked the river when he caught up to her.

"Stop!"

And because he didn't want to tackle her, he ran up and caught her around her waist, pulling her against him, easy. He braced his hand on a pillar in the gazebo, breathing hard. "Stop. Please."

"Let go of me." She turned in his arms, pushing against his chest.

"Not until you promise to stop running."

"Fine," she snapped.

And yeah, he should let her go, immediately, but, shoot, he'd missed her, and with everything inside him, he just wanted to wrap both arms around her and hold on. To breathe in the scent of her skin. Look into her eyes and see…well, there was a part of Coco that must still love him. He believed that with everything inside him.

Or maybe just hoped for it with the power of every heartbeat.

But he didn't want to be that guy, the one who scared her, used his brute force on her. Made her feel helpless and small.

He let her go.

She stepped back, her mouth tight. Her hood had fallen off, and he nearly reached out and touched her hair, black as night, and startlingly bold and beautiful, despite his love for her usual red.

It only made her gray-green eyes stand out in a bright and terrible beauty, especially when sheened with tears.

"I'm sorry," he said now, not sure why. "I just didn't want you to get away. Why did you run?"

She wrapped her arms around her waist. "I…" She swallowed and looked back at him. Wiped a hand across her face. "I'm not sure why I'm crying. I'm just—"

"Wow, I've missed you."

Her eyes widened.

Oh, that sounded pitiful and heartbroken, but—

"Please tell me you're okay." Because he'd almost forgotten that she'd been shot just over a month ago. "Did you—are you—" He ran his hand behind his neck, squeezing tight. "RJ said you were shot."

His heart fell when she nodded. "But I'm okay. I'm healing."

His jaw clenched against a horrible roaring in his chest. "Did I hurt you?"

She shook her head.

His chest uncoiled from the terrible knot inside. "I…I was worried."

That got the tiniest of small, tentative smiles. He wanted to reach out and touch the side of her mouth, capture it.

"I noticed," she said. "How many messages did you leave?"

Oh. Those. "You…got them?"

She nodded. "But I was afraid to answer. I didn't want… well, maybe RJ told you that—"

"Yes." He held up his hand, glancing around. There weren't others out here, but just saying the words—*assassin*, *Russian general*, and maybe even *conspiracy*—felt like it might alert some FSB tracking system. They *were* in the former Soviet Union. "I know everything."

Her eyes widened, and he might have been imagining it, but it seemed she had paled, her breaths shallow.

He couldn't stop himself from putting his hands on her shoulders. "It's okay, Coco—"

"Kat. I'm Kat now."

He drew that in. Um, *never,* but he didn't say that. "So,

26

here's the plan. You're an American citizen, so you don't need a visa to get into the country. I've got a flight out in a couple days. We'll leave tomorrow with the team, go to the US Consulate in Vladivostok, tell them you lost your passport, and they'll issue you a temporary one. Then we'll fly out with the team and—"

"No." She backed out of his grip. "I'm not leaving, Wyatt. I…I appreciate that you came all this way, but…I can't leave."

He had nothing, her words reaching in to steal his heartbeat. His breath.

His entire future, the one that still made him look into the stands in hopes she might be there, cheering for him. Waiting for him after practice.

In his world, where she belonged.

"You're in danger here, Co—Kat." And yeah, he was pleading, but, "Please come back to the US with me. I can keep you safe—"

Even as he said it, it sounded hollow. He wasn't Tate the bodyguard. Or Ford the Navy Seal, or even Knox or Reuben who had their own brand of toughness.

He was just an athlete. And a cover model—yeah, that had made him feel silly, but Nick Coyote, his publicist, said it was good for his image.

Wyatt had wanted to turn all the copies face in on the newsstand.

So no, Wyatt probably couldn't protect her. But he wanted to, and maybe that counted, right?

"You'll be safe on the ranch" was all he could come up with.

She was shaking her head. "I…I just can't, Wyatt. But I did bring the evidence you need to prove that RJ is innocent." She pulled out a jump drive, a tiny USB stick, and held it out to him.

He stared at it as if it might be a bomb, his world sort of exploding.

"No—" He met her eyes. "No. I want *you*, Coco. I want— please." And now he couldn't stop himself—he touched her face, earnest. "Please. I haven't...I miss you. And I—"

"You have plenty of friends," she said, looking away, a flash of hurt in her eyes.

He frowned. Shook his head. "I don't—"

She swiped his hand away from her. "It doesn't matter. I can't leave. I *won't* leave." She looked back at him, and a tear slid down her face.

It shattered him as it dripped off her cheek.

And he just...

Oh, no, he kissed her. Because he'd lost his head and he didn't know what else to do to show her how he felt, so he slid his hand behind her neck, bent down, and pressed his mouth against hers.

He was desperate and pitiful, and oh, how he'd missed her. He drank her in, kissing her with so much of himself outside his body, he didn't have the strength to rein it in.

And heaven help him, for a second, it worked. Sure, at first she froze, probably from shock, maybe anger, and if she'd fought him in the least, he would have let her go, but...

But she grabbed his shirt with a fist and held on. And in a glorious, beautiful, breathtaking moment, her mouth softened and she kissed him back, as if she missed him too.

He gentled his kiss, moved his arm around her, pulled her against him. She'd always been such a perfect fit in his arms, and even now, the old feelings rushed over him, hot, a strange sort of homesickness he hadn't tasted in years.

Coco. He'd take a thousand more hits at goal for this moment, to feel her body relax against his. To know—

She leaned away, shaking her head, her hands pushing against him. "No, Wyatt...no, no—"

He let her go, her words like fire, flashing over to scorch him. "Coco, *c'mon*—"

"You can't kiss me and then just walk out of my life." She pressed her hands to her mouth, shaking her head. "Don't— it's not fair."

Not. *Fair*—? "Walk out of *your* life—what are you talking about? You're the one who left! Who..." *Broke my heart.* "You left *me*. Twice—no, *three* times."

She looked away. "Twice because once you didn't even notice I'd left."

He stared at her. *What?* "Coco, I don't get it. I don't understand *any* of it. Why you came to me in Russia two years ago. Why you even left Montana in the first place. You…" And then, he couldn't take it. "You broke my heart, okay? I thought after we…" His voice wavered, and he swallowed hard. Fought the urge to reach out to her again. "I thought we meant something to each other."

Her breath hiccupped. "We did, Wyatt. But…" She shook her head.

The kiss was right there, lingering between them, and the way she kept looking at him, half fear, half hope.

A huge part of him could swear she wanted him to kiss her again.

But maybe he couldn't read her anymore.

Still, he couldn't let it end again. Not like this. He fought to school his voice, away from desperate, back to rational.

Nobody played well with their emotions spilling out everywhere.

"Listen. I know we have something. We always have, and I…I want you to come to America. With me. I want us to be together. Be *happy*."

Her jaw tightened at his words, her eyes sparking. "Yeah, well, guess what. Life doesn't give us what we want. And happily ever afters don't exist and…our best hope is to survive. I appreciate that you came all the way over here, Wyatt. But I can't go with you."

"Why not—"

"I can't!" She clenched her jaw. Swallowed. "Listen. I'm sorry, but…you should just forget about me."

Forget—?

"Take this home and clear your sister."

She shoved the USB drive into his hand and closed his fingers over it.

Then she met his eyes.

His had started to blur.

"Goodbye, Wyatt." She swept her hand across her cheek. "And, by the way, great game. You deserved to win."

Then, while he gaped at her, she turned and ran out of his life.

Again.

———————◆———————

So, that wasn't at all how her clandestine meeting was supposed to go.

With Coco blubbering her way through some flimsy explanation that probably made no sense, shoving the USB drive into Wyatt's hand, and for the third and probably final time, fleeing.

Apparently, that's what she did best. Run. From the only real family she'd ever known, from the love of her life. She'd even run from the shadow existence she'd pieced together in Moscow as the personal computer genius-slash-hacker for one of the most powerful generals in the Russian military.

Her father.

A man who'd recently nearly been assassinated. A man whose daughter was probably a valuable pawn to nab, manipulate, and hold hostage.

Aw, maybe she *should* have said yes to Wyatt's really bad but earnest escape-from-Russia plan.

She nearly did. Nearly stepped back into those amazing arms and let him rescue her.

Wake up, Kat. She did *not* need rescuing, thank you. She'd been on her own since she was eighteen, and frankly even before that had learned how to take care of herself.

Coco slid into the Lada parked down the street from the Intourist Hotel, locked the door, and sat in the darkness.

Stared at the hotel.

She could go back inside. Tell him the truth. *I can't leave Russia without my son. Our son.*

She closed her eyes, imagining how that might play out.

30

Shock? Certainly. Anger? Most definitely—and rightly so. She should have told him she was pregnant five years ago, or three, or two or…anytime over the past year when he'd tried to chat with her online.

No, *when* she told him, it would have to be the perfect place and time.

And most importantly, when everyone was *safe*.

She started the Lada and pulled out, driving down Karl Marx Street, turning off onto Lenin Street, then onto a side street toward one of the older buildings at the end of Lermontova, and parked in the lot. The nine-story apartment building was one of the newer ones, but she passed by a monument of a World War II era tank on her way inside.

These newer apartments came with security codes at the door, and she punched in the code and entered. The difference between the Russian streets and the apartments could be startling—going from crumbling buildings, weedy, broken parking lots, and trash-littered alleys to bright and shiny, clean and new apartments. She took the lift up to the ninth floor and hit the buzzer.

The inner door opened, and a blonde woman, her hair cut short in a bob, answered. She wore a pair of leggings and a flannel shirt rolled up to the elbows. "Hey," Sarai Novik said through the window in the metal door as she inserted the key into the lock.

It whined open.

"Hey." Coco stepped past her.

"You don't look so good. You all right?"

Other than her puffy face and the fact she'd only stopped crying? "Yeah, I'm fine. I just…oy!" She stepped over the threshold into Sarai's four-room apartment and was nearly mowed down by a five-year-old on a bike riding down the hallway. She caught the handlebars, dodging the front wheel.

"Vitya, I told you—no riding your bike in the house," Sarai said and shooed him off the bike.

He could wreck Coco with his smile. Blond like his mother, with hazel-green eyes like his father, Roman, and a little older than Mikka.

Coco simply stared at him as he dropped his bike by the door and scampered down the hallway to his room.

"He's got the energy of three boys," Sarai said, motioning Coco to the kitchen. "Roman installed a jungle gym in his room, complete with a pull-up bar and a rope swing so he could burn some of it off. But he's more exhausting than a roomful of trauma patients." Sarai patted a kitchen chair. "Let me take a look at your wound."

"I'm fine."

"Sit down."

"It's healing fine," Coco said, but sank into the chair, pulling off her hoodie. She tugged down her waistband enough for Sarai to look at her wound, now a bright, angry red scar.

"Want to talk about it?"

Coco sighed. "No." Yes. "I saw someone from my past."

Sarai probed the wound, then got up. "And…?" She turned the heat on under a tea kettle, the Russian way to solve every problem.

The door lock bolts slid back, and Sarai turned just as her husband, Roman, walked into the room. A former special ops soldier, he now trained militia and other spec ops types. Vitya ran down the hall, and his father scooped him up.

Roman had spooked Coco the first time she'd met him, at the train station. He'd worn a black sweater, a pair of black pants, and sort of blended right into the night. He'd materialized only after York practically carried her off the train, his help volunteered by an American consulate director they'd met in Moscow.

The consulate director just happened to be Sarai's brother, David Curtiss. And a friend of Roman's.

With short hair and probing, hazel-green eyes, Roman had borne the grim look of a soldier as he drove them to his flat. York told him about their run-in with the Russian mafia, who York believed had hired the assassin, and finally the circumstances of the shooting, namely said assassin finding them in a dark alley in Yekaterinburg.

Roman had agreed to hide Coco, under his physician wife's care, as Coco healed.

York didn't know Roman either, but the two hit it off in a camaraderie born from understanding the sacrifices of patriotism. York had left her under Roman's protection while he returned to Moscow and tried to track down Gustov.

He'd called last night, needing help with a hacking project, with the news of the meet, and the reality that he'd be delayed. Hence Coco's field trip to the hotel.

She probably would have found herself at the hotel anyway, her traitorous heart begging to see Wyatt.

Why oh why did she always set herself up for heartache?

Roman set Vitya down and patted his bum. "Time for bed, *lapichka*. Scoot."

Sarai got up and headed down the hall, running her hand over Roman's arm as he headed into the kitchen.

"So? Did you make the handoff?" Roman asked.

"The USB drive? Yes, I gave it to Wyatt Marshall."

"That hockey player?" Roman said. "I saw his picture on television."

Roman had played a little hockey himself, back at university.

"And you think this Wyatt is capable of carrying the drive out of the country?" Roman turned a chair around and straddled it, leaning his folded arms against the back.

"Yeah. Although he wasn't happy about my not going with him."

On the stove, the tea kettle whistled. Roman made to get up, but Coco shook her head and got up instead. She'd lived here long enough to earn her keep.

She dropped loose black leaves into a tiny teapot, then poured the hot water in, letting the chai steep. She put a cloth over the small teapot.

"He wanted you to leave the country with him?" Roman was looking at her as she sat down. "Why?"

"I guess…well, he's worried about me…" Oh shoot. She'd left out the part where… "He and I…we had a…"

She didn't know what to call their relationship. Not a fling,

33

because that meant it was short-lived. Hello, she'd been in love with him for nearly a decade. And not an affair, because that made it tawdry and illicit.

It wasn't tawdry. Just…under the radar. And, maybe not as pure as it should have been.

But in truth, Wyatt was the love of her life.

Roman said nothing.

"I loved him. And I thought he loved me. But…" She drew up a knee. "But that was a long time ago."

"I see," Roman said. "Back when you lived in America?"

She nodded.

"Before you moved to Russia."

"And, during. I went back to Montana for a short time not long after I moved to Russia. We saw each other then, but… well, he was just getting his chance to play for the Blue Ox, and I didn't want…" She swallowed, looked away. "I didn't fit into his life anymore."

Roman was just watching her.

She got up to check on the chai. The silence pressed into her back.

"So…you think he came here to find you?"

She drew in a breath. "I don't know."

"But he wanted you to leave with him. It sounds like he thinks you fit into his life. You might consider taking him at his word."

"He doesn't…understand. And if he did, he wouldn't want me."

Roman got up and turned the chair around. "A man doesn't go to another country and risk his life to rescue the woman he doesn't want. Trust me, I know this."

She stiffened. "I can't leave Russia, Roman."

He frowned. "You're an American, right?"

"Yes. But—"

"You'd be safer in America is my guess."

Sarai had come back to the door and now folded her arms, leaning against the doorframe. "We love having you here, but Roman is right—"

"I can't leave Russia!"

Sarai recoiled, frowned, and Coco closed her eyes, wincing. "Sorry."

"What's going on?" Roman said quietly. Carefully.

She drew in a breath. Glanced at the chai.

"Sit down, both of you," Sarai said and pulled out three cups from the cupboard.

Roman sank down into his chair.

Fine. Coco also sat down. Took a breath. "I can't leave because I...I have a child."

Nothing. Sarai continued to pour chai into the cups. Roman's mouth stayed a grim line, his hand flat on the table.

"He's Wyatt's."

Roman's eyebrow raised. "No wonder he wants you to leave—"

"He doesn't know."

Sarai set down the teacup in front of her. Pushed a sugar bowl and a spoon her direction. Then she retrieved cream from the fridge.

"I've tried to tell him, three times now. When I first got pregnant, then a year later, when I went back to Montana for a visit, then a couple years ago in Moscow and...yeah, I was trying to find the courage to tell him today. But..."

She dropped in a sugar cube, played chase with it around her cup with her spoon. "How do you say that, really?" She looked up, and her gaze met Sarai's eyes. Then Roman's.

"Hey, Wyatt. Great game. Your son would have loved to see it. Oh, who?" She returned her gaze to her cup. "In my head, I have this perfect time to tell him, and it was five years ago when I was at his college hockey game. I went with his sister, Ruby Jane—the one who I was helping escape Russia, by the way—with the intention of telling him. But while we were visiting, his father had a heart attack and..."

She took a sip of the tea. Her stomach clenched, and she hadn't realized she was so hungry.

Roman and Sarai hadn't moved.

"It was crazy—the fact that I even got pregnant. We'd

only slept together once and…well, I don't know what I was thinking…"

"There's usually not a lot of thinking going on." Roman looked at Sarai and winked.

"Yeah, well, I was so in love with Wyatt Marshall, I lost my head. He was home on Christmas break, and we'd gotten caught making out in the hay mow during Thanksgiving. And it just sorta…sparked something. I was eighteen, and he was twenty and one night his family went to town for some church event, but Wyatt and I stayed home to…well, I don't remember what excuse we made up, but I knew what I wanted."

She could close her eyes and way too easily be back in Wyatt's arms in his skinny twin bed in the room he'd shared with Ford and Tate. Which felt weird, but then…well, she hadn't cared.

"Truth was, I had been in love with Wyatt for years, and in my head I believed we'd end up together. And that he loved me too." She looked up at them. "When I found out I was pregnant, I didn't tell anyone—I wanted to surprise him. I was so…" She shook her head. "I thought he'd be thrilled and ask me to marry him, and we'd have a family and live on the Marshall Triple M and…"

Her eyes always burned when she got to this part. "While I was at that game, his father suffered a heart attack and died and suddenly everything changed. Wyatt changed. He was so…angry. He quit school, tried out for the Edmonton team, didn't make it, then tried the Blue Ox in Minnesota. He landed a position on their amateur team, and just like that, he was gone. And I was alone. And scared. And ashamed. So I moved back to Russia."

"Where your father lived."

"He'd kept tabs on me for years, even though we were supposed to act like he was dead. He took me in and helped me…well, Mikka lives in an orphanage in Belogorsk."

Sarai touched her arm, squeezed.

"It wasn't my choice. I kept Mikka with me for the first year, but then my father said he'd unearthed a kidnapping plot and said it was too dangerous for Mikka and me, and even for my father to keep him. He had to remain anonymous. He started out in an orphanage not far from St. Petersburg, but then we started to move him. He's been at the home in Belogorsk for two years."

She gritted her jaw against a familiar burn in her throat, her eyes. Kept her voice even as she said, "I visit him as often as I can. He knows me."

She looked away again, her eyes on fire, glazing over. Shoot. She'd thought she'd be used to the ache by now.

"I'm sorry, Kat."

"That's why I went back to Montana to visit. I thought, maybe, if I told Wyatt about Mikka, he'd want us back. He'd tell me to move to America and…"

"You'd be a family."

She wiped her cheek with the palm of her hand. Since when had she turned into such a baby? She was the daughter of a Russian general—she knew hardship, *hello*.

"Wyatt had just made the pro team, and he was so excited. And I just couldn't…well, he barely paid any attention to me anyway, so I figured I was nothing to him. Just a…" She couldn't say the word *fling*, so she lifted her shoulder. "I came back to Russia and lived the best life I could."

She didn't want to tell them about the shame of his visit to Moscow two years ago, so she omitted it and went straight to— "I know he deserves to know, but…"

"But he'd demand to take Mikka too," Roman said.

She hadn't thought of that. Coco looked at him. "Or not. He doesn't even know Mikka—"

"He would want to know him," Roman said, nothing of a waver in his voice, and that only made her chest burn.

"Maybe I *should* have left with Wyatt. Mikka is safer if no one knows about him. If I leave Russia, I take the assassin with me."

"You can't leave your son," Sarai said, more of a statement than a question.

Coco shook her head. Closed her eyes. "No. I can't. I'm

just not that strong."

Sarai moved over to her and pulled her into an embrace. "I think you're plenty strong, honey."

The embrace was sweet, but with everything inside her, Coco wanted to push away, run back to that hotel and... and...

You broke my heart.

Oh, she was such a fool. Here he was in Khabarovsk, looking for her and...

And if he kept it up, trying to find her, the assassin might find *him.*

The thought caught her up, stole her breath.

Yes, better for him to leave, and pronto.

"No one would expect you to leave your son," Sarai said softly, letting her go.

"But if I stay, Mikka stays in danger."

Sarai's eyes widened.

"Just imagine if he'd been with me when RJ showed up, an assassin on her tail? He might have been killed."

Roman's jaw tightened and he glanced at Sarai.

"Listen," Coco said. "Damien Gustov knows that *I know* that he tried to kill my father. I don't know what his end game is—kill me, hold me hostage—but whatever, I'm in danger. And because of me, so is Mikka. And frankly, Wyatt." She looked at Roman. "Even you guys."

"I can protect my family, Kat. You're welcome here," Roman said.

She wanted to believe him, but the thought of anything happening to Vitya or their daughter, Zia...

The only way to save Mikka—and Wyatt—was to disappear.

Maybe forever. "No. I need to leave town," Coco said, finding her feet. "Tonight."

Roman's mouth tightened. "I don't like it."

"Where are you going?" Sarai said, ignoring Roman.

"I said goodbye to Wyatt. Now, I'm going to say goodbye to my son. And then, I'm going to disappear."

She held up her hand to Roman's deep breath, the fore-play to his building argument. "I've done it before. I can do it again. And trust me—this time I won't be found."

3

Wyatt sat on the Intourist restaurant patio, the USB drive on the table next to his smart phone. The view overlooked the darkened Amur, stars sprinkled overhead like eyes blinking in disbelief at his failure.

"Is there something wrong with your meal, sir?"

Wyatt glanced at the waitress, a pretty, skinny brunette with her hair in a bun. She wore the black-and-white dress of the hotel staff. He wasn't the only one sitting in the outside seating area, but she'd swung by often enough for him to sense that perhaps she wasn't doing her job well.

"It's delicious. I just…I'm not hungry."

He'd purchased a plate of smoked salmon and a pint of Baltika 3, but it swam in his gut and he might have made himself sicker.

He hadn't had a beer in three years.

"Can I offer you something else? Maybe a hamburger?" She said it like a Russian, *gambooger*.

"No, thanks." He offered her a smile, and she smiled back. And it simply hurt. Because he was a nice guy. And frankly, had tried to be the kind of guy worthy of Coco, especially after…

Well, after he realized what she meant to him.

Apparently, he didn't mean the same to her.

"I'll take my bill," he said.

She moved away, and he reached for the phone, dreading

the call. But RJ was probably pacing the floor of the great room back at their family ranch in Montana, so…

She picked up on the first ring. "So, what happened?"

"What time is it there?" He noticed Jace walking into the patio area with Deke and Kalen.

"Two-thirty in the morning—did you see York?"

"No, actually…" He took a breath. "Coco showed up."

The waitress led them over to a table near his. Perfect.

"What—is she okay?"

Wyatt could imagine his sister, her dark hair pulled back into a messy ponytail, dressed in faded jeans and a flannel shirt, barefoot, maybe sliding onto a high top chair at the kitchen island. She'd been hiding out at the ranch for the better part of six weeks, and she was probably going stir crazy. He didn't blame her for sitting by the phone.

"Yeah. She's fine. I think she's fine." The way she'd kissed him…for a moment practically inhaling him, yes, she'd been *very* fine.

"She's not—I mean, I know she's been recuperating, but…really? She looks healthy?"

"Healthy enough to take off in a sprint after she saw me." Oh, he hadn't meant to admit that part, or for his voice to carry.

Jace looked his direction.

Wyatt cut his voice low. "She seemed surprised to see me."

Silence. "I hope York is…did she say why he didn't meet you?"

Oh. He hadn't thought to ask, so stunned by Coco's appearance. "No. But she did give me the USB drive. She said it has everything on it you need."

"Copies of the emails that show I was set up for Stanislov's assassination?"

"I haven't checked it, but I'm guessing yes. She seemed pretty confident."

"Why didn't she come with you? I don't—Wyatt, did you do something?"

"What? No. I practically begged her to come back with

41

me. She said she couldn't."

"She's probably afraid of getting you hurt."

He stilled. "Wait—*what?*"

"Just that there's an assassin after her—after us. And maybe she thought—"

"I'm hardly helpless, RJ. I can take care of myself."

Silence.

"Seriously?"

"You're not a soldier, Wy. You're a hockey player, and yeah, I get that you're tough, but…"

"And *Coco* can handle herself?"

"No, but—well, York is there."

"He didn't show up, RJ. And she didn't mention him, so my guess is that she's on her own."

RJ drew in a breath. And maybe he shouldn't have said that because it did sound…now he was really going to be sick.

The waitress swung by, picked up his half empty bottle, his plate of food, and dropped off the check.

"You can't leave her there—"

"What do you want me to do? She *ran away* from me!"

Oh. Shoot. The wind caught his voice, carried it to the nearby tables. He turned his back to Jace and the guys, cut it low again. "She doesn't want me in her life. And I'm a stupid man to keep chasing after someone who just keeps leaving me. No. If she wants to stay in Russia, I can't drag her kicking and screaming back to America—"

"Wyatt—she is in danger."

"I *know!*"

Oh, maybe he should just give up the attempt to keep his emotions under wrap. "I know. But like you said, I'm no superhero. I can't save her—"

"I never said you weren't a superhero."

"You know what I mean. I'm getting on the train tomorrow, going to Vladivostok, and heading home with the team."

Silence. And shoot, but his kid sister might be crying, for the muffled breaths.

He felt like crying too. *Happily ever afters don't exist.* He

42

should probably let that truth sink in, take root. Stop trying so hard to believe.

He was such a pitiful romantic, it made him ill. So no, it wasn't the fish. Or the beer, but his broken heart that turned his body to poison.

"I gotta go. I'll see you soon." He hung up. Picked up the USB drive. Looked it over—small, about two inches, but the drive was a 32-gig, so it probably held a fair bit of information.

He dropped it into his shirt pocket, swiped up the check, signed it with his room number, and got up.

Jace glanced up at him. Wyatt nodded to him.

"Guns—you okay?"

Deke and Kalen had turned too, and the last thing he needed was the team thinking he might be falling apart.

Like Jace said, he was a leader. If he didn't have Coco, the only thing that remained was his team. His career.

Time to get back in the game. "I'm good, Coach."

Coco's voice clung to him as he headed to the elevator banks. *Our best hope is to survive.*

Yeah, well, he was very good at that game.

The elevator arrived and he got in and leaned against the wooden walls as it shuddered up to the second floor. He got off, slowing as he remembered the last part of their conversation.

And, by the way, great game. You deserved to win.

She'd been at his game? Wow, he'd completely forgotten that part.

He shook the thought away. It didn't matter because hello—She. Didn't. Want. Him.

He stuck his key in the door. It unlatched and he opened it.

For a second, he thought he might be in the wrong room. The mattress was off the bed, turned over, the bedsheets cast off. A chair at the table had been overturned, every drawer in the bureau pulled out, his clothes thrown across the room.

Ransacked.

Wyatt took a step inside. Stilled. What—?

He took another step, his entire body prickling. *Get out.* He felt the words more than thought them.

He turned—

Wyatt had been body slammed thousands of times, knew how to take a hit, but this one came sharp and fast, a blow centered in the middle of his spine.

He hit the door, cracked his jaw, but turned fast and got his arm up before the fist found his jaw.

He wasn't a street fighter—or spec ops, thank you—but he knew how to tussle, on and off the ice.

He sent a punch into the man—about four inches shorter than himself, blond, a wicked scar across his jaw, clubbed ears—but the assailant took it like he'd been grazed and came at Wyatt.

Wyatt sidestepped him and grabbed his arm, sending him into the wall. The man whirled and jabbed his elbow into his ear.

Wyatt's head spun, and he stumbled, hitting the bureau.

His attacker kicked him in the chest, and he went down.

Get up, get up!

He could almost hear the chanting, voices from the past.

He rolled, found a shoe, and flung it at the attacker, scrambling to his feet just in time to ward off another hit. He landed a right—the man grunted, and Wyatt grabbed him, whirling him to the wall. The man hit the table—the vase of roses went flying, crashing in shards against the wall.

The man bounced off, grabbing Wyatt's shirt.

Then he slammed his head into Wyatt's and threw him back.

Wyatt stumbled, pain exploding through him, dazing him. He hit the nightstand, fell off it, blinking fast.

Had the presence of mind to get his hand around a book that had fallen and slammed it against the man's head as he jumped on him.

It barely slowed him down.

Wyatt caught the attacker's fist, throwing his own, kneeing the man over his head, into the nightstand.

Get up!

The lamp had fallen and he swiped it up and threw it at the attacker, who had bounced away. It smashed against the wall as he rolled away to his hands and feet.

Too late. The man jumped on his back, his arm around Wyatt's neck, pressing against the carotid and jugular and in a second, the room dimmed.

No! He jerked back, putting everything into his movement, and his head hit the man's face.

By the shout, he'd broken something. Hoo-yah, as Ford would say.

The man fell, and Wyatt turned and sent his fist into his face.

The man stumbled, hit the balcony door, and Wyatt threw up a protective arm as the door shattered.

The man rolled out onto the cement.

"What the—"

Jace's voice came barreling into the room just as the man on the balcony climbed to his feet.

His face was bloodied, his nose gushing, his eyes hard.

Then he smiled and held up the USB drive.

Oh— Everything else dropped away, Jace's shouts fading as Wyatt leaped through the door at the man.

But the thief took two steps and jumped off the balcony.

"No!" Wyatt lunged toward the edge but hands around his waist pulled him back.

"Guns—breathe!" Jace, bigger than him, holding him, dragging him to the corner of the balcony.

"He's got the drive!"

Then Deke and Kalen were there, eyes big, Deke staring out into the night.

"Who was that?" Kalen asked. He had just enough wild-eyed crazy in his goalie genes to go after him, maybe.

"Let me go, Jace," Wyatt said, elbowing his coach.

Jace barely grunted, but let him go. "You're not going over that balcony."

Deke was staring at the room. "You did this?"

"No!" Wyatt let out a dark word and didn't care. He stood at the edge of the balcony, searching.

Lights lit up the path, but the man had vanished.

"Did you see where he went?" He looked at Kalen.

"Yeah. Out into the parking lot." Kalen pointed down the path into the darkened lot.

Wyatt hung onto the rail, breathing hard. Yeah, now he hurt. His back, his ribs, and he'd taken a shot in the jaw.

"What did he want? Money?" Kalen asked.

"No—it's…nothing."

"Paparazzi." Jace growled. "What did he steal? Pictures?"

Wyatt looked at him, and he must have worn horror in his expression because Jace held up his hands. "I was just…it's a guess."

"Who do you think I am? What—nude photos? A sex tape?" He spit out a gathering of blood in his mouth. "Wow, I thought you knew me better than that."

"I thought I did." Jace's mouth tightened into a grim line. "But you've been acting so off. What are you into, Wyatt?" He glanced at the destroyed room.

And that's when the door banged open. In strode three black-uniformed guards, guns drawn. "Militia!"

"Great," Jace said and put his hands up. Deke and Kalen did the same.

Wyatt too, only he stepped forward. "*Vso.* Okay." The little Russian he knew.

But apparently it wasn't all okay, because they came forward and ordered the four onto their knees.

Then he was zip-tied and hauled up beside Jace, Deke, and Kalen.

"I guess you're going to give that interview after all," Jace growled as they led them out of the hotel room.

Admittedly, this wasn't exactly how York wanted to die. Hands behind his back, his neck cinched tight in a noose that hung from one of the grimy overhead pipes, his feet balancing on the rickety arms of an old office chair.

No, he had hoped—maybe it was a crazy thought, really—to die in his comfortable bed, maybe sixty or so years from now, surrounded by a family. That was the crazy part. Family. A home. Which included a wife.

So maybe it was just a crazy dream after all. Besides, a man who lived by the sword died by the sword according to his deceased preacher father, so maybe this was a fitting end.

"The Bratva doesn't bluff," said Slava. Yeah, York had managed a first-name basis with his torturers. Why not? Because they certainly knew him.

Of course they knew him—he'd been on the trail of assassin Damien Gustov for the better part of three years and had finally gotten close. Too close.

So close Gustov had sent in a few thugs to slow him down.

Which, at the moment, was working if York couldn't get the last of the plastic severed from the zip tie holding fast his wrists. He'd been working on it with a piece of chipped cement for nearly an hour.

Quietly.

While Slava and his buddy Vasily hit him.

While York slowly fed out the information they thought he was so keen to hold on to.

Yeah, he knew that the Bratva was behind the assassination attempt on Russian General Boris Stanislov, one of the troika who had his finger on the Russian nuclear missile system. Thankfully, Stanislov was a moderate, more interested in American capitalism than conquering the world.

It wasn't that hard to figure out the grand plan—take out Boris. Into his government cutout would step Arkady Petrov, hardliner, comrade, believer in the Communist way.

Aka, today's mafia boss. One with long political strings and a taste for global expansion.

York let all that information trickle out in grunts and pieces as he concocted his escape plan. Because while he always knew he'd die like this, frankly, he had things to do.

Like find Ruby Jane Marshall and tell her that she'd changed him.

Or at least gotten far enough inside that he'd started to wonder if he could, possibly, change.

She'd opened up a tiny fissure of hope within him, one that had released some pretty long tamped-down desires. Home. Love. A fresh start that didn't include lies, living with one eye over his shoulder, and the perpetual screaming in his head that he'd long learned how to hide.

She made him feel free, and shoot, after a decade in his own cruel prison, he needed that like a man needed air.

Um, and literally, he *needed air*, because the noose had this inconvenient way of landing on his windpipe and shunting off his breath.

Too bad they'd gotten tired of hitting him and had shortcut to the finale because he had plenty more in him. But no, they'd thrown a rope over the four-inch pipe above him, forced him onto the chair, and issued their final questions.

York kept his voice easy. "I'm not lying to you, Slava. I'm telling you, we have proof that Gustov tried to kill the general. Not just emails from him to the American woman he set up, but I saw him myself."

Only a little white lie. He hadn't actually seen the shooter the night of the assassination attempt. Mostly he'd been looking at naive RJ standing in the spotlight for the world to blame as the shots rang out.

He'd had to do something. Which ended up being a rescue from the FSB and an epic escape from Russia.

There. He'd gotten one wrist free. And that was all he needed. But he didn't move, just held the cement piece in his fist.

"Where is the woman?" Slava was leaning against an ancient desk, his foot precariously placed on the chair, ready to kick it out.

York tasted the blood pooling on the side of his mouth. His bruises had calmed to a dull ache rather than the sharp pain from movement. That would all change as soon as he figured out just exactly how he was going to wrangle himself out of this moment, incapacitate Slava and Vasi, escape the abandoned office building probably located on the outskirts of Moscow, and hightail it to the airport in time to intercept Kat in Khabarovsk.

Tell her to leave the country.

And stop the very bad person who'd been sent to kill her.

That thought alone could cause a prayer, albeit thin and desperate, to the Almighty to watch over her. Not that York really had any pull with God anymore, but Kat was a good person. And she deserved protection.

Which meant he needed to keep it cool with Slava. "What woman?"

"The one on the train."

Yeah, Slava needed to be more specific because technically, there'd been two women on the train with him from Moscow to Siberia last month. Kat, and the other, Ruby Jane, the woman they were most likely talking about.

Since RJ was safe in America, maybe that was a truth that wouldn't cost him. "She's back in America. Safe. Where you can't touch her."

It was the way that Slava smiled, the way he looked at Vasily, who was leaning one shoulder against the grimy wall, that raised the little hairs on the back of York's neck.

But no, there wasn't a chance that Gustov could track RJ to the remote Montana ranch where she was hiding.

No. Way.

"Listen, we know it all, and you're not going to get away with any of it. We know that the Bratva *hired* Gustov to kill General Boris Stanislov last month. That after it failed, you pinned the attempt on an American tourist, RJ Marshall."

Well, not exactly a tourist, because she technically worked for the CIA as an analyst, but she'd been here on a tourist visa. Okay, procured illegally, thanks to a contact she found through the agency, a contact who had given her York's name.

He owed Roy for that. At the moment, he didn't know if that was a good or bad thing. "We know that you chased us through Moscow and tried to kill us on a train to Yekaterin-burg. Alas, she got out of the country."

Taking a terribly large piece of his heart with him. A loss he was still trying to figure out, not to mention cope with.

Shoot, he had vowed to himself he'd never be in this place again. Caring about someone, worrying about them, fearing someone like Gustov might hurt them.

Admittedly, it had him off-balance. Which was why, prob-ably, he hadn't heard Slava and Vasily get the drop on him in his safe house.

The same safe house where York had kept RJ for a week while he was trying to figure out how to save her life.

A big part of him regretted not going with RJ when she'd begged him to leave the country with her. Shoot, what was his problem—

Oh wait.

Anger.

Revenge.

Justice.

Protection.

Yeah, all very good reasons to stick around and make sure Gustov was out of the game, for good.

Then maybe he could go back to being the guy he'd always thought he'd be. The son of missionary parents. The good guy.

Except, there was that small issue with the CIA. But he'd have to face it sometime.

Until then...

"Let's get this over, huh?" He glanced down at Slava's foot, back at the guy, then up at the pipe above him, maybe two feet.

Vasily frowned.

Slava rose, as if to kick out the chair. Or at least threaten him.

York was tired of being threatened. Of feeling helpless, of only getting to fight back.

Now.

He leaped from the chair, both wrists finally free, and wrapped his arms around the pipe overhead, kicking away the chair.

Slava fell forward, and York grabbed him around the neck with his legs. He ripped the rope over his head, pulling himself free.

Then he dropped, slamming his fist into Vasily's already jacksaw nose on the way down.

Vasily roared. Yeah, it hurt, didn't it?

He landed hard with his knee in Slava's face, turned and sent his fist into his chest, right below the sternum where he could empty Slava's breath.

Then York turned to the raging bull.

Vasily roared, launching at him. He slammed York back, onto the grimy cement floor, and for a second, York's head spun, the hit so hard it felt like it had turned his bones to dust.

He managed to get an arm up to protect his head from Vasily's fists and in the meantime, lifted the knife from Vasily's belt.

Yeah, he'd seen that, and since Vasily wasn't using it...

Two quick stabs to the kidneys and Vasily howled, jerking back.

He ended it fast, with the knife to the man's jugular, then pushed him away.

Slava was still gasping for breath and York debated a second before he walked over, looked into Slava's eyes, and shook his head. "Tell Gustov that I *will* find him."

Slava's mouth was moving, but York didn't stick around to listen just in case the two had friends. He swiped his phone and his wallet off the desk and headed out of the building.

Vasily's fist had opened up the blood at his mouth, and his jaw burned, but he hustled down the hallway, pushed through the door, and found himself on a side street somewhere in Moscow.

Past midnight, given the waning of the stars, although they were hard to see against the lights of the city. A wind picked up the dust and grime littered in the alleyways, and not far away, he heard the rumble of a tramvai, the city train.

He needed a taxi to the airport because right now Kat was meeting Wyatt Marshall, handing over life-, no, world-saving information, and he needed to convince her to go with him.

Back to America.

Find RJ. Stay safe.

Let him handle Damien.

Except, he had this gut feeling, given his call to Kat some twenty-four hours ago, that she had a different escape plan.

"Wyatt? I'm meeting *Wyatt*?"

He wasn't sure why this was such a big deal—according to RJ, they were family friends. So, "Yeah, meet Wyatt. Give him the USB drive, and do what he says."

Maybe it was that last part. Kat failed the *Takes orders well* part of her kindergarten evaluation. She had her own mind—and a quick, sharp one at that.

If only she'd stayed on the phone longer, he might have convinced her. After all, at the time she was giving him Damien Gustov's hidden home address, something she'd tracked down from the massively hidden but hackable IP address on Gustov's emails to RJ, the ones where he set her up to be accused as a killer.

York had tucked the phone in his pocket, attached his earpiece, and quietly broken into Gustov's high-rise apartment building. Five upscale rooms, with a kitchen that looked out of the space age. Black furniture, brass lamps, spare, tidy, and precise.

Exactly what he expected for the private domain of one of the world's most lethal assassins.

He'd found the burner phone in a safe in the office, one that Kat had helped him hack into, thanks to the digital entry, and that's when he hung up.

Because he'd found a call list and needed the help of David Curtiss, or more specifically, his wife, Yanna, who yes, had the initials FSB in front of her name, but was as invested in finding the killer as York was.

He'd returned to his safe house to wait while Yanna

tracked down the contacts—all five of them—and discovered one of them had booked a flight to Khabarovsk in the last twenty-four hours.

She'd sent York pictures on his cell phone and it turned him cold. The woman had long dark hair, tattoos up her arm, and right in the center of the back of her neck, an eight-pointed star.

A Bratva woman—rare and lethal.

A closer look at the tattoos on her arm—a rose with barbed wire wrapped around it—told him she'd been in prison before she was eighteen.

He'd been dialing Coco again when Slava tased him.

His not-so-gentle wakeup came at the other end of Vasily's beefy fist.

York hadn't a clue how long he'd been down, but he looked like he'd spent the night in an alley. So maybe no decent cabbie would pick him up.

As he ran toward the metro station, he knew three things in the pit of his gut.

If Kat wasn't on a flight to the US, then she was in serious trouble.

Damien Gustov was in the wind.

And York *was* going to survive this and find the woman he loved—no, not loved, but maybe *needed*—no matter what it took.

Now Coco felt like a fugitive. Funny, it wasn't until she packed her backpack—her only possessions her laptop, external hard drive, a handful of necessary cables, headphones, a sweatshirt, and change of clothing—that she felt as bereft as she appeared to be.

Wounded. Her hair dyed a raven black, and she'd lost weight. A glance in the hall mirror told her that it only turned her more gaunt. No wonder Roman was worried about her when he dropped her at the train station. So worried that—

"Listen, I told you about how Sarai and I finally got to-gether—that I had to sneak into a part of the country that was under siege to pull her kicking and screaming out of trouble. And she hated me for it—but it saved her life. Eventually, she forgave me and she realized that I did what I did because I loved her." He took a breath and looked her in the eyes. "Are you sure you don't want to take this chance to go with Wyatt? Because it feels like the same crazy thing."

"And what about Mikka?"

"I can get Mikka, get him out of the country—"

"What kind of mother would that make me—leaving my son behind in Russia for others to rescue?"

Roman's mouth tightened and yes, she could hear the weird hypocrisy in her statement. Hadn't she let other people, for the most part, care for and raise her son? But no—she'd sent him packages every month. Went to visit regularly. Called and told him she loved him. It was no different than sending him away to boarding school.

She did it to keep him safe, and that thought centered her and allowed her to meet Roman's hazel-green eyes with a look that said, "This is for the best. For everyone." Then she hauled her pack out of his Lada and headed into the station.

The train to Belogorsk left the station late, so she sat on the bench, her backpack clutched to her, watching for signs of York. Or Gustov, or frankly, even Wyatt.

She couldn't pry from her gut the sense that she hadn't seen the end of him.

Oh, shoot, even hoped so. Because his touch still lingered on her skin. The taste of him, the sense that in his arms, the world stopped terrifying her.

She was safe.

But no one could keep her safe but herself, so, yeah, she hoped desperately that Wyatt was in his hotel room sleeping. And tomorrow, got on that train to Vladivostock, the oppo-site direction of Belogorsk.

She boarded and found her spot in second class, in the open car filled with sleeping berths. She opened the bench seat, took out a blanket and pillow, then shoved her backpack in the space and closed it.

A woman in her late twenties sat down opposite her. Long black hair, she wore a T-shirt and a pair of jeans. A tattoo of what looked like black roses wound up her left arm, and it looked like a complete sleeve because it even edged out of the neck of her T-shirt. "*Prevyet*," she said.

Coco gave her a smile, then curled up on the bench seat. Not as comfortable as the private berths, but her funds were low and she didn't want to take out more money from one of her various bank accounts in case Gustov might be hunting her. She'd find a place en route to—

So she didn't know exactly where. Out of Russia and someplace where she didn't need a visa. She had options— both a Russian and an American passport. She could travel to Ukraine or Kazakhstan, maybe even to Belorussia on her red passport. Then switch to blue and head into Finland or the Czech Republic. She could even set up shop in Germany.

Or she could board a flight to Alaska. She'd heard of people getting lost in the wilds of the back country. As long as she could snag bandwidth she would be fine. Go back to working for her father.

She pulled her phone from her back pocket and scrolled down to York's number. He hadn't contacted her since his cryptic call telling her to meet Wyatt.

She dialed as the train lurched out of the station. It went to voicemail—no surprise—and she cupped her hand over the speaker. "York. It's me. I dropped off the…uh, package to Wyatt. I'm on a train to Belogorsk—" Oh shoot, maybe she shouldn't have said that, but oh well— "And then I'm disappearing. I'll leave word through Roy when I get…someplace."

Roy. Their contact in Europe who had originally alerted RJ to her father's danger.

"Don't worry about me. I'll be fine." She clicked off. Turned her phone off, just in case Wyatt decided to call her and break her heart, and slid it under the pillow.

Then she drew up the blanket, pounded her fist into the

pillow, lay down on her back, and closed her eyes.

Sleep. She needed sleep. Because her body was starting to ache and yeah, maybe running hadn't been the best idea for her shredded, now-healing insides.

A conductor came by offering tea, but she shook her head. *I know we have something.*

She closed her eyes, willing Wyatt away, but the moment she did, his hand was behind her neck, his lips against hers.

She opened her eyes. Across from her, the woman had lain down, also on her back.

We always have, and I…I want you to come to America.

She rolled over, curled her knees up. Closed her eyes again.

His arms came around her, holding on to the reins as they rode one of the ranch horses through the pastures, the scent of summer in the air, the brush of his early beard against her neck.

She rolled onto her back.

I want us to be together. Be happy.

Her jaw clenched, and she threw her arm over her eyes.

Coco, I don't get it. I don't understand any of it. Why you came to me in Russia two years ago. Why you even left Montana in the first place. You… You broke my heart, okay?

Yeah, well, it was break his heart or…or…

He'd done his share of breaking *her* heart, thank you. Like when she'd showed up at the door of his hotel.

How she hated the memory.

Hated it. Loved it, and sometimes, now, in her weakness, let it wash over her.

Even if it hurt.

Maybe she shouldn't have come—she was practically a glutton for pain. She should have given in to her impulse to turn and, well, run. But no, she'd stood in the hallway of the Vega Hotel in the middle of Moscow. He had one of the executive, aka party, suites. The music slid out from under the door in a pulsing mix of Russian pop and American hip-hop. Which meant probably a mixed crowd inside.

She was about to knock when room service showed up, a

cart roughly the size of a hockey rink filled with champagne and chips and dip and pizza which said yes, there were probably Americans inside.

The room service attendant knocked at the door, and she held her breath.

Wyatt answered. He was dressed in a pair of faded jeans, a blue oxford unbuttoned two down and was grinning, looking over his shoulder, laughing at something. He wore a mid-season beard, his hair long and tucked back behind his ears, and…he looked happy. Without her.

She drew in a shaky breath. *Run.*

Then he turned to receive the food and spotted her standing across the hall and froze.

Yeah. *Hi.*

For a second, their past flashed through his eyes, the flirting, the texts and phone calls while he was at college.

The night he'd pulled her to himself and kissed her like she was more than just his kid sister's best friend.

Her throat thickened.

"Coco?"

She turned and sprinted down the hallway. What had she been thinking—that she'd show up and he'd be alone, staring out into the darkened Moscow skyline pining for her? Sheesh, she had read too many romance novels, for sure, and—

"Stop!"

His hand hit the wall above the elevator button just as she pressed it. Her breaths came hard, running under his, and she closed her eyes a second before he grabbed her by the shoulders, turning her into the wall.

When she opened them, his gaze was trailing over her, as if to confirm it was her, then fixed on her eyes. Oh, he had beautiful eyes. Whiskey brown with flecks of gold when he got serious or intense. They practically shimmered now. "What are you doing here?"

She reached up to push his hands off her. "I don't know, okay?" Her voice shook, and she wanted to just press her hands over her mouth, back away from him. The lift was taking an eternity—

But she knew exactly the answer to that question. *I'm here because of Mikka. Because you're a father and*—

"I've been trying to find you for a year," he said, cutting his voice low, almost a growl. "Ever since you came to Montana—I'm sorry. I know I was a jerk that weekend, but…you vanished." He'd taken his hands off her shoulders now, but hadn't backed away, his body too close to her space. If she ran, he'd catch her.

"I know. I just…"

"You live in Moscow?"

She nodded. Glanced at the lift. *Please.* "I'm a computer tech." Not really a lie. She could do this…not lie.

"How did you know—oh wait, the tournament."

"Your posters are everywhere."

He grinned, one side of his perfect mouth sliding up, and oh, it did devastating things to her heart. "Did you see my game?"

Her traitorous head nodded. "You were fantastic. How many shots on goal?"

"Nearly a hundred."

And he'd saved every one, practically a superhero in the crease, kicking, stretching, nabbing the pucks as the Finnish team bombarded him. "Your defensemen need a little work."

The lift dinged.

She couldn't move. Or maybe simply didn't want to. Not with him smelling freshly showered. He'd filled out even since she'd seen him a year ago, his body tighter, his shoulders defined. Not a wasted inch on him. His jeans hung low, and through the neck of his shirt, dark hair peeked out. He hadn't had that when…

Oh boy. *Run.*

The doors opened.

He looked at the lift with a hint of what she thought—hoped?—might be panic. "Don't leave. I…" He glanced back down the hall. "I can get rid of everybody. It's just a casual after-party. The team is—well, they can celebrate somewhere else."

Then he took her hand. His was strong, warm, and it sent a shock of pure electricity through her body as he wove his fingers through hers. "Please don't go."

His eyes held her captive and what could she say?

He did shoo everyone away, down the hall to one of the other players' room. Deke, maybe, but she didn't pay attention to the crowd.

Just Wyatt, who kept some of the food and set the table for them. She stood at the picture window, still not quite sure how she got here. The moon had come out to shine upon the light of Izmailovo Park, with its faux-ancient buildings, towers, bridges, and onion-domed turrets. "I've never seen it from this far up."

Inside the words were stirring, the night nearly perfect. *We have a son, Wyatt.*

"I can't believe you're here." Wyatt came up behind her, his hand on her shoulder. "I contacted RJ, but she said she hadn't heard from you, and…I'm sorry how things turned out the last time…well, in Montana."

She nodded.

"I didn't expect to see you, and the team photographer wanted pictures of my life on the ranch for publicity and…" He sighed. "I'm sorry."

"You're apologizing that the woman was in love with you?" She looked up at him, remembering too well the woman, a good five years older than Wyatt showing up to take his picture, flirting with him like he might be a teenager. "Yeah, that was hardly your fault."

He laughed and leaned down, nuzzled her neck. "Wow, I've missed you. Nobody gets me like you, Cookie."

Oh no. He'd gone right for his pet name. And the last of her reserves simply, well, crumbled. "How is your drawing coming along? Still trying to be an artist?"

He drew her back to the table and she sat down opposite him. "No. I…" *Spend my free time visiting our son.* She shook her head. "Work. It keeps me busy."

"I get that. If I'm not playing, I'm practicing or icing down or weight lifting or answering interviews. It's been a crazy year, and Coach says he's starting me this year, so it's going to get crazier." He picked up a piece of pizza, folding it in half before he took a bite. "Eat something. I ordered a lot of food. You're way too skinny."

Oh. Uh.

She must have frowned because his smile fell. "Oh, Cookie, I'm sorry. I didn't mean it like…" He put the pizza down and took a drink of his water. Wiped his mouth. Then he leaned forward, his gaze in hers. "You are still the prettiest girl I've ever seen."

She caught her bottom lip between her teeth.

He touched her face, his fingers whispering over her skin. "I've really missed you."

She didn't want to ask or argue with him, didn't really want to believe anything else but his words. So she let herself lean in to him when he curled his hand behind her neck and pulled her forward to kiss her.

He'd been her first kiss, at the age of eighteen, stolen after he'd cajoled her out to the barn to slap around a tennis ball. They'd been fighting for it as it rolled behind a wheelbarrow, and then, suddenly, he'd fallen into a stall and taken her with him.

She wasn't sure how the kissing happened after that, but suddenly his mouth was on hers and she was lost inside a place she'd only dreamed of. Wyatt's arms around her, his lips on hers. And sure, Ford had messed that up, thank you, by finding them and making a ruckus out of the escapade, but nosy kid brother Ford wasn't here now.

Now, it was all Wyatt, his mouth sweet and tender, drawing her in to himself as he stood them up. He reached behind her, caught her legs, lifting her around him, so she could kiss him face-to-face, settle her arms on his shoulders. Then he just held her there, kissing her so thoroughly she'd forgotten why she'd tracked down his hotel, sneaked into the lift, followed the party up to his room, and tried to find the courage to talk to him.

Wyatt made her feel safe. He was gentle and caring, and even as he brought her over to the bed, even as he settled her down into it and pulled her into his arms, she felt cocooned in his presence. Big. Solid. Focused.

He took a breath, as if he might be nervous, and it sent a funny feeling through her, like maybe he wasn't quite as changed as she thought.

Wasn't the big time hockey player with the flock of women.

Maybe Wyatt was still the shy boy who'd cried the first time they were together.

She wanted to believe that.

He'd kissed her neck and then raised his head and met her gaze. Swallowed, a question in his beautiful eyes.

Yes. She'd nodded. "I've missed you too, Wyatt."

Oh, she still missed him, and as the train lurched, she rolled over, pressing her hands to her face, trying to hold herself together.

Because if she could, she'd stay right there, in the last good memory between them. In the place where she always belonged.

Wyatt's embrace.

4

Wyatt rued every single Russian spy novel he'd ever stayed up late reading—le Carré, Forsyth, Follett, Lee Child, even Tom Clancy—because every torture scene had rolled into one, settled into his bones, and turned him desperate by the time an officer came to get him.

The grousing from Jace, Deke, and Kalen hadn't helped—even after Wyatt had told them everything, three times, emphasizing the fact that he had *no idea* why someone would want to rob him.

He was turning into a pretty decent liar.

But as the officer shoved him, still cuffed, down into a metal chair and shut him in a room that had KGB written all over it, Wyatt considered rethinking his answers.

Yes, nude photos. And he wouldn't cop to sex tapes—hello, that felt too tawdry to even lie about—but he had a litany of possible explanations. Whatever it took to get him out of these zip cuffs and on the train to Vladivostok in the morning.

The door opened and a woman came in. Blonde, midfifties, she wore a thin line of red lipstick, cool blue eyes, and the uniform of a militia officer.

"I'm sorry for the delay," she said, offering a smile he didn't quite believe. She sat down in the chair across the table. "We were busy gathering evidence." She placed a long manila folder onto the table. Opened it up. He recognized the handwriting of the officer who'd taken down his initial statement.

At the time, he'd also been bleeding, holding a compress to his nose, and trying to wrap his brain around the fact that he'd lost the only evidence his sister had of her innocence.

Sometime later, as he sat in the cell—a chipped and dour eleven-by-eleven cement dungeon that stirred up visions of gulag and Siberia and had Deke praying under his breath—Wyatt realized that if Coco still had the USB in her possession, she might have been the one attacked.

Which led him to the fact that maybe someone saw her hand him the device in the garden at the hotel. And that meant that someone had been following her.

Or him.

Which gave all sorts of credence to the idea that a real live and deadly assassin was very truly after Coco. And probably RJ.

And Wyatt had beat him up.

See, he could have been a SEAL. So, hoo-yah.

Except, well there was the fact that Wyatt had lost the evidence.

But if he could find Coco, maybe she could reconstruct it.

Except, he *couldn't* find Coco. Not without help, and certainly the woman across the table wasn't a great bet.

In fact—and this was where the spy stories kicked in—he didn't know who to trust.

Probably no one.

"No problem," he said now and flashed her his best smile. "I'm glad to answer any questions."

She glanced up at him and raised an eyebrow.

Oh, that might be too much cooperation, maybe. They wouldn't believe him from the start. Which might mean bright lights, toothpicks, maybe even waterboarding.

He liked his water frozen, thank you.

He stopped smiling. "I've already given my statement—"

"Just a few questions."

Her English was good. British, with an accent.

"Why was this man in your room?"

Oh, he got to start with the big lie, huh? What was it that

Ford said once—or maybe it was Tate. Lie with the truth attached. "He was there to steal something, probably."

"And what could that be?"

Wyatt lifted a shoulder. "Money? My credit cards? I don't know. This isn't the first time I've had someone break into my hotel room. Once, in BC Canada, I found an entire fan club sitting in my suite, wearing only—"

Oh. Maybe not *that* story. "I asked them to leave. Because I'm not that kind of guy." He slowed his words down. "I know it sort of looks like that—my publicist is big on getting me cover gigs—and then there was this ad for the sleep number bed and they put me in the bed with this woman I didn't know, but she wanted to know me, if you know what I mean, and that got super awkward because like I said, I'm really not that guy. I haven't even had a girlfriend. Ever. In college I sorta dated this one girl from my econ class, but that was because she was smart, and yeah, I guess I might have used the fact she liked hockey to get some help, but I *didn't cheat*—I draw the line there. It was all studying. And I scored a C in that class, which was actually amazing, because I hate numbers and—"

"*Stoy!*"

He recoiled. "Sorry."

She pressed her hand to the table. He stared at it. Fat fingers.

"So, you don't know why this man broke into your room."

His voice caught in his throat. Uh.

"Calm down. We are just trying to find your attacker."

He must have looked afraid. Which was very, very close to the truth here, so he let out a breath. Swallowed. And dodged the question. Which was a legitimate technique his publicist taught him about talking with the press. "I...I just walked in and there he was. And he jumped me, and I fought back. He went over the balcony, and that's the last I saw of him." There. All truth.

She stared at him. Pursed her lips.

A knock came at the door. "*Minutichkoo!*"

Oh, that didn't sound calm at all.

Another knock, and he offered an apologetic smile. "I have this sort of pregame routine where I listen to music while I warm up. I have to stretch out, a lot, and I get in this sort of zone, away from the other players—and really, I have to because being a goalie is sort of your own island. You can't hide out there. So, I just get in this place, you know, where I'm listening to *Here Comes the Boom*, or yeah, I do sometimes zone out to *All I Do Is Win*, but that's a crazy song, so that's not my go-to, but I have a whole playlist, and I just get down into the zone, visualizing my saves. Over and over, sinking them into my head and just forcing my body to feel it. Because you can't think when you're out there on the ice, you just have to know—"

"Oy," she said and got up.

He closed his mouth as she opened the door. Said something in Russian, glanced at him, and left.

Huh.

He sat there on the chair, shoulders hurting, trying not to think about the second tier of interrogators, and really, what did it feel like to be waterboarded? And no, he actually didn't want to find out, and probably he couldn't hold out any longer, and—

And Coco was out there, and the man who'd taken the USB drive was after her and...

He was getting out of here and finding her, no matter what it took.

The door opened and a man walked in. Tawny brown hair, built—clearly gym honed—but he had the gait of someone who knew his body, knew how to hurt someone.

A sweat beaded along Wyatt's spine. But he just swallowed and met the guy's hazel-green eyes with his own, ready to go another round.

Yep. So ready.

So—

"So, you're Wyatt, Kat's friend."

He stared at the man. He wore a black sweater with leather

shoulder pads and now folded his arms across his impressive chest.

Probably, Wyatt couldn't take him. But he'd give it his best shot. Go down swinging. "Why?"

The man raised an eyebrow. "So here's the deal. I know what really went down in that room. I know she gave you the jump drive, and what I need to know is—do you still have it?"

Oh these guys were good. Very good.

Wyatt needed a drink. Water.

Okay, maybe something stronger than water, but right now, his throat was closing up, fingers digging into his chest, and—

"I'm a friend."

Wyatt's eyes widened. That's what they all said. Especially in a Lee Child novel. What would Reacher say? *I don't know what you're talking about.* No, no, Reacher would say something like, *In two minutes, I'm going to be out of these cuffs and you're going to wish you were already dead.*

Why didn't *those* words come out of his mouth?

The man frowned. Sighed. "Listen. My name is Roman. My wife Sarai and I have been taking care of Kat since she showed up on our doorstep a month ago, wounded. She went to meet you today on orders from a friend named York. And I know where she is. Trust me yet?"

Wyatt nodded, a little too enthusiastically for his taste, but, "Where is she?"

"Did the assailant get the USB drive?"

Wyatt stared at him, and for a moment, he was in the zone. The one where he stared down a wing, eyes on the puck, feeling his next move in his bones, knowing exactly how to react. "Tell me where she is."

Roman cocked his head. "On one condition—after you describe the man who took the USB drive, you get on the train to Vladivostok with your team and go straight back to America."

"And you've lost your freakin' mind." Wyatt pulled at his bonds. "Coco is in trouble, and I'm not going to let anything happen to her."

"Neither am I. I'll find her, put her in protective custody. But first—is there a reason to worry about the USB drive?"

"Yes!" And shoot, he let out a word that betrayed the fact he might be going off the rails.

Tuck it back in, Guns.

"Yes. He took it. A blond guy, maybe five ten or more, good with his hands. A professional. He had a scar on his jaw and clubbed ears. He jumped me, but I think I broke his nose."

Roman held up his hand. "Breathe, Wyatt."

Wyatt narrowed his eyes at him.

"I really am on your side." He started to get up.

"Who was that man?"

"If my guess is right—and we're still tracking down CCT footage to see if we can find him on the hotel cameras—his name is Damien Gustov."

And ding, ding, ding, that rang a bell because that name matched up with the name RJ used when she'd relayed her horrific get-out-of-Russia-before-you're-killed-by-a-hit-man story.

Wyatt went cold, his shoulders simply rising and falling as he tried to get back up, mentally, from his crash onto the ice.

Gustov had the drive. Had probably followed him from his meet with Coco to get it.

And who knew but he was on his way to kill Coco right now.

"Where. Is. *She?*"

"I think I'm going to let you cool off right here in holding until the train leaves." Roman headed for the door.

"Where is she!" Wyatt stood up, knocking the chair over, rounding the table, heading straight for Mr. KGB.

Roman turned, something lethal in his expression. "Step back." He didn't raise his hands, didn't move, but his entire body had tightened, and Wyatt recognized it.

Ford and Tate did that too when they were snapping into some kind of warrior mode.

Well, it had nothing on angry athlete. Hello, he wasn't helpless.

He'd nearly taken down a killer, thank you. Broken his nose.

He might be cuffed, but he could still do damage.

Would even feel good about it.

"She's on her way to a city called Belogorsk. And then, she's leaving the country."

"But you *will* catch up to her," Wyatt said softly, not sure if he was playing along or pleading.

"I will. And I'll keep her safe." Roman's gaze met Wyatt's. Held it. "I'd like to think you'll stay put if I let you go back to your hotel."

Wyatt said nothing.

"Yeah. I thought so. I'll have the guard bring you a blanket."

Then he opened the door and led Wyatt back to holding.

Coco had missed out on so much of his young life. And if she made the decision to leave, she'd miss out on the rest.

Coco stood outside the high fence of Orphanage 23, the sun over the houses of the small Russian city of Belogorsk, fingers of light cascading down the dirt roads, around the two-story blue and green wooden houses, and into the back yard of the group home.

Dew glistened on the playground equipment—slides, a wooden swing set, a merry-go-round, a sandbox filled with toy trucks, soldiers, and tanks. A couple tricycles sat under the overhang near the door.

Small, but cute, the sprawling one-story, orange stucco detski home was outfitted better than most, with a gymnasium, a media room, new beds, an educational center. It sat tucked away in a neighborhood with houses and gardens, pets and other children running down the streets. Just another family amongst many.

That was, if no one looked at the fencing that cordoned off the place. And what no one could see were the security cameras hidden in the oak and linden trees that surrounded the yard.

She couldn't help but see it as a prison. For children.

Twenty children lived here, most of them abandoned, but a handful, like Mikka, had parents who visited.

Some of those parents were people like her—single mothers who couldn't keep their children.

Only one had a private nanny hired to care for him.

Her father had found the place in a village time had forgotten. The best kind of hiding place, really. Coco had helped set up the surveillance, had vetted the children who lived here. Her father had hired the security guard who acted as one of the children's physical education teachers. A man who was probably tired of his life in the FSB or the Spetsnaz and wanted to settle down with his family.

A man with something to lose if Mikka should be found.

With the recent passing of the law that excluded foreigners from adopting children from Russia, Mikka was safe from mistaken red tape. He wasn't going anywhere, and no one was getting in without her knowing about it.

It didn't feel any less remote, untenable, and terrifying, especially for the children inside. But sacrifices had to be made…

Oh no, she was starting to sound like her father.

Coco wove her fingers into the fence, watching as the door opened and children ran into the yard.

If you're not careful, you're going to get your son killed.

The words could still take her apart, that terrible moment the next morning in the hotel room in Moscow.

She'd spent the night, the entire night, in the arms of the man she loved. And every moment was as beautiful as she'd hoped it might be. Wyatt was gentle, and this time she hadn't been quite so afraid.

In fact, it might have been him who'd been more afraid, asking her in a voice she barely recognized if this was what she wanted. Meeting her eyes with a vulnerability that suggested maybe he wasn't quite the player the tabloids made him out to be.

"I've missed you so much, Coco." His words whispered into her ear, the scratch of his beard on her skin. He'd trembled in her arms.

He'd reminded her exactly why she'd fallen for him. There was no going back now. As soon as he returned from his early morning practice, she'd tell him about Mikka. *We need to talk, Wyatt.*

He'd take them both back to America. Marry her. And she would live the life she still longed for.

Then the knock at the door. She'd thought he'd left his key behind, or maybe ordered up room service, like last night. She'd drawn one of the hotel bathrobes around her and answered the door.

Just like that, all her dreams shattered. Because Colonel Natalya Smolsk stood on the other side, dressed in the uniform of the FSB, her dark brown hair pulled back. "What have you done, Katya?"

For a second, Coco had forgotten. Forgotten that she was not only Russian but the daughter of one of the most powerful men in the country. Maybe the world.

Forgotten that she didn't really have choices. That she'd never had choices. Forgotten that her life didn't belong to her.

Forgotten that she didn't get to change her life, escape, live in the world she'd dreamed of. That chance died when she'd abandoned her life in Montana and fled back to the man she thought would protect her.

In truth, the general *was* protecting her. It just felt...

Natalya stepped into the room, shutting the door behind her. "Get your things—"

"No."

Oh, the look on Natalya's face.

Coco knew her father's security chief would have a reaction. She just hadn't expected it to be pure disgust. Especially as her gaze traveled the room, from the empty champagne glasses to the pizza box to the rumpled covers.

Yeah, Coco had felt naked.

"Did you tell him?" the colonel snapped.

"He's Mikka's father."

"He's no one. And you are someone. And if you're not careful, you're going to get your son killed."

Cold slivered through her.

Because she didn't know if that was a threat or a warning.

She got dressed. "I want to talk to him—"

Natalya grabbed her arm and pulled her out of the room.

Two of her thugs-slash-FSB officers stood outside the room, one of them by the elevator.

Coco's eyes filled. "But he won't understand—"

"He's a stupid American hockey player. Do you seriously think you're the first woman who's spent the night with him since he's been here?" She turned to one of the men. "What is this—number five?"

Coco had gone numb, down to her toes.

As the lift opened, Natalya turned to her. Laughed. "It's not like he loves you." Then she pushed her into the lift. They took it to the garage, shoved her into a car, and took her back to her father's dacha outside the city, until the tournament was over.

Not long after, her father moved Mikka to Siberia. And with that move, any chance of Coco leaving.

Except, leaving was the only way to keep him safe now. Because her father wouldn't let anything happen to his grandson.

Please.

She drew in a trembling breath as she spotted Mikka.

If possible, he'd grown an inch, his brown eyes brighter, his smile more infectious, and his hair darker, with sweet Wyatt-like curl at the ends.

He looked like a miniature version of his father and could wreck her on the spot. She tightened her grip around the fencing as he ran for the slide and climbed up the ladder. He wore the blue jeans she'd sent him and a lightweight canvas jacket and a pair of boots. The entire orphanage had received clothing in a package she'd sent from Moscow—one more way to hide him among the masses. He got to the top of the slide.

"*Smotree!*" Look at me!

One of the women—yes, his private nanny, a middle-aged woman named Lana—waved to him. She had no children and had been an elementary school teacher. "*Ya smatroo!*"

He raised his arms and slid down.

His feet caught under him, however, and he pitched forward, landing on his hands and knees.

Oh—Coco wanted to run to him, pick him up, especially when he cried out. He got up, lifting his scraped hands, running over to Lana.

She blew on his hands, then picked him up and hugged him.

Coco's heart nearly shattered into pieces.

Mikka pushed away from her and scampered over to the swings, clearly recovered.

Coco gripped the stupid lion she'd purchased at a kiosk in the train station. He was probably too old for stuffed animals, but really, what did she know? She wasn't really his mother—just the woman who'd birthed him. A visitor in his life.

Lana, who drank a cup of tea and chatted with the other two teachers, was more of a mother to him. She wore her brown hair short, a thin coat over her pants and shirt.

Did she read stories to him? Sing to him at night? Coco's throat tightened.

At least her own mother hadn't left her in Russia when she'd fled the country. No, she'd dragged Katya, albeit kicking and screaming, out of the only world she'd ever known and settled her into the back country wilderness of Montana.

Coco had never felt so abandoned, so alone in a world where the language felt unwieldy, despite the rules of English she'd been taught. She didn't understand the customs or how to live in this new world.

It had terrified her.

Then her mother had died of leukemia and abandoned her completely. If it hadn't been for the Marshalls, for Wyatt…

No, she couldn't do that to Mikka.

And, maybe she shouldn't even be here. Because he wouldn't understand.

He was getting old enough to remember her. To ask questions.

Maybe it would be better for him if she were simply a dream. A hazy recollection. She could still send him money. In a few years, her father would send him to an elite boarding school somewhere in Europe, and he'd have a brand new life. One that could build a future for him. What could she give him, really?

Coco turned, and a dog in a nearby yard barked at her movement. It alerted the woman sitting on the porch, and Coco froze.

Lifted a hand.

Lana got up, glanced at Mikka, and then headed over to the fencing. "Katya?"

"*Prevyet.* I…I was in town and wanted to see Mikka."

"Of course. I'll get him ready for you—"

"No. I just…I'll just stand here and watch him."

She'd hired Lana because of the way she had looked at Mikka, a softness in her eyes, as if she could truly love him. She now gave Coco a smile, the same softness in her eyes. "Come in and spend time with him. He knows you. He has your picture by his bed. He will want to see you." She cast her gaze on the bag, the lion peeking out from it. "And he'll be delighted with the gift."

Coco didn't know why her eyes glazed, but she seemed to have no mind of her own when Lana motioned her to the gate entrance. She pressed in the digital lock and opened it.

A couple children were riding the merry-go-round. A couple more looked up from where they were teeter-tottering. She walked over to the edge of the play yard. Mikka was digging in the sandbox, motoring a truck through a tunnel he'd made. His dark brown hair fell over his face—he probably needed a cut, but it reminded her so much of Wyatt, she just wanted to touch it. He pursed his lips, making a motoring noise.

"Mikka, someone is here to see you," Lana said.

Mikka looked up, first at Lana. Then at Coco.

She held her breath.

His concentration dissolved into a slow, perfect smile. "*Mamichka!*"

Oh—uh—

He got up and sprinted toward her. She had enough presence of mind to crouch. To open her arms.

To catch him when he flung himself into her embrace.

He caught her around the neck, his strong little body melded into hers.

She pulled him against her. He smelled of the laundry soap, and perhaps his morning kasha, and the outdoors, and crazily, a little like Wyatt, as if he embedded the skin of his son.

Coco could do nothing but hold on and weep.

I'm assuming your plan ends with assassination?

Yes.

If you kill him, we'll never have the opportunity to discover who hired him and what he is after. Or how he works. Or his alliances.

"Seriously, RJ? An old *Alias* rerun?"

The voice, not on the television screen, jerked RJ's attention from the drama and over to where her big brother Reuben leaned against the doorframe to the wood-paneled den of the Marshall family ranch home.

Reuben wore the mantra Big Brother well, from his rank in the Marshall family to his actual size. The former smokejumper-slash-sawyer-turned-ranch-foreman had the shoulders of a buffalo, his arms thick, not a spare inch around his waistline. No wonder he'd won awards in high school for his football prowess. But the man was a gentle giant and his voice was soft as he came into the den and sank down on the recliner.

"It's 2:00 a.m. What gives?"

RJ sat on the sofa, a knitted afghan pulled up over her, a mug of hot milk in her grip. Darkness pressed against the windows, and the house smelled of tonight's pot roast and homemade bread.

For a prisoner, she was living well.

She shrugged, not sure where to start. "This is my favorite episode. It's where Will finds out that Sydney is a secret agent. She saves him and blows his mind."

"You were addicted to this show when you were a kid. I remember you saying you wanted to be like Sydney when you grew up."

He smiled. She didn't, painfully aware of what she'd said.

What a joke she'd turned out to be. Oh, she'd had big, high-flying visions of who she'd be. And a crash-and-burn reality.

She lifted a shoulder, keeping it casual. "Mostly, I watched it for the romance between Vaughn and Sydney."

"You've been down here every night for…well, at least the last couple weeks. And that's just since Gilly and I moved in permanently. What's going on? Does this have to do with your…event in Russia?"

Event. That was one way to say it.

Another could be Idiotic Attempt to Save the World. As if what she did mattered. As if she could be a hero like Ford, or frankly, any of her brothers.

Apparently, she would always be just the girl who needed saving. Something her nightmares reminded her of every night. The residue of tonight's nightmare, another rerun of her bare escape from a killer, still buzzed under her clammy skin. Even now, a half hour later, she could still hear the gunshots that had taken down Boris.

Still feel York's hands on her as he grabbed her and told her to run.

She was still running.

And he was still in Russia, trying to keep her safe.

Or maybe not. Maybe York had forgotten about her. It wasn't like she was Sydney Bristow or he was Vaughn.

She ran her fingers through the golden fringe of the afghan. "Every time I close my eyes, I think about Coco and leaving her bleeding in some Russian alley…"

Coco. Their foster sister.

Out of the corner of her eye, she saw Reuben's mouth tighten. Oops. He'd always been a protector, looking over his little sister like a mastiff.

He reminded her so much of their father. Quiet. Faithful. Strong. Brave.

Not unlike York.

Oh for Pete's sake, she really had to stop thinking about the man. About his dark blue, pensive eyes trying to read her. The way he pulled her to himself, held on to her as if…as if…

As if he was trying to… Save. Her. Life. Because she needed rescuing.

She needed a good dose of reality. Namely, that she was a peon CIA analyst—*former* CIA analyst, thank you—and he was some kind of 007-slash-Jason Bourne who had risked his life to get her out of Russia.

A superspy who'd kissed her.

Oh, how he'd kissed her.

Sometimes, she simply stopped and hung on to that kiss. The way he'd pushed her against the wall and kissed her like he might be pulling his heart from his body to give it to her. He'd tasted of desperation and danger and what-if and *if only* and she had let herself believe—for that moment—that maybe he could love her.

I could find you when this is over.

York's words, spoken in his slight British accent, probably meant to convince her to leave him.

On the screen, Will was following Sydney as she dragged him, wide-eyed and terrified, to safety, and yeah, maybe this wasn't the episode to watch.

Because she wasn't Sydney. She was Will…in over her head.

Yes, her feelings for York had everything to do with the fact he'd saved her life and nothing at all to do with reality.

"I never did hear what exactly happened," Reuben said, picking up the remote and turning off the television. "You came home, and you went quiet and we didn't want to pry. But now I'm prying."

Oh.

"All I know is that Ford was completely freaking out," Reuben was saying. "I suppose we all were—after you were blamed for shooting that general."

"General Boris Stanislov," she said. "He's one of the troika—one of the three Russian leaders who can deploy nuclear weapons. He's a moderate and has been a supporter of peace and nuclear disarmament." And was Coco's biological father. But she left that out because Coco had hidden that truth for years when she lived in Montana.

Boris had sent her to the States with her mother to hide after she'd nearly been kidnapped.

"And they thought you tried to kill him, why?"

She reached for the half-empty bag of Doritos she'd found in the pantry and pulled out a chip. "Because I was standing on the street corner near the restaurant when he came out. And someone had slipped a gun into my purse. I'm not sure it would have taken much more than that—I was in the country on a fake visa, something hurried I got through our contacts, so…"

Reuben just stared at her.

"I was trying to *stop* the assassination."

Reuben's mouth tightened into a dark line. "And York? Who is he?"

York. Ex-Marine. Attached to the CIA somehow. A fixer, maybe. And her contact in Russia. "He works in transportation." She said it exactly how York had, straight-faced, without a hint of irony.

A raised eyebrow from Reuben suggested the same response she'd given York.

"No, really. He helps people get in and out of the country."

"Mmmhmm," Reuben said. "Did Coco hook you up with him?"

Coco. Aka, Katya Stanislova. The woman they knew as Coco Stanley.

"No. Actually, I was…in need of some help and York…" Found her. The man had materialized from nowhere right after the shooting to grab her. Had practically tackled her into an alley to save her from the FSB. Brought her to his safe house.

Risked his own life to get her out of the country. "Hid me, then arranged for me to meet Coco. He didn't know we knew each other."

"Why Coco?"

"She was—is—a hacker. See, when I found out about the assassination threat against the general, I contacted a man who I thought could stop it. Turned out that those emails routed to someone else—a man named Damien Gustov, an assassin who was hired to shoot Stanislov."

"And frame you for it."

"Yes."

"Why?"

"We don't know—we think he works for the Bratva."

"The Russian mob?" Reuben drew a breath. "You were running from the *mob*? RJ—you're not…well, you're *not* Sydney Bristow. What were you thinking?"

And no, she wasn't deluded, but thanks for that, Reuben. She pulled the afghan to her chin. "I *wasn't* thinking, okay? I was scared, and I didn't know what to do. I just knew that…" She swallowed, her throat thick. "I know I was stupid. I got in over my head. I know it's my fault Coco got shot—"

"What?" Reuben leaned forward. "No it's not."

"Yeah it is. We took the Trans-Siberian train—me and Coco and York—and York had to kill this guy—"

Reuben stilled. "This guy *killed* someone?"

"No, I mean, he was a Bratva agent, and he'd found us, and York—he was defending me. And then he threw him off the train, but he was worried that others would find us, so we got off but…" She closed her eyes, pressed her hands to her face. "That's when Ford found us, and that's when Coco was shot."

Reuben had gone quiet, and when she brought her hands down, he also wore this pained, sort of thin-lipped, grim look.

She wanted to reach out to him, let him pull her into his massive arms.

"Someone started shooting at us. And Ford and York ran down the alley to stop him and…" She shook her head. "Oh, Rube, I was so stupid. I started running after York, and Coco grabbed me, pushed me back, and that's when she was shot. If I hadn't been so—" She reached up and wiped her cheek. "You're right. I'm not Sydney Bristow. I'm just stupid and now…" She swallowed. "Every time I close my eyes, I'm back in that alley with Coco's blood on my hands, listening to her whimpering while York and Ford fight with an assassin, while I sit there and…unravel."

Yeah, that's the word for it. Since that day she'd been slowly unraveling, losing pieces of herself. Not sleeping, her eyes reddened, eating too many cookies, and *hiding*.

Yes, hiding was exactly what she'd call it. Hiding from a Russian assassin, sure, but hiding from her mistakes. Hiding from her regrets.

Hiding from the fact that she wasn't at all the person she'd wanted to be.

A superspy didn't wake up in a cold sweat crying.

A superspy didn't spend hours binge-watching television because she was afraid to sleep.

A superspy didn't sit by the phone hoping the man she'd walked away from would call from the other side of the world.

She wasn't anything but super pitiful.

"I can't go back to work either to try and find them because when Ford and I fled Russia, we found out that the CIA had put a hit on me too."

Reuben's eyes widened. "What—?"

"The Chief of Station at the embassy in Russia, a guy named David Curtiss, said that he'd also heard rumors that there was a rogue group working inside the CIA and they had made me the prime suspect."

"The CIA can't kill their own people."

She lifted a shoulder.

"Is there no one you can trust? No one you can talk to?"

"And tell them what? I have no evidence. Not until Wyatt gets home with the information Coco is giving him."

Reuben just stared at her. Then, quietly. "*What* did you say?"

Oh. So maybe Wyatt had left big bro out of *that* conversation.

"Wyatt is in *Russia*?"

She bit her lower lip. "A hockey tournament."

"Slash secret mission," Reuben said, shaking his head.

She looked away. "If he gets hurt, that will be my fault too."

"And there we are, back in the cave."

She looked at him, and he raised an eyebrow. He had inherited their father's dark hair, his solemn, steady demeanor, and sometimes he reminded her so much of Orrin Marshall it turned her inside out.

"What do you mean?"

"You know what I mean. Sometimes, I think you never left that cave you and Ford were trapped in when you were twelve. You always blamed yourself for the fact that he didn't go for help."

"I begged him not to. I was scared to be left alone, and because of it, we nearly died."

"You and Ford are like two sides of the same coin. He always blamed himself for not having the courage to leave."

She shook her head, but Reuben got up and sat down next to her on the sofa. Put one of his big arms around her and pulled her to his chest. He was warm and safe, and she just wanted to sink into his embrace and let him tell her that everything would be all right.

While she sobbed in his arms.

But superspies didn't cry either.

"Sydney Bristow always knows exactly what to do. But not me. I ran to Russia, thinking I was brave and smart and…"

"And now you're having nightmares."

She closed her eyes.

"I understand getting in over your head. I once thought Gilly had died in a fire and I just…I lost it. I couldn't think, I couldn't move. I completely fell apart."

She had a hard time imagining that. "I guess I realized that I'm not who I thought I was. I planned to come home, dig up evidence, save the world. Instead, I can't sleep, all I do is eat Doritos and bake sweets and I jump at every noise I hear. I'm not me. I don't know who I am. Or what I'm supposed to do."

"I know who you are, Rubes." Reuben kissed the top of her head. "And if you need time to get yourself back together, you're welcome to stay right here on this sofa." He picked up the remote. "Even Sydney Bristow needs rest in between saving the world. Now, hand me those Doritos."

5

That's about the closest I ever want to get to a gulag. Thanks for that, Wyatt." Deke was folding down his bed in the private compartment of their train car. The man looked—and smelled—exactly like Wyatt. As if he'd spent the night in his clothing on a hard, wooden bench in some chilly cement Russian prison cell with urine stains in the corner. They'd eaten Wyatt's definition of gruel for breakfast—runny oatmeal with specks of brown he dearly hoped were raisins. His gut clenched with the memory.

At least someone had packed his gear. He'd found it deposited in his train compartment when the militia dropped him, Deke, Kalen, and Jace off at the train station.

Wyatt had received an extra-special escort by a quiet and large FSB agent to his train car. A glance out the window revealed said agent wasn't taking chances on his escape.

"Sorry about that," Wyatt said. "I don't know why they felt the need to detain you guys too."

Deke opened his duffel bag, also packed by someone on the team, and retrieved his headphones. He glanced at Wyatt. "I got your back, Guns. But next time you suggest a goodwill trip to Russia, I'm out." He settled the headphones around his neck. "And I don't understand why we couldn't fly of out Khabarovsk to Seattle."

"We have some sort of meet and greet in Vladivostok the consulate set up," Wyatt said, scrolling through his phone, which he'd found in his duffel bag. No calls from York or his sister.

Or Coco. Not that he expected one, but…

Please let her be okay.

He'd spent the night replaying his conversation with the FSB agent—Roman?—in his head. *I'll keep her safe.*

Yeah, maybe.

The train jerked, then eased forward. Wyatt braced his hand on the wall, still staring out the window.

I know we have something. We always have, and I…I want you to come to America. With me. I want us to be together. Be happy.

He should just sit down, let the train take him away from this nightmare. Leave the shards of his broken heart in his destroyed hotel room.

Deke leaned against the back wall, legs on the sofa, arms folded, eyes closed. The guy could sleep anywhere—he'd snored himself into REM last night on a chipped wooden bench. Jace and Kalen had been in the cell next door, and Jace had shouted a couple times, not nicely.

Jace wouldn't even talk to Wyatt as they drove to the train station.

Yeah, this would be a fun trip home.

Except maybe he shouldn't go home. Maybe—

You should just forget about me.

That would be like forgetting how to breathe.

Wyatt pressed his hand to his chest and sat on the bench seat. Stretched out and closed his eyes, trying to ignore the deep ache in his hips. Oh, Russia was so very fun.

The train bore a rhythm that reminded him very much of the countless bus rides, early in the morning or late at night. The rides he'd learned to sleep through, exhaustion embedded in his bones. Now, he lay on his back, forcing himself to stop thinking about the fact he'd failed.

Oh, he'd failed.

Failed to bring Coco home. Again.

Please don't go.

His voice tugged him back through time to that moment

by the elevator in Moscow when he'd seen the rest of his life, everything he wanted, right there within his grasp.

A pro career doing what he loved. Travel. Money. And... Coco.

He couldn't believe it when he'd opened the door and saw her standing there in the Russian hotel hallway, as if she'd simply materialized.

She looked good. The kind of good that stopped his heart, stole his breath, shut out the rest of the world. She'd cut her red hair short, and her gray-green eyes wore just enough surprise, just enough fear for him to see the girl he'd wanted to protect back at the ranch.

Except, they *weren't* back at the ranch where Ford and the rest of his nosy brothers could interfere with his life.

Just him and Coco, and there was no way, no how he was going to let her walk out of his life again.

Please.

Of course, he'd said none of that. Just an astonished, "Coco?"

What he should have said, if all of his brain had been working, was, *I'm sorry. I missed you. I love you.*

Yes, even that.

He didn't know when he'd started loving Coco Stanley, but he hadn't realized how he'd kept it bottled inside.

Seeing her standing there...it all rushed over him in a cascade that could probably bring him to his knees.

She turned and practically sprinted toward the elevator.

What—*wait!* So, he shouted at her. *Shouted.* "Stop!" But he'd never been good at taming his emotions, unless he locked them away, like he did in a game, so he sprinted down the hall after her.

Slammed his hand against the wall to try and stop her from hitting the button. And when it didn't work, he'd grabbed her, spinning her around.

She had her eyes closed. As if he might be scaring her.

That slowed him down to a near halt.

He hadn't meant to be rough with her. Suddenly she felt

so fragile, so breakable under his grip, it scared him a little.

But for some reason he said, stupidly, "What are you doing here?"

Which really meant *You look amazing*—but emerged as cold and maybe even bullying.

She pushed him away, fire in those beautiful eyes. "I don't know!"

She was angry with him.

Maybe he should have expected that. He'd barely spoken to her the last time he'd seen her. The commotion of the visit, the fact that the team had sent a photographer out to take shots—it all went straight to his thick, arrogant head.

Coco had tried to talk to him that first night. He saw her standing outside the den where he was giving an interview with the photographer.

An interview that probably looked very much like a date, with the woman sitting too close to him.

Shoot, and him letting her.

Then he looked up and saw Coco standing there, and everything—*everything*—that happened between them rushed into his head.

Coco, it's not—

She walked away. All the way back to Russia.

But she was here now, and he might never, ever get another chance, so—

"I've been trying to find you for a year. Ever since you came to Montana—I'm sorry. I know I was a jerk that weekend, but…you vanished."

He didn't want to move too far from her.

Especially since the elevator was moving toward their floor.

She said something about her living in Moscow, about her job, talked about the game, maybe, but he wasn't listening.

Just scraping through his brain for a way to make her stay.

The doors opened.

Right then, yes, the panic hit full stride.

"Don't leave. I…"

His first thought. His *only* thought. Behind him, the music from the party in his room drifted down the hall. Just a few of the guys, some women they'd met during the tournament.

Not even his idea—thanks, Deke. But his agent liked to cultivate this image of him as some sort of playboy. Apparently, it sold covers. And made him a most-wanted celebrity for paparazzi.

He wasn't a player. Had never been. But he did like to be liked.

Coco looked past him, as if she wasn't sure, and it sparked the tiniest flare of hope.

So he took her hand.

It was just as soft and fit so amazingly well into his strong, chipped grip. He wanted right then to tug her to himself, the stir of longing so deep it rocked him. *I love you.* "Please don't go."

He held her beautiful eyes, not daring to breathe.

She nodded. His heart restarted, and he practically sprinted down the hall to kick Deke and the rest of the party out of his room.

He'd lost his mind after that. Barely remembered their conversation. Probably he tried to explain the weekend on the ranch. He knew he'd made her laugh. And called her too skinny—shoot, she'd always felt a little small around him and his family.

But she *was* skinnier than she'd been a year ago, as if she'd had a hard year, and while she said nothing, his heart broke a little to know that she might not be okay.

With everything inside him he wanted to protect her.

He did remember telling her she was pretty...a sort of spilling out his heart that followed him leaning forward to kiss her.

Oh, he'd been aching to kiss her.

More even than that first time, two years prior, in the barn.

He still wanted to choke Ford for finding them. Poor Coco nearly ran from the barn in a full-out sprint.

Her kiss then had ignited something inside him he couldn't

douse. And a month later, when he came home for Christmas break, it flashed over. He'd known it was wrong. Known he was taking advantage of her, maybe, but...

She hadn't seemed hesitant, and he was just as afraid as she was. And not just of getting caught but...

He knew that Coco was the only girl he'd ever love.

Ever give himself to.

Shoot, holding her in his arms had practically turned him into a baby. He might have even cried.

The first time between them had been awkward and rushed and not at all what...well, and how could it be? He was a little ashamed of the fact that it had happened at all. That he'd let his emotions trample over everything his father had drilled into him.

But he wasn't his father. Didn't want to be. He'd long ago walked away from the Marshall family expectations.

He wasn't really a Marshall, and he knew it. He just carried the Marshall name.

Not the Marshall family hero and honor genes.

Besides, nearly all the guys on his college team had girl-friends. The kind who stayed overnight.

So he'd followed his heart and...

Shoot, it hadn't been *at all* how he'd imagined it. They hadn't talked about it either. But that night she'd walked inside his heart and never left.

And despite the press and the games and the after-parties, that was still true. She was his one. His only.

His Coco.

Tonight...tonight would be exactly what he wanted for them. And yes, maybe he was still stepping over his moral upbringing, but he'd saved himself for her. Only her. And hadn't broken that internal vow since.

"I've missed you so much, Coco."

In his heart, he was hers, for life. So, he'd reached out and kissed her and she sort of melted into him like she, too, had missed him. She tasted of home and the piece of himself he'd been missing, and the little sound of surrender she made could make him weep again as he picked her up, drawing her closer. She slid her arms around his neck, and the smell of her skin wound through him, and he lost himself.

Not that he wanted anything but to find himself in her arms again.

But maybe she didn't want that, and for a second, after he'd brought her over to the bed, the thought that…well, that maybe they'd made a mistake the first time pierced him enough for him to raise his head. Meet her eyes, stir up the courage to ask—"Are you sure?"

She nodded her answer just as he got the words out. "I've missed you too, Wyatt."

Oh, he wanted her. And not just physically, but her heart. Wanted to tell her about the craziness of playing goalie for one of the best NHL teams in the league, to hear about her life in Moscow, and to trace out his dreams for them.

He wanted to stay right there, holding her, and not come up for air.

Except, he had early practice. So he'd left her in their warm bed, tangled in the sheets, with a kiss and a promise to return. *We have to talk, Wyatt.*

Yes, they would. About all their tomorrows.

He'd even brought a couple of coffees back to the room. The *empty* room.

She hadn't even left a note.

If it weren't for the fact that she'd shown up in the Blue Ox fan forum a few months later, or the fact that his publicist made him answer postings, he might have never found her again.

The forum certainly wasn't the place to bare his heart.

You should just forget about me.

Not hardly. But he couldn't take her walking out of his life again.

Except, something about the way she'd kissed him, looked at him…

Coco is in trouble, and I'm not going to let anything happen to her.

His words to Roman came back to him, solidified in his

chest.

The train jerked, and he opened his eyes. The early afternoon sun hung high in the window, heating the red vinyl seats. The train swayed, and out of the window, they passed tiny blue or green farmhouses with ornate windows and coal smokestacks. The occasional cow or goat wandered dirt streets.

He'd traveled back to World War II or 1, into a different world, a different time.

Deke was snoring.

Wyatt got up and opened the door of the compartment, not sure where he was going, just that...

Well, the burning in his chest wouldn't let him sit.

"Oy, look at who showed up."

He glanced down the corridor, and leaning up against a window, her arms braced on the railing, was the brunette reporter from the bar. Nat?

He tried out her name, and she smiled. "You remembered."

She was wearing a pair of black jeans that might have been painted on and a T-shirt printed with some Russian band on the front.

"You're traveling with the team?" he asked, and *obviously*, but he didn't know how else to account for her presence.

"A girl's gotta make a living."

He didn't know what to say to that except...

"Wait. Are you really a reporter?"

She made a face, looked away. "Yeah, sure."

Oh.

He stared out the window. "Have you ever heard of Belogorsk?"

She nodded. "It's a village west of Khabarovsk. About a six-hour train ride, the other direction."

In the distance, another tiny town rose from the horizon. "Are we stopping here?"

"Probably. Not long, but long enough to get something to eat and—"

"Wanna make some money?"

She looked at him, raised an eyebrow.

He held up a hand. "No. Not like that. I mean..."

And the crazy thought appeared out of nowhere, formed, and took possession. "I need to get off this train. And on a train to Belogorsk. And...I could use a translator."

She made a little noise that sounded like disbelief.

"Really. That's all."

She considered him. Glanced down the hall. "How much?"

"I have five hundred dollars, cash—"

"Not rubles."

"Dollars."

"*Vso*. Done. Get your stuff."

And now he was back in a le Carré novel. But he wasn't leaving Russia without one more shot at saving the girl he loved.

Even if he ended up in gulag.

She couldn't leave this child.

Coco stood in the play yard of Orphanage 23 at the end of the slide, watching as Mikka climbed to the top, his teeth gritted.

He was a charmer, this boy of hers. She'd stayed with him all day, through his morning classes—read aloud time, crafts, some gymnasium time—took tea with Lana and the other teachers during nap time, and now, as the sun began its slide into the far horizon, she followed him around the play yard, pushing him on the merry-go-round and swing and digging tunnels with him in the dirt.

"Is it my birthday?" he'd asked when she gave him the stuffed lion this morning, and the question had made her want to weep.

What kind of mother only showed up for her child on his birthdays or holidays or...

She didn't deserve this golden boy.

He had Wyatt's strong jawline, his dimple on the right

cheek, those long dark lashes and brown eyes flecked with the gold that made him a prince. And when she tickled him, his laughter embedded her bones with joy.

"*Smotree!*" he shouted now as he stood at the top of the slide.

"*Sidee—*" Sit. She patted the slide.

He grinned at her, eyes shining with a familiar mischief. But he sat and pushed himself off.

She caught him at the end, picking him up, twirling him around. "You're so brave and strong." *Just like your daddy.*

Mikka wiggled out of her arms, running toward the merry-go-round.

"He'll be fine," said Lana, standing behind her. The woman stood with her arms crossed over her body. "He's a smart boy, and he'll understand."

Coco watched as he climbed onto the merry-go-round, holding onto the railing, pushing with one foot. "How can he? I don't even understand." She shook her head. "I hated my mother for moving us from Russia. And I was ten years old. *And* had recently nearly been kidnapped. I understood why my father sent me away." She ran her hand over her cheek. "I still hated it. It wasn't until she got sick that I forgave her. By then it was nearly too late. She died of leukemia when I was fourteen."

Lana touched her arm. "She did what was best for both of you. And she saved your life."

He was running now, trying to keep up with the spin.

"Mikka, be careful!"

He pulled himself onto the spinning ride.

"Maybe I should take him with me." She glanced at Lana. Behind her, the smells of dinner—some sort of beef soup with fresh dill and potatoes—sneaked out of the kitchen. Probably it was better than what she'd feed him. She subsisted on ramen noodles and cold cereal.

"Where would you go?"

The answer came easily. "Montana. Back to the Marshall Triple M. It was the last time that I..." She swallowed. "The last time I felt safe."

Lana said nothing.

"They have this big family. Reuben—he's the oldest. He left home years ago, though, to fight fires. The next brother, Knox, took over the ranch. Tate is a couple of years younger—he was in the military. Wyatt plays hockey. And then there's Ford." She shook her head. "I saw him last month. He's a Navy SEAL."

"Spetsnaz."

"Yeah."

"Which one is Mikka's father?"

Coco glanced at Lana. About her mother's age, Lana wore a soft smile. "You never said who his father was, but I am guessing it's one of those brothers."

"Wyatt."

Just admitting it felt like exhaling after being underwater.

"I fell in love with him nearly the first time I saw him and…"

"You still love him."

She shrugged. "It doesn't matter now. Wyatt doesn't know about Mikka, and he never will."

Mikka was hanging on now, throwing his head back, his hands and legs wrapped around the bar. Enjoying the ride.

Reminded her of Wyatt as he skated, so much enjoyment on his face it could fill her soul.

Or break it into pieces.

"In my dreams, I live on the ranch with Mikka and Wyatt." She couldn't believe she voiced that. "But that will never happen."

"It sounds like a lovely dream," Lana said quietly.

The merry-go-round slowed, and Mikka sat up, turned, and slid off.

"Careful!" Coco shouted, but Mikka landed hard on his backside.

She went to run to him, but Lana held her arm. "Wait."

Sure enough, Mikka climbed to his feet and scampered off to the swings.

"He is a tough boy," Lana said.

He'd have to be.

"Where will you really go?" The question was innocent, she was certain, but any real answer could put Mikka in danger.

"I don't know. Off the grid for sure."

"And Mikka?"

"In a couple years he'll go to live in boarding school. Maybe under a new name."

Which meant she may never find him.

He climbed aboard a swing.

"You are strong too, *maya lapichka.*"

She didn't know why, but the words stirred up the past, and even as she looked at Lana, she saw her mother lying in a hospital bed, holding her hand.

You will survive this, maya lapichka. You will bloom and grow into an amazing woman. Someday, even a mother. But in all things, remember. You are strong. And you are not alone.

Yes, actually, she was. Very alone. She gritted her jaw against the ache in her chest rising to consume her.

"*Smotree!*"

She looked over just in time to see Mikka jump off the swing into the air.

"Mikka!" Now it was Lana's voice that joined with her own as Mikka landed in the dirt, falling onto his hands and knees.

Coco beat the woman to him, picking him up. His lip trembled, his eyes sheening.

"You're okay," Coco said and pulled him to herself. "You're okay."

"He's bleeding," Lana said, and Coco pulled him away. Sure enough, from his nose trickled a line of blood.

She set him down and pinched his nose while Lana ran to the house for a towel. "Does it hurt?"

He shook his head.

She picked him up and carried him to the house, meeting Lana at the door. Pressing the towel to his nose, she brought him inside to the kitchen. She set him on the small, long kiddie table and crouched in front of him.

Blood had spilled onto his shirt.

Tears filled his eyes. "*Mnye zhalka.*"

"It's okay, baby," Coco said. "It was an accident." She checked his nose. The bleeding seemed to have stopped.

"I didn't see him hit his face," Coco said to Lana.

"He gets them a lot," Lana said, holding a clean shirt in her hand.

Coco tugged up his shirt, and he held his hands up for her to lift it over his head.

A slow horror washed over her as she saw his body. Bruises, both large and small, some gray-green, some a deeper purple. They darkened his arms, his torso.

She looked up at Lana, who handed her the shirt. Coco took it but kept her gaze in hers. "He's got a lot of bruises."

Lana crouched next to her, as if to examine him. "He's a boy. He falls down a lot. But I'm sorry, I didn't notice there were so many."

She swallowed, her throat thick. They weren't...uh...

She'd vetted this place, had looked into Lana and her history. Nothing suggested abuse.

As she looked at the bruises, they didn't seem to be pressure marks, as if he'd been grabbed, but rather bumps and bruises.

Still, her hands shook as she pulled the shirt over his head. Then she picked him up and walked over to the sink. Lowered her voice.

"Do you like it here, Mikka?"

He was moving his head away as she washed his face so she stopped. Met his eyes. "Do they hurt you?"

She really didn't care that Lana was standing just a few feet away and could hear her.

He shook his head.

She finished washing his face and set him back onto his feet.

Lana came up to her. "He is safe here."

Coco couldn't read her expression, but that didn't matter.

She turned to Lana. "I'm trusting you with his life—"

"I know." Lana's eyes sparked. "No one loves him like I do."

The statement could dig a tunnel through Coco, but she nodded. "How often does he have nosebleeds?"

"Sometimes at night. Sometimes after he plays."

Mikka scampered back outside, laughing. He didn't bear the fear of an unloved, abused, or even neglected child.

"And how long has he been bruising?"

"I don't know. But sometimes he cries at night because his bones hurt."

A chill shivered through her. "Does he get sick?"

She shook her head.

So maybe it was nothing, but— "When is the last time he saw a doctor?"

"Last fall. He got a complete checkup. He's fine, Katya." Lana touched her arm. "I promise. He's just an active little boy."

Coco followed her back to the yard where she and the other teachers called the children in for dinner. Tried to chase the worry from her head as they ate and then as she pulled him onto her lap for a story.

Mikka held the lion in his arms as she read, his own body tucked close to her. She wanted to lock the smell of him inside her, along with the picture of his smile, the joy in his beautiful eyes.

She settled him in his bed, one of ten in a room. Kneeling beside it, she reached inside to find the person her mother had told her she was.

"Mama has to go now, Mikka, but you remember this. You are strong." She kissed his forehead, then pushed his dark brown hair from his face. "And you are loved."

"Will you come back for my birthday?"

She pressed her hand to his cheek. "If I can."

He rolled over and pulled the lion into his embrace, and she could barely breathe.

Lana waited for her by the door. Without a word, she

pulled Coco into her embrace.

Coco let her, her jaw tight, then pushed her away and without a word grabbed her backpack and headed away from the orphanage, trying not to look back.

Trying not to break into a thousand pieces right in front of her son.

Be strong. Be a Stanlisov. Be…

She broke out in a run, breathing hard until she turned the corner. Then she leaned against the building and pressed her hands to her face.

She was a terrible mother. But she was just trying to keep him safe, right?

Just keep moving. She finally managed to pull herself together, to breathe out the terrible grief in her chest. *Don't look back.*

The dirt street was quiet, just a couple dogs barking at her through fences. She headed down the main street under the glow of a street lamp, onto the cobblestone sidewalk.

Her heartbeat banged against her empty chest as she walked through the semidarkness to…where? She hadn't thought all the way to the moment when she had to leave.

Maybe a hotel—the Intourist Hotel was usually located near the train station.

Or maybe right to tonight's train—

Footsteps behind her made her stiffen.

Clearly, she was still a little paranoid. She hunched her shoulders, put her head down, and stayed under the lights of the sidewalk.

The cadence of the footsteps quickened, rushing at her. She turned to look—

"Run!"

The voice came from across the street and she got just a glimpse—a man, solid, quick, and with enough urgency in his English—*English!*

"Run, Katya!"

Behind her, a woman was running at her. Dark hair, tattoos up her neck—

The woman from the train?

Coco screamed as the woman leaped at her.

She at least remembered to throw her backpack before she turned and fled down the street.

York was tired of getting there too late.

He hadn't been able to keep Tasha, his girlfriend, from being run over.

Hadn't been able to warn RJ of the setup.

And now, he was two steps too short from stopping Tattoo Tanya—his name for the assassin the Bratva had sent—from hurting Kat.

He'd taken a flight from Moscow straight to Blagoveshchensk, then hopped a train to nearby Belogorsk. Frankly, he hadn't the foggiest idea why Kat had gone to Belogorsk, of all places, but he'd downloaded a Google map on the train.

A town of sixty thousand in the middle of Siberia.

Maybe she'd come here to hide. He'd tried to call her nearly a dozen times, but the calls went to voicemail and he'd nearly done something stupid and called Yanna, his contact with the FSB, to see if she could track her.

Instead, York had gotten lucky.

He'd seen Kat walking toward the vokzal while he was getting a chebureki from a kiosk. Almost didn't recognize her with her dark hair, especially in the shadow of the hour. But she wore jeans, Converse tennis shoes, and a backpack.

She might be Russian, but she dressed like an American.

Only then did he catch her tail. A woman also, given her slim figure, dressed in black. She wore boots, her hair long. And she walked just far enough behind Kat as to not be obvious.

His gut clenched, and he'd shouted, took off running.

Run, Katya!

Tattoo Tanya took off too, something glinting under the streetlights in her grip.

This wasn't going to be a clean kill.

Kat had flung her backpack at her, but Tanya batted it away.

It slowed her enough for him to make up those two steps. York practically flew over the curb and tackled Tanya before she could stick the knife into Kat's neck.

Which left him dodging a lethal slice into his gut as she went down. He grabbed her wrist and slammed it against the ground. She hung on to the weapon, but he hit it again, and it released from her grip.

His tackle had landed them on a grassy area off the sidewalk, and she kicked him off her and rolled to her feet.

He did not want to hit a woman, even one trying to kill him. But she rushed him, and he stepped to the side and gave her a hard push.

She hit the dirt and rolled, coming up with the knife.

"Aw, c'mon."

She came at him, slashing, and he dodged, narrowly missed a hit, and grabbed her arm.

She kneed him hard. A shot of agony spiked through his head, but he hung on even when she hit him in the face.

"*C'mon!*" He ducked his shoulder, rammed it into her chest, pulled on her arm, and flipped her over onto her back.

She landed with a whump that should have taken out her breath. But she grabbed him and pulled him down with her. He rolled backward, still holding her wrist, grabbing her other to keep the knife from slicing through him.

The weapon came up between them, he turned to face her, and in a movement he couldn't have stopped if he'd wanted, her body weight slammed down on top of him.

The knife slid between ribs into her body.

She swore at him, lying over him, her blood hot on his body.

He pushed her off onto the grass, the knife protruding from her chest. She gasped for air.

They were hidden beneath a trio of linden trees.

"York?"

SUSAN MAY WARREN

Kat's voice turned him. She stood on the sidewalk, her hand pressed to her mouth. "Is she—"

"Yeah. Or she will be." He got up, painfully aware of the blood that saturated his shirt. He unbuttoned it, ripped it off, and wadded it into a ball. He turned to her. "Let's move."

He grabbed her arm and pulled her into a space between buildings. Gestured to her pack she'd retrieved. "You got a shirt in there?"

"Big enough for you? No. But I have a sweatshirt that might fit." She swung her backpack down and pulled out a black sweatshirt.

He barely squeezed into it, pulling up the hood. He looked like a freakin' teenager, so he pushed up the arms. It didn't help, but he wadded the shirt up and shoved it into the front kangaroo pocket of the sweatshirt.

"Here." She handed him a bottle of water. He washed his hands, wiped them on his pants, then took a drink.

His hands were shaking as he replaced the lid. Handed the bottle back.

She took it without words and slipped it back into her backpack.

"Let's go." He led her out of the alley and quick-walked toward the train station.

It had all happened so fast, neither of them said anything for a long moment. Not until he walked past the train station and turned down a shadowed street.

"What's going on? How did you find me?"

"You called me, remember?"

"I…but, who was that? I saw her on the train—"

"She works for Gustov. One of his assassins, I think."

Her breath shagged out, ruffled and thick.

"You're going to be fine. We just need to lie low until we can figure out our next move." They passed Lenin Street and then turned down a side street—Partizanskaya Street for the patriots. He spotted a two-story blue-and-white building with the Gostinitsa over the door. Hotel.

Out of the way, cheap, but by the sign, it had internet and

a café.

The lobby was empty, and Kat wandered over to a fish tank as he booked them a double room. Two beds, second floor, near the end of the hall.

York came over to stand by her. "C'mon."

She drew in a breath.

He hadn't seen her in a month since he'd dropped her off at Roman and Sarai's apartment, and now he took a good look at her. Thin, pale, and not a little shell-shocked. Yeah, well, being on the run did that to a person.

"I'm a fish," she said quietly. "Just swimming. Going nowhere. People watching me."

"Oh brother. Let's go." He put his arm around her, and they took the stairs to the second floor.

The room was clean, the wallpaper gold, the bedspreads a light blue. He turned on the lamp between the beds, and the light pooled on a wooden floor, a thin scatter rug.

She sank down onto the farthest bed as he walked over to the window and drew the shade. Then he turned to her.

"What are you doing in Belogorsk?" He didn't mean his tone—except, maybe he did because frankly, he was still shaking a little from the knockdown with Tanya, her blood in the cracks of his hands, despite the brief washing.

"Aren't we going to talk about the body we left back there?"

He just looked at her a moment, then headed to the bathroom, tore off the sweatshirt, and washed himself. Then he pulled out his sodden shirt and washed it out. Blood ran down the drain, but he scrubbed his shirt as clean as he could, then wrung it out and hung it over the shower.

He grabbed a towel, draping it around his shoulders as he emerged and leaned against the doorjamb.

She was staring at him.

"My question first." He raised an eyebrow.

"I came to visit my son."

If Tanya had risen from the dead and burst in through the door, it would have surprised him less. He blinked at Kat, trying to wrap his—

"Yeah, I have a son. Almost five years old. And he lives here in Belogorsk in Orphanage 23." She said it with her gaze hard in his, but behind it, he saw the hurt, the pain of her words.

So he said nothing. Just swallowed. He wanted to ask about the father, but maybe he'd died. Or just wasn't in their lives.

Or maybe he was, and Kat just didn't want to mention him.

Really, it didn't matter. "Why would you come here? It just puts him in danger."

And that was the wrong thing to say because her eyes filled. And she so didn't deserve a dressing down from him, of all people.

She'd gotten shot on his watch, thank you very much, so there was that.

"Sorry." He walked over and sat on the bed opposite her.

"No, you're right. I just…" She pressed her hands to her face. It jarred him a little seeing her so unraveled.

Kat was always put together. Always organized. Always— well, she lived with the slightest edge of paranoia, so maybe this was the other side.

"I just had to say goodbye."

Oh. His throat thickened. Right.

Because if she was going to disappear that meant… "I guess I *don't* understand. How is it you have a son and he lives…here?"

Tears lined her cheeks as she looked up. "My father convinced me—well, I mean, I agreed, but—it's just safer for him, you know?"

No, he didn't know. Because he'd grown up without his parents and it *wasn't* better. But he didn't say that, clamping the words inside.

"I mean, if anyone knew who he was, they could kidnap him, hold him for ransom, and—"

"And put pressure on your father, the general."

She wrapped her arms around herself and scooted back on the bed. Leaned her head against the headboard. "Yeah. It's why he sent me and my mother to Montana—there was a kidnapping attempt made on me."

"But you were with your mother—"

Aw, shoot, he shouldn't have said that because she looked so suddenly beat up. It occurred to him that she'd probably told herself that a thousand times.

"Sorry. I'm just trying to wrap my mind—"

"I was scared! I had this baby, and I didn't know what to do, and my father...he helped me. I know he's not exactly the warmest coat in the closet, but he convinced me that Mikka would be safe and that I could visit him all the time, and I did—I *do*. Every chance I get. He lives with this woman named Lana, and he's strong and beautiful and happy, except..." She closed her eyes, the tears still running down her cheeks. "Except I think he might be sick."

She inhaled, her breath ragged, and looked at him as if he might have answers.

Not a one. "What kind of sick?"

"I don't know. Lana says he's fine, and he *is* an active boy, but he's got bruises and is getting bloody noses and it..." She wiped her face again. "It reminds me of when my mother first started getting sick." She drew in another long breath. "She died of leukemia."

Oh, Kat.

And he wasn't sure if he should reach out and pull her to himself.

He didn't do big emotions. They sort of snarled up inside him and cut off his breathing. Close to how he'd felt the first time RJ had kissed him.

Full-out panic followed by a confused desire.

He felt none of that now, however, just a deep sorrow. But before he could move over and reach out to comfort her, Kat shook her head and bounced off the bed.

"What are you doing?"

"I'm going back there to get him. I'm going to take him to

Khabarovsk and have Sarai test him."

"What about the doctors here?"

"What about them?" She rounded on him. "This is my son. And I'm sorry, but the medical care in America is...well, it's light years ahead of the care here. If he's sick, we're going to America."

He stood up. "Calm down. As far as I know, that woman who followed you is the only person Gustov sent after you. Mikka will be fine tonight. We'll go back first thing in the morning and get him, okay?"

She looked up at him, her eyes big. Nodded. "We have security there, too, so..."

"See? He's going to be fine. You look wiped out. Go to sleep. I'll keep an eye out for trouble."

She sank back onto the bed. Considered him a moment then rolled over onto her side. "You're a good man, York. I can see why RJ loves you."

She closed her eyes.

He sat on the bed, stared at his wrinkled hands, and tried not to let her words cut off his breathing.

Because maybe the very last person RJ should love was him, despite his feelings for her.

In fact, in his gut he knew he probably wasn't the kind of man any woman should love.

6

W hat are you going to do after you find her?"

The question came from Nat, who sat across from Wyatt. She had wound her hair up into a bun this morning and was reading a newspaper offered by the conductor when she'd trolleyed by with her food cart earlier.

Nat hadn't tried, not even once, to suggest anything beyond their business arrangement. Just done her job, from helping him escape the train to purchasing him a ticket back to Khabarovsk. When they arrived, she hustled them through the station to catch yet another train, this one overnight.

What had happened to airplanes, he wanted to know, but when he'd asked, she'd told him no airplanes landed in Belogorsk.

It was a little like saying a plane wouldn't land in Duluth, Minnesota. Although, yeah, he'd been there a few times and he wouldn't want to land in Duluth, Minnesota, either.

"I don't know," he said now. He hadn't gotten any further in his head beyond step one: find Coco.

Step two might be to convince her to come to America with him.

That was the extent of Wyatt's plan as he tossed the night away on the hard berth of the sleeper car in their private coupe on the train to Belogorsk.

He spent some time thinking about Jace's shouts as the train pulled away without Wyatt, hightailing it across some village train platform in the boonies of Far East Russia.

Wyatt might be in a smidgen of trouble when he got stateside.

Finding Coco was worth it.

Finding her, and getting to the bottom of why she'd say something as impossible and idiotic as *Just forget about me.*

He wasn't that guy, and he was about to prove it. Maybe that's all she wanted—a guy who wouldn't let her go. Who chased after her.

He should have done that two years ago probably, instead of letting his hurt keep him paralyzed, cut off his breathing, and leave his heart in shreds. But he'd been young and stupid then.

Today, he was on a train to a remote town in the middle of *Siberia.*

He'd bet Tate and Ford had never been to Siberia.

"She'll be surprised to see you, no doubt." Nat gave him a soft smile over the top of her newspaper. "Do you know why she's in Belogorsk?"

He shook his head. "I was just told she was here."

"By?"

He didn't want to tell her. But, "The FSB."

"Is she in trouble?"

He couldn't decide if she was pretty or simply handsome. Shapely enough, she had a sort of edge about her that, if he didn't know better, would tag her as military. Lean, spare, and with an awareness of people who walked by that seemed reminiscent of his brothers. He'd put her in her late thirties, maybe, not the typical age for a woman in her, um, profession.

Maybe she *was* a reporter.

"No. Nothing like that," he said.

"Then what's the urgency?"

Good question. Desperation, maybe? "If I don't, then I...I feel like I'll never see her again."

Hopefully Nat wasn't taking notes for her exposé on goalies who'd been hit too many times in the head.

"You Americans are so romantic."

He snorted. "No. I have four brothers. Trust me, we're not romantic. They're all cowboys—"

"My point exactly."

"Don't believe everything you read."

"I know. I'm a reporter." She winked but put down her paper. "So, why this girl? Why now?"

He looked out the window. The train had started to slow as they'd entered the outskirts of the city, the outlying suburbs congested with blue and green painted houses, tall fences, cement garages, and dirt streets. Such a disparity with the cities. He spotted an elderly woman pumping water into a container in the middle of the street.

"She's the one who got away."

Nat said nothing, and he looked over at her.

"She's…I've been in love with her since I was sixteen."

"Really?"

"She came to live with my family after her mother died, and we spent the summer together. I taught her how to drive and to ride a horse, and she would shoot tennis balls at me in the barn and…I don't know. She was quiet and she listened to me. She made me feel like I wasn't the strange one."

"Why are you the strange one?" Nat asked as she folded the newspaper and set it on the seat beside her. She picked up a sugar cube balanced on the side of her cup, then dipped it into the tea and put it in her mouth.

Huh. "I don't know. Maybe it's because I play hockey and… well, I guess I've always played hockey and no one else in my family does. My uncle played, and I got the bug when he came out to visit with my cousins from Minnesota one Christmas. We had a tiny rink in town that we used for recreation, and he took me down there and slapped some pucks around, and that was it. My mother signed me up for a local peewee team. I played wing back then, and I fell in love. And not just with the competition, but the sport. The quickness of gliding over the ice, the toughness of it, the skill it takes to handle a puck, even the teamwork. Maybe that was it—I was a middle kid in the family and felt pretty much invisible. My brothers loved the ranch, but I didn't. And I think my father knew it—there was always something off between us. I didn't feel a part of them. Then suddenly, I had something of my own. Hockey. And I was good at it—really good. I don't know what it is, but when I'm on the rink, I feel almost invincible. Like...I was born to play."

He looked out the window. The train was moving deeper into the city. "As I got better, I had to move away to play—I spent the summers at hockey camps, and when I was sixteen, I moved to Helena to play on a traveling team. I lived with my coach and his family. Coco came to live with us the summer before I moved."

He turned back to Nat who was looking at him, listening.

"I was pretty freaked out, but she'd just lost her mom, so we sort of bonded over feeling like our lives were crazy around us." He smiled, the memories sweet. "But together, we were safe. I felt seen, and maybe she did too."

Nat said nothing.

"She's the only girl I've ever loved," he said quietly. "And I blew it. Somehow, I blew it. I mean—I don't know why, or how, but...okay, I might know why, but I didn't mean to... screw up. I thought..." He shook his head. "Last time I saw her, I let her go without a fight. I was stupid and hurt and angry. This time...this time, I'm probably still stupid and hurt and angry, but I'm also...well, I know what a jerk I can be, and I don't want to be that guy anymore."

He hadn't a clue why he might be unloading all this onto a stranger. Stress maybe. And she just sat there and listened. But even as he spoke, he felt something shift inside him. A resolve, maybe.

Or perhaps just him hunkering down into the zone. He looked again at Nat. "Yeah, she's in trouble. She needs me, and I'm going to be there, like I should have been before. I'm going to keep her safe."

And once she duplicated the information that had been on the jump-drive—yes, he couldn't wait to tell her he'd lost that—then his sister would be too.

"If she's traveling," Nat said, "she'd do it by train. You have no idea why she'd come here?"

"No."

"So, we'll wait for her near the station. Eventually, she'll come back."

She made it sound like they might be a couple wolves, stalking their prey. Maybe they were. And who knew how long they'd have to camp out?

But absent any other plan...

He watched as his tea shivered in the glass snugly fit into a metal holder. He'd eaten a hard roll with what might have been raisins inside. What he wouldn't give for some eggs and crispy bacon—and not the raw version they served in the dining car.

He packed his gear as the train pulled into the station, a long yellow and white building with multiple tracks edging up to platforms. Greeting them in the center of the cobblestone square stood a bronze statue of Lenin. Pigeons scattered as travelers, some with rolling bags, others with duffel bags, moved toward the train.

None of them were Coco.

He hiked his bag onto his shoulder and followed Nat out of the train, across the platform, and into the building.

A light crowd of travelers sat on wooden benches, their bags tucked between their legs. An overhead ticket counter listed prices to various locations. A couple—a man in a leather jacket, a woman with a red plaid dress—sat at one of the round tables in front of a café.

None of *them* were Coco.

"Let's go outside, by the door," Nat said and headed through the station.

They emerged to the other side and scattered more pigeons. Overhead, the sky had turned a bright blue, the sun still peeking over the horizon, the clouds wispy. A beautiful day for late August, the temperature cool enough to warrant his suit coat but with hints of heat. He got a couple looks as people passed him, and he considered that he could probably use a shower, a shave.

The train station overlooked a bus stop, a row of vendors in blue tin-sided kiosks. Nat gestured to one of them. "I'm going to get a chebureki. Want one?"

He hadn't a clue what that was, but he nodded, his stomach a beast.

She headed out across the street, and he wandered over to the edge of a raised flower garden and sat down.

A bus pulled into the stop across the street and people streamed out, most of them headed toward the station. A woman with a pram strolled by.

Belogorsk had all the makings of a storybook village, no sense of the chaos and rush of the city.

Why Belogorsk?

Coco already had a sort of mystery about her. When she first showed up in Montana at age ten, sporting a Russian accent, she was the town curiosity. His mother had invited her old friend over to the ranch, and Wyatt found Coco in the barn watching the goats.

You can pet one.

She looked at him as those beautiful gray-green eyes widened. *Won't they bite?* Only she said it in her accent. *Von't zhey bite?* It sort of knocked him over.

"No," he said and climbed over the fencing to pick up one of the skin and bones baby goats. He held it out to her.

She stared at him, and he reached out and took her hand. "Trust me."

She considered him a moment before nodding, and he placed her hand on its body, the hair more wiry than soft. Then the goat shivered and bleated, and she yanked her hand away and laughed.

He'd only been twelve, but he was a goner for that laugh. High and sweet and it found his bones and never left.

Sometimes, when he closed his eyes, he could still hear it. Even—

Oh. He jerked, and yeah, laughter, somewhere—it came from ahead of him, across the street.

Just like that, there she was, walking along the cobblestone pathway as if she'd emerged from some side street.

He'd almost missed her.

Wyatt bounced to his feet, intending to shout but—

She was walking with a man. Nearly as tall as Wyatt, maybe, dark blond hair, square-jawed, he had his hands in his pockets, as if casual, and he was smiling at her.

A dark fist went around Wyatt's heart.

She'd come to Belogorsk to meet a *man*.

Just...forget about me.

Yeah, maybe he should have.

He glanced over and found Nat standing in line at the kiosk. Debated. Looked back at Coco. She was disappearing down the street.

Nat had money and could take care of herself. He picked up his duffel and dashed after Coco, calling himself a fool.

But he still couldn't get it out of his gut that she was in trouble.

Maybe this guy had something to do with it.

He cut across the street, kept them a good distance from him, and followed. They reached the end of the long block, then turned onto a dirt road. He hung back, staying in the early morning shadows. She was gesturing with her hands as she talked. He was a big man, wide shoulders, a steadiness about him as he walked as if...

Oh, man, this guy could be military.

FSB?

Wyatt quickened his pace but didn't catch up.

They stopped at a tall gate, the entire house fenced off, and as he tucked himself in behind a hatchback, he noticed the play yard out back.

A school, maybe.

The gate was opened by a man, and Coco and her friend went inside.

Wyatt crouched behind the car, feeling like an idiot.

Maybe he should just go in there. But what would he say? *Hey, Coco. Funny meeting you here. I was just...in the neighborhood.*

You should just forget about me.

He cupped his hand over his eyes. Oh brother. He should just... Move. On. Apparently, she had.

Maybe. *Shoot.*

He was about to get up when he heard the laughter again, only this time it was higher, brighter, and he looked up to see Coco emerge from the gate, holding the hand of a little boy.

A cute kid. Tousled brown hair, a grin on his face. He wore a lightweight canvas jacket, a baseball hat, and a pair of jeans. Maybe about four or five years old.

And holding his other hand—the blond man. He carried a bag.

Coco stopped and crouched in front of the kid. Wiped his cheek with her thumb, then kissed his forehead.

She wore an expression that looked so familiar, it spiraled right to his bones. A smile, an affection in her eyes, a joy he hadn't seen since...

Moscow.

That morning when he told her he would return.

But when he had, she'd been gone.

So maybe he'd just been deluding himself about that joy.

Except—

Wyatt couldn't move. What if...what if that was why she left? Because she had a...child? *Wyatt, we need to talk.*

Everything turned to ice inside him. Who was this kid?

She took the little boy's hand again and walked with him down the street, the boy swinging in his steps between her and the man, laughing.

The hand in Wyatt's chest cut off his breathing.

Coco had a son. He saw it in the shape of the little boy's face and that smile, those lips—

His throat thickened.

They drew closer and he should probably hide better, but he still couldn't move.

Coco had a son and *hadn't told him.* Clearly he'd misread everything in Moscow, and...

His stomach turned. What if she hadn't...well, what if

he'd seduced her into something she hadn't really intended on doing and shame made her run from him?

Wow, he was a jerk.

Wyatt put his hand out on the car, bracing himself, and that's when he felt something behind him, the cool nose of metal pressed into his back, right at the base of his spine.

"Don't move."

Nat. He recognized her voice, the soft tone, but this time with the steel edge of warning.

He stiffened, glanced over his shoulder. "What—?"

She stood behind him, her face hard, eyes narrowing. "Just keep your mouth shut. We're taking a walk."

A chill slid down his spine. That's what assassins said a moment before they walked someone to the edge of a ditch and dropped them.

He held his hands up because that felt right and stepped out from behind the car.

Coco looked up, still thirty yards away.

Time stopped. His heart punched against his rib cage as her smile vanished and her jaw slackened.

The guy next to her frowned, his gaze sliding off Wyatt to the woman behind him.

"Wyatt," Coco said, so softly he actually didn't hear it, but saw her lips move.

"Move," snapped Nat and gave a little push with her gun. Or he thought it might be a gun. Felt like a gun.

In a Jack Reacher novel, it would be a gun.

He took another step forward.

Coco picked up the boy, was holding him against her, as if trying to protect him.

The man stepped in front of her, and didn't *that* do just a little damage to Wyatt's heart.

He should be the one stepping in front of her.

"I just want to talk to Katya," said Nat.

"Natalya?" Coco said. "What—what are you doing here?" She took a couple steps toward them, but the man in front of her turned and said something to her.

She stiffened.

Glanced over his shoulder to Wyatt. Or maybe Nat. *Nata-lya*, she'd called her.

Coco knew her.

"Listen, I don't know what's going on—" Wyatt started.

Nat barked something in Russian, which he interpreted as *Shut up*.

Nice. Not only had he not listened to Coco, but he'd helped a killer find her.

"I just need the jump drive, Katya. Then we can all go home."

Wyatt froze. Coco met his eyes.

"This is the one from Moscow, isn't it?" Nat said, now in English. "The man you spent the night with?"

Oh, nice. Turn it into something tawdry.

"Give me the jump drive, and I give you your lover."

Her *lover*?

"She doesn't have it," Wyatt said, loud enough for Coco to hear. "She gave it to me."

A hiccup, a beat, and then, "And it was stolen from me at the hotel."

Another beat as Coco's eyes widened.

"That's very bad," Nat said quietly.

"So, that means we can all go home, right? No harm, no foul—"

There went that Russian word again. "Move." She pressed into his spine and he started walking toward Coco.

"Natalya, please," Coco said, then switched into Russian and began to talk.

More steps.

The man in front of her turned around, his hands up, shielding her. Wyatt could like him for at least that much.

"Stop," the man said.

Yes, good idea. Because every step closer meant Coco was closer to the gun.

Wyatt's mind raced through scenarios. What would Tate and Ford do? Probably enact some super awesome spy trick where they turned and grabbed the gun and disabled the shooter in one smooth move.

Wyatt wasn't that awesome. But he didn't have to just stand here and let the skinny brunette assassin shoot him. He took another step, drew in a breath, and—

"Run!"

He jerked back, his elbow about shoulder height to Nat and slammed it hard into her body. It jerked her grip loose, and he rounded on her and tackled her to the ground.

The gun fired, and for a second, he jerked. But no, he wasn't dead, so he grappled for her gun hand as she boxed him in the ear, then brought her knee up.

Sorry, but he'd spent half his life tussling with people on the ice, getting sticks in the face, in the body, between his legs. And sure, he didn't have padding, but—

The slam to his head felt like a brick, exploding against his temple. She must have picked up something from the street—a rock, maybe—but in a second, his world pitched, turned into slats of gray and black. He rolled off her, his vision churning.

Shouts and grunting near him, but he couldn't make them out. His ears were ringing, and his head just might explode.

Screaming. He put his hands over his ears to keep it from piercing his brain, shredding it.

Then another shot.

And his vision faded to black.

Coco needed a moment to breathe. To piece together exactly how—what—had just happened.

To travel back three minutes to when Wyatt—*Wyatt*—appeared out of nowhere, as if he might be out for a morning stroll, in the middle of Belogorsk.

Hey, Coco.

Had he said that? It seemed like maybe, because he'd given her that signature lop-sided smile, a little apology in his whiskey-brown eyes, as if chagrined.

He always looked a little like he wanted to apologize to her.

At least lately.

Then she'd tracked past him to the woman behind him.

Natalya. From her father's security force. She wasn't dressed like an FSB officer, however, wearing a black T-shirt, a pair of jeans, and boots. The woman looked like she might be a—

"She's here to kill you." York's voice, low and tight as he turned in front of her, literally putting his body between hers and Mikka's.

What—? "She works for my father."

"Why else would she be here?"

"I just need the jump drive, Katya. Then we can all go home."

York met her eyes. "See? Why does she want that drive?"

Coco shook her head.

And that's when Natalya drove everything home to a fine point. *Give me the jump drive, and I give you your lover.*

York blinked. His gaze went to Mikka. "Really?"

She opened her mouth, not exactly sure what she planned on saying when suddenly, "She doesn't have it."

Oh, no. Wyatt—stop talking—

"She gave it to me. And it was stolen from me at the hotel."

Her breathing cut out then. All the emails, all the compiled evidence proving RJ's innocence…

Breathe. She still had copies on her cloud storage—if it hadn't been hacked.

"Natalya," she said. "I don't have what you want. But I can get it. Please—let him go—"

"Stop," York said, turning his back to her, to protect her.

And probably he could, somehow, but he didn't have to because Wyatt started acting like some kind of superhero. "Run!"

She wasn't exactly sure how, but he ended up on the ground, wrestling for the gun with Natalya. It went off, and

Coco screamed and raced with Mikka for cover behind a nearby car.

York took off in a dead sprint, but not before Natalya scooped up a nearby brick and slammed it into Wyatt's head.

He rolled off her onto his back, writhing.

"*Wyatt!*"

"Stay there!" York barked at her as he jumped on Natalya.

She couldn't watch. Because she'd seen him with the woman yesterday, and…oh, was this her life now? She couldn't trust anyone she met or knew? Coco turned and brought Mikka close, putting her hands over his ears. "Close your eyes, Mikka."

She, too, closed her eyes. Until a shot went off again, and she couldn't stop herself from looking up.

York bled from his shoulder on the ground, and Natalya was on her feet, searching, probably for them. "Katya, this doesn't have to end badly."

Really? Felt like it.

York wasn't done. He lunged at Natalya, hooked her around her knees, and she went down, slamming hard into the dirt.

Just like that, she stopped moving.

Silence. The sulphuric smell of gun powder stirred the air, mixed with the metallic scent of blood in dirt.

York scrambled up next to Natalya. She lay face down, blood pooling beneath her head. He pressed his fingers to her neck, then rolled her over.

"She's still alive, but her head hit the brick when she fell. It's bad."

The brick she'd used to clobber Wyatt, who also lay like the dead in the street.

As if reading her mind, York scrambled over to Wyatt.

She followed, picking up Mikka. "Is he—"

"No. He's just got a doozy of a goose egg and probably a concussion." He rubbed his knuckles into Wyatt's sternum. "Wyatt. Come back to us."

She could have wept when he stirred. Setting Mikka down,

she knelt beside Wyatt. His eyes fluttered.

"We need ice or a cold pack," she said.

"We need to get out of here," York replied. He glanced at Natalya. "Why did she want the jump drive?"

Coco had nothing. Wyatt stirred to life, and she ached for him as he woke wincing.

"Shh, you're okay," she said.

His eyes found hers.

And he most definitely wasn't okay. "Coco—oh—I thought—"

Then he rolled over and retched, mostly bile, but she had to look away.

He sat back, wiped his mouth.

She reached out for him, but he pushed her hands off him. "I'm fine." He looked at her again. "Are you okay?"

"Yeah."

She glanced at Natalya. Her eyes were rolled back into her head. "York...uh—I think she's dead."

Wyatt's eyes widened. "York?"

"We need to get off the street," York said. "Those shots will bring militia. And when they arrive and find Natalya..."

Coco nodded and got up, reaching under Wyatt's arm to help him, York on the other side.

Wyatt found his feet, obviously still woozy. He looked at York. "Huh," he said, and she had a feeling he still hadn't found himself.

"C'mon, buddy. You're a long way from home." York put Wyatt's arm over his shoulder, and Wyatt let him, a little evidence of his wound. He held his hand to his head over the growing bump.

York picked up Mikka's bag, then Wyatt's and put them over his shoulder.

Coco picked up her backpack and Mikka. Didn't look at Natalya sprawled in the road.

She put her hand over his eyes.

She couldn't just leave her in the road—

"Oy! What happened?" The voice turned her, and Lana

was running down the road after them, just behind their security man.

"It's a terrible story, but—she fell and hit her head." York, the half-truth spilling out of his mouth in a matter-of-fact tone.

Coco was a little shaken at how easily he let that information spiral out. And how easily he'd also left behind the woman at the train station.

She knew him from her friend Tasha, who had dated him before her death. Knew he'd been a Marine working at the embassy. Knew he'd worked in some covert position in the CIA.

Knew that something terrible had happened to make him resign.

Now, a darkness spread through her gut, into her bones as he said, "Call the morgue. They can pick her up."

Like she was refuse.

But Natalya had been…well, sort of her friend.

Maybe.

"Let's go," York said and turned down the street.

Mikka was trying to wiggle out of her grip, so Coco turned to Lana. "I'm so sorry—we have to catch the train."

"Go," Lana said and kissed Mikka once more. Coco couldn't look at Natalya's body as the security guard put his jacket over her.

She followed York, hustling to catch up.

When they rounded the corner, back onto the street, she let Mikka down and took his hand. He looked up at her, his smile gone. "It's going to be okay," she said, squeezing his hand, trying to believe it. "We're just going on a little trip."

After her conversation with York last night, she'd put together a few details. Like once she got Mikka to Sarai, got him checked out, she'd get him an American passport. Or at least a birth certificate. As her child, he could travel into the United States under her documents.

She'd go to America. Hide in Kansas or somewhere.

If Mikka was sick, she'd tap into her father's vast wealth

and get him the best medical care on the planet.

And then Wyatt had to walk back into the picture. He'd stopped leaning on York and now simply walked, albeit slowly, his hand pressed to his head.

She caught up to him. "How did you find me?" Oh no, that wasn't exactly the first thing she wanted to say to him.

He glanced at her, his mouth tight. "The FSB. Although after what just happened, I'm not sure who is lying to me."

Oh, and that hurt. But why would—

"Roman."

Recognition of the name flickered in his eyes.

"He told you where I was? How did you—"

"He questioned me down at FSB central, thanks. After someone broke into my hotel room and tried to beat the snot out of me while stealing the jump drive you gave me."

And that very definitely sounded like an accusation.

"Sorry—"

He blinked. "I'm not blaming you. I'm just saying—it's gone, and I don't have the first clue what is going on, and maybe I should have just...stayed on the train to Vladivostok."

Her mouth tightened. Yeah, maybe.

Especially when his gaze fell to Mikka walking beside her. It held a touch of sadness, a little anger, maybe. "He is your son, right?"

Oh. She nodded. And right now...she should, she could—

He looked at York and suddenly she got it.

Wyatt thought the child was York's.

Oh. Boy. He'd clearly been hit in the head a few too many times, because he had to be very, very bad at math.

Or perhaps not, because one good look in the mirror screamed the truth. Her son looked *exactly* like his father.

They had the same dimple, the same eyes, the same hair... shoot, even the same gait.

Clearly, Wyatt wanted nothing to do with the little boy.

Her heart broke all over again.

"I'm sorry I told Nat where you were. I thought...well, I thought you were in trouble. Turns out *I* was the one in trouble." He gave a wretched laugh and shook his head. "I'm sorry I didn't listen to you. You're right. I should have just gone home. I don't know you at all."

She dropped back and tried not to cry.

They reached the station, and York led them inside to a bench. "Stay here. I'm going to get us tickets. I'm sure there's a day train leaving soon."

She sank down on the bench beside Wyatt, who leaned forward, his head in his hands. She drew Mikka onto her lap.

"Where are we going, Mama?" Mikka asked, in Russian.

"We're going to see Mama's friend. She wants to meet you." She pressed a kiss to his cheek. He giggled and wiped it off.

Wyatt's gaze turned to them. He frowned. Met Coco's eyes.

Yes, Wyatt, he's yours.

But she didn't say that. Not here, not now.

Maybe, frankly, not ever.

York came back. "We're in luck. The Trans-Siberian passes through here in about an hour. We'll take that to Khabarovsk."

"Good," Wyatt said. "The sooner I can get out of here, the better."

Coco looked away and determined not to cry.

7

He'd really been walloped. Because Wyatt couldn't get past the idea that he was missing something, that all the pieces weren't puzzling together.

Coco wouldn't look at him. Instead, she had pulled her little boy onto her lap, reading him a book, her black hair—he still couldn't quite get used to that—tucked behind one ear, her voice in low Russian tones.

She was a good mother—he could see that much. And Mikka was cute. He'd introduced himself when they reached the private train compartment, holding out his hand to Wyatt, grinning.

Wyatt kept looking at York, trying to find the resemblance. York was blond, square-jawed, his gaze serious as he leaned back on the bench beside Coco, his arms folded as he stared out the window.

Thinking.

Probably about how colossally Wyatt had messed up.

Wyatt leaned his head back on the seat, and Coco looked up. "Don't go to sleep."

"Yeah. I got it." Not like he *could* sleep—his head wanted to leave his body with the pounding of his headache. And the residue of Coco's scream.

Not to mention his stinging words that he very much wanted to take back—*The sooner I can get out of here, the better.*

He hadn't meant that. Exactly.

Because pitiful him, now that he was with her again, the thought of leaving her made him want to curl into a ball and surrender to the pain.

Except...so much for hoping that she was pining for him. Clearly. Not.

He looked again at York. "You're the guy who got my sister out of Russia."

York said nothing. Finally, "How is she?"

"Fine. Back at the ranch, hiding. She'll freak out when she finds out that some guy stole the information that will clear her."

"Describe him."

"Blond. A wicked scar across his jaw, clubbed ears."

York glanced at Coco. "Gustov."

"The assassin."

York nodded. "Which means he knows for sure that Coco and RJ are onto him. Perfect."

"Hey. It's not like I invited him into my hotel room to watch the game, have a couple beers. He tore it apart, attacked me, and tried to *kill* me, thanks."

York glanced at his head. "Apparently, that's a trend."

Wyatt gave him a look. "How was I supposed to know that she was some kind of—of—who was she?"

"She worked for my father," Coco said, pulling a stuffed lion out of Mikka's bag and handed it to him. "She was head of his security."

"Your father. You mean General Boris Stanislov?"

Silence pulsed between them.

Finally, "You should have said something."

"I was in America to hide. It's not something I wanted broadcast to the world."

"I wasn't the world. I was the guy who..." He glanced then at York and shut down the rest of his words. "I cared about you."

"I know." Her mouth tightened. "But my mother asked me not to, so...and I had my reasons."

"I'll bet you did. As it turns out, you're very good at

keeping secrets."

If his head hadn't been throbbing before, it would have split open with her stinging glare.

Mikka slid off the bench and climbed over to sit next to Wyatt. Coco started to reach for him, but Wyatt held up his hand.

He was just a kid. And a tough one at that. He spotted a bruise on his jaw, where he must have fallen. Wyatt held out his hand, and Mikka grabbed it to pull himself onto the bench.

He sat beside Wyatt, playing with the lion's long tail.

Wyatt didn't know why, but the sudden injustice of it all settled into his bones. Coco had a child. With York—or maybe not York, but still, this jerk was in her life—*their* lives—and Wyatt wasn't and...nope, it wasn't fair.

Because when he gave her his heart, and his body, he'd given it all away.

Coco was his girl.

Had been his girl.

Wyatt closed his eyes against the burn in his throat, his eyes.

"Don't sleep."

"I'm not sleeping!"

He opened his eyes, aware that he'd raised his voice. Mikka was watching him with a wide-eyed gaze. "Sorry, kiddo. I'm just...tired."

"He doesn't understand you," Coco said.

He looked at her. "I know. I just... He's a cute kid, Coco. I'm happy for you." Sorta.

Yes. But...he also wanted to weep.

York was back to looking out the window. "Why would your father send Natalya to get the jump drive? How would she even know about it?"

"Why did you think she was here to kill me? Maybe she came to make sure that Mikka was safe."

"She had a *gun* on him."

"Yeah. But...her job is to protect me."

"Maybe she was trying to protect her from *you*," Wyatt said, not sure why, but frankly, he didn't trust this guy.

Not only did the guy—well, maybe he didn't exactly murder Nat, but he would have, Wyatt knew it in his gut. And there was a cool presence about him that may work for Jack Reacher, but Wyatt still didn't trust him.

Especially since he seemed to be cozying up to Coco when he was supposed to be...oh, RJ. "How, exactly, were you involved in the assassination attempt and the framing of my sister?"

York looked at him, his expression unmoving. "I wasn't. I saw she was in trouble and jumped in."

"What are you getting at, Wyatt?" Coco asked.

"I'm just saying, this guy has secrets written all over him. What if Nat knew that he was dangerous—"

"I am dangerous. But not to Kat. Or RJ. Or you, although I'm rethinking that."

"Wyatt, he's right. York is on our side. He saved my life—"

"I know, I was there." Although he'd had a hand in that, hadn't he?

"No. Yesterday. One of Gustov's associates tried to kill me and..." She swallowed. "He...um..."

Wyatt just stared at York. "You killed him."

"Her," he said. His chest rose and fell. "It was an accident."

"Sure it was."

Coco looked at Mikka, who was sitting back in the corner of the bench, winding the lion's tail around his arm. She stood up and spoke to him in Russian, and he slid off the bench. "We're going to find something to eat, although I've lost my appetite. It's a good thing Mikka doesn't know English or I'd be wringing both of your necks. No more talk about murder, assassination attempts, or anything else scary around my son."

Wyatt ran a hand behind his neck.

York looked out the window.

She slid the door closed behind her.

Wyatt couldn't take it. "Are you his father?"

A beat, and York just stared at him, his mouth opening.

Then he closed it. "No, I'm not."

The breath he'd been holding released. "Do you know who is?"

Slowly, York shook his head. Kept shaking it. Then rolled his eyes and looked again out the window.

"What's that for?"

"You just... Nothing."

"I don't get you, York. I know something happened between you and RJ. I'm not stupid. But—what, you're with Coco?"

"Are you kidding me right now?" York rounded on him. "Seriously?"

Wyatt recoiled. "What—?"

"I'm not with Kat! I'm...with no one." He shook his head. "Don't be an idiot."

He'd let that pass. "Then what are you doing here?"

York pinched his finger and thumb against the bridge of his nose. "I'm here because I was tracking down Gustov when I got jumped. While I was figuring my way out of that, I realized that Kat might be in danger, so when she texted me that she was headed to Belogorsk—and then disappearing after that—I knew I had to get to her."

There was too much for Wyatt to unpack, so he picked the one that mattered most. "Disappearing?"

"That's what she said."

"Was she taking Mikka with her?"

"No. My guess is that she went to say goodbye."

And so much of this wasn't making sense, but, "Why would she say goodbye to...I don't—"

"Mikka doesn't live with her. To keep him safe, she did the same thing her father did to her—made Mikka live away from her."

"Why is Mikka in danger?"

"Because this is Russia, not America. If someone found out Mikka's identity, they could take him and use him to leverage the general."

Oh.

"But...why didn't she just move to America?"

York sighed. "I don't know."

Wyatt did. "He lives with his father, doesn't he? And he won't let him leave." It was a guess, but if Wyatt had a son like Mikka, he wouldn't let him out of his sight.

York blinked. "No. He lives—it's an orphanage."

"An orphanage. Is his father dead?"

"I don't think so. At least... Not. Yet."

"So, let me get this straight. She lives in Moscow, and her kid lives in the middle of Siberia?"

York raised his eyebrows, touched his nose again.

Huh.

"So, she was just going to say goodbye to him? Leave him...here? While she went...where?"

York lifted a shoulder.

But yeah, it fit.

Because that was Coco. Leaving people behind without a word. Except, "But now, she has him. Where are you going?"

"She thinks he might be sick, so she's bringing him to a doctor friend in Khabarovsk. If she needs to, she'll take him to America."

Right. "What kind of sick?"

"Leukemia."

"Oh, geez. Her mother died of leukemia." He leaned his head back against the seat, closed his eyes.

"Don't—"

"Stop."

"That was a pretty good crack."

He opened his eyes. "I play hockey for a living. Goalie. I know what it feels like to take a shot to the head."

York offered a tiny smile. "RJ says you're good. You play for a professional team?"

"The Minnesota Blue Ox. Three years, the last two as their starter. Except, now that I've jumped the train...yeah, I'm not sure what's going to happen."

"Jumped the train? What's that short for?"

"No. I really jumped the train. In some town called Spassk.

The team was on their way to Vladivostok to do some meet and greet and I just couldn't get it out of my head that Coco was in trouble. It was the way, well, the way we left it. I begged her to leave the country with me. And she said she couldn't. And now I know why."

York looked away.

"I wish she'd trusted me enough to tell me," he said quietly. "We were together in Moscow and...she took off. And I never knew why." He looked at the door. "It was because of Mikka. I wonder if the guy ever knew—"

"Oh my gosh, you are such an idiot!"

Wyatt recoiled. York was rubbing his forehead, shaking his head. "This is so not my business, but geez, man, you are so freakin' blind."

"Hey. Listen. I know this is hard for her. It's not a picnic for me either. I love her—she's my, my *soul mate*. Or I thought so, and I show up here thinking she's been missing me for the last two years—and frankly, that isn't my fault because she is on the hockey forum for the Blue Ox all the time, and we chat and she never once, *not once* mentioned her son. Or having another boyfriend—or what, did she marry him?"

He paused, stared at York who was simply deadpanning him, a sort of disgusted look on his face. "What if she married him? Is she divorced? What if she was married to him when we...when we—" He shot a look at York who now looked a little horrified.

Agreed. "Okay, yeah, we had a one-night stand in Moscow, but it wasn't like that for me. I love—loved her. I wanted to marry her. I know I should have led with that—I mean, I know better. I was raised better. But she has this way of getting under my skin and my brain sort of turns off, and I just get into the zone, sort of like I do for hockey, you know. Where you just feel it, and know it's right? Like I know when a wing is going to take a shot and my body just reacts. And that's what happened. She was there, and I missed her so much, and I just reacted. And no, I don't really regret it, except, maybe...I should have asked a few more questions. But then she was gone. And nothing's been right after that. I'm still playing, but there's something missing, you know? I keep thinking that it's because I left myself back in Russia, with Coco, and if I can just find her again and tell her how I feel… but maybe I've got this thing all wrong. Maybe she didn't love me, but it seemed like she did, and now I look at her with that kid, and he's so cute, and she's such a great mom, and there's something wrong with me because it just makes me want her even more—"

"Oh, for Pete's sake, man. The kid is your son. He's yours."

Everything went silent. In his head. In his body. Not even the thump of his heart.

"Take a good look at him. He's got your eyes and your hair, and…geez, man, did you see the way he looked at you? He knows it too."

"But he's…too old. I mean, he's what—"

"I don't know. Five?"

Five.

Five years old. Oh. No.

Their first time. Oh, Coco.

Wyatt looked at York. Closed his mouth. Swallowed. "I got her pregnant that night."

"Whatever night you're referring to, I'd say that's a yes."

Wyatt pressed his hand to his chest. "Oh…uh…"

"Wanna rethink everything you just said?"

What he wanted to do was rethink his entire life.

———◆———

For the past four hours, Coco had experienced the happy ending she'd longed for. At least, deep in the secret parts of her heart.

She just wanted to snapshot this moment.

Mikka lay with his head on Wyatt's lap, sound asleep, his little lips askew, and even drooling a little onto his jeans. Wyatt's hand rested on his tiny body, almost in a protective embrace.

A fatherly protective embrace. Which might be as much as she should ever expect given the fact she hadn't told him the truth.

She simply didn't know how to form the words. *Wyatt, so, the little boy you've been playing with for the past four hours? Teaching him how to win a thumb war? Kicking that tennis ball you always carry down the hall to you? The one who erupts into laughter when you tickle him? Yeah, well, he's yours.*

She'd stood at the entrance to their private berth, watching Wyatt stop Mikka's crazy throws, not unlike he'd done with her back when she'd been a scared little girl fresh out of her home country.

He just had this way of making everyone feel safe. As if they mattered.

She'd never seen her son so happy. Wyatt had bonded with Mikka so fast it took out pieces of her heart. It almost made her think that maybe he'd figured it out. But he'd said nothing to her, no, *Hey, Coco, got something life-changing to share with me?* when she'd returned to the compartment, so…

She had to find a way to tell him.

But not with York around, because, well, this was a private conversation. Not just the news, but the fact that she'd spent five years not telling him. Five long, stolen years.

So, as happy as she was to see Mikka curled up against Wyatt, her stomach was in a hard knot by the time they reached Khabarovsk.

Wyatt started to reach for a sleeping Mikka, but when his eyes closed hard, probably against a rush of pain from the now horribly bruised and swollen head wound, York stepped in.

Picked up the kid and threw him over his shoulder.

Wyatt picked up Mikka's bag, as well as his own, and braced himself as he rose from the bunk.

"Sarai should check out your head," she said.

Wyatt wouldn't look at her. She had noticed that too. Ever since she returned from the dining car where she'd purchased Mikka a milk and chips, Wyatt had practically ignored her.

Well, except for a couple strange looks that seemed almost pained. But he had been hit on the head, so maybe...

No, something was definitely off with him because he nodded. "Good idea."

Huh.

York carried Mikka off the train, across the platform, and into the train station, Wyatt and Coco behind him. She had to practically run to keep up with him, and it reminded her of the last time they'd been in K-Town, when he'd practically carried her to Roman's house.

She was tired of showing up wounded or on the run or in desperation. Someday she wanted to be the heroine of the story instead of the victim.

York was waiting by a cab when she caught up to him. He nodded inside, and she climbed in. He handed her Mikka, who had just started to wake up. Wyatt squeezed in next to her, and York got in front.

Mikka raised his head, trying to get his orientation.

Wyatt looked over at him and smiled.

Oh her heart was going to burst because when Wyatt smiled, Mikka grinned back and...

"Wyatt, I need to talk to you," she said quietly.

He glanced at her, frowned, but nodded.

"Later. After I talk to Sarai—"

"Sure," he said, but his response felt sharp, almost cutting. He tousled Mikka's hair.

The driver let them off at Roman's nine-story building, and she took Mikka's hand as they headed to the door. It buzzed and they went inside and climbed into the lift.

Sarai was waiting in the doorway, frowning. She glanced at York, then at Mikka, her eyes big. "Is this—"

"Yes. My son, Mikka."

She crouched. "Hey there."

"He only speaks Russian."

"Of course he does," she said and switched into his native tongue, offering him a cookie. Mikka beamed.

Sarai set him up with a treat at the kitchen table, then

emerged into the hallway. "I didn't expect you back so soon."

Translation: *ever.*

"Roman is out with the kiddos."

More translation: *or he'd have questions.*

"So, what's going on?"

Coco gave her a quick rundown of her medical fears, ending with, "I just need to know if I'm overreacting—"

"You're never overreacting when it comes to children. I need to draw blood, but I have a kit here. I'll take it to the clinic to run tests, but I can get them rushed and we can get labs back by tomorrow." Sarai touched her arm. "It's going to be okay."

Coco noticed Wyatt leaning against the doorframe, his arms crossed, his jaw a hard line.

"I'm going to make a call. I'll be back in a bit," York said and slipped out of the apartment.

"Let's get this over with," Wyatt said and headed into the kitchen.

Sarai glanced at Coco. "That's Wyatt?"

She nodded.

"And—?"

Coco shook her head. "And please don't say anything."

Sarai raised an eyebrow, looking over her shoulder to where Wyatt was sliding onto the bench next to Mikka. "I don't think I need to. One look in the mirror…although, your man looks pretty beat up."

"He's not my man anymore."

"Mmmhmm," Sarai said.

Seeing him trying to steal one of Mikka's cookies, making her son laugh, Coco very much wanted him to be.

Coco hadn't a clue how this was going to turn out, but she feared to dream.

As Sarai drew Mikka's blood, Wyatt held him between his legs, his big arm around Mikka, his voice in his ear. Coco cried with Mikka's tears, and shoot, if Wyatt didn't have tears running down his cheeks, too, at Mikka's whimpers.

"I'll take this down to the hospital and ask them to run

the right tests," Sarai said, putting the vials into her purse.

The door buzzed, and she went to let York in.

"Can we use your internet?" York asked as he came in. "Kat needs to do some work."

Oh. Right. RJ's information.

"Computer is in the office," Sarai said. "Password is this long number written on a Post-it on the desk."

"Kind of defeats the purpose—" York started, but Coco gave him a look.

"Thanks," Coco said.

"Vitya has a bunch of trucks in his room, and if you want, Zia has books in hers. I'll be back with dinner."

Sarai let herself out.

Wyatt picked up Mikka and tossed him over his shoulder. "We're going to go zoom-zoom." He headed down the hall in search of what Coco thought might be the trucks.

Zoom-zoom.

Oh, that was too cute for her own good.

York motioned with his head down the hall.

"So, I checked in with Yanna, our favorite FSB agent, about Natalya and she said that she's been rogue from the FSB for six weeks."

"What?" Coco pulled out a chair in front of the desk, running the mouse to activate Roman's laptop.

"Yeah. Apparently, your father's been practically apoplectic about it, and the FSB has been trying to find her."

"Not looking hard enough."

"She killed two of her men before she left."

Coco didn't want to suppose who. She knew most of the agents on her father's detail.

She logged on with Roman's crazy sixteen-digit random password and accessed the internet. "Here's hoping that my cloud hasn't been hacked."

Her breath let out when she found the information. "It's still here."

York produced a jump drive.

"You're handy," Coco said and downloaded the

information onto the drive.

"What's in the packet?" York asked.

"Gustov had two folders in his online email account. One contains the emails between him—masking as you—and RJ. And it proves that he intercepted the emails and set her up to be in the wrong place at the right time for the assassination attempt."

"And the second?"

"Dating emails."

"Huh?"

"Yeah. As far as I can tell, they're emails from a dating website he belongs to."

York just stared at her.

"I went in and grabbed everything he had, but I only transferred the one file onto the disk."

"Download the dating files too."

She frowned at him but slid them over onto the offline storage drive.

"I keep trying to figure out why Gustov hasn't deleted those email files."

"Maybe he didn't know I had them."

"I always wondered how he found us on the train. Only your father, David, and Yanna knew we were headed to Siberia."

"Natalya was there when my father suggested it."

"Could be."

"Except, how did Gustov figure out that I was in Khabarovsk...oh no."

York looked at her.

"Your email account. You store your emails online too. He's emailed you before—it would only take a hacker like me to break in, read them—"

"And figure out where you were, what evidence you had."

"So, he hops on a plane for K-Town, shows up at our meet, and grabs the drive."

"So then why didn't he access his drive and delete the emails?"

"Maybe he couldn't access the internet."

"Why not?"

"What if he was traveling? Got on a plane or a train. You know how sketchy the internet and even cell service is in remote parts of Russia."

"Which is why Natalya didn't know he had the drive." York got up and moved away to the window. "Maybe he hasn't had a chance to contact her."

"I injured him." Wyatt had come in, his arms folded, that massive shoulder propped against the doorframe. "He was bleeding when he went over the balcony. He might have gone to a hospital."

"And then jumped on a plane."

"What—and lost his cell phone?"

"Nat was on the train with me for nearly twenty-four hours," Wyatt said. "Even if he did call her, the messages might not have come through."

"And if he got a train or a plane…"

York was looking at her. "If he read my email, he knows where RJ is. I've been writing to her. He could track her ISP address. If he thinks Natalya did her job…"

"RJ is the only loose end," Wyatt said.

"Excuse me." York pushed past Wyatt.

Wyatt watched him go. Turned back to Coco. "Mikka is asleep. I tucked him in to the lower bunk in Vitya's room."

She reset her encryption on her cloud, then logged out. Pulled the jump drive out of the computer, got up, and handed it to Wyatt. "Hang on to this one."

He slipped it into his pocket as she stepped past him into the hallway, over to the bedroom.

Shadows pressed through the window, the night falling in great swaths. Mikka lay on the bottom bunk, his breathing soft. She knelt beside him and ran her hand over his face. "I'm so afraid he has cancer."

Wyatt touched her shoulder. "I know."

She pressed a kiss to Mikka's cheek, breathing in the smell of him, the fact that right now, in this moment, they were safe.

She stood up and turned to Wyatt.

"About…that talk…"

He drew in a breath, those brown eyes latching on to hers.

"He's your son, Wyatt."

"Yeah," he said quietly. "I know."

Her eyes widened and crazily started to fill. "You know? How?"

His gaze fell on Mikka, his mouth lifting in a half smile. That dimple emerged. "He's just like me, isn't he?"

She covered her face with her hands, her shoulders shaking.

"Aw, Coco. You should have told me." Then he reached out and pulled her into his arms, that wide, strong chest, rubbing her back as she started to weep.

"It's going to be okay," he said, his own body starting to tremble. "I promise. I'm not going to let anything happen to you. Either of you." Then he simply lowered his cheek to her head and held her as he, too, quietly fell apart.

At least RJ hadn't forgotten how to make cupcakes. Or muffins. Or cookies. Or cinnamon rolls and even a stack of buttermilk waffles.

If she wanted to go undercover in a bakery, she'd be golden.

Except, she wasn't undercover, and frankly, was gaining weight like Knox's prize baby bucking bull, now six months old. He was cute, too, with his big brown eyes, those reddish-brown ears poking up every time she walked out to the corral.

She wasn't quite so cute, probably, dressed in her yoga pants and a T-shirt, her dark hair pulled back. And flour. She wore her flour like the champion of cupcake wars, down her apron, across her chin, up her arms.

That was the price of excellence.

That, and Tate's smile as he reached for another cupcake. "So, is this a thing now? Late-night baking?"

Outside, the night pressed against the windows, the glow of the kitchen holding it at bay. Holding back, too, the nightmares that awaited her upstairs.

So, "Yeah. I do my best work at zero-dark-thirty."

Tate gave her a look even as he peeled the wrapper from the chocolate cupcake. "I know about PTSD, sis. You can't bake your way out of it."

"I don't have—"

"Seriously. You were shot at. Had to escape Russia. There's an entire genre of books about escaping Russia, so don't tell me that's not traumatic. You have PTSD, and it never really goes away—you just get better at pushing through."

She opened the oven and pulled out her final tray of cupcakes. Set them on the island of her mother's remodeled kitchen.

"I'm trying."

"Reuben says you've been binge-watching *Alias* again. Listen, I get it. I think I watched all six seasons of *Lost* when I got back from Afghanistan. That's about 120 hours of my life I'll never get back." He ate half the cupcake in one bite. Made a noise of appreciation.

"Yeah, well, I've been helping Ma harvest the garden, canned some tomato sauce, made some pickles, and even sorted through more boxes of Dad's books to donate to the library."

"That's real high-action stuff there, Sydney."

"Maybe I'm not...well, Sydney Bristow. Have you ever thought of that?"

He finished off the cupcake. "Of course you're not. She's a made-up television character. You're a real kick-butt heroine who did something scary and noble and nearly got killed doing it. You're allowed to...bake. But the fact is you can't cook...or binge-watch...away your fears. You have to get it in your head that you're safe now, and no one is going to show up in the backyard and try and kill you."

She raised an eyebrow.

"I hardly think this Russian is going to hop the pond and track you down in the middle of our ranch."

"Why not? Glo nearly got killed here."

Tate's mouth tightened into a dark line. "Points to you. But—"

"You're probably right. It's just an excuse to hide out and get my feet under me. But I've called my boss a dozen times and she's not answering me. And I've been shut out of my access to my computer, my files, and any research I could get done. I'm just twiddling my thumbs here, and it's driving me crazy. As soon as Wyatt gets here with the information from Coco, I'm going to DC. I'm going to slap it on her desk and…"

"Maybe you don't." Tate got up and went to the fridge, opening it. He grabbed the milk. "Maybe you give the information to Reba Jackson."

"The VP candidate?"

He took out a glass from the cupboard. "And Glo's mother. She has connections—she's on the Armed Services Committee. She could get you cleared."

He filled his glass with milk and turned. He was dressed in a black T-shirt and a pair of very faded jeans hanging low on his hips, and in the light, with the dark window behind him, he looked very much like the off-duty bodyguard, former spec ops soldier he was. Even with his tousled brown hair and haze of brown whiskers.

He and Glo had arrived just a few hours ago, surprising them. Apparently, Glo and the country band she played with—the Yankee Belles—had a few days off from their tour with NBR-X, a professional bull-riding show. Knox and Kelsey had stayed on the tour, thanks to Knox's job as the livestock supervisor.

Tate took a drink, and it left a white mustache. "Come with us to Seattle." He wiped his upper lip with his sleeve.

"What—why?"

"Glo's mom is having a political rally there. You can see

Wyatt—I think the Blue Ox have a pre-season exhibition game with one of their junior teams—the Thunderbirds."

She hadn't heard from Wyatt for a couple days—not that she was worried but…oh, fine! Yes, she was worried.

"Listen, don't you want to…stop *baking* and—"

"I don't know what I want, okay?" She was transferring the cupcakes she'd just pulled from the oven onto a baking rack. The heat bled through to her fingers, and she yanked one away and put it into her mouth.

"I'm thinking maybe it's just as dangerous for you to be here."

"Go to bed."

"I can't sleep." He set down his glass and sighed.

Tate sighing never boded well. "Why not?"

He made a face. Then he reached into his pocket and pulled out a tiny velvet box. "Because of this."

She reached for it, but he yanked it away. "Promise not to say anything?"

"Hello. CIA. I can keep a secret."

"Wash your hands. This cost me three months' pay."

She grinned at him and washed her hands. Then she opened the box. "Oh, Tate."

"Think she'll like it?"

"White gold or platinum?"

"White gold. It's called a halo center, it's got like eighteen tiny stones around the outside, and that's a one-point-two carat diamond—"

"It's impressive."

He grinned like a ten-year-old, and her heart wanted to burst for him.

"She'll love it. When are you asking her?" She handed him back the ring box, and he looked at it one more time before he closed the box and stuck it back into his pocket.

"I don't know yet. I thought…here, but…now I'm not—"

"Don't be such a pansy. Take her out to the waterfall and propose. Tomorrow. At sunset."

"Really, you think—"

"Yes. Because that thing is burning a hole in your pocket, and if you just keep carrying it around, she's going to notice and then the surprise will be wrecked." She walked over to him and took his handsome face in her hands. "No one deserves a happy ending more than you, Tater. Make it happen." She kissed his cheek, painfully aware of the burning in her chest.

She was happy for him. But…

But wow, she missed York. And they barely knew each other.

Tate drew her close in a hug. "You're going to bounce back, kiddo." He let her go. "But you stop baking. You're getting squishy around the hips."

She hit his chest. He grinned as he stepped past her and swiped another cupcake on his way upstairs.

Maybe she should go to Seattle. It seemed like a good idea. She couldn't keep hiding forever. And really, Tate was right. She might totally be overreacting to the threat of Damien Gustov. After all, he was all the way over in Russia.

She was frosting the last of her cupcakes when her cell phone buzzed on the counter. Please let it be Wyatt, except she didn't recognize the number.

Wiping her hands, she grabbed it. "Hello?"

A breath, then. "Oh. Wow. I was worried."

Not Wyatt. The voice was low, deep, soft. Powerful. Accented. And it hit her entire body like a wave of heat washing over her, settling into her core. "*York?*"

"Yeah, it's me. Sorry. I guess we've never talked on the phone, but…hey." A deep sigh came over the phone, and for some reason she imagined him in some dark corridor or on a train or even in his safe house, dressed in a pair of black jeans, a black shirt, his dark blond hair rucked up thanks to the stress that layered his voice.

"Hey," she said. "You okay?"

Another sigh.

"York. What's going on?"

"I think Gustov is on his way to you."

She reached out and flicked off the lights to the house.

WYATT

Silly, and just a gut reaction, but…

She might be overreacting. She probably didn't need to scoot down in the corner of the kitchen or better yet, sneak over to the pantry and close herself inside it.

"Ruby Jane?"

"I'm good. I'm just…um…" Oh, her voice wavered. And now she sighed. "I miss you."

She winced. Really? She had to go there? They'd exchanged a few emails, all business, and frankly, maybe she should stop dreaming of something romantic blossoming between them—

"I miss you too."

He did?

"You do?"

"Of course. You're not here to annoy me or get me into more trouble. It's downright boring."

She grinned, unable to account for the crazy tears that edged her eyes. "You got yourself into trouble, double-o-seven."   •

He laughed too, and the rumble of it slid under her skin, simmered there. "Where are you?"

"Still in Montana. Specifically, I'm sitting in the darkened pantry, but it's not usually where I spend the night."

"Right. Me either. I prefer a grimy alleyway myself."

"Now you're just bragging."

"I wish. But really…are you okay?"

She closed her eyes, leaning her phone against her shoulder. "I am. I can't wait for Wyatt to get here with Coco's information. It's time I come out of hiding."

"About that—he's still here."

Oh. "I thought he was traveling with his team."

"Things got a little complicated. He'll fill you in, but I'll try and get him on a flight out of town tomorrow. Um…I don't like you being in Montana. I think…well, the short of it is that Gustov attacked Wyatt in his hotel room—"

"What—?"

"And he got the jump drive."

"Oh no—"

140

"But Kat was able to restore the information. So he has a duplicate. But…we think that maybe Gustov hacked into my emails and…well, he knows where you are."

He knows… "Is my family in danger?"

"I don't know. You, for sure, but—"

"Tate wants me to go to Seattle and give the information to Senator Reba Jackson. She's running for VP, but she has contacts that could clear my name."

"I don't hate that idea."

Silence.

"I wish you were going to be there." More silence, and a hand gripped her chest, started to squeeze. "York?"

"Yeah, uh. So…Ruby Jane. I…"

A pause and she closed her eyes. Please, don't—

"I know we had something—and I know what I said, but… you don't really know me or the guy I've been—am—and…"

"Stop."

He drew in a long breath.

"I don't know your past, but I do know enough about the guy you are to tell you that you're wrong about what you're going to say."

"Which is—"

"That I should just let you go. That you have a promise to keep to yourself, which means doing some things that…well, that you don't want to talk about."

"I killed someone yesterday."

Oh, York.

"She was an assassin, after Kat, but…and then today… the fact is, I didn't really take a good look at my life until you walked into it, and it's not…it's not one that is conducive to a happy ending, Ruby. I'm not a…good person."

"York. You're not a bad person. A bad person wouldn't be running his hand around the tight muscle behind his neck, wishing he hadn't had to hurt anyone."

His breaths came out tremulously.

"York, listen to me. I don't know what the future holds. And yeah, I do…I care for you. But the only promise you have to make to me is to not let go of the guy who saved my life. Who risked his to get me out of the country. Who is on the side of right."

His voice dropped. "I wish I'd met you…well, years ago. I wish I was on your postcard ranch right now, in the closet with you. I'd have you in my arms, and…well…that's probably all I need to imagine right now."

She could probably imagine more, but yeah, he was right. "And I wish I hadn't thought I was some sort of superspy saving the world."

"Except then General Stanislov would be dead, and the world would be in upheaval."

"There's that."

"Yeah. There's that."

She imagined him grinning.

"You know, I haven't been stateside for nearly a decade."

"I think it's time."

He made a noise, she hoped of assent. "Please stay alive, Syd."

"You too, James."

She waited for an *I'll find you*, but the line clicked off. She held the phone to her heart.

And said it for him.

8

Wyatt just needed a game plan. Something to wrap his mind, his emotions around, something to center him.

Something to keep him sane. Because every cell in his body wanted to let out a scream.

Hit something, again and again.

Or maybe just field a thousand shots on goal, one after another, letting them hit his pads, slapping them away with vengeance.

Anything but stand with his back to the wall in the crowded living room, listening to the blonde American doc tell him that his son was going to die.

He might be over-reacting because she didn't have a firm diagnosis yet, but the fact was, she wouldn't suggest further tests if he wasn't sick.

Coco sat on the sofa, her face bone white as Sarai explained.

"He has elevated white blood cells in the sample we took, but we need to run a complete blood count and a panel of other tests. It has me worried enough, however, that he needs to be hospitalized for those tests ASAP."

Sarai had arrived home thirty minutes ago, not long after Roman, who had returned with their daughter, Zia, and son, Vitya. Cute kids.

Not as cute as Mikka. The second Coco had returned to the train car after York told him the news, the moment Mikka

143

looked at him, grinning, Wyatt was a goner.

Sheesh, he should have seen it right off. That tousled brown hair, those big eyes. He looked *exactly* like Wyatt had as a kid, and York was right. *You are so freakin' blind.*

Apparently.

Or just so wiped out by the very notion that Coco would have had a child—*his child*—and not told him.

But he'd swallowed back any words and focused on his son.

Mikka. Short for Michael, probably. Or, in Russian, Misha.

For an almost five-year-old, he had good reflexes and decent eye-hand coordination. He could catch a ball, got back up after he fell down, and his laughter when Wyatt tickled him had embedded his pores.

Wyatt wasn't leaving Russia without his son.

His. Son.

Why didn't you tell me?

He'd vowed to himself on the train to keep it calm. And he had—oh, he had, all the way to Khabarovsk, through the ordeal of holding down Mikka when the doc drew blood, and even as he tried to cheer him up with a pile of Matchbox cars.

He'd even held it together when Coco came into the room and confessed the truth, finally.

But the words, secrets, lies, and even heartlessness shook free as he held her, and he couldn't seem to tuck them back inside.

Breathe. He'd practically screamed it in his head. And then…yeah, Wyatt had completely fallen apart, like some pansy.

He also didn't blame himself for pushing her away. For the rough scrape of his voice as he'd tried to pull himself together.

"You should have told me." He'd kept his voice at a whisper, still fighting to close his mouth, to keep the cascade at bay. "Four years of his life, Coco—and I missed all of it. I'll never get that back."

She'd stepped away from him, her eyes lifting to his.

Swallowed, and right then he had a flashback of the look she'd worn so many years ago when he'd arrived back on the ranch after being recently picked up by the Blue Ox.

Cute photographer trailing him like she might be his girlfriend. Yes, he'd been a bit of a jerk that weekend. But it didn't mean Coco had to lie to him about the most important thing in his entire life.

He had a *child*.

"I wanted to tell you," she whispered, a glance at Mikka, an unspoken request to take this conversation outside the room.

Fine, they'd have this conversation in the hallway. York was still outside of the apartment, in the corridor, and Sarai had left, so—

Wyatt closed the bedroom door behind him and turned to her.

Coco looked so small, despite the way she folded her arms and tightened her jaw, a tiny hand grenade.

He didn't care. "Really? And how hard would that have been?" Emotion still shook his voice, the residue of letting it crest over him. But he was quickly balling it back up, finding his game face.

He wanted answers, and he wasn't going to let his hurt get in the way.

"Pretty hard, as it turns out," she snapped. "I planned to tell you when I came back to Montana, but you had moved on."

Moved on? "That wasn't my fault. You left first."

"Then I came back. I wasn't the one who was snuggled up with some chick on the sofa—"

"So you were jealous. That's the reason you kept my son from me?"

She went a little white, as if he'd slapped her. "No. I...you were just starting your pro career, and I thought, well, I was worried—"

"That I wouldn't have room for him in my life." He drew in a breath as she lifted a shoulder.

And shoot. For a moment he got a good look at the person

he'd been back then. Arrogant and driven and...

Okay, so, "What about two years ago, in Moscow? When we..." He lowered his voice. "There was no one in the way then."

"That's why I went to the hotel. To tell you."

Silence, and finally, "But...?" His voice hovered just above a whisper.

"But..." She swallowed. "I..." Her eyes welled up. "I couldn't."

"Couldn't? Or didn't want to?"

Her silence left him to fill in the blanks.

I didn't trust you. I didn't want you to be his father. I...didn't want you.

Yeah, so he pretty much was figuring that part out.

"It was dangerous."

He just stared at her. "For whom?"

"For Mikka! If someone had found him—"

"No." He shook his head. "That's not good enough, Coco. He could have come home with me, with—"

And there it was again. *Us.* Except, maybe she didn't want an us.

Just forget about me.

Her jaw tightened.

"Wow, you're right. I must have been hit in the head too many times, because it's taken me until *right now* to get it. You really *don't* want me, do you?"

She looked away.

"Well, that's just perfect. And tough luck, because whether you want me around or not, here I am. And like I said, I'm not going to let anything happen to you."

Her eyes flashed and she turned back to him, and he was hunkering down for a response when Sarai's husband came through the door.

Roman. *The FSB agent.*

They stared at each other, Roman blinking, one hand on his son's shoulder, his daughter balanced on his hip. He let the little girl slide to the floor as his gaze went to Coco. "Are you okay?"

The man said it in Russian, but Wyatt figured it out.

She nodded. Glanced at Wyatt. And said something in Russian he *couldn't* figure out. But by the look on Roman's face, his pinched mouth, it had to be something along the lines of *Why did you tell him where I was?*

Well, Wyatt had questions too. "I thought you said you were going to find her. You *promised* me." He took a step toward Roman, who pushed his daughter behind him.

"Are we going to have trouble?" Roman said quietly.

"Hey, *hey*—" York had come in behind them and now pushed past all of them. "Step back. We're all friends here."

Not hardly. "He told me that he'd find Coco and tell her about Gustov taking the drive—"

"I called her, twice," Roman said. "It went to voicemail."

"What?" Coco said. She pulled out her phone. "I don't have any new messages."

"I called you too," York said. "To warn you about Gustov's assassin."

"Gustov sent an assassin?" Roman said. He glanced at his children and said something to them in Russian. They headed into the family room and turned on the television.

"Two of them," York said. "One of them was on the train with her to Belogorsk."

Wyatt stared at him, a cold horror dragging up his spine. "*What?*"

"Call me," Coco said, ignoring him, and looked at York.

Of course she did. Because he was the superhero here.

York took his phone out and called her.

It didn't ring. "It's going to voicemail."

Coco was looking at her phone. She headed into the kitchen, put the phone on the table, and pried open the back of it. She pulled out her SIM card. "I don't think this is mine."

Silence.

"A SIM card contains user identities, personal security keys, contact lists...stored messages..." Coco looked up. "If someone took my SIM card, they could access my cloud information."

"And track phone numbers and even stored addresses," York said.

"Like our ranch," Wyatt said and glanced at Coco. She nodded.

"But how did they get it?" Coco said.

"What if it was switched on the train, while you slept?" York suggested.

"But why not just steal my phone?"

"Clearly he—and I'm guessing this was Gustov's work—wanted to be able to reach you. So, Natalya put a new SIM card in."

"So he could call me?"

Wyatt drew in a sharp breath.

Coco let go of the phone like it burned her.

Wyatt had pressed his hand to his gut, the thought of this guy calling Coco, his voice in her ear making him a little ill.

And that's when Sarai had come home.

If he wasn't feeling ill before, her news about Mikka's test results had him nauseous.

"So, what's next?" Wyatt said now, leaning up from the wall.

"He needs to go to America," Sarai said. "I have a friend who works at a children's hospital in Seattle. We can go there, and she'll get him fast-tracked. We'll probably need a bone marrow aspiration and a biopsy. We'll also do some tests to look for surface markers on the cells, maybe even a lumbar puncture—"

"Yes, he's going to America," Wyatt said. "As soon as we can get him on a plane."

"Except, not with Kat," York said from where he sat on a straight-backed chair, and the room went quiet. Wyatt would have been sitting also, but after two days on a train, his hips were practically on fire.

He couldn't pace sitting down anyway.

"What—? Why not?" Coco frowned at him.

"Because we have to assume that Gustov knows you're

still alive."

"Why?"

"Because none of the people he sent to kill you succeeded."

The room again went quiet.

Roman shot a look at York. Frowned.

York ignored him. "Listen, the best way to do this is to separate you two."

"What—?" Coco said.

"No—!" Wyatt's voice overlapped hers.

"Yes," Roman said. "If Gustov is after Kat, then Mikka is in danger. But if he travels with Sarai as a patient, she can get him in the USA under an emergency medical visa, even under an assumed name."

"I'll go with them," York said. "I have a name or two I can use."

If York thought Wyatt was leaving his son in another man's hands—

"Wyatt," York said, looking at him. "I need you to get Kat out of the country."

Huh. He didn't know why, but having the man turn to him, confidence in his eyes, did a strange thing to Wyatt.

As if someone had just taken a shot on goal and he'd gloved it.

"No problem," he said. Except, "Any bright ideas on how?"

"Isn't your team in Vladivostok?" Roman asked.

"Maybe. I don't know how long our layover was there."

Roman got up. "Then we need to get you on a train. Tonight. You two can fly out with the team."

"Wait," Coco said, rising fast. "No—I'm not leaving my son!"

York had gotten up also, and now he strode across the room. Grabbed her shoulders and met her eyes.

"I will not let anything happen to your son. As long as I have breath inside me, I will protect him."

Coco breathed in his words. Then he looked at Wyatt. "I give you my word."

Wyatt met his eyes. Nodded.

Coco sat back down, her breath tremulous.

Sarai scooted in beside her, put her arm around her. "It'll be okay, I promise."

York headed down the hall to the office. "I'm going to book us plane tickets."

"Come with me," Roman said quietly to Wyatt.

Oh great. "More waterboarding?"

Roman frowned at him. So maybe that wasn't appropriate, but he still didn't like the guy.

Roman led him into the kitchen. Turned to him and shut the door. "I have a buddy in Seattle. He used to be a Russian cop. He works for the Seattle PD now. I'll email him and tell him what's going down. He'll protect you—"

"I can protect Coco." Even as Wyatt said it, it sounded stupid, but...hey, hadn't York just tasked him with getting Coco stateside?

And there went Ford in his head, asking him how he was going to get her out of Russia. *You don't have a visa, you don't speak Russian. You're a hockey player, for cryin' out loud.*

Yeah, well, for a hockey player, he hadn't completely stunk. If he omitted the leading an assassin right to Coco part.

And getting hit on the head—a wound that still throbbed. Sheesh. Still...

"His name is Vicktor. He's married to an American named Gracie. I'll give you his number."

Wyatt nodded.

Roman met his eyes then. "Don't do anything fancy. Or stupid. Just go to Vladivostok and get on a plane. Stay with your team. Gustov won't approach you if you're surrounded." His voice dropped. "Sarai *will* take good care of your son. I promise."

Wyatt glanced away, toward the darkened window. Saw his own reflection—the bruise on his forehead that swelled down to his eyes. The three-day beard growth, the greasy hair. He needed a shower and a shave and maybe a good look in the mirror to help him wake up and realize he wasn't in a dream.

"You didn't know."

Wyatt turned back to Roman. Frowned.

"Coco said that you didn't know."

Aw. "*You* even knew about Mikka?"

Roman nodded.

Nice. Coco trusted the FSB before she trusted him.

Well, he had about two days to prove that he could be the guy she needed.

The guy to keep her safe.

What was it that York said...as long as he had breath in him?

Yeah, well, ditto.

Drop the puck. Game time.

This was no different than every other time she'd had to leave her son.

Except, this time she wasn't doing it alone.

Coco didn't know what it was about saying goodbye to Mikka while standing next to Wyatt. Or watching Wyatt say goodbye, his jaw tight, his eyes shiny as he gave Mikka a hug. For some reason, knowing that he too had to kiss Mikka's forehead, close the door behind him, and leave their son in Sarai's care made her feel like, well, maybe she didn't have to bear the pain alone.

Or maybe she did. Wyatt hadn't exactly spoken to her since his outburst some two hours earlier at Roman's flat. *You really don't want me, do you?*

She'd been so stunned by his words she hadn't moved, her own retort clogged in her throat. Because it wasn't like she was going to fall at his feet like some sort of lovesick fan.

He had plenty of those, thank you.

Call it her dumb Russian pride, but in that moment, she heard Natalya's words. *It's not like he loves you.*

No, she might have said. *You didn't want* me.

She wanted to strangle York for his stupid suggestion that

Wyatt bring her with him to Vladivostok. But maybe he was right—if her life was about dodging assassins, then Mikka was better off away from her. And with York, who actually knew how to defend him.

Oh, that wasn't fair. Wyatt was big, tough, and at the end of the day, well, he'd delivered his *No problem* as if he regularly sneaked in and out of former Communist countries.

Roman dropped them off at the train station, and Coco bought a ticket with Wyatt's money—a private coupe.

Wyatt dumped his duffel bag on the top bunk, made his bed on the lower bunk, and lay on it, one arm up to brace his head. He'd taken a shower before they left but hadn't shaved, and now the fragrance of fresh soap and the cotton from the sheets drifted over to her. She sat on the berth, staring out the window to the lit tracks, her heart folding over into itself.

"He's going to be okay. We'll see him in Seattle," Wyatt said, not looking at her.

"He'll be scared and is probably feeling abandoned." She drew her legs up, locked her arms around them.

"Just like you felt when you came to America." He looked at her then.

She couldn't bear the tenderness in his eyes. "Maybe." She blinked, looked away.

The train lurched forward and eased out of the station.

"Why did you come to America? You always said that your father died, but apparently, that isn't true, so…"

Her mouth tightened.

"Sorry, maybe I shouldn't have phrased it like that. It's just that…" He sighed, then rolled over onto his arm. "I'm reeling here, Cookie."

She closed her eyes. Pressed her fingers into them, her voice quiet. "For the last five years I've pictured how I might tell you that you had a son." She opened her eyes and met his. "It was not like this."

He nodded, his mouth pinched at the edges. "Not how I wanted to find out either, to be honest."

"I was going to tell you I was pregnant that weekend I

went to your hockey game in Helena. When you played for the Bobcats—"

"I remember that weekend," he said softly.

Of course he did. That was the weekend his father had died.

"I remember looking up in the stands, and you were wearing that crazy hat with the bobcat ears. You wore your hair long then, and it was shiny red and caught the light, and I nearly let a goal in."

Oh.

"I couldn't stop thinking about you after…" His mouth closed. And then he broke her heart again by shaking his head. "I'm so sorry that I…" He winced around the eyes. "I think I must have taken advantage of you, twice. I was stupid and inconsiderate and—"

"And I said yes, just as much as you did. Both times."

He surprised her by looking away and reaching up to thumb away a tear.

"Wyatt?"

He shook his head.

"I don't regret anything—"

"But I do!"

If he'd stabbed her in the chest, it would have hurt less.

He sat up, put his feet on the floor, his hands rubbing his head as if trying to pry the words from his mind. "I knew…I knew it was wrong. I mean—yeah, I loved you—wow, I loved you, but all my life I'd been raised to wait, you know? Until marriage? And even though I'd lived away from home for years, I still knew that. And sure, I was probably the only virgin on my college team, but …" He finally looked at her. "It meant something to me, Cookie. It meant *everything* to me. And yet, I walked away from you with so much shame I could hardly breathe. I thought my father could see right through me to what we did, and I practically sprinted back to college. But I loved you so much, I was at war with myself. I longed to see you. And I was terrified I'd screwed things up so badly between us that you'd never talk to me again."

He blew out a breath. "And then you were there. I so wanted to make everything perfect and golden between us—like it was before…but I didn't know how, so I thought I'd propose. We'd get married and then everything would be put right, and I could stop walking around with this cannonball on my chest, you know?"

She just stared at him, stuck on the words *shame* and *propose* and most of all, *regret*.

He regretted making love to her.

Regretted, probably, Mikka.

She tightened her jaw, willing herself not to cry. Because he'd been angry with her, frustrated, and even accusatory.

But he hadn't once said he was glad he'd met Mikka.

"And then RJ got the call about Dad."

She remembered that too well. Halfway through the third period of the game. He'd been found out in the field, riding fence by himself. A heart attack.

RJ had waited until the end of the game—a win—until she told Wyatt. He'd turned stoic and cold and hadn't even cried at the funeral.

Now, his eyes sheened with tears.

"I just had to run. To forget—so the day after the funeral I hopped a bus for the juniors, up in Edmonton." He looked up at her. "And you went to Russia. Pregnant."

She nodded.

"Oh, Coco, I'm so sorry. You must have been freaking out."

She drew in a breath, not even sure how to start. "I was. But it wasn't the first time I had to start over. Or was alone and afraid."

He flinched, and she didn't care. Steeled her voice. "I came to America because I was nearly kidnapped."

He stared at her with something of horror in his eyes.

"I was ten years old. Back then, my mother lived in Moscow—she and my father weren't married, but I saw him often. He was in the military and he'd show up when he was on leave, sometimes for weeks at a time. Then he got elected to the Duma, as a part of the liberal party, and suddenly, my mother and I were put under FSB guard. I had a driver to and from school. We moved to a secure building, and for the first time I realized that I was different. I was in an English-immersion school, but my mother pulled me out and began to tutor me at home. The one thing she still let me attend was art classes."

She unlatched her arms and put her legs down. "One day, I had a different driver. I didn't recognize him, but he was nice to me. He drove me to a café and told me that we'd get ice cream. I was ten—and maybe he thought I wouldn't know better, but something felt off. So when we went into the café, I went to the bathroom and locked it. When he found out, he tried to get in, but I started screaming. He turned off the lights in the café to force me to come out, but I refused."

She wrapped her arms around herself and stared into the darkness outside the window. "I still remember sitting there in the dark, listening to him yell, banging on the door."

Wyatt's reflection stared back at her, his jaw tight.

"I heard shots and it wasn't until I recognized my father's voice that I unlocked the door. The man who tried to take me was dead—he'd been shot. And so had three other people— co-conspirators, I think, but I don't know."

She looked at Wyatt now. He was leaning forward, his hands folded, looking at them.

"We left for Montana a few days later, and I didn't see my father again until I was eighteen."

"You were told to say he'd died for your own protection," Wyatt said quietly.

"He said it was up to me to keep myself—and him—safe. So, I kept his secret."

"And that's why you hid Mikka."

"My father is now a very powerful man. People could use Mikka—"

"Or you—"

"Yes. Or me to influence him."

"You could have come back to Montana. Even if we

weren't together, you're always welcome at the Triple M. My mother loves you like a daughter—"

"You weren't the only one who was ashamed."

His eyes widened.

"I knew your family was religious, Wyatt. It's probably why I like them. You all had this belief in God on your side, and I desperately wanted to believe in that too. So I hung on to your family like it might be a blanket over me. Especially after my mother died. And then…then I did the unthinkable."

A beat, and he raised his eyebrows.

"I slept with the golden son of the family."

"I'm hardly the golden son—"

"You were on television. Your dad watched every single Bobcat game."

Wyatt blinked at that, frowned. "He did?"

"Yes. Absolutely. And I was about to destroy everything by getting pregnant."

He swallowed.

Oh, she hadn't realized how much she wanted, in that moment, for him to say *You wouldn't have destroyed anything.*

His silence told her the truth.

She'd been right, oh so right, to run away.

"I would have said yes if you'd proposed, Wyatt," she said quietly.

He looked up at her.

"Which is why I had to leave."

"Cookie—"

"It's my life. I have to leave to protect people. My father. You." Her throat thickened. "Mikka."

"Not anymore."

He reached out for her, but she pulled her hand away.

"Coco—"

"No, Wyatt. The only thing different now is that you know about Mikka. He's not any safer. And now, neither are you. I bring trouble into people's lives." *And if you're not careful, you're going to get your son killed.* "You should have forgotten about me, like I said."

"Are you *kidding* me?" His outburst reeled her back. "That would be like forgetting...forgetting how to breathe."

Oh brother. He was so dramatic. "Hardly. You forgot me the moment you left Montana. My showing up a year later only got in the way."

"What—?"

"You'd think I'd figure it out but no, I had to be a glutton for punishment and show up again, two years later."

"In Moscow? Coco, my heart nearly stopped when you showed up at my suite."

"I remember."

He just blinked, staring at her. Then, "Wait. You don't think...that I didn't want to see you?"

"I didn't know what to think."

"And...after?"

She drew in a breath and lifted a shoulder.

"You don't think that was just a one-night stand for me, do you?"

"One of a series, maybe."

"One of a...who do you think I am?"

"I don't care who you are—"

"Well I do!" He scooted forward and grabbed her wrist. She tried to twist it away, but he didn't let it go. "Coco, listen to me. Look at me, please."

She gritted her teeth. Looked at him. His eyes were earnest in hers.

He let her wrist go. "I admit I let my publicist create a few stories, but none of them are true. I am not a player—"

"Please—"

"You are the only woman I've ever been with!"

"What?" She stilled, looked at him.

He held up his hands as if grasping for something, then curled them into fists. "Coco. I've been faithful to you since that first night. I meant it when I said you were my one and would be my only."

Even as she stared at him, she heard his voice, soft in her ear, young and eager, but oh so ardent. *I love you, Coco. You are my one. And you will be my only.*

"That was five years ago," she whispered.

"I know," he said.

"And not once—"

He shook his head.

"But, Natalya said…"

He frowned. "Nat? From the train Nat?"

"She was my father's chief of security, and she found me in your suite that next morning. Told me that not only was I jeopardizing my son's safety by being with you—clearly, my father feared my telling you the truth—but she said that…" Oh, she didn't want to say it.

"Said *what?*"

"That I was just one of many girls you'd slept with in Moscow."

A word emerged from his mouth, one she'd never heard him say. But it about summed up her opinion of Natalya.

"She lied, Cookie. Sure, I had a party in my room, but I swear, that was all. Deke and Kalen and a bunch of other guys were there, and it never ended up with…well, anything but some crazy pranks. I swear to you that I've never loved anyone else. Physically or emotionally."

Crazy tears burned her eyes. She pursed her lips, nodding. "But it doesn't matter, because…"

"Because what? Because you don't want me?" He nodded harshly. "Yeah, I get that part."

What—? "No! That's not what I meant."

"Sure looks like it. I practically begged you to leave with me—"

"I told you I couldn't, and now you know it was for Mikka's safety."

"It seems like it was about spite. Paying me back for breaking your heart."

"Seriously? Wow, you think I'm that person?"

"No! Or, yes. *I don't know.* I came back to that hotel room with flowers and another stinkin' marriage proposal in my head and you were gone. Vanished."

"If you were so brokenhearted, why didn't you say anything? You know it's been me on the hockey forum—"

"Pride."

She stared at him. He looked away, his expression wretched.

"I thought you didn't want me. But I couldn't stop talking to you. Holding out hope. I think somehow I got it in my head that you were in trouble. And...then you were."

Then she was.

And he'd come running to save her. Only to discover... Mikka. *Oh, Wyatt.*

His voice softened, and he looked at her, his beautiful eyes glossy. "Cookie, if I could, I'd start all over with you. Do things right. Honor us both."

She drew in her breath, needing to know the truth. "Wyatt. Do you...do you like Mikka?"

His mouth opened. Closed. He swallowed, and a tear dripped onto his cheek. "He's amazing," he said, his voice shaking. "He's so amazing I can hardly breathe around him. I'm crazy about him, Cookie." He reached out and took her hands. "Thank you."

She frowned.

"Thank you for keeping him safe. For taking care of him. For not...for not doing the easy thing and..." He shook his head. "Thank you for having him. I promise you will never be alone in this again. I'm here now. And I'm not going anywhere."

She wiped her hand across her cheek. "I'm so afraid you're going to get hurt...that you're both going to die because of me."

"And I'm so afraid that if I close my eyes, when I open them you'll be gone."

She let a beat pass. "Then maybe you should lock the door."

Another beat. Then a small, sweet smile hinted up his face. "It's already locked."

"Really?"

"Really," he said. "I'm a goaltender. My job is to foresee

trouble and stop it."

Huh. Maybe he could keep her safe.

He slowly dropped to his knees before her, between the two seats. "I'm not going to get hurt, Cookie." He took her face in his hands. "Have you not met me? I'm the tough one of the Marshall family."

She took his face in her hands. That beautiful, amazing, handsome face.

He might have seen trouble coming, but it had found its way into the compartment anyway. "No, Wyatt. You're the softie."

Then she kissed him.

Wyatt. Sweet, romantic Wyatt, who wore his heart outside his body, despite his tough act. He tasted of coffee and a husky, deep familiarity that she could never forget. But instead of swooping her into his arms, he kept the kiss gentle, calm, his mouth tender against hers. Maybe because she was trembling.

Or maybe because he was.

He leaned back then and met her eyes. "In case you're wondering, tonight's a no. Because we *are* starting over, Coco. But I am going to find a way to wedge myself onto that couch and hold you."

She laughed as he did just that, tucking her close to him, her head on one of his arms, the other around her waist, warm, heavy. Solid.

"Go to sleep, Cookie. You're safe now."

So, maybe there were such things as happily ever afters.

9

I f Wyatt didn't move, he couldn't destroy anything.

Every morning should start like this. The sun cast in around the drawn shade of the train compartment in streams of gold and red, and the *clack-clack* of the tracks as the train moved was already coaxing him back into sleep.

Wyatt couldn't remember when he'd slept so well. Maybe it was the way Coco was tucked into his arms, small and perfect, her head below his as he lay on his side. Her legs were trapped inside his, his arms around her body, and she too slept, her breaths deep and peaceful.

Maybe because they didn't have anything to regret.

No. He'd held on to that word as kisses deepened last night, as he'd moved up to draw her into his arms, curling onto the couch with her. But the no in his heart had risen, instead of a warning, to a sweet, perfect line of protection.

As if he'd nabbed a puck in the crease, stopping the sirens of failure.

No. Because his words had thundered in his head like a voice. *If I could, I'd start all over with you. Do things right. Honor us both.*

She smelled good, and he drank it in without guilt. That, and the feel of her skin against his lips as he pressed them to the side of her neck.

She roused, glanced over her shoulder at him. "Hey."

"Hey," he whispered and let a grin slide up his face. "We're almost to Vladivostok."

She reached out and lifted the shade, wincing as the sun crested into the room. "Yeah. I can see buildings—looks like we're getting close. What's your plan?"

His plan. He liked that she asked that—as if she were depending on him. As if she trusted him.

Maybe that's what happened when a guy said No for the both of them.

"I remember from our itinerary that our flight leaves pretty early. I think we're on a charter, but I don't know for sure. I'm going to catch the team at the airport and make sure you get on that flight."

She said nothing, just curled her hands around his arm. Her thumb moved in small circles, tiny eddies of warmth.

He refused to let his mind travel anywhere but right now, right here. Her, fitting perfectly in his embrace, their tomorrows unblemished. "You're so small. I was always worried I'd crush you."

"I'm pretty durable," she said.

"Yes, you are." He kissed her behind her ear. "I have some time off before the season starts back up. Maybe we could go to Montana. I'd love for Mikka to see the ranch."

She drew in a long breath.

"He's going to be okay. I'll get him the best medical treatment, whatever it costs." It hadn't occurred to him that Mikka didn't have medical insurance. But it didn't matter. Money was the least of his worries.

"I wish I could believe that. It just feels like, well, good things don't happen to me."

He was about to argue with her, however, when—

"I wanted to be a Marshall with everything inside me."

Really? He must have made a noise that accompanied his surprise because she nodded.

"I looked at your lives, compared them to my broken one, and did everything I could to belong to your family."

That thought took a swipe out of him. Because sometimes he felt he'd spent his life trying to run from his overachieving family. "Why?"

"I don't know. Your mom, maybe. She was always so at peace with her life. Safe. She had all these kids and your dad so clearly loved her, and I wondered what it might feel like to have a family like that."

Oppressing with the expectations? The competition? "My family was far from perfect."

"Yeah, I know. I saw the fights you and your brothers got into. But at the end of the day, you all ate dinner together. You prayed together. You showed up for each other."

He didn't know what to say to that. Especially since, "My father only attended one of my hockey games my entire life." Shoot, he wasn't sure why he'd said that. He didn't want to destroy her vision of his family, but— "He hated that I played hockey instead of working the ranch."

She rolled over then. "Wyatt, that's not true. He was immensely proud of you. Like I said, he never missed one of your games on TV."

"Probably because my mother watched them. *She* came to my live games."

Coco frowned, as if sorting through her memories.

He rolled to lean against the back of the couch. Oh. He let out a moan as fire shot up his stiff bones to his hips. He'd wedged himself onto the couch like a pretzel and now his body was fighting back.

"Are you okay?"

"Yeah, just...this couch is tiny."

"Maybe you're just too big." She grinned at him. "But maybe that's why you're such a great goalie—you take up most of the net."

He let out a rumble, half laugh, half irony. "I used to play wing."

"You did?"

"Until I was thirteen. I think that's what makes me such a good goalie—I was a great wing. I knew how to handle the puck and make goals." He closed his eyes, almost feeling the chill of the rink in his nose, down his spine, mingled with the sweat of his efforts. "I loved to hear the roar of the crowd when I'd steal and take it down the ice. And when I scored..."

So different from now when the only cheering he heard was when he failed.

And of course, that was for the opposite team.

"In fact the last game I played wing happened to be the only game my father saw. I had a great game that night. I couldn't believe he was in the stands, and I wanted to impress him. It was against this team from Missoula—we were in a tournament in Helena, and I was hot. I scored three times. We were up five to four when I stole the puck again. I was chased by one of their defensemen, and he slammed me into the boards—which, by the way, was illegal in peewee hockey. But it happened, and I was mad. I'd lost the puck, lost the goal, and he took me down. I could hear my dad in the stands shouting at me. 'Get up. Get back in the game!' I just lay there on the ice, like an idiot, and his shout shamed me. I sort of lost my mind. I got up and just tackled the kid who'd hit me."

He'd lost the roar of the crowd in the swell of fury in his ears.

"There were penalties on both sides, but it didn't end there. I was so angry this kid had turned my dad against me that after the game, when I spotted him in the tunnels, I jumped him. He was a big kid—bigger than me—but I didn't care. I lit into him. His entire team came out before mine did, and pretty soon I was at the bottom of the pile, biting, kicking, being kicked, bleeding, fighting in this sort of crazy red haze. I didn't even hear the shouts of the parents until my dad was right there, in my face, hauling me up. I'd broken my nose, my lip was torn, and my eye was swollen. But I could see his disgust just fine. He looked at me and shook his head, and said, 'Who are you? This isn't how a Marshall behaves.'"

His throat thickened, even with the memory. "I was shocked. I thought he'd...I dunno. Stick up for me, maybe. Or say something about the game. But he was *ashamed* of me."

He looked down at her. "The rest of my brothers sort of worship my dad. Like he was some paragon of wisdom and spiritual fortitude. I saw him as judgmental and biased. He loved his cowboy sons. Me…not so much. That night he said, 'Either change your name or change your ways.'"

She was frowning and put her hand on his face.

"Why did you change your position?"

He made a face. "His words got to me, at first. I started thinking that maybe he'd like it better if I saved goals instead of making them."

"You changed for him?"

"It seemed like a way I wouldn't get into so many fights. A goalie has to be steady. Tough. Unflinching. I thought maybe that's what he wanted me to be. Once I got there, I discovered I was good at it—better, even, than being a wing. But it didn't matter—my father never went to another game."

"I'm sorry."

"It's okay. But I took his words to heart and decided to change my name, at least on the inside. I poured myself into hockey, into my team, and I eventually moved in with my coach, in Helena."

"I remember. I really missed you."

Her eyelashes made her eyes seem huge in her face. "I missed you too." He moved, and another spike of heat riveted into his hips. He winced.

"Something *is* wrong, Wyatt. What's going on?"

"It's my hips. I just need to stretch."

She made to disentangle herself, but he held on. "I'm fine."

"Really? Because now that I think about it, you seemed pretty sore after your game the other day."

The fact that she'd seen his game went straight for his heart and squeezed. Wow, he'd missed her. He reached up and wove his fingers through her short hair. "I like it black. It's mysterious."

"Stop changing the subject. Are you hurt?"

He ran his thumb along her cheekbone. "Yeah. Maybe. It's a goalie injury—it's called a labral tear, or a tear in the fibrocartilage around my hip joint."

165

Her eyes widened. "Do you need surgery?"

"Not yet. I was supposed to rest it after last season and maybe do some PT, but, well, I was busy."

"Running around Russia trying to find me?"

He made a noise, caught by the desire to kiss her nose.

"Wyatt—"

"Yeah, so maybe I'm not good at resting. But there's also this other goalie—Kalen. I took his place a couple years ago when he had surgery for *his* labral tear and…"

"And you're worried he'll take your place if you slow down."

"I'm not in that much pain."

"*Yet.*" She sat up. "If you continue, could you take yourself out permanently?"

He lifted a shoulder.

"I know I said you were a softie, but you're also just like your brothers. Stubborn and too tough for your own good."

"Hey—!"

"I once watched Knox get bucked off a bull, limp to the side of the arena, and the very next round, climb on the back of a bareback bronc. And get thrown *again.*"

"My father always said you had to get back on the horse—"

"Your father was the worst of all. He went out riding alone in some back field—"

She stopped, her eyes wide. "Sorry."

"No, you're right. He was as driven as the rest of us—and got in over his head."

"Hockey is your life. Don't mess around with this."

For a second, Jace's words roared back at him. *What if it crumbled? What would you have left?*

Wyatt was staring at it. Or at least half of his answer.

The other half was on his way to Seattle.

"I can't quit now, Cookie. What if Mikka needs treatment? He has no US insurance—and treatment costs money. My contract is up in a year. If I'm injured, no one is going to pick me up."

"This is where your mother would say, 'Trust in the Lord

with all your heart. Lean not on your own understanding.'"

"Really? You remember that?"

"It was on a plaque in the kitchen. Hard to forget. But she said it too. And other verses. She used to stand at her kitchen sink, singing hymns. *Be Thou My Vision...*"

"I remember that. My dad's favorite hymn. He had it written on a piece of paper on his desk."

"I know you don't want to be like him, Wyatt, but the fact is, you are *a lot* like your dad."

He recoiled.

"I mean that in a good way—you're tough. Driven to leave a legacy. And now you want to provide for your family."

Wyatt pushed himself up from the couch. "Funny. Sometimes when I'm playing, I look up in the stands, just like I used to when I was twelve, and I wish...I imagine that he's there. Watching me." He gave her a chagrined smile. "Silly."

She took his face in her hands. "Not silly. Not silly at all." Then she kissed him.

And he wanted to focus on just her, the taste of her lips, the fact that she hadn't run away from him. But Jace was bothering him again. *You're still looking for something, trying to grab something that just keeps flying by you.*

No. He had what he wanted right here in his grasp.

And now, he was bringing her home.

Wyatt, for the win.

———————◆———————

She'd read the text under the groggy 4:00 a.m. sunrise.

RJ probably should have gotten a couple more hours of sleep instead of tiptoeing down the stairs and back into her crazy espionage life.

But frankly, RJ was tired of hiding.

Which was why, when her mother showed up in the kitchen with an *And where do you think you're going, young lady?* she didn't put up more of a fight.

Still, she should have never dragged her mother into this

mess.

The voice had turned RJ from where she stood in the kitchen, looking at the coffee pot. No, *willing* it to brew more quickly. She wanted a quick and painless escape from the ranch, one that didn't broadcast her intentions for the scrutiny of her mother, her nosy brother Reuben, or even Tate and Glo, although her little trip had been his idea.

One she'd been ruminating on for the last twenty-four hours. *Tate wants me to go to Seattle and give the information to Senator Reba Jackson. She's running for VP, but she has contacts that could clear my name.*

York had even endorsed it with his *I don't hate that idea.*

Especially since he thought Gustov was heading her direction.

She needed to leave, for the protection of her family, and hope that Gustov hadn't figured out where she lived.

It didn't hurt that York had texted her. The one night she'd had a fairly decent night's sleep and she'd missed his text.

On my way to Seattle. Meet me? Renaissance Hotel. Room booked in your name. York.

She didn't recognize his number, but then again, he used burner phones like any good spy.

On my way. She'd texted her answer back just as the sun slid into her bedroom, then packed her meager belongings and tiptoed downstairs.

The decision felt easy. And, frankly, it was about time.

Harder, however, to explain it to her mother, how she'd felt sidelined, lost. Even a shadow of the person she thought she was. So she kept it simple. "I'm leaving."

Her mother was dressed in a pair of leggings, an oversized flannel shirt, her brown curly hair pulled back. She set a duffel bag on the floor. "Good. It's about time."

Not the response she'd expected, but— "What's with the bag?"

"Well, I am assuming you are considering taking your old Chevy Malibu beater, the one you left behind when you graduated from college, and frankly, that's going to get you to Missoula at best. Which means you need to take my truck. So I decided to go Thelma and Louise on you. Hurry up with that coffee, we have miles to go."

Her mother walked over to the cupboard and pulled down a travel mug.

RJ just stared at her. "What is happening here?"

Ma opened the lid of the cup, looked inside as if checking if it were clean. She walked over to the sink to rinse it out. "Haven't used this in a while."

"Ma?"

She shook out the cup, grabbed a towel. "Tate told me about your trip to Seattle to see Reba Jackson, and I thought... we don't spend enough time together—"

"I've been here for nearly seven weeks."

"I know. Most of it binge-watching *Alias*, making cupcakes, and helping me can pickles. And brooding."

"I haven't been—"

"Yes, darling, you have. And I understand." She reached for the coffee pot and filled her mug. "After your father died, I was absolutely shell-shocked. I wandered around for about a year not knowing what to do with myself, not sure who I was anymore. So much of my life had been tied to your father. I didn't know how to do it alone. And then one day, I realized...I needed to stop looking at my grief and all the disappointments and start looking at what I still had."

She capped the lid. "You and your brothers. This ranch. All this, and Jesus too. And I realized that I could go forward, trusting Jesus to carry me, or stay stuck. So, one day at a time, I stopped letting my grief have me and started giving my hurt—and my fears—over to Jesus. In exchange, He gave me peace."

She walked over to the refrigerator. "It's not about forcing yourself through the pain, honey." Opening the fridge, she pulled out a couple apples, a container of yogurt. "It's about exchanging your heart with the Lord's." She set those on the counter. "You will heal, Ruby. But not by trying to ignore your wounds or heal them with other things. Watching *Alias* will not make you braver. And we both know that cupcakes are of the devil." She winked.

RJ just stared at her, her throat thick. "Ma, you can't go to Seattle with me."

"Yes, actually, I can." She nodded to the coffee pot. "Better get your mug filled up. I want to get to know this Reba Jackson. Especially if we're going to be related." She opened the yogurt and grabbed a spoon. "I can't believe Tate proposed."

Out by the waterfall at sunset, just like RJ had suggested. Her job here was finished.

"Fine," RJ said. "But why don't you just go with Tate and Glo? They're leaving later today for Helena."

"Travel with those two lovebirds? Yeah, that sounds fun." She wrinkled her nose. "Listen, we're due a girls' trip anyway. Remember our last outing, to Vegas?"

"Ma. You were terrible. I tried to take you to a show and you covered your eyes the entire time."

"So Vegas wasn't my cup of tea. Frankly, I don't think some of those shows should be anyone's cup of tea, but it doesn't mean I don't like a good adventure." She finished off her yogurt, dropped the spoon into the sink, and picked up a mesh bag, reaching for the apples. "Let's go, sweetheart. Daylight's burning."

Huh.

They stopped for a coffee refill in Missoula, and by the time they hit Spokane, her mother suggested elevenses.

"So, tell me about this York guy you won't talk about." Her mother raised her eyebrow over a glazed donut from Dunkin'. She'd taken the wheel, her coffee mug wedged into the seat beside her. Her mother always looked dwarfed in the giant Chevy Silverado she'd refused to sell after RJ's father died.

Now, she wore a pair of aviator sunglasses and definitely emitted a Susan Sarandon air as she pulled back out onto I-90.

RJ supposed that made her Geena Davis, Thelma, the meek housewife who fell for the sexy thief, Brad Pitt. Yeah, that sounded about right.

"He's blondish. And quiet. And he was a Marine."

"So, shoulders."

"Ma!"

"And knows how to stand up to you is my guess."

"What?"

She glanced over at RJ. "You wouldn't like a man who couldn't stand up to you or your brothers."

Scarily true. "He and Ford got into it in Russia."

Her mother nodded, her lips pursed.

"Ford won."

A smile tweaked her face. "Of course he did."

She didn't add that the only reason was because she'd distracted York with a scream. "He worked for the CIA in some capacity."

"So, a friend from work." Her mother passed a slow-moving orange Kia.

RJ laughed. "Yeah, that's it."

"Where's he from?"

"Wisconsin. Raised by his grandparents. His parents were killed when he was a kid, but he didn't tell me the details. He had an uncle who was a Marine—that's why he enlisted."

"So how'd you meet?"

She hadn't exactly filled her mother in on her Great Escape from Russia, although she knew the summary. "He... works as a travel agent. Helped me get out of Russia."

Her mother sighed. "Okay, honey. If that's what you want to go with."

"It's that—or the ugly truth."

"I'd like the truth, please. I know you were accused of assassinating a Russian general."

"Coco's dad, actually."

From her mother's quick intake of breath, she hadn't known that part. "Did you see Coco?"

"Yeah. That's why—oh, Ma, I'm so sorry. There's so much you don't know."

"Like why Wyatt is in Russia right now? And the real

reason you've been hiding out on the ranch? And even why Tate came home to check on you?"

Oh. "Yes, those things."

"Let's see. I've got about four free hours. I can probably squeeze you in."

"Fine. But you have to promise not to freak out and drive off any cliffs."

"Have another donut and start at the beginning."

RJ reached for the bag. "It all started with a message I got from my boss, Sophia Randall. I'd been traveling with her a lot, and when her contact reached out with the message that he thought General Stanislov had a hit out on him, I tried to contact her. When I couldn't find her, I took the meet instead."

When her mother said nothing, RJ stared at the road in front of them and told her the story.

Two hours later, they hit Ellensburg, Washington, and stopped for lunch.

"So, what you're telling me," her mother said over a McDonald's chicken sandwich, "is that Wyatt went to Russia to find Coco and clear your name?"

"Mmmhmm."

"Oh, that boy." She picked up a fry and dipped it into ketchup. "He's always been the romantic one."

Huh. She hadn't thought about that before. "Wyatt has always seemed a mystery to me. I missed a lot of his growing-up years, with him playing away from home."

"Yes. Maybe that wasn't the best idea, but your father saw his potential and wanted to give him every opportunity to succeed. It was hard on him—Orrin wanted him to live at home, but he knew he couldn't move our entire family to invest in Wyatt's sport, so he found a friend in Helena who Wyatt could live with." She picked up her soda. "Problem was, your father never did feelings well. He hardened himself from Wyatt in an effort to let him go. I'm not sure Wyatt ever got that. I think he felt distant from our family because of it."

"Is that why you didn't come down hard on him after

Ford found him and Coco in the barn?"

Her mother fingered her napkin. "No. He was a grown man by then. In college. Besides, I knew he was in love with her. And frankly, Coco was in love with him. A little embarrassment goes a long way. I do know that something happened between them—maybe at Christmas. Maybe at your father's funeral. Maybe they had a fight, I don't know. Whatever it was, it made her leave, and for that I regretted not stepping in. Maybe I should have protected her more."

RJ reached across the table to squeeze her mother's hand. "Is this what this road trip is about? Protecting me just a little longer?"

Her mother winked, then wadded up her food wrappers. "Maybe I am hoping to meet this York fellow."

"He texted me this morning. Asked me to meet him in Seattle."

Her mother raised an eyebrow.

"It's not like *that*, Ma. He's probably got information to help me—"

Her mother made a humming sound, nodding.

"What?"

"I knew something lit a fire under you. Now I know why God nudged me awake and told me to pack my bag."

"Oh brother."

Her mother winked at her again and grabbed her trash. "Let's get moving. I need to set up my surveillance."

RJ laughed. Her mother didn't.

Now she knew where she inherited her superspy genes. "Please don't tell me that you brought a weapon."

"Then don't look in the glove box." Her mother slid into the passenger seat. "I didn't get a conceal and carry if I didn't intend to use it."

Huh.

"Where are we going?"

"The Renaissance Hotel."

"I hope I brought enough ammo."

"Oh for crying in the sink."

Her mother grinned.

Mid-afternoon traffic was light as they hit Seattle and wound their way downtown. RJ spotted the Space Needle in the distance rising over the skyline.

"There's the parking garage," her mother said, looking up from her phone, where she'd been navigating.

RJ pulled in, the clearance just over the Silverado's roof.

She wasn't sure how long she might be staying, or…well, the entire thing felt a little weird.

So maybe she didn't mind having her mother along. Could be better than a brother.

Or even alone. Because yes, she trusted York. But she didn't know…well, maybe he was right.

She didn't exactly know him that well.

Why had he suggested a hotel to meet, instead of, say, a coffee shop?

She got out and looked at her phone. No reply to her message. She sent another one. *I'm here.*

"He said he booked me a room. In my name."

Her mother had gotten out, pulling her satchel over her shoulder.

"You don't have the gun in there, do you?"

"Doesn't do me a lot of good sitting in the glove box, does it?"

"Oh, please, Ma—"

"Calm down." She looped her arm through RJ's. "I haven't yet found a reason to use it."

RJ rolled her eyes but headed to the elevator banks.

They exited into a lobby with tall bookshelves cordoning off sofas and reading areas. RJ approached the copper-topped reception desk, smiling at the woman in the dark suit.

"I have a room here in my name," she said and decided that sounded awkward, so, "Ruby Jane Marshall?"

She reached into her purse and pulled out ID and a credit card.

The woman reached for the ID. "The room is paid for, with an incidentals card on file." She handed over a couple card keys. "King suite. Fifth floor."

"How far is Pike Place Market from here?"

"C'mon, Ma."

She found the elevator bank and took them up to the fifth floor.

"I clearly need to get out more often. I hope you can see the ocean from your room."

They exited, and she followed the numbers down to her room.

Paused outside the door. Looked at her mother, her breath caught.

"Having cold feet?"

"I just…what if I've been dreaming up any feelings he has for me?"

Her mother put her hands on her shoulders. Turned her. "Listen. Remember what I said about moving forward? You just have to open the door. Take a step inside. That's all. And, I've got your back."

This time RJ didn't roll her eyes. "Thanks, Ma."

Her mother kissed her forehead. "That's what moms are for."

She opened the door.

The smell hit her like the soaking of a wave, rancid, fresh, but not so pungent that she knew to turn, run.

No, she waited until she got into the parlor of the guest room before her steps told her to slow.

"Honey, something doesn't feel—"

"York?" Please, let it not be—

No answer. And yes, she should have stopped right then, listened to the waver of her mother's voice, the press of her hand on RJ's arm, but no, it was that not so latent curiosity gene, her draw toward danger—probably also inherited from her mother—that urged her forward.

Into the doorway of the bedroom.

She froze, a scream wedged like a brick in her throat.

"Oh…" Her mother's hand tightened on her arm. "Oh… God, help."

175

A woman in her late forties, dressed in black pants and a formerly white oxford, lay on the bed, her throat slit, the bedding saturated, her skin deathly white.

RJ took a step toward her.

"What are you doing—"

"That's my...that's my boss, Sophia Randall." She took another step.

Yes, most definitely dead. RJ turned and stared at her mother.

The woman had her gun out. A tiny 9mm Sig Sauer. "Ma, put that away—"

"RJ! Are you here?"

The voice jerked her gaze past her mother, who was turning, and right on the man who came barreling into the room, slamming his hand on the open inner door.

Blond, wearing a dark leather jacket, blue jeans, and a black dress shirt. He looked a little worn out—darker whiskers, something of fear in his expression.

"York!"

And then a shot went off, probably more of a reflex than an aim, but the sound of it bulleted right through RJ.

She screamed. Shrill and quick before she had a chance to clamp her hand over her mouth.

A hole embedded the door where York's head had been a second earlier.

He'd ducked, and in some superspy move that she should have expected, had already disarmed her mother.

Who was shaking. "Are you okay?" Gerri gasped.

RJ stood there like an idiot, gasping for breath as York took two more steps into the room, shoved the gun into his jacket pocket, and grabbed RJ.

He pulled her to himself with almost a violence, breathing hard, his arms so tight around her she might not be able to breathe.

She'd never been able to breathe around him. Not really.

She clung to him, trying not to shake.

"Are you hurt?" he said, his voice raspy. He put her away

from him, looked her over, glanced at the woman on the bed, then looked over at her mother.

"Good shot."

"Good miss," Gerri said, her hand on her throat. "Are you okay?"

He nodded, slipping his hand down to RJ's. "But we need to get out of here."

He tugged her toward the door.

"Wait—I don't understand. Didn't you send me here?" RJ stumbled after him, out into the parlor. "And that's my boss—how did she—?"

"Later." His eyes were bloodshot, and he definitely looked wrung out. He turned to her, touched his hand to her face, his expression a little stripped.

She pressed her hand over his. "You're here."

"I'm here," he said quietly.

She drew in a breath, her heart stopping to measure the moment. York, his blue eyes holding hers, the grim set to his jaw, but the smallest tweak of a smile up his face. She gripped the edges of his jacket, not wanting to let go. Ever.

Then his gaze flickered over to her mother and he dropped his hand.

"That's my mother," she said.

"So that's where she gets it," he said. Offered her a quick smile. "Nice to meet you, ma'am."

He turned back to RJ. "We'll figure it out later. For now—let's get out of here."

He headed toward the door.

Her mother followed him. But on her way out, she glanced over her shoulder at RJ. "I definitely approve."

Oh brother.

She followed James Bond and M out into the hallway and down the exit stairs.

They weren't dead.

Coco hadn't run away.

And, just maybe, they were going to live happily ever after.

If, that was, they lived through the next ten hours in the back of an Aeroflot cargo plane.

So maybe she shouldn't start planning her wedding yet.

Not that Wyatt had proposed. And even if he had, she wouldn't be able to hear him.

Not with the earphones muffling the engine noise.

Still, she tried, leaning over to shout at him, facing him so he could read her lips. "Are you sure you're going to be okay?"

It was only the fiftieth or so time she'd asked, but she was getting worried. Starting with this morning when Wyatt had practically turned a shade of chalk as he picked up his duffel bag and limped off the train.

The guy was hurting, and why not? He'd shoved his six-foot, three-inch body into a five-foot space and pretended to be comfortable.

All so he could hold her in his arms.

All so she could feel safe. *I think somehow I got it in my head that you were in trouble. And...then you were.*

She simply couldn't get past the idea that he thought she'd abandoned him...and he still showed up to rescue her.

What kind of man did that? *I swear to you that I've never loved anyone else. Physically or emotionally.*

Her stomach was roiling, and not just because the plane had just survived a jostling of air pockets somewhere over Japan.

How could she have been so very wrong?

Because she'd only seen what her fears—and hurt—had allowed her to see. That he didn't really want her. That nobody really wanted her.

She needed to stop translating everything through the lens of her greatest fears.

"I'm fine! Sit down!"

She didn't actually hear him, but he had enunciated so clearly, it was comical.

She sat, her back against some ridiculous foam padding

strapped to the hull of the plane, her body on a hard, wooden bench. She was shivering under his jersey, and according to her watch, they still had ten hours to go.

Wyatt's arm went around her and pulled her close. He was shivering too.

Perfect. They weren't going to die from an assassin's bullet. Just good, old-fashioned hypothermia.

It was her fault, really.

She'd never been to Vladivostok and hadn't realized the train station was about fifty thousand miles from the airport.

She'd also been lulled into a false sense of security when York had texted Wyatt with the news that they'd gotten an international medical pass for Mikka. They were booked on a flight to Seattle later that morning.

Which meant York, Sarai, and Mikka were probably already in Seattle. So, she could release the tightly knotted breath she'd been holding since leaving Khabarovsk.

They'd disembarked the train near the harbor. Ocean-going vessels were moored at long piers. Seagulls strutted down the boardwalk, and a great bell clanged from a nearby tugboat. The air stirred with brine and seaweed and the piquant odor of fish.

Wyatt had been trying to text his teammates while she flagged down a cab under the sunlight of a beautiful day.

That was the first time she asked if he'd be okay.

He looked up at her question. "I'll be fine. We just need to get to the airport. I can't get a hold of Deke. Or Kalen."

The wind raked through his brown hair, the sun lifting the copper from his beard, and when his brown eyes settled on her, the otherwise cool day heated to molten through her entire body.

He'd behaved himself last night.

And while yes, she knew it was so she'd feel safe, a deeper part of her easily remembered…

Well, *remembered.*

Admittedly, his words *I walked away from you with so much shame I could hardly breathe* felt a little like she'd been slapped, but maybe he was right. She couldn't exactly look Gerri Marshall, her foster mom, in the eye after that.

She'd trampled on their trust as much as Wyatt felt like he'd trampled over his family's values.

So probably, he was right. Starting over could keep them from opening old wounds, maybe.

A taxi had driven up and she'd waved her hand, nabbing it. "Aeroport?" she asked, and the woman, in her mid-thirties, tattooed, and with her blonde hair pulled back, nodded.

Coco had a momentary flashback of the woman on the train. Then Wyatt settled in beside her in the back seat, his presence large and in charge, and her heartbeat settled back down.

He put his arm around her as they drove north of the city. "I got ahold of Deke and he said they were already aboard the flight."

She leaned forward and asked the woman to drive faster.

The shiny, mirrored blue airport terminal rose in the distance. The driver pulled up, and Wyatt was nearly out of the car before it stopped. He handed the woman a wad of dollars and got out.

He couldn't stifle his moan, however.

Coco kept up with his long legs by nearly running. He hit the terminal building and strode down the corridor, past purple sofas and a long information desk, and toward the Korean Air gate.

He already had his passport out when he approached the desk. She dug out hers from her backpack. The last time she'd arrived in Russia, she'd used her American passport, with a visa her father had obtained for her.

Once inside, she switched to her Russian credentials.

It felt odd to be reverting back to her American self. But she smiled like an American and stood next to Wyatt, a little small in his shadow.

"We need to get on the flight with the Blue Ox hockey team," he said. "I'm booked on it and I need one more ticket."

The woman across from him was Russian but wore the

red uniform of the Korean airline. She typed in his name, then took Coco's passport and did the same.

"I'm sorry, but the flight has already pulled away from the gate."

"No!"

The outburst came with a slam onto the desk and even Coco had jumped. Wyatt let out a breath. "No. I need to get on that flight."

"I'm sorry, sir, but—"

"Are there any other flights out today?" Coco asked sweetly, her good cop to his Cujo.

"I'm sorry, this is the last flight until Thursday."

Both Coco and Wyatt blinked at her. "That's *five days.*"

"You could ask Aeroflot, but their next scheduled departure is three days from now."

Wyatt's jaw had tightened. Ho-kay. She slipped her hand into his, squeezed.

He looked down at her. "Nope. We're getting out of here. Today."

He took her hand and headed toward the Aeroflot desk. "I need you to translate for me."

She nodded.

Her words to him last night about being just like his father—driven, stubborn, and downright tough—came back to her as he talked first with an Aeroflot official, then someone in the back room, and finally, an Aeroflot flight manager.

Somewhere in there he started handing out dollars. Lots of them.

"Where did you—"

"I came prepared to bail you out of gulag if I had to," he said.

"I would've had to have committed murder to need that much bail money," she said as they finally exited the terminal, walking out to a cargo plane. An Antonov An-12.

He glanced down at her and lifted an eyebrow.

"I would never do that."

"Your buddy York did."

"Actually, both were sort of accidents—"

"Whatever. I don't like him."

"Your sister does."

He drew in a breath. "One problem at a time, please."

The side door was open, a ladder leading up to the hatch. He climbed up and inside, and she followed.

"Sorry," he said.

Yeah. Well, "This is what ten thousand dollars buys you?"

He made a face as she slid onto a hard bench. Between the benches was cargo—giant boxes strapped into the center.

"I hope they show a movie."

He sat down, grimacing, onto the bench.

"Oh, Wyatt. You're going to be in so much pain."

"I'll be fine." He unzipped his backpack and pulled out his Blue Ox jersey and handed it to her. "You're going to get cold."

"No—what about you?"

He reached over and pulled her close. "I'm a hockey player, remember? We're made of ice."

Hardly. The man had molten fire living inside him. Especially when he looked at her like that.

A man—maybe the captain—came back and handed them earphones.

Right. Oh, this would be ultra fun.

Wyatt made another face.

And she just couldn't stop herself. "This is the best ride home I've ever had."

The airplane had rumbled to life around them. "Put on your headphones, smarty pants."

That's when the shivering had started.

And it was getting worse.

Around her, even the plane was shivering.

Next to her, Wyatt got up. She looked at him, and he held out his hand.

"What's going on?" she shouted, but he said nothing, just pulled her toward the hatch at the front of the plane. He muscled it open.

Beyond lay the crew quarters and the door to the cockpit. The warmth of the crew quarters flooded around her. Wyatt shoved her inside and closed the door behind him, pulling off his earphones.

She did the same. "What are you doing?"

"Getting my money's worth." The compartment was empty and he gestured to a couple side-by-side seats with faded green velour covers that had seen better days, but at least they wouldn't rattle her teeth from her head. She sat.

Wyatt eased down next to her.

"It's bad, isn't it?"

"I could use some ice," he said quietly and gave her a half smile.

"What if it gets worse? What will you do?"

A flicker of what looked like panic flashed through his eyes, then he blinked it away. "I don't know, actually. Being a goalie is all I am."

"That's not true. I've seen you in front of the camera. You're funny. And super photogenic."

"Ha."

"What about the ranch?"

"No. I'm not a cowboy. I'll leave that to Knox."

"Apparently, your brother Reuben is taking over."

"That's what I heard. He and Dad were inseparable until he got hurt his senior year of high school. Was in a plane crash and broke both his legs."

"I think I remember that."

"It was right after you moved to Montana."

He put his arm around her again, and she leaned against him, staring out the window at all that blue.

"You know, the first time I met your family, it was at a family campfire. You weren't there—I think you might have been at hockey camp. They were roasting marshmallows at your backyard fire pit."

"Ma loves to do that."

"She taught me how to make a s'more. Your sister brought me a kitten from the barn and I sat there, petting that kitty,

WYATT

the sparks from the fire dancing into the night, the mountains in the background, chocolate on my tongue, and I thought… this must be what it feels like to know you're going to be okay."

His arm tightened around her.

"My father sent me to a private hospital in St. Petersburg to have Mikka. It had all the latest technology, plus a private birthing center. Mikka wasn't an easy birth, and it wasn't like my father was there—"

"I'm so sorry."

"When they brought him to me, he was all swaddled up, his chubby face sticking out, and I took him and just held him in my lap like I had that kitten. I rubbed my thumbs on his fat cheeks, over his perfect lips, and I sat in front of the window of my suite, staring out at the skyline and I thought…how will I keep him safe?"

He pressed a kiss to her forehead.

"And then I thought…I'll name him Marshall, after his father."

Wyatt's breath caught.

"That's his real name. Marshall Stanley, or, in Russian, Marshall Marshalovich Stanislov."

Beside her, Wyatt had stopped moving.

She looked up at him.

His eyes had filled, his expression wrecked. "Marshall? I assumed it was Michael."

"Yeah, well, you've been assuming a lot of things wrong lately."

"That would make him Marshall…Marshall?"

She nearly didn't say it. "I had to keep a part of you, and this was the only way I could think of."

He shook his head. "Coco. I love you. We belong together. You to me. And me to you. And we always have."

This time when he kissed her it wasn't the soft, chaste kiss from last night. This held an outpouring of emotion and hope and passion that had her holding on to his shoulders, trying to keep up.

184

Oh, Wyatt. *I love you too.*

She was worried for nothing. Mikka was on his way to Seattle, and he'd be okay. She'd marry Wyatt, and maybe someday they'd move to Montana and...

The plane shook. But she held on to Wyatt and for the first time stopped listening to her fears.

10

He wasn't too late.

This time.

York had gone cold when he'd arrived at the hotel room, the door slightly ajar, and in a second, his brain went right there, to RJ dead in some macabre pose.

A chilling gift from Damien Gustov.

But RJ *wasn't* dead. That thought drilled through York as he led RJ and her mother out of the hotel, down the street, and toward the relative safety of the sea of fish stalls, ethnic eateries, crafters, flower vendors, and buskers of Pike Place Market. The perfect place to hide inside while he figured out his next move.

But oh, RJ had gotten a raw and brutal reminder of the danger of being around him.

Gustov was making this cat and mouse game very, very personal.

York had a grip on RJ's hand, glancing over his shoulder occasionally at her mother—*her mother*—who'd taken a shot at him with her Sig Sauer.

He'd simply glimpsed the gun, his reflexes kicking in to save him.

He hoped he hadn't hurt the woman when he disarmed her. That too had been pure reflex, but he'd pulled back before he did anything serious, like bring her to the ground.

Poor woman had been shaking when he turned to RJ and

yanked her into his arms.

Ruby Jane.

Despite himself, he nearly moaned with the sight of her. Just seeing her beautiful eyes widen as he appeared in the doorway of the hotel had heated him all the way through to his bones. Made him realize how cold he'd been.

She looked amazing—her dark hair pulled back from her face, wearing a pair of faded jeans and a red T-shirt. He'd wanted to kiss her, to stop time and just escape into the realization of the moment.

RJ. Her eyes shining. Glad to see him.

He didn't deserve the way she looked at him, like he might be her hero.

This could not end well for either of them. Because it wasn't only Gustov that he was running from.

If the CIA knew he was back in the United States, he could find himself in a whole new layer of trouble.

"Where are we going?" RJ asked.

"Pike Place Market." He again shot a look at her mother. She was keeping up, her expression set on determined. Reminded him of RJ when she fixed her mind on something. The woman noticed him looking at her and gave him a small smile. "Sorry about shooting at you."

"You had the right instincts," he said. "If it wasn't me coming through that door, it could have been someone worse."

"Like Damien Gustov?" RJ said now, her fingers laced through his. "Do you think he was the one who texted me?"

They stopped at a light. Across the street, a ferry had pulled up at one of the long piers. Down the boardwalk, the massive Seattle Great Wheel loomed, the briny smell of the harbor mixing with the scent of oil and debris from the busy port. To the east, the neon red Public Market sign rose above the farmers market.

"This way." They crossed the street.

"York—what's going on?" RJ said. "I don't understand. How did you find me?"

"He sent me a text too, although I thought it was from you. Told me to meet you at the hotel."

They crossed the street, passing the first kiosks of the market—tulip vendors, fresh donuts, a pottery shop, a busker playing a guitar.

"He— York. What. Is. Going. On?"

He pulled her down a side street and into a building.

Chaos. Exactly what he was hoping for. Fish vendors, their wares stacked three bins deep, shouted at customers, tossing fish across tables. Snow crabs, lobster tails, and shrimp were embedded in piles of ice. Freshly caught fat salmon, cod, and halibut lay in piles, their skin shiny. Overhead fans stirred their fishy odor into the air.

Across from the fish market, a specialty meats vendor was giving out samples of salami, other processed meats hanging in links from the ceiling.

Down the tiled aisle, fresh flowers—gerbera daisies, English roses, and birds-of-paradise—emitted a robust mix of fragrances.

More importantly, everywhere he looked, tourists, shoppers, and vendors provided the perfect cover.

"In here." York pulled them into an alcove next to a vegetable vendor, hiding them behind a crate of purple cabbages.

Then he turned to RJ and just let himself take her in.

I could find you when this is over.

His last in-person words to her, spoken in the middle of a dark train station alley in Yekaterinburg over six weeks ago.

He hadn't imagined they might come true.

Had intended on leaving them there, a what-if that could never materialize, except in his dreams.

Only, this wasn't a dream, was it? Because Gustov was playing a game of chess and York hadn't a clue to his next move.

He'd call it a nightmare.

"Are you hurt?" He cradled RJ's pretty face, running his thumbs over her cheekbones, meeting her eyes.

She pressed her hands to his. "I'm fine. Are you?"

"What are you doing here? Why aren't you on your ranch?" He blew out a shaky breath. "What if I hadn't been able to get to you?"

Her eyes widened, and shoot—that wasn't what he wanted to say at all.

No. What he wanted to do was pull her to himself and kiss her, oblivious to the onlookers and even her mother, who was standing three feet away.

Probably not a great idea, even though the woman was averting her eyes as if trying to give them a moment. Especially if he wanted to keep his heart from careening off the edge, taking her hand, and simply making a run for…well, anywhere.

Off the map, forever.

Yeah, if he could, he'd simply disappear with RJ. Change their names.

Erase their pasts.

Live happily ever after as John and Sally Smith.

"What am I doing here? I thought you texted me. I thought you *needed* me," RJ said.

Oh, and…okay, yes, he did. Because just being around her made him feel less…less alone. He wanted this woman in his life—and the realization of it could take him out at the knees. Especially if Gustov won.

So he ignored her statement and the hurt in her eyes, cutting his voice low to focus on right now.

Not tomorrows.

Not what-ifs.

Not the fact that he was in way over his head. "So you got the same text I did—the one telling you to meet me at the hotel?"

"Yeah. This morning, early. I…I texted you back and even tried to call, but I got no answer."

"That's because I didn't send it." He took her hands in his, met her eyes. "I was so worried. When I got off the plane, I got your text, but I had your number, so I knew it wasn't from you. I knew—"

"Gustov sent it."

"Maybe. Probably. He stole Kat's SIM card—probably got the phone numbers off that and used them to text us."

"Coco? You saw her?" This from RJ's mother. She was pretty too. Curly brown hair tied back in a bandanna. She wore an oversized flannel shirt, leggings, and running shoes.

"Yeah, actually. She's with Wyatt, on her way to Seattle."

The woman's eyes widened.

York stuck out his hand. "I'm York, by the way."

"Gerri Marshall." She took his hand. "Thank you for helping get my daughter out of Russia."

Oh, that. His mouth lifted in a smile. "Yeah, well, she was doing just fine on her own."

"Hardly," RJ said. "So Coco is okay?"

"Yeah," he said. "She seems to be on the mend. The past month she's been staying with the sister of David Curtiss—we met him in Moscow, remember? Sarai is an American doctor and she and her husband live in Khabarovsk..."

Gerri was pressing her hand to her heart. "Where is she?"

"I'm not sure. But I know where she will be." He stopped there, not sure exactly how much he should say.

"Why would Gustov text us to meet him—and then kill my boss?" RJ said. "I've been texting her for the better part of six weeks, and she never once texted me back. Has she been dead all this time?"

"She hasn't been dead for that long, given the smell and the color of the blood."

"She was killed to send me a message," RJ said.

"Or used to frame you for murder."

"Which means Gustov is here, in Seattle."

"Maybe. I don't know. If he's working with the Bratva, he could have simply had one of their associates kill her."

"The Bratva," Gerri said. "The Russian mob is behind this?"

"Members wear a star tattoo on their bodies," York said. "The guy who attacked us on the train wore a star tattoo, so yes, we think they're involved somehow."

"Do you think Sophia figured it out? Maybe the rogue CIA group that framed me is also behind this."

"I don't know what to think. Just that..." Okay, fine. York gave in to the urge to draw her close, tucking her body in next to his. "I'm so glad you're not hurt. I got the text as I was walking off the plane, and all I could think was that I was going to show up—"

"And find my dead body. Like you did Tasha's."

He closed his eyes. Yes. That.

She held him back, lowering her voice, soft in his ear. "This isn't your fault, York. Just so you know that."

"He's making it personal." His voice betrayed more emotion than he'd like. "He knows I...I care about you. He wants to hurt me."

"Why would he want to hurt you?" Gerri was looking at him, frowning.

And see, this was why he shouldn't be here, holding her daughter, allowing himself into their lives.

Because he got people he loved killed.

"The assassin who is after us also killed his girlfriend, Ma," said RJ, pulling away from him but still meeting his eyes. "And he kissed me and sent the picture to York—"

"He kissed you?" her mother said.

She made a face.

York wanted to hit something, the memory of the picture turning his gut. "I've been hunting him for the past three years."

"And now you think he's in America," said Gerri.

"I don't know. But I do know he's still playing the game. I need to get you both somewhere safe."

"I want to see Coco," Gerri said. "Take us to her, and then...well, we'll talk about safety."

"And I need to see Wyatt," RJ said. "He has the information I need to give to Senator Jackson. She's on the Armed Services Committee, Tate thinks she can clear my name."

"How are you going to get close to her?"

"My brother Tate is engaged to her daughter. And she's

doing a rally in Seattle tomorrow."

He let himself smile. "Yeah, that could work." *Please, let it work*. "Let's go." He took her hand.

"We can take my truck," said Gerri. "It's back at the hotel."

"No. If Gustov was watching, he might know your license plate number. We need to keep this easy—we'll Uber it to the hospital."

"The hospital—?" Gerri said.

"It's...well, you'll find out when we get there." He started to lead them out of the stall, but RJ put her hands on his shoulders. Looked at her mother.

"Go watch the fish mongers."

Gerri glanced at York. "Good thing I like you." Then she winked and walked away, down the aisle.

"What—"

But RJ had turned to him, something sparking in her eyes. "You found me," she said.

Then she kissed him.

And this kiss wasn't the faux kiss she'd given him in the park in Moscow when trying to hide from authorities. Or even the one on the train, more of a release of the pent-up fear between them. No, she had a confidence in her touch, as if hearkening back to the RJ he saw standing under the streetlights, hoping to intercept the general, save his life. This RJ didn't need rescuing, but frankly was reaching out to rescue him, because if it were up to him, he'd probably—well, he knew himself too well to let himself reach for her.

To let himself want her.

But crazily, she wanted him.

And he knew he shouldn't, but he gave himself over to her, tired, for once, of holding himself back, of punishing himself for his mistakes, of believing he couldn't have this.

A life.

The house and the family and the wife and dying happily in his bed at the age of ninety.

As she moved her arms up to play with his hair, she molded herself to him, and he just hung on.

Turned them so that he could rest his hand against the wall, use it for support as he deepened his kiss.

And sure, there were fish flying around, but he ignored them and tasted the relief, the desire, the hope she gave him.

This was worth coming back to America, regardless of the cost.

He finally leaned back from her. Touched his forehead to hers.

"Syd, what are you doing?" he whispered.

"I'm welcoming you back to America, soldier." She pressed her hand to his heart. The one pounding through his chest.

He took her hand. "The war isn't over yet."

"I know. But there's the two of us now."

And shoot, but those words sank into his bones and lit them on fire.

The two of them now.

He leaned back. "There's something I need to tell you, RJ."

She glanced at her mother, then back to him.

"Coco has a son. And he's very sick. That's why we need to go to the hospital."

"She has a son?"

He nodded, and the words *And his father is your brother* hedged his lips. But he'd already overstepped once. Maybe he should let Wyatt tell the rest.

"Yeah. And I need to make sure he's safe."

"Why?"

"Because I'm responsible for him."

She frowned, considering him for a long moment. Then she nodded.

But oddly, she dropped his hand as they headed back out of the market.

Wyatt was a *father*. More importantly, he was a father to

a little boy who was probably scared and maybe in pain and alone and—

With everything inside him, he was going to be the best father on the face of the earth. Teach Mikka how to skate and shoot and if he wanted, play goalie. Read him stories, play zoom with him, tickle him, rock him to sleep.

His son would know him. Have the dad the kid deserved, starting with the fact that *nothing* was going to get between Wyatt and the Seattle Children's Hospital.

Not customs.

Not a rainstorm.

And especially not his rather irate and unreasonable coach, Jace Jacobsen.

Unfortunately, Jace had spotted him at Sea-Tac Airport while loading up the team bus. Of all the bad timing…

Maybe if Wyatt had seen Jace making a beeline for him as he stood on the sidewalk waiting for his Uber, he still might have been able to dodge him.

The storm had delayed all the incoming flights, landing them one after another. They rode through it for nearly six hours, clanging and bumping through clouds and wind pockets.

At least it gave him a reason to hang on to Coco.

Will you marry me? The words had traveled out of his heart nearly to emerge from his lips a number of times, but frankly, he didn't want to do it on a rust bucket An-12.

He wanted to propose over candlelight and dinner, do something right for a change.

In fact, he was going to do it *all* right, starting with making sure his son had the best medical care in the nation. According to his text from York, they'd landed in Seattle hours ago, and Mikka was already checked in.

"Marshall!"

The voice brought Wyatt around, and he drew in a long breath as Coco put a hand on his arm. "Who's that?"

"My coach," he said as Jace strode up to him. He looked better rested than Wyatt, had probably ridden in first class instead of on a ratty, lumpy jump seat.

Wyatt felt like he'd ridden the entire way in the luggage compartment, his ears still buzzing, and he could hardly move from the pain in his hips, thank you.

Jace wore a suit jacket, his earbuds hanging from around his neck, and radiated a sort of anger reserved for when he was contemplating pulling Wyatt from the game.

"Hey, Coach." Wyatt kept his voice easy.

"Do you have any idea what it did to me to leave you behind in Russia?" Jace snapped. "Sheesh—in *Siberia*, Guns. I had nightmares all the way home of how I was going to tell our General Manager I'd lost our best goalie."

Best goalie. He liked that. "Sorry." He put his arm around Coco. "This is my...uh..." Girlfriend? The mother of his child? "This is Coco. She grew up with me—she's—" Oh, he didn't have a clue how to explain her presence in his life.

Wait. Yes he did. The best thing that ever happened to him.

"Hi," Coco said, saving him and putting out her hand. "I'm actually a long-time fan of the Blue Ox and Wyatt's family."

Jace shook her hand, but his gaze flickered over to the way Wyatt held her.

"I don't understand," Jace said. "Do you live here—are you picking him up?"

"No, I was in Russia. We flew over together."

Jace frowned. "And that's what I can't figure out. I thought ours was the last flight out. How did you—"

"Hitched a ride on an Aeroflot cargo plane. We got to the airport right after you took off. Listen, Coach, I gotta run—"

Jace shoved a barrier hand on his sternum. "Not so fast. We're on our way to practice. I don't know what you've been up to, but I fully expect you to get on this bus. Right now."

Practice. Wyatt glanced at Coco, who suddenly wouldn't look at him.

"I have something to do—"

"We have an exhibition tomorrow with the Seattle

Thunderbirds, and I know it's not a match, but it's for charity.
And part of the publicity clause in your contract."

Oh nice, Coach, pull out the contract.

Coco was pulling away. "I think our Uber is here."

Maybe Coach read his expression because he raised an
eyebrow. "The crowds show up to see you, Marshall."

"What about Kalen? Can he—"

"Sure. I can play Kalen. Are you ready for that?"

Wyatt's entire body stiffened. "What does that mean?"

"I think you know what it means. I start Kalen, and I'm
looking at him for the starting line."

"Nice. It's one practice, Coach—I'll be at the exhibition
tomorrow, I promise."

Coco was leaning into the open door of a Subaru.

"Practice starts in one hour. At the Thunderbirds practice center." He shook his head. "I don't know what's going
on with you, Wyatt, but you need to get your head back on
straight. You're a Blue Ox, and we expect you to act like it."

Jace turned and strode back to the bus.

"Wy? You ready?" Coco stood by the Subaru, her door
open.

He walked over and squeezed into the car, his knees
against the vinyl seats.

"Seattle Children's Hospital," she said.

He looked out the window as the driver got on I-5 and
headed north.

Are you ready for that?

Jace's question seeped into his aching bones. Every muscle
in his body burned, right down to his mitochondria, and his
hips could make him curl into the fetal position.

I've been breathing hockey since I was seven years old. It's who I am.

"Are you okay?" Coco said. "Are you sure you should miss
practice?"

"And leave you and Mikka alone at the hospital?"

She touched his arm. "What about…I just…"

His mouth tightened.

"We need to look at this realistically," she said finally.

"You have a job that causes you to travel. You aren't going to be able to stick around in Seattle if Mikka is sick. And if he's not…well, he needs to live somewhere stable." She took a breath. "We can't travel with you, Wyatt."

Her words dug a hole through him.

What if it crumbled? What would you have left?

He wasn't ready for it to crumble. Coco was right, but her words suddenly took him out and he was sprawled on the ice on his back, struggling to get back on his feet.

What had he been thinking?

"Let's just get to the hospital."

Hockey is all I have. It's my whole world.

He blew out a breath even as they pulled up to the hospital.

What if he had to give up his career to take care of Mikka?

Inside, Coco headed straight for the information desk and presented her name. The receptionist looked it up. "Here for Mikka Stanley? You're listed as the mother."

Coco nodded. "And this is his father." She gestured to Wyatt.

His father. The word wrapped tentacles around his chest and squeezed.

The woman printed stickers and handed them over. "If he's here longer than a day, we'll issue you wristbands."

Wyatt slapped the sticker onto his chest and followed the woman's directions through the lobby with the cartoon drawings of forest animals and woods to the bank of elevators.

They got off on a floor with lime-green carpet, a children's play area, and a reception desk.

Coco inquired about Mikka.

The whole thing felt surreal. One day Wyatt was worried about stopping shots on goal, the next he was a father. And now he was following Coco down the carpeted hallway of a children's cancer ward, trying to steel himself against a deep, bone-chilling horror that one of these gaunt children could someday soon be his.

But he would do this. Be there for every surgery, every needle poke, every waking moment his son needed him.

Because he was his father.

Coco stopped at an open door and knocked, then walked inside.

Wyatt's entire world skidded to a halt.

What—?

His mother stood at the bed, holding Mikka's hand, waging a thumb war. The kid was laughing, dressed in a pair of new pajamas with trucks on them, his brown hair tousled, his stuffed lion clutched under his other arm.

His mom looked up.

Wyatt had nothing. He stood there, stripped, unable to move.

Especially when her gaze softened on Coco and she moved around the bed, her arms open. "Coco. Sweetie. I missed you."

Coco, too, seemed undone, unmoving even as his mother folded her into her arms.

RJ was leaning against the window, frowning, and by the wall, York had shoved his hands into his pockets, looking rueful.

"Hey, Wyatt," York said.

Wyatt just stood in the doorway and swallowed.

His mother had released Coco and now took her face in her hands. "York says this darling boy belongs to you. He's a beautiful child, Coco."

Coco's eyes had filled, a tear dragging down her cheek.

Huh.

That's when he got the slightest shake of head from York. As if…

If York hadn't said anything, then…

"Um…so…how are you here, Ma?"

"Road trip with RJ." His mom came over and drew him down into a hug. "I'm so glad you made it home safely. When RJ said you went to Russia to play hockey—and to bring Coco home, well, *of course* you did. You and Coco were always special to each other." She patted his cheek.

He frowned and glanced at RJ.

She was looking at York, her mouth pinched.

Mikka flung his arms around Coco. Wyatt didn't understand the words, but he could figure them out. He hoped for the same reaction someday.

His mother was looking at the little boy with such a soft expression.

And suddenly, the fact that he'd...

Who are you? This isn't how a Marshall behaves. His father's voice sliced through him.

He had the sudden urge to slink from the room.

Behind them came another knock. Sarai came in, dressed in a white lab coat, wearing one of those stickers, followed by another doctor, a Korean woman, her dark hair cut chin-short.

A blonde nurse in her mid-twenties, dressed in an orange top and pants with fish on them, followed. As the two doctors came over to the bed, the nurse smiled up at him, her eyes widening. "Are you Wyatt Marshall? Goalie for the Blue Ox?"

The question came so far out of the blue it felt like he'd been high-sticked across the head, his life rushing back to him.

Wyatt Marshall. Goalie for the Blue Ox.

Yes. That was him. He nodded.

"Are you visiting the children's cancer ward today?"

He glanced at Coco.

And then, for some unknown reason buried only in his subconscious, he nodded again.

"This little guy is special. He's from Russia," she said and came over to take his blood pressure.

Sarai sat on the bed. "Hey, Coco. Wyatt. We're all checked in, and we ran the first panel of tests. They should be back soon."

He didn't know why, but Wyatt couldn't move.

Sarai turned to Mikka and spoke in Russian.

Coco was nodding, her face pinched. She reached out for Mikka and pulled him back into her arms.

And in his gut, Wyatt knew it was bad.

Are you ready for that?

No. Yes. Oh, he didn't know what he wanted.

He loved Coco. And he loved Mikka, too, but…but the life he'd dreamed for them hadn't included an instant family.

Hockey is all I have. It's my whole world.

His instincts just took over, and he found himself moving into game mode, not thinking, not feeling, just…

"I gotta go to practice," he said and turned. His legs obeyed, and like the coward he was, he fled the hospital and the life that certainly couldn't belong to him.

Wyatt was leaving?

Leaving?

Coco turned, but he was gone before she could call after him.

Which she *wouldn't* do, thank you.

The silence in the room rose up to choke her as Wyatt's steps disappeared down the hall. Because oh, she'd been right. Frustratingly, painfully, regretfully right.

For all Wyatt's honorable, romantic words, he *didn't* have room for Mikka—or her—in his life. And as soon as his *real* life rose up to remind him of everything he would be sacrificing, he ran.

She half expected him to smile big, maybe offer to sign autographs. *Yes. I'm Wyatt Marshall. Goalie for the Blue Ox.*

Oh, shoot, she shouldn't blame him. Wyatt had lived for hockey since long before she met him.

Her mistake had been falling for a man whose heart was already taken.

Now she'd just have to figure out a way to protect Mikka too.

Sarai had briefly stopped talking when Wyatt left.

"Um, I have to, uh…" RJ got up and left the room. Probably to run after her stupid brother.

Of course, York went after *her*.

Which just left her with Gerri Marshall, who had stepped

back, watching, a wrinkle across her brow.

Coco hadn't a clue what to say to her.

Meet your grandson?

No. Not now. That would be a longer conversation that by rights she should have with Wyatt, the coward, by her side.

Besides, Mikka was clinging to her, small and afraid in her arms. She climbed on the bed with him and pulled him into her lap.

"*Mamichka*. What took you so long?"

"I got here as soon as I could, little man."

"Should I wait until Wyatt comes back?" Sarai asked, still in Russian. "I shouldn't have spoken Russian—"

"You were telling Mikka about the procedure. Of course you need to speak in Russian." She kissed his head. "Mama will be with you the entire time." Her eyes filled then as Sarai went on to explain the specifics of the bone marrow aspiration.

"We'll be taking a bone marrow sample and biopsy from his hip bone. He'll be on his side. It'll take about thirty minutes. We'll inject a local anesthetic, and that will probably sting a little, but we'll make sure he doesn't feel anything, just a little pressure. The results will take about a day to get back."

She looked at the other doctor, the Korean woman with kind eyes, and flipped into English.

"This is my friend Dr. Nancy Lee. She'll be doing the procedure."

Dr. Lee shook Coco's hand. "Nice to meet you."

She looked at Gerri. "And is this Grandma?"

Coco looked up, frozen, the question holding her hostage.

Gerri just smiled. "Of course it is." She stepped up and shook Nancy's hand and winked at Coco.

Oh. Right. Because Coco's mother had died and left Coco in the care of Gerri. So, yes, that would sort of make her a proxy grandmother.

Never mind the truth.

"Let's get started," Dr. Lee said. "You ready?" She directed her question at Coco, who wanted to shake her head, her entire body trembling. Not in the least ready.

Coco couldn't move.

"Let's get this over with," Gerri said, meeting Coco's eyes.

Yes. Right. Coco nodded.

Behind her, a nurse had entered, carrying a tray of supplies.

Coco got off the bed and came around in front of Mikka, pulling up a chair to sit beside him. Took his hand.

Gerri pulled up a chair behind her. And took *her* hand. Squeezed.

As the nurse prepped Mikka, positioning him on his side, then stepping aside for Dr. Lee to prepare his hip with sterile cleanser, Gerri started to sing.

Her voice was soft, sweet, and directed toward Mikka.

Jesus loves me, this I know. For the Bible tells me so...

The song stirred inside Coco, awakening a memory of her sitting on the floor of the big house, in front of the fire, the wee hours of the night clouded in around her, quietly weeping.

She hadn't heard the steps on the stairs, hadn't realized that Gerri had come down until she felt the soft wool of the afghan settle on her shoulders.

Then Gerri sat beside her, put her arm around her, and pulled her close. Humming, then singing.

Little ones to Him belong.

They are weak, but He is strong.

Her eyes filled, and in her memory she laid her head on Gerri's shoulder.

"You are not alone, Coco," she'd said softly. "And right now, you don't need to be strong. God is with you. And He will rescue you."

She hadn't exactly known what Gerri meant, because with everything inside her she'd wanted to curl up in front of the hearth and never get up.

Now, holding Mikka's hand, she just wanted to lean in again to the shoulder of this woman who had, somehow, miraculously appeared to wrap her arms around her.

Around them.

Sarai had her hands on Mikka's body, speaking to him in

Russian, and Dr. Lee inserted the local. "Don't move, Mikka."

He whimpered, and his eyes filled, but Coco held his gaze, her eyes filling also. "You're such a brave boy."

Gerri continued to hum as Dr. Lee finished the local, waited until it took, then quickly proceeded with the biopsy.

"You'll feel pressure, but not pain, Mikka," Sarai said, but his eyes widened anyway, and he cried out.

"Stay still."

He was whimpering, however, and starting to wiggle.

"Mikka, stop!" But Coco was crying so hard that her word came out sharp and frightening.

Mikka started to scream.

Gerri got up and pressed her hands on his body and started to pray.

"Lord, You are great. You are mighty. And You can heal this little body. And in Jesus's name we ask for Your peace for Mikka and for Coco and for these doctors. And for complete healing, by Your power."

A heat radiated through Coco's body, Gerri's words finding her bones, steeling them.

Mikka stopped screaming, looking up at Gerri with his big brown eyes.

"You are our rescuer, Lord, and right now, deliver this sweet boy because You love him. You delight in Mikka. You see him, and he belongs to You. Because of that, we put Mikka's body, his life, his spirit into Your safe hands."

Mikka had settled, his eyes still on Gerri.

"All done," Dr. Lee said and put the specimens into bottles onto the tray.

Gerri touched Mikka's face. "Such a brave boy. Just like his father."

Coco looked up at her.

"Really?" Gerri said, her eyes shining. "You don't think I didn't recognize my son in this cute little boy? Those brown eyes, that unruly brown hair, the dimple? The way he sticks his tongue in the side of his mouth when he's bearing down, trying to win at a thumb war?"

Yes, Mikka did do that.

The nurse finished bandaging Mikka then patted his leg. "All done, Mom."

As they were packing up, Sarai turned to Coco. "I thought maybe, while we're waiting, we could run some blood tests. If we need to pursue a bone marrow transplant, it would be good to see if you might be a match."

"Of course," Coco said.

"What about me?" Gerri said. "Because I'm the *grandma*."

Sarai smiled. "Okay, Grandma."

"I think you should call me *Grandma Gerri*, how about Gigi? I think it has a nice ring to it, don't you?"

Coco just stared at her.

"I'll send someone in to draw blood," Sarai said as she left the room.

Coco slid up to the bed and pulled Mikka into her arms, smoothing down his hair. "I...I wanted to tell you, but I didn't know...I mean—"

"It was before you left, wasn't it? Probably even before Orrin died?"

She nodded.

"Thanksgiving? When Ford caught you—"

"After that, when Wyatt was home for Christmas."

Gerri had slid back into her chair and now gave her a smile, a nod. "I wondered if something hadn't happened between you two. My son always loved you. I know you loved him too." She squeezed Coco's hand. "Why didn't you tell me?"

Coco wiped her cheek. "I was ashamed. I knew...well, your family doesn't make mistakes—"

"Oh, please. *Honey*. We are epic with our mistakes. You've heard the one about Reuben leaving home because his little brother stole his girlfriend? Or Tate being arrested for a drunk and disorderly? We make mistakes like everyone else. The difference is that God *doesn't* make mistakes. So..." She touched Mikka's leg. "This little guy is a gift to all of us, just like you were. Are."

Coco looked away, her eyes blurry. Aw, she was just tired

from the crazy trip over the ocean.

And the fact that she'd been so tragically right about Wyatt.

"You probably don't know this, but you came to live with us right about the time Wyatt was moving out."

Yes, actually, she did. Because she'd longed for Wyatt to stay.

"I was worried that we were going to lose him. And then you came to live with us, and it was game over. I liked to imagine that he came home to see us, but in truth, I think his heart belonged to you. Wyatt is my romantic, and once he gets something in his heart, he doesn't let go."

Mikka's breathing deepened as he fell asleep against Coco's chest.

"It's also his folly. He sets up an ideal, and when his life falls short, he doesn't know how to adjust, so he goes back to what he knows. He did it after Orrin died, and I think...well, how long has he known about Mikka?"

"About thirty-six hours." She made a face. "I was going to tell him that summer when I came back to the ranch. No, actually, I was going to tell him the weekend that Dad Marshall died, but—"

"All our lives changed that day. And Wyatt didn't handle *that* well at all. I think in his head he had hopes to make it to the NHL and then somehow his father would—"

"Be proud of him? Show up for his games?"

Gerri frowned, but nodded. "Orrin loved Wyatt so much he didn't want to stand in the way of his dreams. It killed him to let Wyatt move to Helena, but he did it because he knew it was best for Wyatt. As for going to his games...I think it simply reminded him too much of the fact...well, the fact that he'd wanted to play hockey too, like his brother. But his father needed him on the ranch. At first, he feared letting Wyatt get so attached to something that could backfire."

"Except it didn't."

"He saw very early how good Wyatt was at the sport. And then, when Wyatt switched to goalie, he really lit on fire." Gerri brushed Mikka's hair back from his face—probably he needed a haircut. "I remember the day Orrin came home and told me that he thought we should send Wyatt away. It was like cutting off his arm, but he did it. *We* did it. Because we were his parents, and you do anything for your child, even if it hurts, right?"

Yeah.

"Wyatt puts his heart into everything he does. It's what makes him special. He doesn't hold back... My guess is that he gave you his whole heart, Coco, back when...when Mikka was conceived. I think today he just ran into a speed bump."

Given her his whole heart.

The one thing she'd been afraid to do.

"Wyatt has built an amazing career," Coco said. "He's on magazine covers, and everywhere he goes, people know him. He has a big life. And mine is...small. I live in a tiny apartment and my only friend is my computer. But...I never wanted a big life. I wanted..."

"Wyatt."

She nodded. "Except, I never told him that. I wanted him to want me, without...without telling him that I loved him. Instead, I kept leaving him, hoping he'd read my mind. I was so stupid."

"I think that makes you romantic, wanting your white knight. And frankly, Wyatt is just as romantic. He wants to *be* the white knight. You two are the perfect pair. No wonder he loves you."

She shook her head.

"What?"

"He shouldn't. I...I lied to him."

"Love sees past that, Coco. It's not based on what we do or don't do. True love isn't conditional."

Coco frowned at her.

"Do you have a reason you love your son?"

"No. I just—"

"Love him. Because he's yours, right? And you'd do anything for him, wouldn't you? You felt his pain during the procedure—I saw it on your face. You'd be fierce for him if you had to. And gentle and sacrificing if he needed that too."

Coco nodded.

"You delight in him." Gerri pressed her hand on Mikka's cheek. "You would even if he hurt you. Lied to you—and I promise, he will at some point in his life. And you'll still love him. And why not? He's absolutely a treasure."

Gerri smiled at her. "That is how God feels about you too, Coco. And He wants to fight for you. Because you are His treasure."

Of course Gerri would bring this back around to God. But oddly, Coco almost thirsted for it, Gerri's prayer and now her words nourishing on the wasteland of her heart.

"Listen. Wyatt loves you enough to do something crazy like go to Russia to find you. I have *no doubt* that he will come back, his heart in his hands. But you need a deeper truth. I know God brought you into our family because we needed you. But you also needed to know that you were safe. That you weren't alone. And that you had a home."

She squeezed her hand. "You still have that home, honey."

Coco's chest might implode.

"You don't have to do any of this alone. We are with you. God is with you. Commit yourself to the Lord. Let Him deliver you. Let Him rescue you, because He delights in you."

The verse sank into the soil of her heart.

"You don't have to fix this, Coco. You don't have to run anymore. You don't have to figure out how to keep yourself and Mikka safe. You don't have to do *anything* but let Jesus care for you. Jesus loves you, this I know. Because the Bible tells me so. When you are weak, He is strong. Because to Him, you belong."

Coco looked at Mikka, then back to Gerri. "Can I come home?"

"It's about time, honey." Gerri got up and pulled her into her arms. "It's about time."

Coco leaned against her, closed her eyes, and wept.

11

R J! Stop!"
    RJ had gotten all the way outside the hospital build-
ing before she slowed. York had hounded her down the
hallway, into the stairwell, down all four flights, and through
an emergency door at the bottom of the stairs.

She hadn't wanted to take the elevator in fear of him
catching up—

"RJ!"

Shoot. The warmth from the August day rushed over her
and she braced her hands on the brick wall of the building as
York followed her outside. *Breathe.*

"What's going on?"

She didn't even know where to start. Except with the
obvious. "Why didn't you tell me?"

She rounded and he stopped, his hands up, as if she'd
fired a shot at him.

Maybe she had.

"Tell you *what?*"

Hello, she wasn't stupid. She knew York and Coco had a
friendship—that was clear when he'd brought her to Coco's
place in Moscow, hoping to enlist Coco's help to get RJ out
of the country. "Oh, please, you know what."

She'd been so shocked to see her foster sister she'd let Coco's insistence that there was nothing between them bounce
off of her. Believed without a pause they were, indeed, *just*

friends.

Apparently, the kind of friends who had a child between them.

Her heart could break at the fact that poor, unsuspecting Wyatt had gone to Russia to save Coco.

RJ should have probably warned him, but she was so undone by the sight of the little boy, of the way her mother warmed right up to him, challenging him to a thumb war. The kid was cute. And frankly, looked a little like Wyatt, although she could maybe see the resemblance to York too.

"Does Wyatt know?"

York lowered his hands. "Yes, Wyatt knows. I didn't think I should say anything to you until he knew."

Right. Because Wyatt's feelings about being betrayed were bigger than hers?

Okay, maybe.

She winced and turned away from York. "I can't believe that Coco did this to him." She wanted to blame York, too, but he wasn't the one her brother had fallen for, pledged his heart to.

York had simply been guilty of omission. A big, *very big*, omission. "Why didn't you say something? Because you had every chance, really. Anytime during the *ten days* that we were on the run together."

"Was it ten days? Seemed shorter than that—"

"Yeah, well time flies when you're trying to escape the FSB. I can see why you glossed over Mikka's existence."

"I didn't—"

"I can't believe Coco didn't tell me."

"Maybe she didn't say anything because he wasn't part of the equation at the time."

"Wasn't part of the equation?" Maybe he was right. It wasn't like they were dating. They'd had a sort of romantic-thriller relationship, born out of fear and stress.

What had she been thinking?

York was right. She didn't know him at all.

"Is that why you pushed me away in Yekaterinburg?"

"What? No, I didn't—Kat was shot! It was the only way to get you out of the country." He reached for her.

She jerked away from him. "So what now?" Just calm down.

Because he owed her nothing, really. Had given her no promises.

Still, he looked stricken.

"I…I don't know. He's sick, I think. Sarai thinks he might have leukemia—"

Oh. And wow, she got it. What. A. *Fool.*

He hadn't come back to America for her, but for his son. For medical treatment. And no, she didn't blame him for that, not at all.

Her heart went out to the kid. Leukemia. Poor Coco. She'd need RJ's support. And frankly, so would York.

But not quite yet.

RJ turned and walked away, wrapping her arms around herself, just needing a moment to regroup.

She headed for the playground area. An orange-and-blue path wound around a swing set, a merry-go-round, a slide. A couple giant yellow-and-blue giraffe sculptures peeked between cedar bushes.

"RJ! Please, tell me why you're so upset."

"Why I'm *upset?*" She rounded on him. "I'm sorry, I know I'm being a little selfish right now. But, for Pete's sake, York. Why didn't you tell me you had a son?"

He went a shade of white she'd never seen before, as if she'd punched him in the solar plexus, and actually reached out for a hold on the swing set.

It made her stop. Frown.

Really? "York?"

"I…" He swallowed and looked away from her. Blew out a breath. "Yeah, I guess you would have found out. I mean, you are a CIA analyst. I…" He shook his head, swallowed. "It's not like it's classified."

She stared at him and wanted to hit him over the head. "No, it's *not* classified," she said. "It's pretty obvious."

210

"I didn't think…well, I suppose it's not like the information isn't out there. I just thought, well, I don't know why I'd think it would be sealed. It's not like they had any reason to protect me."

What?

He glanced at her. "It happened while I was still a Marine. It was a stupid mistake and I…I'll never forgive myself."

"That might be going a little far. I mean, it's not like, well, things like this *do* happen."

"No. Not to me. I thought I was a better man than that."

Huh. Her too, actually, but she didn't say that.

"She was pretty and smart and innocent, and the first moment I met her, I…I loved her."

Yeah well, Coco was all that and more. RJ might be talking to Wyatt for the way York was describing her. RJ's chest tightened, hating the spurt of jealousy.

What was she doing here, chasing a man who clearly still loved the woman upstairs?

"She was also the daughter of the American Ambassador to Russia, and clearly off limits to a guy like me."

RJ froze. Wait…

"Her name was Claire, and she was a student at the University of Moscow."

RJ's brain simply stopped working.

He walked over to a swing, sat down.

"I was asked once in a while, as part of the personal attachment to the ambassador, to watch over her, and…one night we ended up having dinner. That's how it started—over Cokes and pizza. I got assigned permanently to her detail, and we fell in love. I'd never felt that way about anyone."

She lowered herself into a swing next to him.

"I asked her to marry me, and she said yes. It was a really dumb move, but we were young, and she thought if we were already married when her father found out…"

He took a breath, glanced at her, then away again.

"We eloped. Went to Paris, got married, and thought the world was ours."

He'd been *married*.

RJ just tried to listen.

"She'd told her father that she was taking a school trip. I was young and a coward. I should have talked to her father, but…well, by the time we got back, she was pregnant, and her father had me fired."

Coco's words from weeks past rose like a ghost in the back of her mind. *I think he had something terrible happen to him…*

Oh no.

"I refused to leave Russia, and I was fluent in Russian, so the CIA approached me, and I agreed to…" His mouth tightened. "I had no choice. I wanted to be with her, and she wanted to stay in Russia, so…"

She swallowed, almost not wanting to hear.

"We had a son. We lived in this little two-room flat on the outskirts of Moscow, and we were happy. I wanted to move back to America, but by then, I was making decent money working for the CIA and I thought…oh, I thought I had life all figured out. I could keep her safe, do my job…no problem."

He scrubbed a hand across his chin. "I should have made her leave."

Like he'd made RJ leave? Suddenly his determination to get her out of Russia made sense.

He'd hooked his elbows around the swing chains, his voice, his gaze now far away. "I was asked to follow someone. He was a known smuggler but also a CIA asset working for a local Bratva group, and the CIA wanted eyes on him. Somehow he made me. Must have followed me home. The next day, when I got home…"

A muscled jumped in the side of his jaw. "She'd been taken, beaten, and then hung in some abandoned warehouse. And my son…" He blew out a breath. "He was just under eight months old. I think she was giving him a bath when they broke in."

She closed her eyes. Oh, York.

He looked down at the dirt, his voice weary. "Her father

blamed me. He was right. He left Russia, and…I stayed." He looked at his hands. "I…uh…found that asset."

He said nothing else.

Oh.

"He was important to the CIA and they…well, I'm probably on a disavowed list. I have a feeling that if the CIA knew I was here, I might be in trouble. I'm still useful to them in Russia. Here…I have too many secrets."

He looked at her. "I thought maybe they would have kept Claire and Lucas out of the official report. Apparently not."

Aw, shoot. "York, I didn't know about your son. I thought…" She didn't want to say it, but… "I thought Mikka was yours."

He stared at her as she sat there, the swing moving slightly. Nodded. "I guess that makes sense. But, no. Kat and I… No."

She wanted to rewind time. Go back and be a rational person instead of this drama queen she'd turned into. She'd been watching too much television. "I'm so sorry about your son, York. And your wife."

He looked away, at the skyline to the west, to the sun falling into the horizon. "It was a long time ago. Nearly a decade now. Grief is funny that way—it's gone, out to sea, and then suddenly, it just knocks you over. I don't know why I thought you knew…maybe because I feared you finding out, and…" He blew out a breath. "I told you my life isn't really conducive to a happy ending. I'm not a…good person."

"Yeah, that's why you risked your freedom to bring Coco's son to America. Because you're a bad person."

He glanced at her, then looked away.

"Why didn't you tell me that Wyatt was Mikka's dad? I was so angry with you—I thought all this time you'd lied to me."

"Oh, Syd. I won't lie to you. Ever. But I accidentally let that out of the bag back in Russia, and it wasn't my secret to tell."

"Wow. So, he didn't know?"

"Not a clue. Really. Not. A. Clue. He's real bright, that brother of yours."

"You think?" She looked back at the building. "He had a stellar escape there." She shook her head. "Why do you think he took off?"

"I don't know. But he's also carrying the information we need to clear you, so we need to find him."

"And Tate. I wonder if he's in town yet."

But York had gotten up and now put his hand on her arm. She looked up at him.

"Syd. Claire and Lucas…that was a long time ago. I tried to fill up some of the empty places with Tasha, but…you need to know that you're not some sort of Band-Aid. I…I don't know why, but it's different with you. Very different. I…I always felt like I had to protect Claire, you know? And even Tasha. And yes, maybe you too—" He smiled then. "But you're the first woman who's made me feel like…well, I always thought there was nothing left for me but being a soldier, I guess. But you make me wonder—no, hope—that there's more. And bad person or not…I do want to try for that happy ending with you."

Oh, York. She couldn't imagine what it cost him to say that. He swallowed, looked away, as if it had stripped him of something.

Probably his heart.

She pressed her hand against his shirt. "Thank you for letting me into your life. For telling me about your family. For coming back to America for me, and for helping Coco's little boy. You're a hero, York. And even if you can't get clear to see it, I can."

His blue eyes met hers. "Is your mother nearby?"

She frowned, shook her head.

He smiled. "Good." Then he wrapped his arm around her waist and pulled her into the shadow next to the slide. "Because this is the hello I wanted to give you."

Then he backed her up against the slide, braced his hand over her, wrapped his other hand around her neck, and kissed her.

Really kissed her. His mouth drinking her in, his arm falling around her waist to pull her up against him.

If she'd wondered if he'd missed her, she tasted the truth now.

He was adventure and danger, and yet being held so tight against him sent a current of heat through her that felt almost like safety. No, maybe power.

She was Sydney Bristow, secret agent, in the arms of this man, who could both save her and give her his sweet heart. Her Vaughn.

She touched his dark golden beard, running her fingers into it, and sighed, surrendering to him.

He slowed them down and as if savoring, he kissed her upper lip, her lower, then her cheekbone, the well of her eye, down to her neck.

She could combust on the spot.

He finally let her go, breathing a little hard, and met her eyes. "I missed you."

"I can tell."

He grinned, and shoot, he *was* an assassin because he could slay her with his smile. He lowered his mouth to her neck, his whiskers deliciously rough on her skin. "You taste good. And smell good. And feel good in my arms, and we probably need to check on your mother or go find your brother or *something*, because I could stay here and kiss you on this playground for a very, very long time."

"And what's wrong with that?" she said, taking his face in her hands, bringing him back to her lips.

He made a noise deep in his throat and claimed her lips again, something almost rough in his response. It tunneled through her, turned her inside out.

Wow, she loved this man.

The thought took her breath. *What—?*

But yes. Shoot. She had lost her heart to the spy from Russia.

Right then, her phone buzzed.

He stifled a word as she broke away.

"Tate sent me a text. Says to meet him at the Fairmont

Hotel. He's set up a meeting with Senator Jackson."

York leaned in, his lips by her ear. "Hotel? Okay." He dragged his lips along her neck.

"Funny. Say that *after* you meet my brother Tate."

His blue eyes held a rare twinkle. "Oh goody. Another Marshall brother." He caught her hand. "Let's see. Ford beat me up. Wyatt nearly got me killed. Maybe Tate can get me arrested."

———————————◆———————————

Wyatt hurt everywhere.

But nowhere more than in his stupid, foolish, cowardly heart.

Wyatt sat in the ice tub, his eyes closed, his head back, fighting the moan.

He'd run. Practically *sprinted* away from Coco.

From his son.

Yeah, he was really on his way to being Father of the Year.

"Well, I don't know what you did, but you were in the zone out there." Jace came into the therapy room and shut the door behind him. Beyond the glass walls, the guys were coming out of the showers, dressing, getting ready to head to the hotel.

Wyatt just wanted to stay. Right. Here.

Hide, actually.

"Reminded me of the early days, when you showed up in the Blue Ox practice arena, asking for a tryout. I remembered you from when we were scouting you, back when you played with the Bobcats, and you were good. Crazy good. But you lacked this edge. And then you stepped into the crease for your tryout, a little desperate after failing in Edmonton, and there was something different about you. You'd grown up, maybe. Definitely a different man than the boy I saw in college. Fierce. Driven."

Jace leaned against a therapy table and picked up a roll of tape, rolling it between his fingers. "I can't figure you out,

Guns. First we nearly have an international incident, I spend the night in a Russian prison—that was fun—and then I see you jump the train in some Podunk town. I'm trying to figure out how to explain to the press—not to mention our GM— that you went rogue on us, when you show up at the airport with a woman. A *friend* that you weirdly picked up in Siberia and brought home like a souvenir."

Wyatt's lips tightened.

"I admit, I wasn't sure you'd show up for practice—but then you do and frankly, you play like you have something to prove—"

"Don't I? You were the one who told me you would start Kalen."

Jace set down the tape.

Wyatt got out of the tub, grabbed a towel, and wrapped it around his waist. He was shivering as he walked over to nab a robe from a nearby hook. He couldn't feel his hips. Frankly, his entire lower body.

"You should get the team doc to check you out."

"I'm fine."

"Hardly."

And then, wouldn't you know it, to back up Jace's words, Wyatt turned and his hip flared to life in a bone-deep pain. Gripping the side of the tub, he bit back a groan.

"For cryin' out loud, sit down, Wy." Jace vised his arm and practically pulled Wyatt over to the table.

"I'm just stiff." Wyatt slid onto the table. "Two days on a train, plus a pretty miserable ride over the ocean in the back of a cargo plane."

Jace gave him a look of horror. "A *cargo* plane? Why in the world didn't you just wait for another flight?"

Wyatt lay back. "No flights for a couple days. And Coco had to get here. Her son is in the hospital."

Jace said nothing.

Wyatt looked at him and he didn't know why, but, "He's my son too."

Jace raised an eyebrow.

"I didn't know about him." Wyatt held up a hand. "And before you start thinking it was a one-night stand—"

"I wasn't—"

"I love her. I have for years. I wanted to marry her."

"That's what this trip to Russia was all about? Getting your girl back?"

Sorta. But Wyatt didn't know how to explain it so he simply nodded.

Jace shook his head. "Well, if there's one thing about you, Wyatt, you are singularly focused."

"Thanks?"

"So, why are you here?"

Wyatt frowned.

"Your son is in the hospital. You could have told me that."

Wyatt's throat thickened.

"Oh. Wait. This is about Kalen."

"No, it's not."

"It's about your future with the Blue Ox."

Wyatt lifted a shoulder. "Not really that either."

Jace was quiet. Then, "Is this about being a father?"

Wyatt looked away.

"Sirens. I scored a goal, didn't I?"

His mouth tightened.

"Wyatt—"

"He might have leukemia. Maybe. Oh, please, God, I hope not. He's so little, and just…this amazingly cute kid and…" He stared at the ceiling. "I…I saw him lying there in that bed and I just freaked out. I *left* him there. Just…left him, and his mother like…" He thumbed away the grit in his eyes. "I mean, I *want* to be there for them, but I stood there, and all I could think was, *what if I fail?* What if this kid dies on me? And worse…what if I do something really stupid and I don't know, screw up his life? But the worst part is I…I already blew it. Honestly, I never saw myself as a father. I mean, I love Coco, and I guess a family was out there, but it's always been about hockey, and for a second, I was watching it die. My entire life just…blew up in front of my eyes, and I panicked.

Sheesh, I practically broke a land speed record getting out of there." He pushed himself up, sighing. "I'm such a jerk. Mikka deserves a better dad than me, trust me."

A chuckle made Wyatt look up.

Jace was grinning at him.

Wyatt frowned.

"Of course he does."

Huh?

"Nothing like becoming a father to scare a man right onto his knees." Jace grabbed a high top chair and scooted it over, climbing on to rest his arms on the back. "I remember when Addy was born. I could hardly breathe around her. She was so small, so...perfect. I so didn't deserve her. I had no idea how to be a father either. Mostly, because I didn't really have one."

Oh great. Now Wyatt was going to get a sermon.

"I mean, I *had* a biological father, but he wasn't around. But that didn't stop me from wishing that...well, in my mind, I dreamed he'd show up, see me play, and realize how wrong he'd been leaving my mom and me." He paused, was looking at his hands. "It wasn't until I held Addy that I realized how terrifying being a father is. I looked at Addy in my big hands and all I could think was that I'd used these hands to hurt people."

Wyatt frowned at him.

"We were pretty poor—me and Mom. Hockey was a way to freedom. But if you remember, I was pretty good with my fists."

"You were an enforcer—it was your job."

"Yep. But what you might not know is that I ended someone's career. Boo Tanner. I hit him so hard his helmet came off when he hit the ice. Brain damage. Lived the rest of his life in a wheelchair."

Wyatt had heard he'd killed him, but looking at Jace's expression, this was just as terrible.

"After a while, I got it in my head that I was some kind of monster, and I was pretty jaded. Nobody wants to make a living hurting other people."

Change your name or change your ways. His father's words huddled in his head, and for a second, he saw his father's face, ashamed as he hauled his son up from the core of a brawl.

Ashamed—or horrified?

Even worried? Huh. Wyatt had never thought about that possibility.

"But most of all, I just wanted to prove to the coaches that I had what it took to be a Blue Ox. And I wanted to prove to my father, if he was out there watching, that I didn't need him. That I was just fine without him."

He looked at Wyatt now. "But see…I *did* need a father. And it wasn't until Eden pointed out that I had a heavenly Father who loved me—who I didn't need to prove anything to—that I started to realize that God had actually made me the person I was in order to rescue me and my mom from our lives. He was my good, good Father."

"I had a father, Coach."

"If I remember correctly, your father had just died when you showed up at the Blue Ox arena."

Wyatt stared at the ceiling. Silence pulsed between them. "My father didn't care about hockey. He only came to one game my entire life. I don't think he wanted me to play hockey at all."

Jace had suddenly decided to clam up.

Fine. "You know, when he died, he'd already left something for everyone else? He'd written it down, like he might be expecting to die or something." Wyatt slid off the table. His hips had warmed, the swelling down. "He left Reuben his Pulaski—it's this fire ax he used to have when he was a hotshot. And Knox got his class ring. Tate got his badge from when he was a range cop, and Ford got his letter jacket. You know what I got?" Wyatt slid his feet into his flip-flops. "His *Bible.* Yep. A worn-out Bible. Because while everyone got a piece of his life, he just couldn't stop telling me that I wasn't good enough. That he had to fix me."

"So that's where it comes from."

"What?"

"You're not trying to prove to your father you're a good enough hockey player. You're trying to prove you're a good enough *son*."

"What? I was a great son."

"I am sure you were, Wyatt. You're definitely a great player. You do everything we ask. You show up for events, smile for the press, and even play when you're in pain. And why? Because you want to be noticed."

"Whatever." Wyatt moved to pick up his water bottle.

Jace got off the chair. "I'll bet you thought that if you were just better, he'd show up, right?"

"Get away from me." Wyatt pushed past him, but Jace put his hand on his shoulder.

"If you were just good enough, he'd pay attention to you, like he did your brothers. You'd be one of the Marshall boys—"

Wyatt shoved his hand away, started for the door, then turned. "*I'm* the one in the paper. I make four times what my brothers make. I walk into a room and every woman there—okay, not every one, but a number of them—know my name. I'm *not* sitting on the bench—"

"And if you were?"

Jace slammed into him, bumping him against a table.

Wyatt bit back a howl, rounded on him, and before he could stop himself, he sent his fist flying at Jace.

Jace dodged it.

Wyatt pulled back, breathing hard. "What are you trying to do?"

"Nothing will be enough for you, Wyatt. Because you'll never prove to your dead father that you were enough for *him*."

Wyatt glared at him.

"But you *are* enough to your heavenly Father."

Wyatt pressed his hand against his aching hip.

"You will never stop enough pucks. You will never have enough stats. You will never land on enough covers. Never. Because the problem isn't up here." He pointed at Wyatt's head. "It's in here." He poked now at Wyatt's chest. "You need to hear the same thing my wife said to me. You will not be free of the striving until you hear the voice of your true Father telling you that you are loved. You are delighted in. You are *enough*, Wyatt."

Wyatt looked away, his chest burning where Jace had poked it.

"It's not because of anything you do, but because of who He is. He decided it. And when we get free of the idea that we have to do something to be enough for God to love us, that's when we are truly free. But that striving only traps us. You're enough, and you're loved because God says so. Nothing else."

Wyatt had stopped shivering.

"And that's why it is freaking you out to be a father. Because you already love this kid and you know you will fail him."

Wyatt's mouth tightened.

"Being a father and playing hockey aren't mutually exclusive. But it will cost you something. And your dad knew that, because it cost him you. Maybe that's why he gave you his Bible, Wyatt. Because your other brothers knew him—they lived with him. They knew his life, his words. Knew that he loved them, even when he failed them. But you didn't. You moved away, and…well, my guess is that he wanted to give you what they didn't have…a look at his heart. The man inside. The man who failed, but still loved you."

Jace stepped away from him. "Frankly, kid, I think you got the best inheritance of all."

Wyatt's jaw tightened.

"Get out of here and go see your son. I'm starting Kalen tomorrow anyway, so don't show up for the game."

"Coach—"

"It's not permanent. But I'm not playing you again until you get your hips looked at." He gave Wyatt's shoulder a slap. "That's only because I want you around for the Stanley Cup, Guns. You're my number one." Jace headed for the door. "But you better be glad you didn't connect with that fist."

Wyatt watched him go, then hobbled out after him. He found his bag and changed his clothes, Jace's words like a burr in his chest.

The man who failed, but still loved you.

Wyatt grabbed his duffel bag and walked down the tunnel toward the glass doors. The bus was still loading, and he pushed through, then stood outside, debating.

Coco deserved better.

Mikka deserved better.

And that's why it is freaking you out to be a father.

Overhead, the setting sun had started to bruise the sky, setting the horizon aflame to the west.

Because you already love this kid and you know you will fail him.

He did already love Mikka. It was like a switch flipped on, and seeing him had felt so…overwhelming. And holding him in his arms…yeah, a completeness there, as if…

As if he was in the zone.

He pulled out his cell phone and opened his Uber app. The phone vibrated in his hand and RJ's number lit up the screen. "Hey, sis—"

"Wyatt. Please tell me you have the jump drive."

Oh. Right. "Yeah, I got it. I made sure I kept it with me."

"Can you please bring it to the Fairmont Hotel, downtown? Tate's here with Glo…and Senator Jackson wants to talk to us." She drew in a breath. "She says she can help me if she has proof."

"I got this, RJ. I'm on my way."

And then—he didn't care if the proposal wasn't perfect—he was going to track down Coco and beg her to marry him.

Finally.

It just didn't matter that Wyatt wasn't coming back.

Didn't. Matter.

Coco was strong, smart, and she'd lived this long without him.

She didn't need him.

Really.

Coco lay on the bed with Mikka, his tiny body tucked against hers. He'd woken after the procedure's novocaine wore off and felt well enough to go down the hall to the play area. Now, four hours later, he'd eaten dinner and had fallen asleep watching something on the television.

Coco had wasted way too much of that time watching the doorway, calling herself a fool.

Gerri had fetched her dinner from the cafeteria, as well as picked up a puzzle for Mikka in the gift shop, teaching him how to put it together, even learning a few Russian words.

Gigi. She practically glowed every time he called her that.

Coco would have been so happy she could burst if it weren't for the unbroken shadows down the hallway.

Now, Gerri sat in the recliner, under a blanket, asleep, and Coco was trying to grapple with the hard truth.

Despite Gerri's words, she was in this alone.

She should keep reminding herself that deep inside her soul, she'd expected this.

Well, not *this*. Not her life imploding around her, but she'd gotten so used to Wyatt not really wanting her...

Oh, Coco. I love you.

She closed her eyes against the burn. No. He'd wanted her.

He just hadn't wanted *them*.

Except...*I'm crazy about him, Cookie.*

Oh, she didn't know what to think. Just...he wasn't here. And the longer the hours stretched out, the clearer the fact was that he wasn't coming back.

Wyatt loves you enough to do something crazy like go to Russia to find you. I have no doubt that he will come back, his heart in his hands.

Frankly, she didn't blame him. After all, she'd been so overwhelmed with Mikka she allowed her father to talk her into sending him to an orphanage. She didn't deserve Mikka.

He stirred in her arms, made a noise, and she bent, kissed

his cheek. He smelled of the cotton sheets, the antiseptic on his skin. A bittersweet, sort of sickly smell that she should probably get used to.

What if he had leukemia?

What if she wasn't a match?

What if Mikka was taken from her?

She didn't want to think about the what-ifs. She closed her eyes, her throat thick. Only three days ago she'd actually contemplated disappearing. *Leaving him behind.* In fact, if she hadn't been on the run, if she hadn't gotten shot, she might not have seen Mikka for another month, when she came for his birthday. And who knew how sick he would have been by then?

The thought stilled her. In a strange way, maybe God had saved her son because of the chaos of her father's near assassination.

Gerri stirred in the chair, and Coco heard her voice. *You don't have to fix this, Coco. You don't have to run anymore. You don't have to figure out how to keep yourself and Mikka safe. You don't have to do* anything *but let Jesus care for you.*

She hadn't let anyone care for her for so long, she wasn't sure, exactly, what that looked like. Being weak only got her into trouble.

She'd been weak when she met Wyatt. He made her feel wanted and safe. In fact, her broken, empty heart had always led her into Wyatt's arms.

When you are weak, He is strong. Because to Him, you belong.

She tightened her arm around Mikka. Closed her eyes. Because despite Gerri's words, she knew the truth.

She'd blown it with God. She'd had her chance—He'd given her a fresh start with the Marshall family, and she'd taken their trust and…

Coco, are you sure? My parents…they're going to be home soon—

Shh. It's okay. Yes, I'm sure.

She closed her eyes against the memory and the fact that she'd been the one to suggest they stay home. She'd been the one who dragged him upstairs.

Hadn't let him tell her no.

Wyatt wouldn't be in this mess if it weren't for her.

Not that Mikka was a mess. *He's absolutely a treasure.* Yes, yes he was.

That is how God feels about you too, Coco.

She actually looked over at Gerri to see if she'd spoken. But the woman slept like she'd gotten up with the cows.

You are My treasure, Coco.

She drew her breath in, sitting up.

Looked for Wyatt, that deep voice. But the hallway was quiet.

Jet lag, maybe. She disentangled herself from Mikka and slid off the bed, walked over to the window. She pressed her hand against the dark pane. Outside, the skyline of Seattle glittered, a thousand yellow and green lights pressing against the magenta folds of heaven. The Space Needle spired above it all, the saucer on top lit with an eerie neon green. And over it all, a perfect moon hung, spotlighting the city.

You need a deeper truth. I know God brought you into our family because we needed you. But you also needed to know that you were safe. That you weren't alone. And that you had a home.

The words had awakened a longing inside her that she had long tamped down. Belonging. Safety. If she were honest, she'd been jealous of the way the Marshall family seemed to almost take that for granted. Now, she couldn't help but feel that she was right back where she had been five years ago. Standing on the outside of all that safety and belonging, not sure how to enter in.

You still have that home, honey.

Yeah, well, not if she brought danger to their doorstep.

She wished she still had her phone. She'd left it in Russia, too freaked out by the idea of Gustov using it to follow her. RJ and York hadn't returned after their crazy exit, chasing after Wyatt.

She pressed her hand against her stomach. *Please, let them be okay.* She hadn't thought about the fact that Gustov might be in Seattle.

She could send RJ an email to make sure they were safe. "You okay, honey?"

She turned to Gerri's soft voice. Nodded. "I think I'm going to find an internet café."

"I saw one down by the coffee shop," Gerri said. She glanced at Mikka. "Don't worry about him. I'll be here."

Coco kissed Mikka, grabbed her wallet from her backpack, and headed down the hallway to the elevators. The lights were dimmed, a quietness over the otherwise brightly colored hallway. Ocean creatures—whales, dolphins, clown fish—were painted on the walls, swimming with a blue current.

Maybe when Mikka was better, she could take him out to the Seattle Aquarium. She'd visited once with her mother before she'd gotten sick.

Her mother's leukemia had taken her so quickly, Coco had barely said goodbye.

No what-ifs. Mikka was going to be fine.

She pressed the elevator button and got in. The door closed and she shook away the distant but never absent sense of claustrophobia. Just a remnant of the terror of being locked in a dark bathroom, but sometimes it rose to haunt her.

The first floor lobby was empty. The tile floor was decorated with yet more sea animals, and art deco creatures hung from the ceiling, casting eerie shadows across the quiet, darkened floor. Lights shone in the waiting area, but she skirted it and headed toward the café. It was still open, the scent of coffee reaching out to give her a tug.

Maybe. But she spied the office area and headed into an alcove with a couple monitors and a pay printer.

She pulled out the rolling chair and moved the mouse, the familiarity of the screen a sort of blanket against her frayed nerves.

Maybe she'd send a note to her father too.

She accessed the internet and logged into her email program and sent RJ a quick note. *Where are you? I'm worried.*

Then, yes, she sent a note to her father.

Then, because she didn't quite want to leave, she opened up her cloud storage.

The files from Gustov were still there—so he hadn't yet been able to hack in. She hesitated a moment, then opened the spam folder of dating emails.

So strange. A man like Gustov enrolled in a dating site. She opened a new tab on her browser and accessed the site, MyAmore.com.

The website opened to a dozen pictures of happy couples and a sign-up page, followed by a questionnaire. She didn't even want to imagine what he might have filled out.

She opened the folder. Seventeen total emails. She opened one.

Dear Morpheus. I'd love to meet. Foley Square. April 4, 9 am.
KeiferLuv24

She clicked on the email and opened the inspector to examine the server information. A quick search of the ISP led her to New York City, but she'd have to dig further to find an address.

She opened another.

Morpheus. When can we meet? How about Boylston Street? I'll run by you. Wearing red, number 249.
Tammer21

The ISP address posted to a server in Rhode Island. So, apparently Gustov was a player of some sort.

Had a number of dates on the Eastern seaboard. She'd ask York about it later. Or maybe RJ could dig deeper with her CIA access.

She closed the files, reset her password, and logged out.

The coffee was still beckoning her so she headed into the café. The barista was just wrestling in a stuffed animal display. A teddy bear fell off. Coco picked it up and helped the woman bring it inside.

"We close at 10:00 p.m. You just made it," the barista said, a woman with a nose piercing and green hair, kind eyes. "What can I get you?"

Coco ordered a decaf chocolate mocha, then reached for her money. Rubles. "Sorry. Do you have an ATM around here?"

"No problem. It's down the hallway toward the emergency room entrance, in a little alcove by a side door."

"Thanks." Coco quick-walked down the hall, pulling out her credit card.

The ATM was parked in an indent off an alcove for taxis and other pickups. The area was dark, the door light probably activated by movement. She stepped into the privacy of the alcove and inserted her card.

The door opened behind her, the spill of fresh night air finding her skin. She didn't get a look at who had exited or entered.

In a moment, the machine was spitting out money. She took it, shoved it into her wallet, and grabbed her card.

The hand came around her so fast she didn't have time to scream. And couldn't, really, not with the grip clamping a cloth over her nose and mouth, his other arm pulling her against a hard, unyielding male body.

The chemical smells of the cloth turned her instantly woozy, and overwhelming toxins seeped into her brain, shunting her struggle.

No—help!

The man picked her up, off her feet, and dragged her outside, into the darkness of the pickup spot.

The light didn't switch on.

She tried to kick, her mind fracturing, her world spinning as she flailed against him. She formed a scream, but he had a death grip on her mouth, digging her lips into her teeth. She'd gone light-headed, her limbs turning to rubber.

God—help! The cry lifted inside, a strange, unused reflex, but she doubled down. *Help me! Help!*

Her abductor dragged her into the darkness of the parking

lot, avoiding the streetlights that pooled on the blackened pavement, along a row of bushy cedars.

Oh, no, she was not going to get raped out here in the parking lot, turned helpless by some date-rape drug.

But he didn't throw her down onto the grass. Instead, he backed her up to a sedan, the bumper hitting the back of her legs. Then he took his hand off her mouth.

She took the opportunity to pull a clear breath. To scream. Or maybe it was just in her head because the darkness had slunk in around the edges.

He picked her up and dumped her into the trunk of the sedan.

"No!"

She threw her hands up, but couldn't stop the hatch from closing around her and locking her in darkness.

"No!" She kicked against the coffin, then turned and pushed on the seat. But he must have braced the back seat with something because it wouldn't move.

The darkness was still edging in. No. She gulped, trying to clear her lungs, but as the car fired up and began to back out of the lot, she lost her grip on herself.

If she ever wanted Wyatt to show up, it was now.

With a frustrated scream, she fell into the engulfing darkness.

12

At least he'd finally disentangled himself from the crazy Lee Child novel.

Wyatt glanced up at Tate's buddy Swamp, dressed in the black-and-white attire of a private security agent, and tried to wrap his brain around what had gone down in the Executive Suite of the Farimont hotel.

"So you're the brother Tate keeps bragging about," Swamp said, pulling away from the curb in the SUV.

"Don't believe everything you hear," Wyatt said.

"He's my boss. I have to believe him," Swamp said, grinning. "Where to?"

"Children's Hospital."

Wyatt leaned his head back, scrolling back over the past hour since he'd met RJ and York in the lobby.

RJ had looked at him with a strange mix of compassion and fury as she rose from one of the silver couches by the fire.

RJ met his eyes. "You okay?"

He'd stared at her, trying to puzzle together exactly what she might be referring to. He was still limping, so, "Just a little stiff from practice."

York had his hand laced into RJ's, and Wyatt's gaze only briefly fell on it.

He decided then that once they got clear of all this, he'd have a short but direct heart-to-heart with his sister about the things he'd seen York do in Russia. Wyatt was pretty sure he didn't want his kid sister hanging around a guy who knew how to kill people with his bare hands, accident or not.

She raised an eyebrow, glanced at York, then back to Wyatt. "Um, no, I was referring to your 100-yard dash out of the hospital."

Oh. "Uh. That was...well..."

"I know Mikka is yours."

Wyatt's mouth lifted on one side. "I only just found out."

"I know. York told me."

Wyatt looked at him, not warmly. "He's full of all sorts of information."

"And he's an idiot," York said.

Wyatt glared at him, but, "Yeah, I am. And I shouldn't have left. I over-practiced and I'm out for tomorrow's exhibition." Not to mention the hurt he left in his wake. But, "Does Ma know?"

RJ lifted a shoulder. "He looks like you, and she's not blind, so..."

Perfect.

"Listen, I know I blew it. But I love Coco—and Mikka—and as soon as we're done here, I'm going to go back to the hospital and beg her forgiveness and ask her to marry me."

He dug into his pocket and produced the jump drive. "I should have given this to you at the hospital." He handed her the jump drive. "Coco said that this has all the emails, with the ISP information proving that your email account was hacked, York. And it proves that you were set up, RJ."

She took it. "Thanks."

"Wyatt."

The voice of his brother turned him and he spotted Tate walking over from the elevator bank, holding the hand of his girlfriend, Gloria Jackson. She was way too good for Tate, cute and blonde, a Nashville country star to Tate's backwoods, rough-edged, tough-guy demeanor. Glo seemed to have spiffed him up, however. Tate wore suit pants, a white dress shirt open at the neck, and a jacket, his brown hair cut neat and tight, and no beard, as if he might be respectable.

Huh. "Bro," Wyatt said and met Tate in a hug. "Glo." He hugged her too. "What are you guys doing here? I thought you were on tour with NBR-X."

"We had a few days off, and Senator Jackson has a rally tomorrow morning. I convinced RJ that the senator could probably clear her name, given her DOD connections—"

"And he has big news," RJ said.

Tate glanced at her, and a rare smile lit up his face.

In fact, so rare it startled Wyatt. Tate had a dark and brutal past, so to see him transformed...

No. To see him *at peace.* Tate looked at Glo and grinned, cupping his other hand over hers. "Yeah, we do. But let's go up to the suite. I'd like a sit-rep."

Wyatt glanced at his watch. After 9:00 p.m. But Coco wouldn't be asleep yet—not with jet lag coursing through her body. "Let's hurry. I need to get back to the hospital."

"What?" Tate's eyebrows rose. "Are you sick?"

RJ looped her arm into Wyatt's. "Oh, you two need to catch up." She pulled him toward the elevator. "So much gossip, so little time."

"Nice, RJ."

Tate was eying York. "And you are?"

"York," he said quietly and held out his hand.

Tate took it. "Nice to finally meet you."

No smile passed between them, however, and Wyatt wondered if Tate might be picking up the same vibe he had. A danger radiated off York, the way he looked at someone with an almost suspicious look, his gaze a little unforgiving.

Trouble with a capital T. Or maybe a capital Y.

Definitely not the kind of guy their sister needed in her life.

"Thanks for getting RJ out of Russia," Tate said. "But what are you doing here?"

Oh boy.

"Upstairs," Wyatt said.

They got onto the elevator and took it up to the top floor,

the executive suite. A couple of suits stood outside the double doors, and Tate nodded to them as he let them inside.

The view overlooked Elliot Bay, the shiny lights of the city reflecting off the black waters undulating with streaks of red, orange, blue, and yellow. The massive Ferris wheel glowed, a circle of light against the dark sky.

A plate of cheeses and crackers and an open bottle of red wine sat on the table.

"Celebrating?" Wyatt said as he went to stand by the window.

But before Tate could answer, the double doors to the adjoining room opened, and a woman in her late fifties walked through. She wore her amber red hair up, a loose white silk shirt, and white dress pants. Regal, composed, and as her gaze latched on Wyatt, a smile tweaked up her face. "Wyatt Marshall. Goalie for the Blue Ox. In my suite. I'm having a fan moment."

He stared at her, not sure. Um, "Senator Jackson."

"Call me Reba." She walked over to him and extended her hand. "My husband is a huge Blue Ox fan, so...naturally, I had to start following them too. You had an amazing season—so sorry about the shootout against the Capitals. That was amazing goal tending."

The room had gone quiet around him. "Thank you, ma'am—"

"Reba."

"Reba."

She patted his arm. "By the way, since Tate is going to be my son-in-law, I'm expecting rinkside tickets."

Wyatt looked at Tate, who lifted his shoulder. He glanced at Glo, who held up her left hand. Yowza.

He needed to up his game if he wanted to propose to Coco. Shoot.

"Congrats, bro," Wyatt said.

"Oh, I'm sorry—I thought he'd told you," Reba said.

"It's fine, ma'am," Tate said.

She patted Tate's arm as she walked past him but didn't

correct him, then headed over to RJ. "And this must be Ruby Jane, the international assassin?"

All the air left the room, and Wyatt had the crazy, inexplicable urge to grab his sister and run.

Tate might have been reading his mind because he gave a little shake of his head.

RJ had paled.

Then York spoke up. "Actually, ma'am, that's incorrect—"

"Oh, I know. I'm not unaware of the situation. The fact that RJ sought out embassy help and her claims of being set up—"

"I was set up!" RJ said, but York pressed a hand to her arm.

"I know that too," Reba said as she walked over to the table and picked up the wine bottle. "Boris reached out to me through back channels and told me what happened."

Boris? As in Coco's father?

Reba poured herself a glass of wine. "But, according to the CIA, you're still on the hook."

"Except, we have evidence that she was set up," Tate said. "Copies of the emails, and proof of tampering with York's email account—"

Reba held up her hand, taking a sip of wine.

Tate glanced at Wyatt, his mouth a grim line.

"Do you have it with you?" Reba asked.

"I have it," RJ said and pulled out the jump drive.

Reba held out her hand, and RJ handed it over. "Do you... believe me?"

A beat, then, "Of course I do. And don't worry. Everything will get straightened out."

RJ let out her breath but looked at York. "We have one more problem."

Reba set down the wine on the table.

"My boss, Sophia Randall, was found dead in the Renaissance Hotel. By...me."

"And me," York said.

Reba folded her arms. "Oh my."

"My mother was there too," RJ said.

"What?" Tate said.

Wyatt echoed him. "*When?*"

"This morning—I got a text from York saying to meet him at the hotel. And when I did—I found her body on the bed. Her throat had been slit."

Wyatt looked at York. Only the fact that he knew York had been on the plane with Sarai and Mikka kept him from advancing on him.

Not Tate. "What the—what's going on?"

York took a breath but didn't move.

"Hold up, Tate. He didn't do it," Wyatt said. "He wasn't even here."

Tate stopped and looked at Wyatt. "How do you know?"

"He was on a plane with…with my son." Not exactly how he wanted to share that epic information, but—

"You have a *son?*" Tate said in the tone Wyatt had expected. "Since when?"

"I'll explain later. But he's sick and he needed a medical escort from Russia, so York and this American doc brought him over."

"From Russia? And where were you?" Tate asked.

"I was with Coco. On a cargo plane. Long story."

"Shorten it for the crowd," Tate said. "So…you found Coco."

He nodded. "But not before I was attacked in my hotel room by the man we think is trying to kill RJ."

"Damien Gustov," York said. "He's a known associate of the Bratva, and we think he's the one who tried to kill General Stanislov. And the one who shot Coco last month."

"Who is Coco?" Reba asked.

"Our sister," RJ said.

"Foster sister," Tate amended. "She came to live with us when her mother died."

"She returned to Russia five years ago because…well, she was pregnant. And her father is…" Wyatt blew out a breath. "Her father is Boris Stanislov."

Reba sat and reached for her glass. "The plot thickens."

"She was sent to America to hide from Boris's opposition and is still in hiding."

"And your son? He's been in hiding too?"

"Yes. In a way."

She frowned, but in truth, she didn't need to know the details.

"We recently found out that he might be sick. He's at Seattle Children's being tested."

"I'm sorry," Reba said, and gave him a compassionate smile. "I'm familiar with the stress of having a sick child."

There was something honest about her that he could like.

"So, you're saying that Coco Stanislova is here, in America. And the man who attacked you? Where is he?"

"We think he's here too and probably responsible for Randall's death. In fact, and this is just a guess, but there is talk of a rogue faction inside the CIA who wants to take down Boris and his progressive views and institute Arkady Petrov."

"He's former military. Even more extreme left—a proponent of ultra-socialist ideals," Reba said. "I know of him and the rumors. And the fact that he too might be aligned with the Bratva." She got up, picking up her wine. "So, you think this killer is in America, probably to find your sister and tie up that loose end. Maybe even to get ahold of Coco, right?"

"Because if he has Coco, then he can get to Boris," Tate said. "It's what I'd do."

"Me too," York said.

Wyatt looked at the two. He simply didn't think like this. Assassinations and kidnapping and conspiracies...

All he had to do was stop a shot on goal now and then.

"Where is Coco right now?" Reba asked.

"At the hospital," Wyatt said. "Where I should be." He turned to the senator. "It was nice to meet you, Sen—Reba." Wyatt reached out to shake her hand again.

She held it a moment. "Wyatt, I hate to ask this, but... since you're in town, would you be willing to show up at the rally tomorrow? Maybe give an endorsement?"

He looked at her, a little flummoxed.

She dropped her hand. "I'm sorry. I shouldn't have assumed—"

"Yes," Wyatt said. "It's the least I can do."

"Thank you." She glanced at Tate. "Look into the situation with Randall. We may need to call the Renaissance Hotel and see what you can find out. We need to put a lid on this ASAP. The last thing I need is some reporter making the connection between you and Gloria and your sister and this entire mess."

The room went quiet.

"Ruby Jane, I'd appreciate it if you could stay and give an official statement about the events in Russia."

"Yes, Senator."

"I'm staying with her," York said.

"Of course you are," Reba said. She headed back to her suite, passing by her daughter. "This is quite the family you've chosen. I hope my campaign can survive them."

Wyatt didn't know what to say.

The door behind her closed.

"So, that's the senator," Tate said.

"Her bark is worse than her bite," Glo added.

"I don't care how loud she barks if she can clear RJ," York said.

"Engaged, huh?" Wyatt said to Tate.

"And you're a dad." Tate folded his hands over his chest. "And you—" He turned to RJ. "*You* brought Ma to a crime scene?"

"You forgot to mention that your mother nearly *shot* me," York said.

Wyatt stared at him. "Really?"

"Yep," York said.

Wyatt couldn't help a grin. He met Tate's.

"This family should come with a warning label," York said, shaking his head.

Wyatt headed for the door, but stopped in front of Glo. "Congratulations."

She lifted herself up on her tiptoes and kissed him on the

cheek. "I'll be praying for your son."

Her words filtered in, found his bones. "Thanks."

Tate followed him to the door, then stepped with him out into the hallway. Closed the door behind him. "You okay?"

Wyatt nodded. "I think so. I...I don't know. It's big, you know? Being a dad?"

Tate considered him. "Yeah. Really big. But not super surprising. Coco and you belong together."

He stared at Tate's grin, unmarred by judgment or even doubt, and something moved inside him, and Jace's voice rose.

You will not be free of the striving until you hear the voice of your true Father telling you that you are loved. You are delighted in. You are enough, Wyatt.

"Wy—what's up? You're usually so...I don't know. Camera ready, I guess. But you look like you want to punch someone. I'm still faster than you, but I'm wearing a suit, so..."

"I'm not...if I want to hit anyone, it's me." Wyatt drew in a breath. "I don't know what's wrong with me. When Coco told me about Mikka, I was...yeah, shocked. And then excited—he's a great kid. But then I got to the hospital and..."

"I'm sorry he's sick."

"It's not that—or *just* that. I mean, yeah, it's horrible. And I hate to think of what he'll have to go through. And I'm ready to do whatever it takes for him, and there's a huge part of me that sees me sitting beside him and even giving him blood or whatever, but...then there's another part of my life. The part I've worked myself to the bone to get for the last twenty years and now suddenly, it's here, and I have it. And I'm just having a hard time reconciling them. Or choosing."

"Do you have to choose?"

"Don't I? If Mikka's sick, he can't travel with me. And maybe...I mean, I know guys leave their families all the time, but...I want to be there for him. I want to be a good dad."

"You will be a good dad. A great dad. But here's a news flash—you don't have to figure everything out right now. Just...show up. God has your back. Trust Him to work it out."

"What's happened to you?"

Tate grinned. "Maybe the same thing that happened to you. I found my happy ending."

"You're such a sap."

"I'm not the one who has a forum for my adoring fans. That you check regularly."

"I don't."

"You do."

Yeah, he did. Because Coco was usually there.

Tate laughed, something of chagrin in his voice. "Dad would love to see this. Me, the troublemaker, engaged. Wyatt, the superstar, raising his own little superstar."

Wyatt the superstar? He frowned at Tate. "I'm not the superstar."

"Whatever, Mr. Blue Ox. Dad would shut himself in the den to watch your Bobcat games, and if we disturbed him, he'd send us out to the barn. Thankfully, I wasn't around much for that part. But we all knew who Dad's favorite was."

Tate winked. Then he turned to one of the guys standing by the door. "Contact Swamp and tell him to give my brother a ride to the hospital."

He slapped Wyatt on the shoulder. "See you tomorrow at the rally." Then he let himself back into the room.

We all knew who Dad's favorite was?

Wyatt had taken the elevator down, and Tate's friend, Swamp, had met him in the lobby. He had led Wyatt out to an SUV in the lot, and now he wove through the city, turning finally onto Sand Point Way.

Swamp pulled up to the darkened taxi entrance near the side of the hospital.

Wyatt got out. "Thanks."

Swamp lifted a hand and drove off.

The place was quiet, the hallway dark as Wyatt walked toward the main lobby. He noticed a light on in the coffee shop down the hall, a female barista packing up a display of stuffed animals. He dismissed the idea of a cup of coffee and followed the tile, scattered with geometric ocean life, to the elevator and took it up to the fourth floor.

Mikka's room was dark, and it took a second for him to make out his mother sitting in the recliner reading something on her phone. Mikka lay on the bed, asleep. Wyatt eased the door open a bit wider.

"Ma?" he whispered.

She turned and offered a soft smile. "Wyatt. Honey. I knew you'd come back."

He dropped his duffel bag on the floor, quietly. "Yeah. About that...I..." He ran a hand behind his neck. "So—"

"Oh, for Pete's sake. I know this darling boy is your son, Wyatt. And I don't need to know the details, but he's a joy and a delight. I'm thrilled to be a grandma."

Huh.

She got up, walked over to Wyatt, and put her arms around his waist. "And I love you. So just take a breath."

Oh. Ma. His arms went around her. "I love you too."

She looked up. "And Coco?"

"You know how I feel about Coco."

"Yes, Number One, I do." She let him go. "Where is she, by the way?"

"Downstairs. She left to use the internet café just a little bit ago. She'll be right back."

Right.

He walked over to Mikka, then eased into the chair by his bedside. He could probably use more ice. "How is he?"

"He's good. He had a lumbar puncture today. They got the results back. Sarai says that he has all the markers for ALL—Acute Lymphocytic Leukemia."

He took that in, braced himself for the impact, and nodded. "So, now what?"

"Chemotherapy first, to kill the white blood cells, and then, maybe a stem cell transplant. But Sarai said she'll go over all of this with you tomorrow."

"I guess I should get tested to see if I'm a match."

Her hand landed on his shoulder. "I'm sorry, son."

"No, I'm sorry, Ma." He squeezed her hand. "I know...
well, I stepped over a line with Coco and—"

"Son. You need to let that go. Yes, it was a life-altering
decision, but you know, God is still in control. He didn't take
His eyes off you that day and say, 'Ooh, whoops. Now Wyatt
is off the rails.' He's been with you—and Coco—every step
of the way, and now...now He's brought you back together to
face this. With each other. And with Him, if you'll let Him."

She leaned against the bed, facing him. "I've been sitting
here for the past few hours trying to think what Orrin would
say to you."

"He'd be disappointed."

"Oh, Wy. You don't know your father at all. Sure, he
would have been sad that you stole from you and Coco that
connection that comes from the security of marriage, but in
truth, he was always more interested in your heart than your
actions. For out of the heart is *birthed* your actions."

"I don't know, Ma. He once told me that I needed to
change my ways or change my name. And then he sent me
away. So—"

"Is that what you think? That your father didn't want
you?"

He looked at Mikka.

"Your father sent you away because he believed in you.
He knew you had potential to be great and he didn't want to
stand in your way."

Wyatt shook his head.

"Oh, son. You are so like your father. Your passion, your
big heart, your drive. Your father saw himself in you, and
he didn't want to keep you from your dreams. He was your
biggest fan."

His mouth tightened around the edges.

"Do you still have your father's Bible?"

He glanced at her. And for some reason he didn't want to
admit it, but, "It's in my duffel bag."

A slow smile lit her face. "You carry it with you."

He looked past her, toward the window, the lights of the

skyline.

"You might consider reading it. Especially the inside cover." Then she got up, gave him a kiss on the forehead. "I'm going down the hall to find a vending machine."

He watched her leave through the reflection in the window. Sat for a moment, then reached down and dragged his duffel bag over.

The leather Bible was old, thin, and worn. An NIV version, the cover flimsy and tattered. He'd watched his father carry it to church with him for—well, as long as he could remember. In the mornings he was up before Wyatt, sitting in his leather chair by the soaring stone fireplace in the great room, light splashing upon the pages, his readers down on his nose.

Wyatt opened the first page. *To Orrin from Dad. Matthew 10:39. Remember, that whoever finds their life will lose it, and whoever loses their life for the sake of the Lord will find it.*

Wyatt turned the next page.

A prayer list.

And his name was at the top.

Not Reuben. Not Knox. Not Tate or Ford. Not even RJ, the princess. But Wyatt's name, squeezed in at the top of the long list.

And next to his name, a verse. Matthew 3:17.

Wyatt turned to the gospel, found the verse, and his breath clogged in his chest.

"This is my Son, whom I love; with him I am well pleased."

He had nothing. Read the verse again.

And again.

Jace barreled into his head. *He wanted to give you what they didn't have...a look at his heart.*

Aw, Dad. Wyatt pressed his thumb and forefinger into his eyes, rubbing away the grit in them. But the burning continued. *He was your biggest fan.*

No. How could—

A whimper from the bed opened Wyatt's eyes. Mikka was moaning, as if caught in a bad dream.

The door opened and Gerri came into the room.

Mikka cried out again.

"Oh," she said and moved toward the bed.

"I got this, Ma," Wyatt said.

"I know you do, son."

Then he slid onto the bed with Mikka. The poor kid was shaking, still dreaming hard, so Wyatt pulled him against his chest, smoothing his hair. "Shh."

Mikka shook against him, fighting him, but Wyatt held him tighter. "It's okay, buddy. It's going to be okay."

Finally, his body began to still.

"That's right, little man. Go back to sleep. Rest. Daddy's here. And I'm not going anywhere."

13

She just needed a distraction.

Coco sat on a rough-hewn picnic table, her hands tied behind her back.

The arching hemlock and cedar trees cut off any warmth, the morning dew seeping in through the grimy Blue Ox jersey and into her bones to keep her shivering.

From the hue of the pewter gray sky, it had to be early.

Someone had to have figured out she was missing by now.

The scant wind stirred a pine fragrance into the air and blew ash from the blackened, lifeless firepit. Dead pine needles littered the spongy ground. Parked near it all sat a teardrop camping trailer.

A dirt trail led away from their camping area, and Coco eyed it, gauging the distance between her and the lunatic who was pacing near the firepit, mumbling to himself.

She hadn't gotten a good look at him last night—and thanks to whatever drug he'd given her, the memory was hazy at best. But in the meager light of dawn, he embodied the definition of crazy terrorist, at least in her mind.

Her *panicked* mind.

White. Deeply tattooed arms, gauged ears, and a deep port-wine stain up his neck. He wore a two-day grizzle, his hair almost military short, and bore the build of someone who still took the time to work out.

When he wasn't plotting evil schemes and kidnapping

women out of hospitals.

At least she was out of the grimy, soiled trunk. She'd tried not to let herself drift back to the bathroom in Russia, not to let the darkness find her pores, the nightmares find her soul.

She'd spent the past half hour fiddling with the duct tape strapping her wrists together. The fact that he hadn't bound her feet suggested that even if she did try to run, she wouldn't get far.

He turned abruptly and stalked over to her. Considered her. He had feral breath, cracked, bloodshot eyes, and fit every nightmare of kidnapper her father had seeded in her.

She drew in a breath, trying not to cower, but she'd already made up her mind.

If he tried to rape her, she'd survive. She refused to become a statistic, a random Jane Doe body found in the woods someday, half eaten by wolves, the victim of a rape-murder.

She wasn't going to abandon Mikka. Not when she was all he had.

God, please—

Except, maybe she was on her own, despite Gerri's words to her. *You are not alone. God is with you. He will rescue you.*

She wasn't going to wait around and test out that hypothesis.

And sure, her head still spun, her muscles screaming, still flush with toxins, but if she had to run all the way back to Seattle, all the way back to Mikka, well, hello, she was a survivor.

Her father had taught her that.

Her captor cursed and turned away from her, stalking over to his squatty, teardrop camouflage-painted trailer.

She took off.

Not down the trail to civilization, but toward the edge of the forest. The dark, tangled forest.

Step one—get away and hide.

She'd been perfecting that act for most of her life. Maybe she didn't know what came next.

Live?

"Hey!" Her captor must have seen her escape, and he

called her a nasty name as she hit the edge of the woods and plunged in. She pushed past foliage and jumped downed trees, her feet sinking into the spongy soil.

A branch slapped her face, and she winced as blood pooled in the corner of her mouth.

Fast. Quiet.

Desperate.

The dawn was peeling away her safety, sending shafts of pale light into the forest, thick with the loamy scent of dead red alder and quaking aspen leaves.

Behind her, she heard the heavy footfalls of her captor. Shunted, angry breaths.

The underbrush wetted her pants legs, and she ran off-balance, her head swimming.

Run. For Mikka. For Wy—

She tripped over the root of a hemlock tree. With nothing to protect her from the fall, she hit the dirt, hard. Her chin banged on a downed tree, her body bouncing off the ground, slamming back.

Her captor leaped on her, pinning her.

She screamed, writhing. "Get off me!"

He clamped a hand over her mouth, brought his close. "It don't matter if you scream. Nobody's around to hear you."

Then to prove it, he pulled his hand away.

Laughed.

It was throaty and deranged and slid like a knife under her skin. He grabbed her by the jersey and pulled her up, vising the back of her neck. "Fate's on my side."

He pushed her through the woods. "I couldn't believe it when I pulled up and there you were. Dressed in your boyfriend's jersey, like a sign."

"I don't have a boyfriend." She jerked, trying to get away from him, and he released her neck, grabbing her arm instead.

"You shouldn't lie, little girl. I know Wyatt Marshall is your boyfriend. I heard him tell his brother he wanted to marry you."

Marry?

She didn't react, but...*what?*

"I've been waiting weeks for this. It's perfect. Wyatt Marshall, the golden boy of hockey. I followed him from the hotel but I still hadn't worked out what to do when I pulled up to the entrance. And then I saw you standing there at the ATM, in his Blue Ox jersey, like some high school crush."

"It's a souvenir. I don't even know him."

He shook her then, hard, rattling her spine, and she bit back a cry. "I told you not to lie, little girl."

He pushed her out into the clearing and over to the picnic table. Shoved her down on the seat, then braced his hands either side of her shoulders on the tabletop, and leaned down.

She turned her head away, which left him free to speak into her ear.

"You might live through this, but only if you do exactly what I tell you to."

She gritted her jaw.

He stood up then. Considered her. "It's going to be okay, you know." He sat down beside her, his shoulder against hers. "We're doing this for the good of everyone. And sometimes, you have to do somethin' bad in order to do somethin' good."

She didn't want to ask, but, "What kind of bad thing?"

He said nothing for a long time, then leaned forward, pulling out his phone. He scrolled over to a picture. "This here is my brother, Graham."

Good looking man, blond hair, a tattoo up his neck that looked like flames.

"He died a couple months ago, trying to save our country."

"Was he a soldier?"

He turned off the phone. "Yeah. Marines. Got captured in Afghanistan and was written off by our military. He was sent to a camp for POWs in Chechnya that intended on turning him against the red, white, and blue. And they might have succeeded if Senator Reba Jackson hadn't shown up. She didn't know he was there, but he saw her, helping the terrorists who wanted to destroy America. And he decided right then that he wouldn't let them win."

"Who?"

He looked at her, frowning. "What, are you blind and deaf? Jackson—she's runnin' for vice president."

Something began to ping, deep inside her head, but she just couldn't wrap her brain around it quite yet. "I've been... out of the country."

He made a noise. "Then maybe you don't know the efforts to which my brother and I have gone to save this country we love."

He dragged her up, tugging her across the campsite to the trailer. When he shoved her down into the sleeping compartment in the middle, her heart turned to a rock in her throat. But he only bound her feet with the duct tape, round and round, nearly halfway up her legs.

She wasn't going anywhere, obviously.

"What efforts?" she said. "And what does Jackson have to do with your brother?"

He got up and walked around to the open hatch in the back of the trailer. "She's in league with the Russians."

Huh?

"She was visiting one of the Chechen leaders in the camp. Graham wasn't privy to the conversation, but let's just say she didn't leave with any gunfire. Wined and dined and if that doesn't tell you that she's in bed with the Russians—"

"So *wait*. Senator Jackson had dinner with a Chechen warlord and she's suddenly what, a terrorist?"

He came back to her, holding a black tactical vest made of Kevlar and cluttered with utility pouches. "No, honey. You are."

She froze.

He'd filled the utility patches with something white, and her brain connected the dots.

Explosive material. He stepped toward her and placed the vest over her shoulders.

"No, what—*no!*" She fought him, kicking, but he pushed her down and brought the vest around her, zipping her up into it.

"No, please—I have a son. He needs me."

"Shh. Listen. Like I told you, if you—and your boy-friend—cooperate, no one will get hurt." He finished zipping up the vest, then reached out and pulled her up to her feet, pulling her out of the camper. "And you're saving America, possibly the world. Don't you want to be a patriot?"

"How—how are you a *patriot* by killing people?"

"Oh, honey. I'm not going to kill people. I'm just killing *you*."

He said it with an easy smile.

She began to shake.

He put his hand on her cheek. "Calm down. Listen, this will be easy. Like I said, fate is on our side. I was trying to figure out how to get into Jackson's rally, how to make her confess the truth, and now..." He smiled, leaned down, and kissed her cheek.

She recoiled, looked away.

"Wyatt will do it for me."

"Wyatt isn't going to do anything—"

"Really?" He stepped away from her, pulled out his cell phone, and turned it back on. "I think he is. See, if I tried to get into the rally, even if they didn't have me on some watch list, there's no way I could get to the mic. But your superstar boyfriend will have no problem getting the world to listen to him, will he?"

He stepped back and held up his phone. "Your job is to convince him to listen to you. Smile for the camera."

He snapped a picture of her standing there. "Let's get a short video, just for fun."

"No, I won't—"

"Nothing to say? Really? Because if this doesn't work, then well, yes, it will end poorly. And I'll have to start all over again, and frankly, I'm running out of time. The election is in two short months."

A tear edged off her chin. "What—I don't know what to say."

"Oh, just speak from your heart. In three, two, one—" He

pointed at her, and the green light on the phone lit up.

And then, oh…

This was not how it was supposed to end between them. Wyatt was supposed to come back to her. Tell her he loved her. Protect her.

They were supposed to have a happy ending.

But maybe life didn't work that way, not for her. Maybe she'd been right all along—happily ever afters didn't exist.

If she hadn't lied, hadn't run away, hadn't let her hurt hide the truth from Wyatt…

So, she looked into the camera and said the words she should have said five years ago.

"I love you, Wyatt Marshall. I always have. And I always will. I am sorry I ran away from you. I was scared. Afraid that if I gave you my heart, you wouldn't love me back. But…" Her tears ran hot down her cheeks. "But you do love me, and I know that, even if it was your turn to run."

She cleared her voice and found a smile. "You're my hero. I trust you, Wyatt. And…I don't know what this man wants you to do, but whatever happens…thank you for coming to Russia. Thank you for our beautiful son. I know you'll take care of him."

Her captor lowered the phone. "Aw, that's sweet."

Then he shoved her back into the camper. "I hope he's the hero you believe him to be."

He closed the door.

"Please—don't do this!"

The trailer jerked as he secured the back hatch.

"This isn't the way! Listen, I'm a hacker—I can get your message out!"

The door opened and he stood in the dimness, as if considering her words.

"I could send a viral message into Twitter and get it—"

"Jackson has cronies in every part of the government. Her own rogue faction. They'd shut it down in a heartbeat. No, the only way this gets out is live." Then he picked up the duct tape and pulled out a long swath.

"No, please—" She struggled, shaking her head until he pushed her onto the mattress, kneeled on either side of her, and pasted the tape over her mouth.

"Can't let you get people upset."

Then he climbed off her and closed the door.

In a few moments, they were backing out, the tires crunching over the pine needles, crushing them into submission.

———◆———

Wyatt had slept like the dead, his entire body collapsing in a protective position around Mikka. It wasn't until he felt little fingers playing with his beard that he opened his eyes.

Brown eyes looked up at him, and the kid grinned. *"Dobra Ootra."*

He repeated it back.

Mikka giggled, and Wyatt tickled him even as he realized he'd fallen asleep in Mikka's tiny hospital bed.

The morning light filtered into the room behind a pulled curtain—probably his mother's doing. She slept in the lounger, looking a little older than he liked.

But now she was a grandma. She was allowed to look older.

He leaned up, expecting to see Coco in the other lounger, but it was empty.

For a long second, he just stared at it, frowning.

The door opened and he looked up, expecting—

No. Just Sarai, who came in wearing a pair of dress pants and an oxford shirt, a stethoscope around her neck. She gave him a smile, something forgiving in it.

Oh yeah, she'd seen his great escape.

"We could find you another lounger, Wyatt."

"Thanks. I'm good." He disentangled himself from the bed, his muscles screaming, and he must have made a face because Sarai came over to him.

"You okay?"

"Stiff. Hard practice yesterday."

"So, I suppose Coco filled you in on the diagnosis?" She came over to Mikka and said something to him in Russian, tousling his hair.

"Sorta. I…so, what are we going to do?"

Sarai reached for the blood pressure cuff on the wall. "Are you willing to get tested to see if your blood is a match for a stem cell transplant?"

He had gotten up and was stretching. "Of course I am."

She took Mikka's blood pressure, then let the air out and reattached the cuff to the wall. "I'll have the nurse send in the kit."

She said something to Mikka, who nodded his head, then turned back to Wyatt. "I'll order Mikka's breakfast. Then as soon as Coco gets back, Dr. Lee and I'd like to meet with both of you to go over treatment."

His mother had woken and was now untangling herself from a blanket. Sarai glanced at her. "Why don't you two get some breakfast in the cafeteria?"

"I could use some coffee," his mother said. She had taken her scarf from her head and now fluffed her hair with her fingers, a brown cloud around her head. She looked at Wyatt. "Where's Coco?"

"I don't know. Maybe she went down for coffee."

"Oh, she does love her coffee."

Gerri went over to stand in front of the window. The sun was sliding over the outline of Mt. Rainier to the south, the sky a mottled orange and lemon. The buildings rose, a blue silver, some of the windows glinting orange. He came to stand beside her.

His phone buzzed in his pocket, and he pulled it out. A text, from a number he didn't recognize. He opened it.

What—? A chill flushed through him, and he must have made a sound, something like taking a punch because his mother turned to him. "What is it?"

Coco. Beat up, blood on her chin, her hair disheveled, wearing his Blue Ox jersey and…

He turned away from his mother, widening the picture,

and nearly lost his breath. A vest, with what looked like explosives.

"Wyatt?"

"I...I gotta go...um..." He looked at her, and the concern on her face stripped him. But what could he say? "I'm going to go look for Coco. Get myself a cup of coffee. What do you want?"

"Just something black, heavy on the caffeine."

"Yeah." He picked up his jacket, glanced at Mikka. The little boy was sitting on his bed, his knees drawn up, staring out the window. The sun had gilded his face, picking up the tiniest flecks of red in his hair, and wouldn't you know it, in this light, with this profile, he looked just like Coco.

Strong, stubborn Coco.

He walked over and kissed the top of his son's head. Turned back to his mom. "Hey. I'm going to call Tate and see if he can...well, he might be sending someone over here to sit with you."

She frowned. "Wyatt—"

"I gotta go, Ma."

Then he left, striding down the hallway, his phone to his ear.

Tate picked up on the second ring. "What?"

Wyatt hit the stairwell, started down it, working out the kinks in his bones. "Coco is in trouble. I just got a text and..."

He had to stop on the landing, brace his hand on the railing. "I think Gustov has her. I got a picture of her wearing a suicide vest."

Silence on the other end.

"Tate!"

"What? I'm trying to process. Coco's not at the hospital with you?"

"No—I told you." He blew out a breath and continued down the stairs. "When I got here last night, she wasn't here. And I assumed she was down at the internet café. And then I fell asleep—jet lag and practice—and I woke up this morning and she wasn't here. And now, I got this text and there's a picture. Of her. And she's...she's hurt and—"

He hit the door and found himself outside.

The fresh air swept into him, filled with pine and the scent of the city and even a hint of the bakery down the street. He stopped, looking around, as if he might see her. "She has a bomb vest on."

"Send me the picture," Tate said.

"I need you here, now!" Wyatt stalked down the sidewalk into the parking lot.

"I can't. The senator has her rally this morning. We're on our way to the pier right now."

"I need you here! With Mikka!"

"Calm down, bro. Listen, I'll send York and RJ, okay?"

York. Yeah, he could use a guy with York's skills. "Good."

His phone vibrated. Another text had come in. A video. "I'll call you back." He hung up, and his hand shook as he opened the video.

Right there in the middle of the sidewalk, his world shattered.

Coco stood in front of some trailer, crying, her voice shaking, telling him...*she loved him?*

I don't know what this man wants you to do, but whatever happens...thank you for coming to Russia.

He gripped the phone with so much force it dug into the palm of his hand. "Coco!"

What man?

He looked up and no one was watching. He listened again, and a fist grabbed his throat.

With a shaking hand he forwarded both the picture and the video to Tate.

Then the third text came in.

Meet me on the hospital playground if you want her to live.

He ran.

Wyatt found a man staring at the giraffe sculptures, his back to Wyatt.

Wyatt fought the terrible urge to simply grab him, to tear him apart where he stood.

"No one has to get hurt here, Marshall," the man said as Wyatt got closer.

Then the man turned.

He wore gauged ears, a simple black plug in each of them, his dark hair cut short, and the hint of whiskers. And, oddly, a suit coat, jeans, and a clean blue shirt.

"My name is Alan Kobie, and if you want to see your girlfriend again, you'll do what I ask."

Wyatt gave him a once-over. About six feet tall, the man looked fit, but Wyatt could take him apart in seconds.

Maybe Kobie figured it out because he held up his cell phone. "Don't do anything stupid, Marshall. And here's why."

As Wyatt watched, the man dialed the phone.

Wyatt didn't know what he expected, but not a connection, then a countdown timer to appear. Kobie held it up. 4:59...4:58...4:57...

"What is that?"

"The timer on the vest. Every time I call, it starts the time. When I hang up, it resets."

He hung up.

Looked at Wyatt. Smiled.

Redialed.

The timer started over.

"What is this game?"

"Not a game. I'm saving our country from a terrorist."

"You look like the terrorist." He wanted to take a swipe for the phone. "Hang up."

"No problem." Kobie held up the phone and pressed End. "So here's what's going to happen, Champ. You're going to a political rally."

Wyatt stared at him. "What?"

"Reba Jackson. VP candidate. She's having a rally on Piers 62 and 63 today, in about..." He checked his watch. "Forty-five minutes. And you're going to get onstage and set the world free."

"I can't—"

"Yes, you can. I saw you talking to your brother Tate,

who I know is working for the senator these days. I've been following them for weeks, waiting for this moment. And I know you went up to talk to her."

He'd seen Wyatt yesterday in the lobby of the Fairmont?

"And I know she likes the Minnesota Blue Ox."

Wyatt's mouth tightened.

"I'll bet she found out you and your team were in town for this exhibition and decided to have a little meet and greet, huh?"

The wind stirred the cedar and spruce that surrounded the hospital, lifting the collar of his jacket.

"Did she even invite you to the rally?"

Wyatt said nothing, his mouth a tight line.

"Well, no matter. You attract a crowd wherever you go. I'm sure you can get a moment onstage. And that's all I need. A moment. For you to read this."

He handed Wyatt an index card.

Wyatt read the first line. "I'm not going to tell the world that Senator Jackson is a terrorist!"

"Yes you are. Because she is and the world needs to hear it. But they're not going to listen to me, are they? Never mind that I served my country. Never mind that my brother was killed trying to defend it. I'm not trying to hurt anyone. We never were. We just wanted people to pay attention. And they'll listen to you, hotshot."

"I don't understand."

"You don't have to understand. You just have to say yes."

Wyatt would be the accomplice of a domestic terrorist. Not to mention, if there was a rogue faction in the government, he might be next on their hit list.

"If I do this, my career could be over." PR suicide, really. His gaze scanned over the content of the card, reading too fast to understand it, really.

What he did understand was Coco's words. *Thank you for our beautiful son. I know you'll take care of him.*

She was saying goodbye. Because she thought he wouldn't do it.

"It's your choice, Marsh—"

"I'll do it." He looked up at him. Drew in a breath. "Of course, I'll do it."

"Good. Let's get you cleaned up. You have an audience to meet."

Wyatt's phone buzzed in his hand. Tate was on the line.

"I have to take this—"

"Be wise," Kobie said and held up his phone.

"What?" he said to Tate.

"Sheesh," Tate said. "Is this for real?"

"I...maybe. I don't know." He was walking with Kobie back to the hospital. But there was no way he was letting the guy near his kid.

"Listen, you're right, we need people at the hospital with Ma and Mikka. But both RJ and York have seen this guy, can identify him, so they're coming with me. But York is sending a cop he knows—"

"No!" Oh, he didn't mean for that to emerge, but the last thing he wanted was RJ at the rally, more of his family around this guy.

Kobie looked at him. Wyatt schooled his voice. "Don't bring RJ to the rally. Send her to the hospital. With Ma."

A pause. "You okay, Wy?"

"Yeah. I'll...I'll meet you at the rally."

Another pause. "Are you sure?"

He hung up. Turned to Kobie. "Listen, I don't need to clean up. Let's go."

Kobie smiled. "You're going to be perfect."

Wyatt pulled up his Uber app and ordered a ride.

Thirty minutes later, they'd navigated through traffic and past the Pike Place garage. "Let us off here," Wyatt said and they got out across the street, taking the under highway pass to the Elliot Bay Trail.

The pier had been sectioned off for the event, a great battleship in the background, a trailing line of flags from bow to captain's roost, back to stern. A grand picture of Isaac White and Reba Jackson hung on the side of the battleship, the slogan *For a Safe Tomorrow* in white letters against a red background.

Security lined the fencing that cordoned off the entrance, police and hired security checking the bags of the long line of people filtering into the event.

Already, the place was full, giant speakers pumping out country music. Flanking a platform at the back of the pier, in front of the battleship, were two sets of bleachers filling up with spectators and beside them, closer to the stage, risers for photographers.

Signs and banners waved in the wind off the Sound, the smell of the sea rife with brine and diesel fuel.

The perfect place to meet the everyday man and woman.

Signs dotted the growing crowd—*White for President. Jackson for VP.* More with slogans for peace, power, and prosperity.

"People have lost their minds," Kobie said as they approached the gate.

Wyatt went right up to one of the security guards and pulled out his wallet, flashing his identification. "My brother Tate is head of security. He said—"

He got the go-ahead.

"This is my teammate," he said of Kobie, pretty sure the security guard could see right through him.

But they passed, and Kobie looked over at him and grinned.

He wanted to throw the guy into the Sound. But if he did, the phone would go with him, and—

"By the way, once I make the call, if it's not manually turned off, then…" Kobie leaned over to Wyatt as they passed a group of women holding signs. "Boom."

"Shut it," Wyatt said. He stuck his hands in his jacket pockets, trying not to let Coco's voice trickle into his brain.

"How did you find her?" he said, his voice low.

"Followed you from the hotel to the hospital. She was very cute in her Blue Ox jersey."

Wyatt could be ill right here on the pavement.

They reached the front of the staging area, where a giant

platform stretched across the back. A three-tiered platform of risers was already filled with supporters holding signs and cheering. A couple of them spotted Wyatt and shouted.

They reached the front of the crowd, met another security agent, and Wyatt flashed his credentials again.

"They're behind the pipe and drape," said the officer and pointed to a section of the stage hidden by a red drape.

"I'm staying here," said Kobie, but lifted his phone. "Right in the front. Don't think about squirreling out because the timer starts now."

He dialed.

"Wait—no!"

Kobie moved away, holding the phone high.

Wyatt turned and headed back to the draped area.

It was like entering a portal, the calm before the storm. The pipe and drape partitioned off the staging area at the end of the pier. Waves slapped against the great battleship, and Wyatt couldn't help but notice the two-story drop-off from the end into the murky, cold waters of the Sound.

The backstage was quiet, aides moving around, security agents posted on watch, and in the middle of the quiet cluster, Reba Jackson was reading her phone. She wore a red jacket, a white shirt, and a pair of black pants, her amber red hair pulled back in a loose bun.

She was a very attractive, powerful woman. The kind of woman who could command troops and make policy.

A very capable VP. And potentially, president.

Wyatt didn't know what to think about Kobie's statement.

Tate spotted him and came toward him. "What's going on?"

Wyatt pulled out the card. "I have to...I have to talk to the crowd."

"What—?" Tate grabbed the card. Read it. "This is crazy."

"He's got Coco, and he's got a timer on his phone that if he doesn't hang up in five minutes, she dies. I have to tell this audience that Senator Jackson is in collusion with the Russians, right now."

"It doesn't help that you were just in Russia," Tate said. "As if gathering information on her."

Wyatt hadn't thought about that part. "Sorry."

"Jackson thinks you're going to endorse her, so…she's not going to stop you from taking the stage." Tate looked at him. "I might have to."

He was Benedict Arnold. "Bro—"

"I know. I get it. But this could also be a political nightmare for our ticket." Tate blew out a breath. "Which one is he?" Tate stepped up to the edge of the barrier and moved the cloth.

"The guy with the—"

"Gauged ears. You're kidding me." Tate dropped the cloth. "That's the guy from the San Antonio bombing."

Wyatt nodded. "And apparently, he has a beef to pick with Jackson."

RJ came up, wearing a pair of jeans, boots, a T-shirt, and a jean jacket. "What's going on?"

Wyatt looked at Tate. "I thought she was going to the hospital."

Tate gave the tiniest shake of his head. "She won't leave York."

He turned to her. "Where is York?"

"He's in the crowd," RJ said. "Tate sent him out there to look for Damien Gustov. And I'm looking for him from here."

He wanted to scream. Instead, "I need to go onstage right now, Tate."

"Yeah. I agree. You go onstage. Distract him. I'll get Kobie."

"Alan Kobie? The bomber from San Antonio you had me check into?" RJ looked past Tate to the crowd. "He's *here*?"

Wyatt sent Tate a look, but he didn't have time. "Hurry up."

"What is going on?" RJ said, but Tate turned and headed down to the end, slipping into the crowd.

Wyatt looked at the card. Drew in a breath.

No, his worlds weren't mutually exclusive. Clearly they were connected, one feeding the other, making him whole. But the only one that really mattered was the one with Coco.

Then he took the stage.

He'd been in press conferences all over the world, spoken in live interviews on ESPN, had given hundreds of interviews, but suddenly his hands slicked and his stomach hollowed as the crowd roared.

He heard his name shouted and smiled, waved. He couldn't help but glance down at Kobie.

The man held the phone up.

He couldn't make it out, but he'd already ticked off two minutes in his brain.

"Thank you for being here," he said into the mic.

Just read the card. Kobie was mouthing the words.

"I need to say something about Senator Jackson." He pulled the card out from his pants pocket. Took a breath. *You're my hero. I trust you.*

"I was given this information just recently, just…a few minutes ago, actually, but it's important that I read—"

A shot pinged off the podium. Wyatt ducked.

Screams.

"Shooter!" The shout rose from somewhere in the crowd.

Another shot. The security agent behind him went down.

Chaos erupted, people screaming, running for the exits.

Wyatt spotted Kobie in the crowd, his eyes wide.

Kobie took off running.

Oh, no—*no*—

Wyatt leaped from the stage.

Two minutes.

14

Two minutes to the rest of his life.

Their story was *not* going to end up with Coco in a fire bomb.

They were going to cure Mikka, get married, and live happily ever after.

"Stop him!" Wyatt knew his shouts died in the cacophony of screams, but it didn't keep him from shouting as he raced after Kobie.

The terrorist had headed for the outskirts of the assembly area, behind the bleachers, along the pier's edge.

Wyatt felt like he was bodychecking his way through the line of the Boston Bruins, trying and failing to bodily move people. But he was running out of time. He'd apologize later to the woman he'd sent flying into the press risers.

Kobie disappeared behind the crowd.

Wyatt kicked up his speed. "Make a hole!"

The shooting had stopped, but the screaming hadn't, people running over each other, some hiding under the tiered risers, more simply lying on the pavement, their hands over their heads. Sirens screamed in the distance.

Wyatt spotted Tate in front of him, emerging from the press area. "Get the phone!"

Kobie was fast. He ran down the side of the pier, pushing away obstructions, looking back over his shoulder.

One minute. The clock ticked in Wyatt's head and he

caught up to Tate. Passed him. Kobie was ten feet away.

"Stop! Kobie—*stop*!"

Kobie slammed into a man with a camera, sent him sprawling, but it slowed him down enough for Wyatt to close the distance. Five feet, nearly a hand-reach away—

Another gunshot.

Before Wyatt's eyes, Kobie jerked, tripped.

Fell.

The phone careened out of his hand.

Wyatt had spent years honing his reflexes, his ability to follow a small black object, to nab it out of the air.

He became a goal tender and launched himself toward the phone as it flew across the pier toward the water.

He didn't have his padding, but he cared nothing for his landing as his hand wrapped around the device.

Gotcha.

His body slammed onto the metal lip that lined the pier's edge, the spiny blade ripping through his body. He bit back a noise, the pain exploding through him.

He might have shattered something.

Then he was falling, his body's momentum peeling him over the side of the pier.

No!

He acted on reflex again, the same kind that slapped shots out of the goal to his defensemen. "Tate! Hang up!"

He tossed the phone onto the pier, toward his brother.

The water engulfed him, took him under, the cold like knives to his skin. The suddenness of it stole his breath and he couldn't move, sinking into the briny sea.

The current slammed him against a piling. Jolted him.

He gasped.

Pulled in a lungful of water.

His head spun, but he kicked, swimming for the surface, fighting the urge to cough out the water.

He surfaced, but his body convulsed. His lungs refused air. He vomited in the water, then tried for another breath.

Hang up!

He looked up, coughing hard. "Hang—" More spasms took him.

On the pier, Tate held the phone, nodding at him. "It's done!"

Wyatt struggled to keep his head above water as he vomited again.

A life ring hit the water. He reached for it, shivering, still coughing.

Overhead, a helicopter turned the water to chop, probably a news source capturing the confusion on the pier. He fought the waves, trying to kick over to a ladder that led up to the pier.

He hooked his arm around a rung and emptied his lungs again.

Then he turned to the ladder and fought his way up.

Someone grabbed his jacket, and he looked up to see Tate and York hauling him up.

They dropped him onto the deck.

He hit his hands and knees, still coughing.

"Sheesh, bro." Tate knelt next to him. "You gonna live?"

He nodded. "Coco—"

"I got the countdown stopped. But…"

But?

He rolled over, sitting, still clearing his throat. "Please—"

"Kobie's dead. Head shot. We're not sure who took him out." Tate looked up then, and Wyatt followed his gaze to York. "York took a shot, but we're not sure it was him."

"What?"

York was staring at Kobie's body, some twenty feet away, crumpled and bloody. "I didn't have the angle. Unless there was a ricochet, but my guess is that it was the sniper."

York looked at the buildings across the street, as if assessing a sniper's location from one of the five-story apartment buildings.

"The one that nearly killed me." Wyatt took Tate's outstretched hand, then looked at York. "Gustov?"

"I don't know. Maybe. Sure looked like his handiwork at

the hotel."

"Why would Gustov want me dead? Or better, Kobie?"

"Maybe he doesn't want the information you were about to announce to come out," Tate said.

Wyatt looked at him, frowning. "You don't think it's true, about the Russians…"

"Of course not," Tate said. But he offered nothing more.

"We need to find Coco. Right now." Wyatt walked over to Kobie's body. Already police had established a perimeter around it.

He bent and began to riffle through Kobie's pockets.

"Hey!" shouted one of the nearby officers, but he ignored him.

Tate held up his hand to the officers, walked over and crouched next to Wyatt.

Wyatt emerged with a crumpled receipt and a pair of keys. He unfolded the paper. "It's for a campground. An overnight camping permit."

He examined the keys. "A Subaru car key. And this bunch looks like the kind of keys to a master lock, a padlock type."

"A camper key?" Tate said.

York had followed them and now stood, scanning the cityscape.

"We need a computer hacker," Tate said. "Someone who could trace that phone signal."

"Our hacker might be locked in a car." York's jaw tightened.

"And we'd have to make the call to follow the signal," Wyatt said. "So that's a no."

Please, God. Help me find her.

Wyatt was shaking now, the cold finding his bones. From the pain radiating through him, he'd seriously injured his hip. He was still coughing, too, his lungs probably swimming with diesel fuel.

Oh, why had he left her in the first place? If he hadn't been such a coward—

You're pretty hard on yourself, Guns. But the more you focus on your failures, the more cluttered your brain will be.

He took a breath, trying to think. So maybe he didn't have to have all the answers. And maybe he *was* focused too much on his failures. Sort of went with the job, really.

But maybe he needed to start looking at his blessings.

Like Mikka, back at the hospital, waiting for his daddy to bring his mommy home.

Back at the hospital.

"She's at the hospital." Wyatt grabbed Tate's arm. "He met me at the hospital, and we took an Uber here. He had to have…well, what if he parked at the hospital?"

"He could have parked anywhere and taken a cab to the hospital."

"He said he wasn't a terrorist. He wasn't trying to get people killed."

"Except Kat," York growled.

Tate was nodding. "Let's go."

Wyatt bit back the grinding in his hips as he followed Tate and York through the crowd, toward the exit.

Tate led them over to a black SUV, talked to the agent standing near the driver's door, and by the time Wyatt caught up, Tate had slid in behind the wheel.

York jumped in the front beside him. Of course.

Wyatt slipped into the back seat, stifling a groan. "Go!"

He leaned up, backseat driving as they cut through the city. "C'mon, Tate."

"Sit back! We'll get there."

"Take a right!"

"I can see the GPS—"

York rounded on him. "We'll find her, Wyatt." Something resolute, even lethal in his tone.

Wyatt leaned back. Looked out the window. *Please, God, let her be okay.* His eyes burned, along with his throat and…

Whoever finds their life will lose it, and whoever loses their life for my sake will find it.

The voice was low, solid, and so familiar it felt like his father had sat down beside him. But suddenly, he heard him.

Change your name or change your ways.

His name wasn't Marshall. Or even the Hottie of Hockey. It was *beloved son.*

He'd spent his entire life trying to be someone who mattered. And it had cost him everything. *You're enough, and you're loved because God says so. Nothing else.*

And Wyatt didn't care what anyone thought of him. Let his brothers be the heroes, let his career go up in flames. He put his hand over his mouth, his eyes blurring.

I believe you, God. I give you my fame, my future, and my life. I give it all to You. Whatever happens, please, save Coco. Please, just save Coco.

They pulled into the circle drive near the main entrance. A tiered outside parking lot flanked the east side of the building.

"I don't see a camper," York said.

"There's another lot," Wyatt said. "On the west side."

Tate gunned it around the circle and back out to Penny Drive.

Wyatt looked up but hadn't a clue what window might be Mikka's as they passed the sprawling buildings.

Tate turned into the west lot. More tiered parking, landscaped with spruce trees, flowers, and fully populated near the entrance.

"There!" York said, pointing.

On the third tier, near the back of the lot—an orange Subaru wagon took up three spaces, a tiny trailer hooked onto the hitch and parked horizontally under the shade of a cedar tree.

Tate rounded the top tier and gunned it, coming around the back side.

Yes. Wyatt leaned up, letting out his breath. *Yes—*

The trailer exploded with such force it shook the SUV. Pellets of stone, rock, and debris bulleted the front windshield.

Tate slammed on his brakes.

Tate ducked his head, York doing the same.

Wyatt just stared at the fire, now engulfing not only the trailer, but the Subaru.

What—?

No—*Please*—

He was out of the car, running, hobbling toward the fire. "Coco!"

The heat burned his face and coughed out black into the sky as it consumed rubber and foam and…

"Wyatt—stay back!" Tate grabbed him around the waist, pulled him back.

"No!" He fought him, but York grabbed his arm. "Let me go!"

"She's gone, man!" York said.

No!

His legs gave out and he collapsed onto the pavement.

I trust you, Wyatt.

He covered his head with his arms, shaking.

"Wyatt—"

"Leave me. Just *leave me.*"

Tate stepped back.

And then Wyatt shattered.

She always knew it would end like this. Coco didn't know why she'd expected anything different, really.

She'd been running her entire life, after all, from people who wanted to kidnap her or kill her, use her to hurt the people she loved.

Wyatt would never forgive himself if she died. If this suicide vest went off.

And it *was* going to go off. Because twice it had been turned on, the countdown beeping. The third time it turned off so close to the zeroes, she'd been weeping.

Then abruptly, it had stopped.

She didn't know what game her captor was playing, but she couldn't wait around for another time.

She couldn't leave Mikka motherless.

She knew exactly how that felt. She'd been bereft as she'd stood at the graveside, a sunny day that only burned her neck.

Come home with us.

Not Gerri's voice but Orrin's in her memory. He'd walked back after everyone else had left her alone, and stood like a tree beside her.

She liked Orrin Marshall. Dark hair, a cowboy mustache, he was quiet, commanding, and something about him felt safe. He wore a leather jacket and a pair of dress pants and boots. When she'd looked over at him, he gave her a tight-lipped smile.

"Your mother and my wife were best friends. You have a home with us, Coco, if you want it."

She'd been trying not to cry, her eyes cracked and dry as she stared back at the casket, the fresh earth piled up under a blanket.

"The Triple M is a good place to catch your breath. To heal. To find yourself. And, you're family now, honey."

He'd put his arm around her then, something quick, but substantial enough to seep warmth into her aching bones.

Then he'd turned her, and she'd seen them standing at the edge of the dirt drive into the cemetery. Knox, his hands in the pockets of his suit pants, and Tate, in his Army uniform, freshly out of bootcamp. Ford, also dressed in a suit, looking young and fierce, just sprouting whiskers. And RJ, her friend's face reddened also wearing black.

And Wyatt, looking up at her through his long hair.

They all had waited for her, just on the edge of the property.

You're family now.

The problem wasn't that she hadn't been a Marshall but that she'd never seen herself as one of them. Hadn't walked into the embrace and protection and identity as a Marshall.

She always considered herself a refugee, looking in, not belonging.

Not embracing the inheritance of the family who wanted to adopt her.

You still have that home, honey.

Tears ran into her ears as she lay in the heat of the camper, staring up at the window cut into the ceiling. Trees swayed in the breeze.

What if she stopped holding back, afraid of being abandoned and…gave over her heart? Not just to Wyatt, but the family who wanted her.

The God who wanted her.

Commit yourself to the Lord. Let Him deliver you. Let Him rescue you, because He delights in you.

The tape muted her words, but she heard them in her head. *"Please, God. Forgive me for being afraid. Forgive me for always taking my life into my own hands. I need You to rescue me. Please—rescue me!"*

You don't have to fix this, Coco. When you are weak, He is strong. Because to Him, you belong.

Belong. Her own words rang back to her. *I wanted to be a Marshall with everything inside me.*

Yeah, well, what would a Marshall do if they were tied up with a bomb strapped to their body?

Knox would think his way out maybe, and Tate would have never gotten here in the first place. Ford would use what he had, and RJ would file back through her research to figure out some hidden answer. Wyatt…

Wyatt wouldn't give up. Wyatt *never* gave up.

If she could just stay alive, he would find her, she knew it in her bones.

Think. The duct tape had half-ripped off her mouth, but she couldn't just lay here and scream. Still she worked off the tape with her tongue, enough to breathe.

"Help! Help!" But her voice was muffled inside the trailer.

Besides, who knew where she was?

Think!

Her captor had zipped up the bomb over her body, and it didn't have a dead man's switch, so probably she could take it off without it exploding.

If she could take it off, she could simply run, leave it here to explode.

She was still taped up, sure, but she could reach the window, kick it out. Squeeze through.

And…the man had said that he didn't want her noises to upset anyone—so there'd be people around where he left her.

Hopefully people who could call the police.

You're so small. I was always worried I'd crush you.

She *was* small. And this vest was big. And he had made the mistake of wrapping it around her body like a burrito.

Or a hotdog bun.

She leaned up, and with her mouth grabbed the zipper of the vest, and slowly, her neck aching, managed to move it down an inch, maybe two.

Enough to get her head through the opening.

Then she pushed herself up on the bed to give herself room, bore down, and began to wiggle.

Her body moved inside the vest. She drew in a breath, brought her shoulder blades in and moved her hips.

The vest stayed, her body moved.

Her chin disappeared beneath the collar of the neck.

Yes!

She wiggled harder—

Something snapped. She didn't know what she'd done, but she'd seen movies and knew that probably the vest wasn't made for tampering with.

The beeping started again.

No—!

She pulled her feet along the bed, her hands now clearing the outside of the vest. Gripping the lower edge of the vest, she fought to push it over her head. The vest fully engulfed her head now, but a couple more pushes and she slid free.

She scrambled onto her knees.

Yes, the timer was counting down, two minutes from detonation.

She moved the vest aside, rolled to her back, brought up her legs, and kicked the skylight hard. It cracked, but didn't shatter.

Covering her face, she kicked it again, and the glass broke, sheeting down on top of her, the glass littering the bed around her.

Birds chirruped, as if cheering her on.

She eased her head through the opening, aware of the jagged glass around the edges, but what choice did she have? She wiggled one shoulder through without cutting herself, but the next grazed a crease down her arm.

She could call for help, but the parking lot was empty. Her captor had set her in the corner of the parking lot of —oh, *no.*

She was back at the Children's Hospital.

Coco dragged herself up and stood on the bed, stuck at waist height, her legs still bound.

One minute. She had to get out.

You are strong, maya lapichka. You will survive this.

Yes, she would.

She jumped off the bed, lunging out of the window toward the curved back of the camper. The glass bit into her body, and she cried out as it tore into her, but she fell off the back side of the camper.

Rolled.

She hit the sidewalk, the pathway that circled the hospital, and for a second lay there, the wound in her gut threatening to curl her into herself.

Not yet.

Run!

She rolled over to her knees and tried to hop and scrabble toward the forest.

The explosion blew her forward, propelling her into the woods and shrubbery.

She slammed against a massive cedar tree. It shucked out her breath, and she dropped hard, the world spinning.

The fire turned to an inferno ten feet away, spitting off debris, embers, and black smoke, the heat blistering her skin.

Coco let out a scream as she lay like a worm, unable to move under the lethal haze of black smoke.

Sparks fell to the earth, lighting puddles of fire around her.

Closing in.

15

et up.

"C'mon, Wyatt, there's nothing you can do."

Sirens sounded in the distance, probably someone having alerted the police to the inferno in the Children's Hospital parking lot.

But he heard the siren in his brain, resounding over and over.

Get up.

Get back in the game!

One more failure, taking him down. Only this one he wouldn't come back from—

A scream.

It lifted from beyond the inferno, maybe. Or perhaps just his own imagination, mingling with the siren.

Still, it jerked him to his feet.

York was staring at the fire, his gaze almost fierce, his jaw tight.

Tate, however, was watching Wyatt as if afraid for him.

"Did you hear that?"

Tate met his eyes. His brother always wore an edge in his expression, but maybe loving Glo had filed it away because he looked at him with compassion. "No, bro, I didn't."

"She's alive—"

Tate put his hand on his shoulder. "Stop. No, you're just going to get yourself killed."

Wyatt pushed him away, throwing up an arm to protect himself from the blaze. Black smoke spiraled out from the edges of the car, the camper, the roar almost deafening. "I am not leaving without her!"

"Wyatt!"

Red-hot embers sprayed into the nearby woodland at the edge of the parking lot, lighting it aflame.

"This is a job for the fire department."

Another scream. This one high and piercing, and he looked at Tate. "Did you hear *that*?"

Tate cocked his head.

Oh please, let her not be inside the camper burning to death!

He ran over to the camper. It was engulfed, glass breaking, more sparks spitting free. Maybe he could get inside from the back—

Blood.

He spotted a puddle of red turning to black on the sidewalk under the heat of the fire.

"Coco!"

He skirted the fire already burning into the woods.

And spotted her.

She lay curled against a tree, her knees drawn up, bleeding from her head, her arm, a terrible pool of blood on her shirt.

She'd turned her face away from the flames, her jaw gritted against the heat.

"Coco!"

His voice jerked her, but he wasn't waiting.

A bush lit next to her, spot fires roaring between them, but Wyatt didn't care.

"Wyatt!"

He wasn't sure whose voice lifted behind him as he sprinted toward her.

He took a breath and dove into the furnace.

His still-wet clothes steamed as he knelt in front of her and scooped her up.

"Hang on, Cookie." Then he sprinted back out through

the flames. Fire licked his legs but couldn't latch onto the wet material. He carried her beyond the fire, into the parking lot, to where York met them.

York had shucked his coat, wrapping it around her as Wyatt set her down.

Tate had gone to the SUV.

Wyatt knelt over her, not sure where to start.

She'd cut her head, but that seemed more like a pressure gash.

York took out a knife and rolled her over, tearing her arms free. She gasped, moaning as he moved her arm around. "She's got a pretty bad gash—"

"My stomach—" She moved her hands over her body, and Wyatt caught them in one hand and moved them away as York lifted her shirt.

Blood ran from a deep, jagged wound just below her ribs, as if she'd been stabbed.

"Did he do this?"

She leaned her head back, gasping, and Wyatt cradled her against him.

"No—I broke the window—" She was breathing hard, clearly in pain. But she looked up, found his eyes. "You came for me."

He stared at her. "Of course I did."

Then, suddenly, she began to weep, her body shaking. "You came after me."

Oh, Coco. "I should have come for you years ago." He pressed his lips to her forehead, perilously close to weeping himself.

Tate landed on his knees next to them, zipping open a medical kit and pulling out a cloth. He pressed it over her wound. "Hang in there, Coco. Help is on its way."

The sirens screamed closer, and in a moment, a firetruck peeled into the lot, followed by two more.

"Did you get him?"

"Yeah. He's dead. Shot."

She pressed her hand against his shirt. "You're wet."

"Long story. I'm okay." He folded his hand over hers. "And you're going to be okay too." He followed his words by glancing at Tate.

His brother met his eyes but had nothing for him.

An EMT ran over and knelt next to Tate.

"She has a penetrating gut wound," Tate said.

The man unzipped his bag. "Keep pressure on it." He pulled out a stethoscope and pressed it to her chest.

Coco kept her gaze on Wyatt. "Is Mikka—"

"He's with my mom."

She nodded and folded her fingers between his. "He has leukemia."

"I know, baby. We'll get through this, I promise. I'm so sorry I ran away—I was just—"

"Freaking out. I get it. I've done that a few times myself."

He was crying now, and he leaned down and pressed his lips against hers. "No more running, for either of us."

She touched his face. "I'm ready to go home, Wyatt."

"Her blood pressure is dropping," the EMT said, ripping off the cuff. "We need to get her into the ER."

Wyatt made to pick her up, but another EMT had arrived with a board. He helped move her onto it, strapping her in.

Then Wyatt took one corner as they ran with her to the ambulance.

"Wyatt?"

"I'm here, baby."

He climbed into the back, glaring at the EMT, just in case he thought he might stop him. Not a chance. Wyatt took her hand. "I'm right here. And I'm not leaving. I promise."

Because, hello, he'd gone to *Russia* to find the woman he loved.

And he wasn't going to let her out of his sight.

Ever again.

Because he was a Marshall.

And Marshalls kept their promises.

She was back on the ranch. Coco knew it without even opening her eyes, hearing Knox's deep laughter filter up the stairs from the great room. And Tate's voice, too, as he was probably throwing something at him from across the room.

She sank into the smells of the ranch, cotton sheets and the deep scent of worked leather, the tangy oil from the timber beams.

Safe.

"Boys, don't be so loud, you'll wake her." Could be Gerri, probably with her apron on, making breakfast.

"She's slept too long anyway." RJ, her voice soft, almost anxious.

Sunlight bathed her eyes. She'd overslept, as usual, but if she opened them, the sunshine would stripe her bed through the slats in the shades.

"She's going to be fine."

Wyatt. Softer still, closer, and something about the concern in his voice tugged at her.

That and…what was he doing home? But her pulse leaped at the thought of seeing him. Maybe he was home on break but—

Wait. Her eyes blinked open, and for a moment, she had nothing.

Then the world rushed at her and she woke up fast, whimpering. Sterile room, gray walls, the cool rush of oxygen in her nose.

"Babe. You're okay." Wyatt, standing over her.

Wow, he was handsome. Even with his bloodshot eyes, the worry lines in his brow. His beard had thickened, deepened, and he wore a flannel shirt. She had the urge to reach up and trace the flattened line where his nose had been broken so long ago.

But when she moved her hand, it pinched.

She looked over, found her left arm bandaged. And a gathering of Marshalls standing in the room. Gerri, RJ, Tate, and yes, even Knox. He stood with a woman with long brown hair, his arm over her shoulder.

And standing with Tate, a pretty, petite blonde.

"Hey," said Tate. "Welcome back, Sugarplum."

She smiled at his stupid nickname for her.

"You had us worried," Knox said. He had always intimidated her a little—the man was as somber as midnight. But he had a fierce loyalty about him that made her want to stand in the cast of his shadow. Now, he walked up to her, touched her leg with his strong hand, squeezed. "I knew you were the brave one."

RJ nodded. "Yeah, you should have seen her in Russia—"

"Let's not talk about Russia," Wyatt said. "Ever again."

Behind Wyatt, York made a sound, something of a harrumph. He was leaning against the window. "Fat chance there, champ. You went to Russia, and Russia followed you home."

Coco frowned at him.

"Give it a rest, York," Wyatt said.

"No, what is he talking about?"

RJ rubbed her arms, glanced at Tate, then Knox. "Ma and I found a dead body yesterday at a hotel. We think Damien Gustov set us up."

Coco's eyes widened.

"Guys, really? Right now? She just had surgery." Wyatt took her hand. "You're going to be okay. You made a mess of your small intestines, but they put you back together. But you have a lot of scar tissue, I'm afraid."

He eased himself into a chair, the movement tightening the muscles around his eyes.

"You're hurt—what happened?"

"He's fine," Tate said. "Just made the papers with his super fabulous hockey hands, catching the cell phone that saved your life."

"I fell and landed on my hip. It's a little sore."

She tried to ease herself up, but winced, and Wyatt was right there, moving her hospital bed up.

"But I'm right. This is not over, unfortunately," York said. "Even if we are taking this time-out. My guess is that Damien Gustov fired the shot that killed your bomber."

"Which means he was the one firing at me, at the podium?" Wyatt said.

"He fired at you?"

"Just before I was going to sell out Jackson to the world with the news that she's some kind of Russian double agent."

"Which is crazy talk," said the blonde woman standing near Tate.

"No one is disputing that, Princess Leia, so calm down." Tate took her hand. "But the question is, why did Kobie make up his story—"

"How about to derail the election?" the blonde said. "Because he doesn't want a woman in power who is a moderate and might actually unite the parties?"

"Down, girl," Tate said. He turned to Coco. "Glo is just super protective of her mother's run for office."

Her mother?

"RJ, can you verify his story about his brother and being a POW?" Tate asked.

"Once the senator reinstates me, yes," RJ said.

"She's working on it," Tate said.

"I can't believe we found the second bomber," Knox said. He had his arm around the brunette, his fingers laced through her hand, and Coco took a guess—Kelsey, his girlfriend.

Kelsey seemed serious, like Knox, a little hesitant to smile, but when she looked at him, she fairly glowed.

Good. Knox deserved someone who loved him for the hero he was.

In fact, they all did.

"More like he found us," Tate said.

"You have to admit, if what he said about Reba was true, it gives motive to whoever was shooting at me," Wyatt said. "I mean, if it was Gustov, why would he want *me* dead?"

York leaned up from the window. "To silence you?"

"The world wants to know what it was you were going to say about Jackson," RJ said quietly.

"I'll endorse her, just like I had planned," Wyatt said.

"Damien Gustov works for the Bratva," York said. "At

least that's the working theory. Why would the Bratva want Wyatt dead? Or the information silenced."

"That is, if it *was* Gustov pulling the trigger," Tate said. "We still haven't found the shooter."

"I know how we might be able to find Gustov," Coco said quietly.

Silence.

She looked at York. "I snooped around the dating files."

"What dating files?" RJ said.

"Gustov has emails from a dating site he's active on. Maybe we post something, act like we're interested—"

"No. No way," Wyatt said. "The last thing we need is to be on the run from Gustov here in America."

"We already are," York said. He gestured to Coco, then RJ. "He hasn't tied up all his loose threads—"

"What if he's not here for us?" RJ said suddenly.

All eyes turned to her.

"What if he's here because the Bratva sent him? What if he's here because there's another agenda?"

"Like?" Tate asked.

"Like derailing this election? Or putting someone else in power? Or, I don't know—I mean, why, out of all places, was he in a position to shoot at Wyatt today? What if his real target was Jackson?"

"Then why take out Wyatt? Just warming up?" York said.

"He doesn't have to kill anyone to cause fear," Knox said. "It's enough to suggest that someone is after Jackson."

"Which would only galvanize her base," Tate said.

"Or scare people away from voting for her," York said. "People might think she's too controversial."

"She's a moderate! She wants world peace, for cryin' in the sink," Glo said.

"We need to dig into those emails, Coco," RJ said, glancing at Glo. "See if we can find a pattern. I find it hard to believe that an assassin is looking for a date."

"Everybody needs a friend," Knox said.

And it was so crazy coming from Knox, of all people, that

Coco let out a laugh.

Then groaned. "Oh—"

"See, we shouldn't be talking about this here. Now." Wyatt leaned up. "Sorry. I'll get them out of here."

"No, it's okay." Coco looked at RJ. "I copied all the emails onto my personal online story before I put it on the jump drive."

"Good. I'll start digging into Kobie and Graham Plunkett. And, I'll start looking for clues in the emails."

A knock came at the door and a second later it opened.

"*Mamichka!*" Mikka barreled into the room, dressed in pajamas, dragging Gerri behind him.

He made for her bed, got a knee up, and just about landed on her before Wyatt caught him, his arm around his body.

"Hold up there, little man," Wyatt said, grabbing his legs and pulling the boy to himself. "Your mama just had surgery."

RJ translated for him as Wyatt set him down on the bed beside her.

Coco touched his face.

Mikka leaned forward to kiss her.

"Gently," Wyatt said, then looked at RJ. "Tell him to be gentle."

She did, then Mikka gave Coco a sweet peck on the cheek.

"You'll have to learn to speak Russian, Wyatt," RJ said.

"*Da,*" he said and winked.

And despite the ache in her stomach, the pain coursing down her arm, Coco's entire body soared. Seeing Wyatt, his arms around his son, and Mikka's face lit up, caught in that embrace. Yes, maybe he was right.

Everything would be okay.

"I thought I would find him in here." Sarai came into the room. "So this is where the party is."

"Hey, Sarai," Coco said as the doctor came over to tousle Mikka's hair.

Sarai looked at Coco. "You're a little old for the Children's Hospital, but you were an emergency, and I told them that Mikka was here, so they're making an exception."

"I'm sorry I ran out on you," Wyatt said to Sarai. "I'm ready to take that blood test."

"No need, actually." Sarai smiled, her gaze tracking to Gerri. "Your mother is a perfect match."

Wyatt's mouth opened. "But—"

"Son. If I can get my blood into my grandson, I'm going to do it," Gerri said. "Besides, you have a hockey season to prepare for."

He made a face. "Yeah, actually, I need to take some time off. I have a—"

"Labral tear?" Knox said.

Wyatt looked at his brother. "How'd—"

"Bull riders get them too. All that torsion on the bull. You were walking like a ninety-year-old man."

"Not so old I couldn't take out a terrorist," Wyatt said.

Knox rolled his eyes.

But Coco didn't. She reached out and touched Wyatt's cheek. "I always knew you were the real hero of the family."

"Hey—" Tate.

"C'mon—" Knox.

RJ laughed.

But Wyatt just stared down at her, meeting her eyes. "Does that mean you'll marry me, Katya Stanislova?"

"You have to ask first, Number One."

And then, in front of his entire family, York, and even their son, Wyatt got on his knee.

"Really, right now?"

"Right now. Before you do something crazy and run away again."

"Never," she whispered.

So he asked, those beautiful whiskey-brown eyes holding hers.

And she said yes.

And then her crazy, romantic superhero kissed her, right in front of his family.

"I knew it," Knox said. "I always said Wyatt had a crush on her."

"You did not," Tate said. "That was Ford. He was the one who caught them making out."

"No, seriously, it was me," Knox said.

"It was me." RJ met Coco's eyes.

Wyatt stood up, looked at his family. "No, it was me. Now everybody get out of here and leave me and my fiancée alone."

"I don't see a haymow," Tate said.

Wyatt raised an eyebrow.

"It's about time you became an official Marshall," Knox said, wiggling her toe, then winking on his way out with Kelsey.

"Gigi is babysitting," Gerri said and came over to take Mikka in her arms. "I'm learning Russian too. Like, *das vedanya.*"

Coco laughed.

RJ took York's hand and pulled him into the hallway.

Tate lingered, coming over to her bed with Glo. His smile had vanished. "You were really brave, Coco. And not just today. Having Mikka, helping RJ get out of Russia...you're the Marshall in the room." He leaned down and kissed her cheek. "I'd say welcome to the family, but it's too late."

He looked at Wyatt, grinning. "Try not to screw this up."

"Get out," Wyatt growled.

But Coco laughed, even as Wyatt took her hand, leaned over her. "I think we could find some hay..."

She sank into the sweetness of his kiss, so familiar, so dangerous, so perfect.

She was home.

What happens next...

She might not be Sydney Bristow, but she still wouldn't let evil win.

"We'll get York back, RJ." Tate came up behind her. Put his arm around her.

She stared out the window at the end of the fourth-floor hospital lobby, her arms around her waist, just trying to breathe. From here, the river to the east sparkled a deep blue, the sky clear, and she spotted Mt. Rainer to the southeast poking through the clouds, brilliant, bold, streaked with white against the granite.

Truth would win.

It had to.

"Did Senator Jackson find out anything?"

"Nothing so far. Swamp said he'd call with any updates. You?"

"I'm still shut out of the system." But she had an inside source.

Coco.

She still couldn't believe her foster sister had nearly died. Couldn't believe that Wyatt had walked through flames to rescue her.

But that was Wyatt. The one who never gave up.

And God had protected him, thanks to his still sodden clothing, the dunking into the ocean.

Please, God, be with York.

She closed her eyes. And for a moment, trailed back through the last two hours to figure out how it had all gone south.

We're going to find Gustov and end this.

York had cupped his hands over her shoulders as she'd stood outside Coco's room, staring down the hallway, not sure what to do next. Her mother had taken Mikka down the hall to play, Glo and Kelsey with them.

Knox had been on the phone, maybe to Ford, giving him

an update, or perhaps leaving a voice mail. Ford had been deployed shortly after she'd returned to Montana and she hadn't talked to him since, although she'd heard that his girlfriend, Scarlett was moving to Minneapolis.

Tate had been talking to the dark-haired cop, Vicktor, whom he'd reached out to via York to investigate Sophia Randall's murder.

She'd turned and pressed her hand to York's chest, his heart beating warm and real under hers. "The nightmare continues."

"We will figure this out, Bristow."

"Do you really think Gustov was the sniper?"

York lifted a shoulder. "I just know that I didn't have the right angle. Ballistics will come back with an analysis of the bullet, and then we'll see. One of the security agents went down also—he's going to live, but they can compare the bullets." He wove his fingers through hers. "I don't get it. If he's working for the Bratva, then the Russian mob wants both General Stanislov and Senator Jackson dead. Why?"

"Do you think there's any truth to what Wyatt said—about her being in collusion with the Bratva? Maybe she betrayed them. I need to get my access back, do some digging. And I can only do that in DC."

He touched her face. "I'm going with you."

Oh, it was dangerous, the way her heart jumped at his words. But, "What about the CIA, I mean…are you in danger here?"

"I don't know. Claire's father told me never to step foot in America again, but that was nearly seven years ago. He's probably forgotten me."

"What was his name?"

"Tom Crowley."

She had stilled, the name dropping through her like a stone. "Crowley is the head of our counterterrorism analysis directorate. His team analyzes emerging threats worldwide."

"Is that your department?"

"No, I'm a targeting analyst. We work with assets." *We. Sophia, what did you get yourself into?* She gripped her stomach—what if Sophia had died because of her connection with RJ?

Maybe York read her mind because he put his strong hands on her shoulders again. "I'm not going to let anything happen to you."

She believed him, especially the way his blue eyes could find her bones, steel them. "So, that means you're staying in America?"

His mouth formed a smile. "If you are."

He was leaning in to kiss her when Tate walked up.

Neither Tate nor Wyatt had been especially warm with York, and now Tate wore the slightest frown, glancing at York's hand on her shoulders.

York dropped it. Looked at the other man standing beside Tate. "What did you find out, Vicktor?"

Deeply handsome, with a strong jaw, his dark hair trimmed, no hint of a beard, his blue eyes solemn, Vicktor was former FSB, and she saw it all over his demeanor.

Funny, she sort of felt if anyone could find a Russian assassin in America, it might be this man, Vicktor Shubnikov.

"I got the initial forensic report back on Randall, the woman we found in the hotel. She has deep ligature marks on her wrists and ankles, suggesting she'd been in captivity for some time. She'd been dead for maybe six to eight hours before you found her."

"How'd she get in the room?"

"We're still figuring that out. My men are talking with the hotel staff. It's possible a master key was stolen."

"Any prints?" York asked. He'd taken RJ's hand, weaving his fingers through hers.

"None yet."

"And ballistics on the bullets from today's shooting?" York looked at Tate.

"Still waiting."

Behind Tate, the elevator opened, and two dark-suited

men walked out, down the hall. RJ stiffened. "I think we're about to find out." She wasn't sure why the gait, the set of their expressions made her tighten her hand in York's, but even he had the weirdest response—he stepped in front of her.

And then she realized why.

"Martin," York said quietly to the taller man. Early forties, medium build, dark, almost black hair, he wore a communication wire in his ear. "What are you doing here?"

"Funny, I'm here to ask you the same thing. Turn around, York. We need to take you into custody."

Everyone stilled.

"What?" York said appropriately.

"For the attempted murder of Senator Reba Jackson."

"That's crazy!" Tate said.

York's hard squeeze of RJ's hand kept her from shouting the same thing. He turned, met her eyes. "We're going to get this straightened out." Something in his gaze...

He kissed her forehead. "I will find you."

Then he stepped away from her, put his hands up.

Martin put a hand between his shoulder blades and shoved him against the wall.

"Hey! Is that necessary?" Vicktor said. "He's not a fugitive."

"You have no idea who this man is and what he's done," Martin said. He pulled York's hands behind him to cuff him and growled his statement in his ear.

A chill lifted along RJ's spine.

York met her eyes then, and something in his expression only added to it.

York, what's going on?

They pulled him away from the wall.

"Where are you taking him?" This, she couldn't stop herself from asking. Or walking down the hallway with him.

Martin and his blond crony ignored her. Even when they pushed York into the open elevator.

He'd held her gaze as the door closed. *I will find you.*

Tate had stood beside her in the hallway, in silence. "I'll call Reba, see if she can find out what's going on."

RJ had turned to her brother. "Ask her to reinstate my access. This isn't over. In fact, I think it's just starting. And I have work to do."

Now, two hours later, she still hadn't gotten any deeper into the CIA web. "This must have something to do with Tom Crowley and his anger against York."

"Who is Tom Crowley?" Tate asked.

She didn't know where to start with the answer.

Tate's phone rang. "It's Vicktor."

She turned to face him as he answered. Watched as he frowned, then looked at her and turned away. "When?"

No way. She moved to intercept him, and he looked up at her, pain on his face.

"Are you sure?"

It was those words that sent ice through her, to her bones.

He swallowed. "Thanks. Keep in touch."

He ended the call and looked at her.

And the fact that her brother's eyes glistened, the wrecked expression on his face told her to reach out for the wall.

To lower herself onto the sill of the window.

"It's bad," Tate said quietly. He tightened his jaw and looked away. Blinked.

"Tell me."

A beat, then he took a shaky breath. "So, there was an accident. It was outside town, somewhere in the mountains, so I'm not sure where they were taking him, but the SUV was hit by a semi. It rolled off the road and..." He winced, closed his eyes.

"Tate!"

He met her eyes. "It exploded, RJ."

Nothing. She went numb.

"It rolled down an embankment, hit a tree, and the entire thing exploded. There were..." He swallowed again. "There were no survivors."

"What…"

"Three bodies. They found them. Vicktor says they're going to the morgue to confirm, but…" He reached out for her. "I'm so sorry."

Tate was holding her, but she couldn't feel it. Couldn't even breathe.

No. This couldn't be right.

She closed her eyes, unwilling to let herself believe anything but his words. *I will find you.*

York couldn't be dead.

Because she refused to let evil win.

Author's Note

Regret. Oh, it haunts us, doesn't it? I'll be doing the dishes, or lying in bed in the middle of the night and suddenly, out of the blue, a conversation I had with one of my children a decade ago will surface in my brain and I'll think—oh, no that poor child will need counseling! Because we just don't get it right all the time. But we can't go back and rewrite it—we simply have to live with what we've done or said...or wish we'd said. (and done.)

Worse, those actions sit in our hearts tell us lies. "You're defective. You're not enough." It's called shamed and it makes us stand outside the circle of acceptance. It makes us see through dirty lenses and interpret wrongly the actions of others.

It makes God seem absent in our lives.

But he's not. In fact, he's standing in the circle, beckoning us in, saying, I've called you my child. And I know your regrets and your hurts...and I want to heal them.

"Behold, I make all things new." (Revelation 21:5)

I knew that Wyatt wasn't like his brothers, that he looked at them and measured himself, believing he wasn't enough. Because of his career, he always felt outside the Marshall family. Yes, much of it was his choice, but he still felt as if he didn't belong. And he interpreted his father's actions through his lens of hurt. It set him on a path of regrets. And when confronted with the opportunity to live a different life...well, it scared him. What if he was rejected again? Or worse, what if he lived up to his own poor expectations?

And Coco...well, she just wanted someone to love her, just like all of us do.

"Behold, I make all things new." Including our lives. Our hearts. Our hope.

We just have to trust him enough to walk into the circle. To open our hearts. To believe He loves us.

To give us eyes to see it.

To give us courage to embrace it.

What truth is God beckoning you to embrace today? The one that says...trust me with your regrets. Trust me with your heart?

Trust Him, because you are his beloved child. He is opening his arms and inviting you into the circle.

Thank you for staying with me through this series! One more epic story left—and it is my favorite!

I'm so very grateful to all those heroes and heroines in my life who have helped me bring the Montana Marshalls to life. My writing partner, Rachel Hauck, for always being the voice of wisdom and creativity on the other end of the phone. Alyssa Geertsen, my key beta reader, Barbara Curtis, for her amazing editing, Rel Mollet, who keeps me on schedule, and for her thoughtful insights to bring the story deeper. My talented cover designer, Jenny @ Seedlings Design Studio, and my fabulous layout artist, Tari Faris. Thank you also to my proof readers (any mistakes are all mine!) Lisa Jordan, Lisa Gupton, Bobbi Whitlock and Laurie Stoltenberg. WOW, you catch so many things...you are all such a blessing to me!

And, I'm thankful to the Lord, who is always and forever telling me He loves me. I am His beloved daughter. That I am in his hands. Wow.

Finally, thank you awesome reader friend, for reading Book 4: Wyatt. I can't wait to bring you Book: 5 Ruby Jane—and the epic conclusion of the series!

Susie May

Susan May Warren is the USA Today bestselling, Christy and RITA award–winning author of more than seventy novels whose compelling plots and unforgettable characters have won acclaim with readers and reviewers alike. The mother of four grown children, and married to her real-life hero for nearly 30 years, she loves travelling and telling stories about life, adventure and faith.

In addition to her writing, Susan is a nationally acclaimed writing teacher and runs an academy for writers, Novel.Academy. For exciting updates on her new releases, previous books, and more, visit her website at www.susanmaywarren.com.

Continue the Montana Marshall family adventures with RUBY JANE

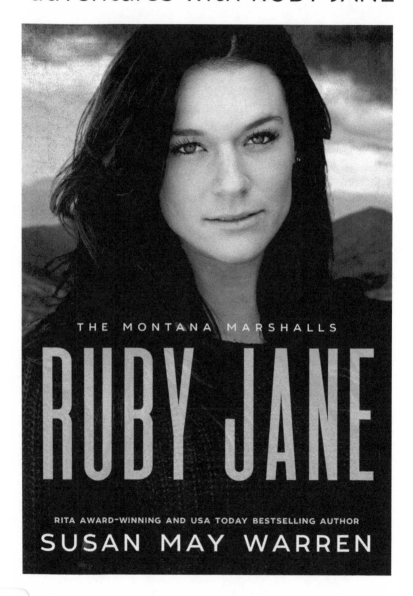

THE MONTANA MARSHALLS

RUBY JANE

RITA AWARD-WINNING AND USA TODAY BESTSELLING AUTHOR

SUSAN MAY WARREN

The man she loves is dead…right?

Former CIA Analyst Ruby Jane Marshall refuses to believe that man she loves died in a terrible car crash in the Cascade Mountains. York Newgate is just too tough for that. And the remains were burned beyond identification of the former CIA officer. She believes he's been kidnapped by the Russian mafia and she'll stop at nothing to find him.

He wants no memory of his past.

Mack Jones has no memory beyond the moment he woke up on the side of the highway, wounded, with the dark sense that he has a past he doesn't want to confront. Especially since he's rebuilt his life in a small tourist town, tucked away beyond the mountains. Mack likes his life tending bar for a local craft brewery and has no desire to dig around in the gray areas of his memory to find out why his body is scarred and he possesses eerie defense skills.

She holds the answers that will unlock his memory, but will it unlock his heart?

When the brewery catches fire and Mack rescues the owner, he makes the news, and Ruby Jane can't help but believe the man on the screen is her York Newgate. But when she arrives to the small town of Shelly, Washington, Mack doesn't recognize her. Is his undercover…or has he wiped her, and their relationship from his memory? And if he has, should she just leave him to restart his life? After all, his greatest desire was to start over, and now he has what he longs for. But what about the danger that stalks him?

And when his past finds them—and Ruby Jane's family—is he still the man who can save them?

The thrilling conclusion to the Montana Marshalls series!

Now available in stores and online.

CPSIA information can be obtained
at www.ICGtesting.com
Printed in the USA
LVHW090804090820
662641LV00011B/541

9 781943 935369